STARS
OVER
STARS

K.D. WENTWORTH

STARS OVER STARS

This is a work of fiction. All the characters and events portrayed in this book are fictional, and any resemblance to real people or incidents is purely coincidental.

A Baen Books Original

Baen Publishing Enterprises
P.O. Box 1403
Riverdale, NY 10471
www.baen.com

ISBN: 0-671-31979-5

Cover art by Patrick Turner

First printing, March 2001

Distributed by Simon & Schuster
1230 Avenue of the Americas
New York, NY 10020

Production by Windhaven Press, Auburn, NH
Printed in the United States of America

For my good friend Lee Allred,
who was of immeasurable help
in the writing of this book

Chapter One

The wind skimming in from the Oleaakan sea bore the scent of brine as well as the crash of waves breaking on the black sand beach below. Heyoka Blackeagle stood on a crest of exposed volcanic rock and gazed out at the aquamarine expanse of water.

The sky of this backwater world was a deep shade of green-blue, the sun, a mellow amber. The afternoon sunlight played over the restless waves so that each, at its peak, seemed topped with diamonds. A strand of his mane escaped its tie and whipped around his muzzle.

His ears flattened. Though he was hrinnti, not human, his adoptive father had raised him far inland on Earth in the Restored Oglala Nation. He had rarely encountered seas until humanity's war with the flek had assigned him to the contested world of Enjas Two.

Now, even two years later, the salt smell of a sea, any sea, brought back that brutal day of fighting, how the gaunt chitinous flek warriors had advanced down the green sand and pinned his unit under impenetrable laser fire. He'd taken a near fatal wound that day and subsequently had to learn to walk all over again. His breath quickened. His claws sprang free and he had to force them to resheathe.

Mitsu looked up and he could see in his human partner's blue eyes that she remembered too. Short and black-haired, deceptively slight for a soldier, she blotted sweating hands on her tan Ranger uniform. It was still crisp and new, the latest cut. She was only three weeks out of Rehab and the shadows that had haunted her for the last year still loomed in her eyes. She lowered her head and looked away. "You shouldn't have requested me."

"It's just a training run," Heyoka said. "You could do this in your sleep."

"Once, maybe." She sat on her heels, a small forlorn figure, and gazed upland into the rich silver-green of the tangled rain forest. "No one with half a brain would trust me at his back now."

Heyoka lifted his muzzle and let the wind ruffle his black fur. She kept returning to that and he couldn't convince her otherwise. At any rate, Oleaaka was not in the direct path of humanity's decades-long war with a notorious hive species, the flek. The enemy had landed here in the past, stayed long enough to damage the environment, as well as exterminate most of the native population of sentients, the timid laka, and leave flek ruins dotted about the planet's six major island continents. Five of the six were still poisoned with heavy metals and uninhabitable.

Then, for some reason never apparent to human scientists, forty-eight Standard years ago, they'd left again, never to return. Perhaps this world was too difficult to transform. Flek preferred their atmosphere thick and noxious, the surface temperature unbearably high. Something, or someone, in this deceptively lovely landscape had defeated them.

Up in the tangled maze of foliage, a delicate six-legged avian cried out and dove. A fleeing cloud of large scarlet insectoids blundered into Heyoka's fur. He swatted at them. Oleaaka was every bit as hot as his native world of Anktan, but flagrantly humid, where it had been dry. The air seemed thick enough to drink here and smelled so damned *green*, he could taste it. Not a problem for humans, of course, who were much less sensitive to odors, but overwhelming for a hrinn like himself.

The wall of leaves at the edge of the forest quivered, then suddenly, Kei and Bey, two of his hrinnti trainees, emerged. They presented a formidable picture, both well over seven feet tall, Kei actually closer to eight, heavily furred, armed with retractable claws, and double rows of teeth, not to mention the laser rifles slung over their shoulders which had been modified for their double-thumbed hands.

It was too soon for them to be back. A snarl rattled low in his throat. They must have used blueshift speed, showing off for the human members of the squad again.

In addition to the obvious external differences between humans and hrinn, hrinn possessed special receptor cells in their bodies to store excess energy which could be released for metabolic overdrive. Only last year, he had learned to control this ability himself so that he could move almost too fast to be seen, but then he'd burned himself out in a battle against the flek on his home planet, Anktan. His body couldn't sustain the effort anymore and he saw the contempt in Kei's eyes every time he looked at him. Hrinn respected only strength and physical perfection.

Accustomed to the loose-fitting robes of their home world, the two hrinn looked distinctly uncomfortable in their Ranger gear. The sleek uniforms with close-fitting

sleeves and legs were only one of many trials hrinn faced
trying to fit into human-based culture.

Bey, the shorter, had a mahogany outer layer of fur with
a cream undercoat: brown/on/buff, a hrinn would have
named it. Kei's fur was almost uniformly black, with only
faint buff patches behind the ears, nearly black/on/black,
as he himself was. Their manes had been cut shoulder-
length, like his, and then bound with heavy cord.

The two were related in some fashion, both being born
of the same Line, Levv, which later he had discovered
was his heritage too. On Anktan, though, grown males
found matrilineal heritage beneath their notice.

Heyoka checked his watch. Ten minutes. A record
find under these conditions, even for his olfactory-gifted
hrinnti recruits, but traveling in blueshift had been an
extravagant waste of energy.

Kei sketched a sloppy approximation of a salute as he
stopped. Heyoka gave him a crisp salute back. "Report,"
he said.

"Recon was right. We found flek ruins, three miles
in." Kei's black eyes were fierce above the ropy laser
scar across his muzzle, relic of a childhood encounter
with flek on his home world.

"'Recon was right,' *sir*," Heyoka prompted wearily.
He saw Bey glance at his fellow recruit out of the corner
of his eye. This was an old skirmish between the two
of them, endlessly replayed. Twice already, since the first
hrinnti class's graduation from boot camp, Heyoka had
been forced to stalk Kei and thrash him unmercifully in
time-honored hrinnti fashion. Fortunately, though Kei was
taller and carried more muscle, Heyoka had trained for
years in hand-to-hand combat. For the moment, he still
possessed a slight advantage.

Kei's massive body stiffened, but he remained silent.

Long simmering anger stood Heyoka's fur on end.
He felt the savage *other* who lived within him, and

all hrinn, awaken. Would there never be an end to this issue? Even though hrinnti culture maintained that obedience was only owed to those individuals who had proved their ability to tear your throat out, Kei should be able to think his way beyond that savage imperative.

"If you intend to become a Ranger," Heyoka said, "then you *will* follow protocol. You will address your superior officers as 'sir'!"

Kei's lips wrinkled back from his gleaming white teeth. "Sir," he said, with apparent disdain.

Mitsu stood, then shouldered her rifle with careful deliberation, affecting, for his sake, not to have noticed Kei's tone.

Leaves rustled, then a third hrinn, yellow/on/white Visht, emerged from the forest, ears laid back, panting hard. Heyoka looked from him back to the forest's green wall. "Where's the rest of your patrol?" he asked Kei. "You have two more out."

"They couldn't keep up." Kei gazed boldly into Heyoka's eyes, giving him brazen challenge.

Heyoka felt a snarl threatening. "Perhaps because you used blueshift?"

"If they can't match our pace, they deserve to be left behind." Kei flexed his handclaws and studied them in the brilliant Oleaakan sunlight.

He would have washed the insubordinate wretch out, Heyoka thought, if he didn't have so damned much potential. As it was, his arrogance had set the tone for far too long now and the other hrinn looked to him for leadership. He had to find a way to get through to him, just as wily old Nisk had finally opened his own eyes back on Anktan. This project was the hrinn's chance to prove themselves more than the barbaric savages humans had long considered them to be. Much more was at stake here than the career of one recruit, or even six.

"Why didn't you check your rally point before returning?" Heyoka said through bared teeth.

"I saw no point in wasting time waiting for that pair of rag-ears to catch up," Kei said in Hrinnti. "And besides, Visht cannot blueshift for very long, so he could watch out for them."

"Go back to the rally point and regroup," Heyoka said.

Kei snorted and plunged back into the trees. Mitsu nodded to Bey and trotted after him, her face pale and set. Heyoka followed. Another showdown was imminent. He might as well get it over at the first opportunity. He was dismayed to find the prospect of a fight did not disturb him nearly as much as it ought.

When he'd first conceived this training program to allow hrinn to enter the Confederation military, he'd hoped to attract the cream of hrinnti society, the best and the brightest. Instead, he'd gotten late culls like young Naxk and outcasts like that rascal Skal, who'd been thrown out of at least three males' houses, misfits like Kei and Bey, who'd been raised in an outlawed Line and, despite their service against the flek, were regarded with suspicion.

One, a rangy pale-gray female named Kika, he'd actually saved from death at the hands of her Line Mother, though she'd always refused to explain the circumstances. And then there was enigmatic Visht, who had come from the farthest edge of hrinnti territory in that region and had almost nothing to say for himself.

At any rate, they had only four more days to smooth the edges before the official evaluators from Ranger HQ arrived to run their own training scenarios. And then it would be too late.

The shade swallowed him, blessedly cooler. The gravity here was closer to Earth Standard than that of Anktan, so his legs had more spring. The leaves of the dominant species in this area were a glossy dark green on top and silver beneath, so traveling the forest was like running through moonlight.

It reminded him of Earth and his boyhood, dark velvet nights spent out on the ridges camping with his friends under the watchful eye of Earth's impressive singleton moon, days of hunting in birch and oak forest, hiking, testing one's self against the elements. His adoptive father, Ben Blackeagle, a retired Oglala space trader, had sometimes gone with them.

He'd thought he'd known what he wanted in those days, who he was, what he would be. But he had known nothing, and understood even less. Sometimes now it seemed to him that his life had not truly begun until that day when he finally made his way back to his fierce home world and began to unravel the mystery of just who and what he was.

Mitsu padded ahead of him, seemingly recovered, once again every inch the seasoned soldier, but her confidence waxed and waned these days. She had been captured by the flek last year on Anktan, then ruthlessly mind-conditioned to believe she was one of them. It had taken weeks after her release for her to begin speaking Standard again, then longer for her to understand what they had done to her.

The best therapists the division had to offer had treated her for months and now said she was as fit as she would ever be, though they recommended a medical discharge. He thought they were wrong. She had been a crack soldier once and would be again, as soon as she got her confidence back, but there were still too many moments when her veneer cracked and he glimpsed the wounded spirit beneath. In a very real sense, she was training here too, trying to find the will to go on and not allow the flek to ruin the rest of her life.

Kei set a stiff pace and Mitsu's shorter human legs

struggled to keep up. "Take the rear," Heyoka said to her as he jogged past.

"Sod off!" she said hoarsely and spurted ahead again, the cords in her neck standing out from exertion.

"Am I going to have to thrash you into submission too?" he said.

"That'll be a cold day!" she snapped over her shoulder.

He surged past her again. "Take the rear!"

She dropped back, her face a white mask of strain.

They had served together now for almost four years, since that day she'd saved his hairy hide as a raw boot, only weeks out of camp. She had a knack for slipping through rough country unseen, climbing like a monkey, employing her small build as an asset, rather than a liability. From the first, she had been extraordinarily observant and quick to react.

At least, she had been, before the flek had gotten to her. The thought still made his own skin crawl. He'd been a prisoner of the flek too, as a toddler, kidnapped from Anktan and sold repeatedly in a flek slave market until Ben Blackeagle, his human adoptive father, had bought him. He knew how the flek treated their captives. He still bore the scars, both mental and physical, to prove it.

Kei slowed, then darted through the foliage to the massive trunk of a tree growing parallel to the damp ground. "Here," he said, then leaned against the mottled red bark.

Heyoka swiveled his ears. Something slipped through the undergrowth about thirty feet away to the north. Fifteen degrees east, tiny toenails scraped as several small green-furred climbers, alarmed by their intrusion, raced for the forest canopy a good hundred fifty feet above. Overhead, avians crooned an atonal song that set his teeth on edge. But, beyond Mitsu's labored breathing, as she struggled to catch up, there was no sign of the two human recruits he'd sent out with Kei, Bey, and Visht.

He'd known Kei and Bey back on Anktan, but the silent Visht remained a mystery. The big yellow male occasionally mentioned the sacred *patterns/in/progress*, which hrinn believed ruled all of life, and regarded Heyoka with a disturbing air of reverence. He'd grown inured to that back on Anktan. His fur's uniformly black over- and undercoats mirrored the physical appearance of an ancient hrinnti hero, the legendary "Black/on/black," a hrinn more powerful than ordinary hrinn sent by the Voice when the need was great. After the defeat of the flek on their world, the hrinn had woven his return to Anktan into legend.

It was all nonsense, of course, based on a tiny nugget of truth. His distinctive coloring did appear to be a genetic marker for the ability to store large amounts of power in his cells and blueshift with ease, but he'd burned himself out, so that no longer mattered.

He circled upwind and sampled the breeze. The acridness of human sweat was just faintly evident to the west. "Come on," he said, and jogged off in the proper direction.

Kei and Bey fell in behind without comment. Bey's ears were down, signalling his unease. Perhaps the seriousness of abandoning one's squadmates was dawning on him, Heyoka mused. There might be hope for that one after all.

They found Aliki Onopa and Jer Kline sitting on a fallen log at the outer edge of the flek ruins. Larger than six football fields, the installation had been studied by Confederation experts for decades, before releasing the site to the military for training maneuvers. Forty-eight Standard years had passed since the flek had been driven from this world, yet he still imagined he caught a whiff of their nose-burning stench.

The white wall was pitted with age and overgrown with vines, so that the massive shape was blurred. All the same, Heyoka suffered a flashback of the last time he'd been this close to a flek installation—*the bizarre pink, green, purple, and blue lights that played over the tall irregular lattices that formed the walls, the ear-splitting screech as the transfer grid came up to full power, shower of sparks . . .*

He shuddered, then glanced aside at Mitsu, who was staring up at the structure with horrified fascination. Onopa and Kline scrambled to their feet and saluted.

"Why didn't you report to the rally point?" Heyoka said.

"Rally point, sir?" Onopa, a sturdy, bronze-skinned woman from Kalana Colony, clenched her fists. "Squad Leader Kei never designated a site. He and those other hrinn took off running and that's the last we saw of them."

Those other *hrinn*, Heyoka thought bleakly.

Kei waggled a dismissive ear. "I did speak of a rally point. If you had not lagged behind, you would have heard."

Onopa flushed.

"You're on report for not following procedure," Heyoka said, stepping between human and hrinn. "You and Bey will police the camp for the next two nights."

Kei's big body bristled nose to ankles. Fight phero-mones sheeted off him in waves. "I am not a servant!"

"You're not going to be a Ranger either unless you stop playing games and use what you've been taught!"

Kei whirled upon him, ears flattened, hackles raised. "Why have you brought us to this empty world, wasting time when there are flek to be killed?" he demanded in guttural Hrinnti. "I did not abandon Levv so I could sneak around in the bushes like a cubling playing at being a warrior! We have weapons now. In the time since we left Anktan, we could have fought thousands of flek and brought much honor to our kind. Instead, we slip through the trees and pretend there are enemies where there are none, all the while holding back at every turn so these whimpering softskins you inflicted upon us as huntmates can keep up!"

"Speak Standard," Heyoka said. The savage *other* who always lurked within him longed to rip Kei's insolent throat out.

Mitsu, who spoke passable Hrinnti these days, gave him a quick glance, but said nothing.

Onopa and Kline, who had not understood more than one word in five, looked furious anyway. "Sergeant, he never even gave us a chance!" Onopa protested.

"That's enough!" Heyoka ordered and the human recruit was at least well trained enough to shut up. Kei snarled and slipped back into the brush. Bey's honest brown face gazed after him, but he did not follow.

"Do you want me to trail him?" Mitsu asked.

"No, he'll come back when he's ready," Heyoka said, his voice tight with frustration.

"That's what I'm afraid of," Mitsu said, shaking her head. She gestured to Onopa, Kline, Visht, and Bey. "Head 'em out, boys and girls. It's time to go back to the playpen."

That might have been funny, Heyoka thought, if it hadn't been so bloody close to the truth.

The voices coming from the clearing around the tall white walls were loud. Third Gleaner paused in her gathering of sweet herbs and tubers. She quite disliked loud noises of any sort. The laka were a steady, quiet people, each committed to that which she did best, never overstepping boundaries or underdoing what must be done. Each tend to her own, as Burrow Matron always said. That was the old, proven way, set down when the world was still soft.

Her two first-hands hesitated above the spiral of a lovely ripe green shellfruit. She trembled as the voices grew ever more strident. Why did they not come to some sort of compromise? Did they actually mean to hurt one another? She crept forward, then peered through the leaves of a spikebush, trying to decide whether to hide or flee. As a gleaner, it was not her function to scout, though sometimes gleaners were required to venture far afield to find enough fresh provisions for the entire colony.

And, if there were danger in this area, then the others must be warned so they could avoid it. The strange two-handed ones came here from time to time, to this place of echoes, where the wind spoke its own language, telling tales of death and misery. They seemed drawn to it almost as much as the laka were repelled, though it was not of their making. The terrible ones, the warriors, had made it. That much was remembered.

Delicate first-hands clasped, she slipped closer and saw a flash of black as one stranger dashed into the forest. The others, who were of two distinct and separate kinds, stared after it.

She had not encountered this second kind before. They appeared to be covered with fur, of all things, one brown, the other black. The first kind was familiar, soft and tan, bearing only a modest amount of varicolored hair here and there. These sought out the laka occasionally and asked questions, but the laka had better things to do than listen. Sooner or later, they went away and left the colony in peace. The laka wanted nothing more.

The black-furred creature called out to its companions, not as loudly this time. It waved an arm and set off toward the shore. The other two followed, one tall and rangy, the other three smaller and more compact, a badly matched set.

Despite their differences, though, they behaved as though they had the same function. How odd, thought Third Gleaner. How inefficient. Either one kind or the other should be best at what was needed here. It was not possible for both forms to excel. She could not get the sight out of her mind as she hurried back to her sisters.

Without seeming to, Bey set his pace so that Mitsu could keep up. She found herself feeling grateful and that just made her madder. What was she doing here on this beguiling amber and green world? Sweat beaded up on her forehead, then stung her eyes. The new tan corporal's uniform, despite being of the latest and lightest weave, designed to wick moisture away from the skin, was stifling.

She was just out of shape, she told herself. It would be all right. She only had to hold on, keep going forward, one step after the other, and somewhere at the end, she would feel like herself again, the confident person she had been before the flek had flayed her mind open.

But that towering white wall! Despite the heat, she was chilled just thinking about it. To stand so close, smell it, remember how flek thoughts had skittered through her head like insects—she felt sick inside, contaminated. The meds had assured her that she was whole again, that there would be no lasting effects, but the truth was they didn't know. No one knew, because they had never been there, never sung the flek's songs or fought at their side.

And she had.

Bey swerved, ducked under a low-hanging branch, then stopped at the edge of a stretch of gleaming black sand. His ears twitched. Onopa and Kline were already there, staring out at the horizon, waiting. Mitsu grimaced. Bey really had held back on the pace.

Blue-green water lapped at the shore and the warm ocean breeze soughed against her face, surprisingly cool on her overheated cheeks. The scent of Oleaakan seaweed growing in the shallows filled the air, cinnamon laced with mint. For a second, she was tempted to shed her boots and plunge into the water, but—she ranked these three grunts and should set a good example. Besides, the way Onopa looked at her, she'd heard the rumors about her so-called "breakdown" last year. She didn't want to give the Kalanan cause to think she was even crazier than she really was.

Blackeagle emerged from the trees, his tan uniform contrasting with his fur. When he'd worn the traditional Ranger black, meant for cooler climes, the uniform had blended better with his fur. He'd recovered from his ordeal on Anktan more readily than she had, though he bore a fresh array of scars and had never quite regained all the weight he'd lost in that last battle. He looked fit, though.

She drew her knife and hefted it experimentally. Blackeagle cocked his head, a question gleaming in his black eyes. "How about some fishing?" she said.

He shook his head. "We have to make camp before sundown."

She looked back over her shoulder at the placid bay. "Why?"

"I don't want to chance Kei getting there first," he said.

"He'd never go into camp alone," she said. "There'd be too many questions."

"True." Blackeagle wrinkled his lips so that his double rows of teeth gleamed.

He was different from before, she realized, just as she was different. They'd both been through hell, but unlike previous actions, not together this time. Perhaps they couldn't function as the efficient combat unit they'd once been. Perhaps that was over too, like so much else.

Get a grip! she told herself angrily. You don't have the right to give up. Better soldiers than you have gone down fighting. That's the least you can do.

She sheathed the knife and turned away to conceal her face. Maybe she'd lost the knack of reading him, but she couldn't count on the opposite being true. "Fish would taste a lot better than those sodding field rations," she said noncommittally.

"What makes you think there's fish in that ocean," Blackeagle said, "or that we could digest them, if there were?"

"Mission briefing said we could eat some of the fruit," she said.

Brush rattled, then Kei stalked out of the trees. He halted a good fifty feet away, where he and Blackeagle sized one another up, as alike in coloration and build as twins, but for the slight mismatch in size.

"Well, Private, we'd about given up on you," Blackeagle said. "What's the matter? Can't keep up?"

Kei snarled and paced restlessly.

"Corporal Jensen, take the point," Blackeagle said. "Lead the squad back to camp."

"I am Squad Leader!" Kei threw out.

"You *were*." Blackeagle looked contemptuous. "But it takes self-control and wits to lead a command and you have yet to convince me that you have sufficient of either!"

Kei's black eyes blazed and he whirled upon Mitsu. "And yet you tolerate this traitor!"

Without thinking, she fell back and drew her knife. Her heart raced and the balmy air seemed suddenly chilly.

"I have told you a million times—she did not betray

us!" Blackeagle's voice held the ring of cold steel as he stepped between them.

"I can fight my own battles, dammit!" she told him. "Get out of the way!"

"I was there! I smelled her!" Kei said. "She fought at their side, spoke their language and would speak no other! You should have let me tear her throat out!"

Mitsu dimly remembered that night, the desperate flek struggle to protect the crystalline heart of their transport grid, the terrible wave of hrinn cutting down the warrior drones, how she had fallen back and directed the battle herself when the flek had lost focus. Kei had nearly killed her that day. Only Blackeagle's quick thinking had saved her life, and his actions had cost him dearly.

"Stand down, Corporal!" Blackeagle said. "That's an order!"

The knife felt right in her hand. Kei was big, she thought, but she had speed and agility on her side. The gravity was lighter here too than on Anktan, which was bound to throw him off. And if he killed her instead, that might be even better.

Blackeagle seized her arm in his double-thumbed hand. "I said 'stand down!' "

Kei snarled as she sheathed the knife, blood pounding in her ears.

"There will be no fighting in the ranks," Blackeagle said, his ears pinned back. "We fight *flek*, not each other!" He looked from Kei to Bey to the three humans. "Is that understood?"

"Yes, sir." Mitsu felt the blood rush to her face.

"Yes, sir, Master Sergeant," Kline and Onopa said.

Bey hesitated, then dropped his gaze, acknowledging submission hrinnti fashion. "Yes, sir."

Blackeagle looked directly at Kei, daring him to further defiance.

"The pattern here is *water/over/trail*," Kei said, "no matter what other name you choose to mask it."

"I thought you didn't believe in *patterns/in/progress*," Heyoka said.

"Since leaving Anktan, I begin to see their relevance," Kei said. "Don't you?"

A low snarl escaped Blackeagle. He turned his back on Kei. "Take the point, Corporal Jensen."

Mitsu slung her laser rifle over her shoulder and headed east. The rest followed, even Kei.

Chapter Two

It was more than ten miles back to the small base camp Heyoka had established for this training exercise and he smoldered every step of the way. What a mess, and it was his fault, not Kei's. He just wasn't getting through. He had to find some way to make him listen.

The hrinn were talented, fearsome fighters who could add much to the war effort, but they had long been classified as a grade seven culture by humans, too primitive and aggressive for assimilation into Confederation culture, little more than savage barbarians.

The battle on Anktan last year had given them a proverbial foot in the door, but at this point, no one was going to equip a hrinnti division and send it off to fight on its own. If hrinn could not be trained to integrate with human forces, they would lose their chance to participate in the larger cultural life of the galaxy, and that failure could only be laid at his feet.

At the front of the column, Mitsu maintained the lead and set a stiff pace, though not one that could tax the hrinnti component of his small force. Kei, for once, kept silent and merely covered ground with great long-legged strides.

The land swept ever upward toward low green mountains that formed the backbone of this large island. Since it had proved impossible to communicate with the laka and discern their names for natural features, Confederation surveyors had numbered the major land-masses of Oleaaka. This particular island continent, third largest on the planet, had been designated Island Three, not a particularly original name, but serviceable. For some reason, Three was the only inhabitable landmass and also possessed the greatest number of relatively intact flek ruins, perfect for military exercises.

Heyoka had seen holos of the laka, a graceful, highly cooperative species, which possessed two pairs of both upper limbs and lower ones. The first pair of arms were slight with four tiny fingers on each hand, used apparently for harvesting and pruning plants. The second pair were heavy-boned and sturdy for tasks requiring strength, rather than precision.

In the holos, they stared out with shy, haunted eyes of varying shades of pink. Their kind had seen the flek come, as had so many other unfortunate species across the galaxy. Of all those, though, only they had also seen them go, without an apparent fight. Flek had transformed the rest of the invaded worlds into sweltering hellholes and none of those other species existed anymore. More than one expert had speculated the laka had survived because they had evolved along the same vaguely insectoid model as the flek themselves. Perhaps their old enemy had hesitated at the last, much as humans might have found some sense of kinship with a humanoid race.

He was overheated and panting by the time they made camp, but Mitsu looked positively ghastly. Months in Rehab had not given her much opportunity for conditioning. She staggered to a halt, leaned over and braced her hands on her thighs, gasping for air. Her skin was flushed, her eyes half-closed.

"Go get cleaned up," he told her.

"I'm—fine!" she wheezed.

"Yeah," he said dryly, "I can tell." He should not have put her in this untenable position, he told himself. He'd thought a return to duty would help, but he should have realized Kei and the others who had fought in that last battle would object to her presence. Another screw-up to be tallied in his column. He stalked away to find Montrose, his second-in-command.

Corporal Abe Montrose was the most gifted of the humans assigned to him to help stage this exercise. Of course, only the most talented of human recruits were selected for Ranger training. That was a given. Still, even among a class of standouts, he was impressive and Heyoka had taken him for his Second.

Montrose was well over six feet with curly dark hair and medium-dark skin. His eyes were almost black, much like a hrinn's, Heyoka thought, and he had an innate economy of words. Perhaps that was why he fit in as well as any human could in this mixed company.

"Any problems, Corporal?" He dropped into a canvas camp chair that creaked uneasily with his weight.

Montrose saluted, then folded his arms behind his back in a stiff parade rest. "None, Master Sergeant."

"At ease," Heyoka said.

Montrose relaxed. "Did you have problems out on the run?"

"We found the sodding ruins." Heyoka flicked an ear. "Beyond that, don't get me started."

"No, sir." Montrose stared tactfully above Blackeagle's head.

Heyoka sighed and stretched until his joints cracked. "This is a *training* exercise," he said. "We have to expect problems."

A glint appeared in Montrose's eye. "And you found them?"

"To the max." Heyoka leaned back and put his hands over his eyes. "This wasn't what I envisioned, when I took this assignment."

"Of course not, sir."

"Go rustle us some rations," he said. "And see that Jensen eats too."

"I'll take care of it, sir." Montrose saluted again and then strode briskly off toward the supply tent.

I must be getting old, Heyoka thought sourly. He flexed his handclaws and raked a black strand of straying mane out of his face. Why else would I be aggravated just because someone agrees with me?

How old was old for a hrinn anyway, he wondered. Was he, at thirty-seven, old? Then he realized that, like so much about his species, he just didn't know.

Kei climbed until he found a flat-topped boulder at a safely private distance from camp. The hillside sloped sharply down toward the invisible sea, thick with trees and silver-green vegetation. This landscape reminded him a bit of Levv's mountain hold, where he and Bey and even the Black/on/black had been birthed. The Black/on/black did not remember, but he and Bey had only left it for the first time less than a year ago, as humans reckoned such things.

The relentless sun beat down on his black fur, making him pant, but he disdained to seek shade. Hundreds of intriguing odors rode on the air: water, warm-blooded animals, insects, a hint of decay, ripening fruits. His nose twitched.

He perched on the rock like a predator overlooking a game trail, then broke the gleaming black laser rifle down into its component parts and carefully set to cleaning each element. The scent of fresh solvent rose in the late afternoon sunlight, while the mindless calls of tiny six-legged avians filled the air. The by-now-familiar drill at least gave him something to occupy his hands when all he really wanted was to *tear* something apart!

Flek scent had been threaded through the ruins, but old and stale. If he hadn't encountered it fresh back on his home world, he probably would not have noticed it at all, so what had been the point of going there today?

Humans were so unfocused, always dithering, end-lessly talking and preparing to fight, but, as far as he could tell, never actually doing it. He had his own laser rifle now and knew how to use it, was well versed, in fact, in the use of a dozen different weapons and demo-lition materials. He had his teeth and claws and ability to blueshift. What more did he need to join the battle with their common enemy?

And why had that traitor, Mitsu, been allowed to run with even this stupid fake hunt? She had been outrageous back on Anktan, maintaining she was flek, when she could have looked in the nearest pond and seen that wasn't even remotely possible. The Black/on/black insisted the enemy had coerced her and the delusion wasn't her fault, but Kei was certain no one could ever have made him believe he was anything but a hrinn.

Perhaps humans were weak-minded as well as soft-skinned and clawless. A low snarl rattled in his throat. No wonder the flek beat them at almost every turn. The Black/on/black should have chosen his huntmates more wisely.

His sensitive nose caught the scent of human on the steamy breeze. He looked up from his work, but the rock-strewn clearing was surrounded by forest and he could see nothing except a hundred intertwined shades of green backed with silver. His hackles raised, he reassembled the rifle in sure, quick motions, then concealed himself behind the outcropping of black volcanic rock.

He was expecting Montrose, who always smelled of soap, or one of the others, Kline of the sour sweat perhaps, but it was Mitsu's scent, thick with new cloth, that strengthened in his nostrils, and from behind, not before him.

"Being a bit careless, aren't you?" she said.

He whirled. The slim form stood behind the bole of a massive tree, rifle in hand.

He bit back a growl. "What business is it of yours?"

"Chow's on," she said. "I thought you'd like to know."

His ears flattened. "I will catch my own food!"

"Never forage off-world, unless you must." She sounded like his instructors at boot camp. Her face was very pale for a human, and looked even more so, beneath that shock of black hair. "You never know in advance whether alien proteins will be compatible with your body chemistry."

Kei had heard this lecture before, but it never made any sense to him. What exactly were "proteins" and "chemistry"? "I will eat when I am ready," he said gruffly.

"Get your rear back to camp," she said and jerked the muzzle of her laser rifle in that direction. "Now."

"No." He retrieved the polishing cloth from the rock and buffed the stock.

"You may look like him," she said, "but you couldn't hold a candle to Blackeagle. He always followed regulations and rules even more carefully than most humans. He took our game and outdid all of us, whereas you can't swallow your pride long enough to see what he's risked for you, for all of you. If you don't qualify, he fails too."

"He is the Black/on/black!" Kei said. "He makes his own pattern, as you say, his own rules! It is for the rest of us to follow!"

"Then get your hairy behind off that rock and *follow!*"
She was flushed now, breathing hard.

She seemed altogether too fragile and young to be
a warrior. He had trouble understanding why one such
as this had not been culled long ago.

"Get back to camp," she said, "and carry out your
duties."

"Police the area?" he said. "That is beneath a warrior.
Why didn't he order you, the traitor, to do it?"

"I would do it in a heartbeat," she said, and her voice
was low, "if it would erase what I did. But it won't, and
he wouldn't let me, anyway."

"You don't belong here!" he said.

"No," she said, "but I am here, for now, and there's
nothing you or I can do about it."

The rising breeze blew his fur the wrong way. He
threw his head back and assessed the sun. It was late.
He should return. The tranquility he had sought here
had been broken. "I was going back anyway," he said.

Mitsu shaded her eyes with her hand. The sun
hung red and huge in the western sky so its twinned
reflection gleamed in her blue eyes. "Yeah," she said,
"I thought so."

Chow was wretched, of course. Heyoka had forgotten
just how thoroughly unpalatable mission rations could
be in the wrong hands. With an effort, he swallowed
the reconstituted eggs and ham. He stood and gazed
around. "Montrose?"

"Yes, sir?" As always, Montrose's trim form seemed
to appear from nowhere.

"Who's the idiot who ruined tonight's dinner?"

Montrose's dark eyes gazed over Heyoka's shoulder.
He locked his hands behind his back. "That would be,
uh, me, sir."

Heyoka flicked an ear. "You did this?"

"Yes, sir."

Heyoka mulled that over. "Don't ever cook for desperate men, Montrose. You haven't the knack."

"No, sir," Montrose said. "Thank you, sir."

"Find me some ration bars," Heyoka said. "They taste like sawdust, but at least they're fresh sawdust."

"Right away, sir." Montrose hesitated, his brows raised.

"Yes?" Heyoka sat down in his camp chair and nudged his plate downwind.

"I called Corporal Jensen when chow was ready, as you instructed, but she never showed up to fill her tin."

"That's probably because she has better sense than the rest of us," Heyoka said.

"Yes—no, I—" Montrose broke off and stared at his boots. "Begging your pardon, sir, but I don't know about that. All I do know is—she's not in camp."

Heyoka jerked back onto his feet.

"And neither is Private Kei." Montrose looked anxious. "I've checked and they're both missing."

Scenarios whirled through Heyoka's head—Kei stalking Mitsu because she had fought for the flek—Mitsu challenging Kei for insulting her earlier—

"We have to find them," he said, trying to hide his panic. "Have the squad fall in."

Montrose dashed off to the mess tent. Heyoka snatched up his rifle and pocketed several spare charges. Which one would he shoot, he wondered, if he did find them fighting? The partner he had fought alongside all these years, or the single best hope for his people?

Kei refused to go unless Mitsu went first. She couldn't decide if this was because he didn't trust her at his back, or if he meant to strike her down at the first opportunity.

Then she realized he could have blueshifted and torn

her throat out whenever he wanted, even in front of Blackeagle, and no one could have reacted fast enough to stop him. Before that last battle, Blackeagle had also been able to reach metabolic overdrive, but he had burned himself out saving her. That was her fault too, like so much else.

The shadows lengthened as they picked their way down through the rocks, thick brush, and the edge of the forest. The background sounds shifted subtly and she thought she could hear the surf, even way up here.

"Why did you defend the flek?" Kei asked suddenly behind her shoulder.

Her stomach knotted and she went cold. She ducked her head and fought to keep her voice level. "Because I was nuts."

"That is not an answer."

"They made me believe I was one of them," she said. Such a simple explanation for such an overwhelming experience. *The white room.* She put a trembling hand to her head. It was all there in her mind, waiting to drown her again. The meds had shown her how to push it away, so that it didn't dominate every waking thought, but they couldn't eradicate the deepest of the conditioning. It would always be with her to some degree.

The rhythm of a flek working song surfaced and it was all she could do to keep her hands from beating it out.

Kei snorted. "Only a soft-brain could be made to believe such a thing!"

"The flek have their ways," she said. "Pray you never have cause to find out."

"I would die first!" he said.

The breath caught in her chest and her throat constricted so tightly it hurt to breathe. "I wish I had," she said.

"Coward!" he said. "You have only to volunteer for

battle, if you wish to die and redeem your honor! Surely
there are human regiments that would take you!"

"No," she said, focusing on the rough ground at her
feet. "There are not. The meds recommended a medical
discharge."

The terrain sloped ever downward. Why had Kei
climbed so high, she wondered. It was almost as though
he were looking for something up here.

"Then fight me!" he said. "Redeem your honor that
way!"

She turned to look up at him, tall against the green-
blue sky, black and massive. Fighting him would be a
certain end to her pain. She could stop trying and just
let death overtake her. She had fought to survive on
Anktan last year and look where that had gotten her.
If she had died, Heyoka could have devoted all his
attention to fighting the flek. Perhaps he wouldn't have
burned himself out.

But if she taunted Kei into killing her, he would be
blamed. The whole hrinnti training project would be
washed out and she would be letting Blackeagle down—
yet one more time.

"You sure are one lop-eared, stupid private," she
said, "I wouldn't dirty my knife with your blood if you
begged me."

A snarl rattled in Kei's throat.

"Get your ugly carcass back to camp and start
policing the ar—"

Kei leaped down in front of her, claws extended,
fangs revealed in a fearsome snarl.

"Nice try, hairball." Her hand itched for her knife,
but she made herself keep walking, detouring doggedly
around him through vines and low-growing shrubs. A
sudden slithering in the grass startled her and she
stopped. Small animals of some sort? Then she realized
the *plants* were moving. How strange. A fibrous

mottled-green vine slid over her boot, snaring her, then another. She leaned down to free her foot.

He whirled upon her. "Stand and fight!"

"I don't fight privates with vacuum for brains," she said, "although, if you play your cards right, I might give you a lesson sometime, if I'm not too busy."

The big hrinn threw back his head and roared. Startled, she stumbled, fell backwards, then tumbled down the green-shrouded hillside. When she hit the first rock, she felt a rib snap. With the second, darkness engulfed her so that she was rolling down a long, onyx tunnel. The third and fourth rocks hardly hurt at all.

Fourteenth Coordinator paused on the rocky ledge and peered out over the tree-covered heights. Ordinarily, laka did not venture on this side of the island. Bad things had happened here long ago. The land itself had been thoroughly savaged and it was rumored traces of that evil still lingered. But, as Third Gleaner had reported, the aliens who called themselves "human" had descended from the skies again and were dug in over here. It was prudent to keep an eye on them.

She heard a piercing shriek which did not match any of the known animal cries in her vocabulary. She craned her head. The disturbance came from below in one of the many ravines carved into this side of the mountain. Of course, such disturbances were to be expected with humans around. It was thought they could be quite violent, when provoked, and it was suspected most of their number were male.

Still, these creatures, strange as they were, never interfered with the gleaning of food from the forest and mountainsides and the wet season was almost upon them. The hatchlings to come must be well fed, so they had the energy to grow and take their place in the community.

She had contributed three sacs herself this time. Eldest Coordinator thought more and more slowly these days. Soon the poor creature would not be able to finish a thought between one sunrise and the next, and someone would have to take her place.

A savage growl erupted from below. Shrubs whipped back and forth as though something monstrous were passing by. Fourteenth Coordinator cringed, then decided to hurry back to the compound. This was no place for a decent laka like herself. She must get back and oversee the harvest, make sure the cultivators weren't wasting their efforts on inferior plantings, gleaners weren't wandering aimlessly, breeders not swaggering about and boasting of the part they would play in the coming ceremony. So much to see after. She was quite too busy to worry herself with these brutish creatures.

The tracks on the outskirts of camp were plain enough. Kei's colossal prints had been overlaid by Mitsu's smaller ones, her boots clearly new. Heyoka signalled Bey and the other four hrinn to fan out and follow the scent trail, which would be more reliable than any sign visible to the eye.

Heyoka stationed Montrose back at the camp to hold down the com. He would coordinate, especially if the search party became separated and, at any rate, someone needed to respond to any messages received from the *Marion*, the ship still in orbit. He couldn't just go off and leave the camp deserted.

Fifteen minutes later, the trail they were following veered up the mountain, over vine-covered rocks, along a tumbling stream that dashed itself to glittering spray every few hundred yards. Gray clouds were gathering overhead and the wet smell of impending rain filled the air. Heyoka took the middle of the column and let the humans bring up the rear.

Bey halted at a pile of boulders, dark against the setting sun to the east. "Here," he said. "They both stopped."

"Any blood?" Heyoka asked as he climbed the last few feet.

"No," Bey said, "but I do smell a trace down that ravine."

"Hrinnti or human?" Heyoka's nose wasn't as keen at this distance as that of those members of his species who had been raised on Anktan. They'd had more practice, he supposed.

Bey plunged down the slope in a controlled slide that looked to end in disaster every second, but somehow avoided it. He disappeared into a mass of foliage, then reappeared seconds later. "It's human blood," he shouted up, "but there's no sign of Corporal Jensen."

Heyoka reached for a calm that he most definitely did not feel. At least there wasn't a body—yet. "What about Kei?" he asked.

Bey's onyx eyes were enigmatic. "He is not here either."

Chapter Three

Since it hurt to breathe, Mitsu decided she wasn't dead. The air against her face was oddly cool and dry, for Oleaaka, and the sound of her ragged breathing echoed as though walls were close at hand. The back of her head throbbed and she couldn't tell if her eyes were open. Everything appeared charcoal gray, but maybe that was just the insides of her eyelids. She'd never paid much attention to them before. She tried to sit up and failed.

"Don't struggle!" Kei said gruffly from above. "You're tangled in vines."

She could feel tough fibers cutting into her arms and neck. Something above flashed in the grayness. Kei's knife, she realized groggily, so her eyes must be open. She flinched.

He put a hand on her shoulder and pressed her down. "No wonder they were able to make you believe you were flek," he said, sawing at a vine altogether too near her cheek. "You're as stupid as one. Even a weteared cubling could have kept her footing up there."

The vine yielded to his knife and she bolted up, then wished she hadn't, as a deep stab of pain made breathing even harder. She hunched over, black dots expanding and contracting before her eyes. "If you hadn't—gotten in my way—" She had to stop and concentrate on taking a shallow breath. "—none of this—would have happened!"

A minuscule amount of light trickled down from an irregular patch of daylight far overhead. Vines had evidently overgrown the hole on the outside, masking its existence, and she'd fallen through into a cave.

She made out the faint outline of Kei looming over her, black against the dimness with his even blacker eyes. "Why in the blazes—did you come down here after me?" She paused to breathe, every inhalation a sharp pain. "It's got—to be twenty feet—back up to that hole. We'll never get out—that way."

Kei sheathed his knife with a jerk. "I did not know how far down this was, when I leaped after you."

"You should know better than to dive headfirst into an unknown situation." She struggled out of the rest of the vines, then put a trembling hand to the wall and braced herself to stand. "Or were you just afraid the fall might kill me and then you wouldn't get to do it yourself?"

"If you passed beyond the Gates of Death, I knew the Black/on/black would not believe you were dead unless he saw your body." Kei's ears flattened. "He's like that."

"Yeah." She pressed her back to the cool rock and stood there, breathing in shallow gasps. "Well, at any rate—we've got to find—another way out."

Kei rotated, head tilted back, nose twitching. The tunnel was perhaps ten feet across, twenty high. "This way," he said finally and set off to the right.

"I hope you're better at navigation than logic," she forced out and followed, supporting herself with one hand against the faint grain of the rock. The light was soon gone and she had to ease along, running her fingers over the rough stone. She stumbled often on unseen irregularities and every jolt brought additional bursts of pain from the broken ribs. Sweat broke out on her brow and trickled down into her eyes.

Ten or so minutes later, a burst of actinic *blue* flashed ahead of her in the darkness. She reeled back, heart accelerating, keenly aware her rifle was still above on the hillside. The afterimage danced on her retinas and Kei's snarl reverberated through the tunnel.

"Is someone down here with us?" she called.

"No." Kei's rumbly voice came out of the darkness, quite a bit ahead of her, by the sound.

"But we must have tripped a sensor. I saw a light!"

"I saw it too," he said gruffly, "but there is no one. If there were, I would smell them."

Then she realized the cavern wall was now vibrating beneath her palm. She pressed her cheek against it. "I feel something in the rock."

Boots scuffed, coming back towards her. She breathed in the musk of Kei's fur, not unpleasant, but as distinctive as Heyoka's. "Yes," he said, "I feel it too." An inhumanly strong hand closed around her arm and double thumbs bit into her skin. "Stay close to me."

"Oh, get real," she said, trying to pull free. "You can't see any better down here than I can."

"No, but I can smell out the shape of the open spaces," he said above her ear. "Come on. I glimpsed another light, not too far ahead."

Mitsu swayed, then caught herself on the wall. "The cave's entrance?"

"Perhaps." He drew her forward, faster than she thought prudent, and she had to trust his guidance, when she would much rather have felt her own way along the wall.

In another five minutes, she saw it herself, a dim, blue, suffused glow, not the mysterious flash of before and utterly unlike outside light, unless hours had gone by, while they were trapped down here, and it was light from one of Oleaaka's four moons. She shook Kei's hand off and eased forward.

The meandering tunnel opened out into a broad gallery. The walls had been coated with a slick, white, sickeningly familiar material and, in the center of the room, sunk into the floor, were a set of glimmering crystals, thick as old-growth trees and taller even than Kei. Blue light rippled up through them like water flowing uphill. She edged forward to touch one with the tips of her fingers. It was strangely warm, vibrating, as though it had just been struck. She traced its length with her finger and the light altered its modulation. She snatched her hand back.

"What are they?" Kei said.

"Transport crystals," she said. Blood pounded in her ears. The white room, she thought. Not again, please. Not again. "Flek transport crystals."

"The trail ends here." Bey looked up, then motioned to Heyoka. "There's blood on this rock, but just a smear." He leaned down and parted the tangled silver-green vines growing along the ground to reveal a hole in the underlying rock. They quivered at his touch, then slithered away.

"A cave," Heyoka said. "Well, that explains a lot. Are they hurt?"

Bey thrust head and shoulders into the aperture, then reappeared. "I don't see them, though their scent lingers along with another trace of human blood."

"Give me a coldlantern," Heyoka said. "I'll try to catch up with them underground, in case they're hurt. You're Squad Leader. Take half the squad and scout downslope for an entrance. If you find it, sweep back this way from the inside until you meet us. Leave the rest here, in case I need assistance."

"May I come too, sir?" Naxk, a tawny young female with black points, stepped forward.

She was small for a hrinn, which had made her a late cull in her Line back on Anktan, but she was very agile. Kendd has missed a good bet with this one, he thought, but physical perfection was everything to the hrinnti Lines. "Good thinking, private," he said. "I may need a backup."

Naxk's eyes glittered, but she betrayed no other emotion. Heyoka rigged his rope and then, compact light swinging from his belt, climbed hand over hand down into the dimness below. A minute later, Naxk had descended and was at his side.

"Leave the rope!" he called up to Bey, then switched on the coldlantern. The light radiated a precise white oval that threw the rocky walls into sharp shadowed contrast. The air was cool, but not dank, so he doubted this cave had been formed by water. Probably it was an ancient lava tube, left over from the birth of the island.

He swung his head, evaluating the scent trail. Kei's path was as plain to him as if it had been drawn in phosphorescent ink. They had gone downhill, which was good. At least they hadn't gotten confused and gone deeper into the cave system. There was just a small trace of blood on the matted vines. It was likely Mitsu had only sustained scrapes.

Naxk turned her lantern on as well and prowled after him at a respectful hrinnti distance. Their shadows bobbed along the uneven walls, over unexpected protrusions and fractures, and he wondered how Mitsu and Kei had fared down here without light.

The scent grew rapidly stronger until he expected

to catch up with them any minute. He would put them both on report, he thought testily, leaving camp like that without permission, wasting valuable training time. They had scenarios to run through, equipment to check, maps to study. They didn't have time for this adolescent nonsen—

He rounded a bend and glimpsed an unexpected blue glow up ahead. Artificial light? he wondered. Had they been equipped after all? Naxk froze, then edged closer, question written into the low cant of her ears. He motioned her forward.

"—is flek," Mitsu was saying. "I know it is!"

Heyoka breached the blueness, pistol in one hand, lantern in the other. He saw a large, roughly oval chamber surrounding a forest of eerie crystalline pillars. "What in the—?"

Mitsu turned to him, one cheek scraped, the hair on the back of her head matted with blood that looked black in this light. "About time you showed up," she said. Her eyes amplified the blueness until they seemed to glow.

"I wasn't expecting to have to pull you out of the fire again," he said irritably. "At least not so soon."

Her face tightened. She flushed and looked away, and he could have kicked himself.

"What we have here, sir, is a set of flek transport crystals," she said in a low voice.

"In a cave?" he said.

"Where better to hide them?" she said.

He set his coldlantern on the floor. The slick white walls seemed to soak up their voices, but he detected a faint hum just below the human range of hearing. "You might be right," he said. "If so, they've stayed hidden for at least forty-eight years while Confederation experts practically dismantled this world, searching for intact flek artifacts."

"They're considerably older than that." The blue light

turned her skin an unhealthy pallid white. "The crystals we destroyed back on Anktan were barely waist-high, and were so delicate, you could break them with a rifle butt, and they'd been growing for over thirty years. These are huge."

So they were most likely hundreds of years old, he realized numbly. Maybe even more. The flek had evidently occupied this planet much earlier than anyone had ever suspected. "But they are always so careful to destroy whatever they leave behind. Why would they leave these crystals intact?"

"They were flek," Kei broke in, "so they were stupid."

Heyoka whirled upon the big hrinn. "By now, you ought to know better than to underestimate them. Flek think very differently from us, but they are not stupid. I only wish they were."

Mitsu looked even shakier than her injuries warranted. He had a sudden flash of that terrible moment, last year, when he had found her among the flek, crazed, unable to recognize him or anyone else from her past life. *The wildness in her blue eyes, the pure High-Flek that was all she would speak.*

She stepped toward the crystals, winced, then braced her ribs with one hand. "They're still active. Don't you feel it? They were left *on*. Flek could come back here whenever they want. Maybe they travel to Oleaaka all the time and no one knows it because they stay down here." She glanced back over his shoulder at the dark passages leading back into the heart of the mountain. "Maybe they're here right now."

"I wonder if the laka know about these crystals," he said numbly.

"We should destroy them," Naxk said. Her lips wrinkled back in a silent snarl as she set her coldlantern on the floor next to his. "Then no one can use them ever again."

"No!" Heyoka said. "And that's an order. No one is to touch them without authorization. HQ put out a lot of heat last year when the Anktan grid was destroyed before they got a chance to examine it. We have to get topside and report this find. I'm betting they have a team here in forty-eight hours."

Mitsu's eyes darted around the chamber, as though looking for a way to escape. Sweat beaded up on her forehead. "But we can't just leave them like this," she said. "*Anything* could come through and we'd never know until it was too late."

"We'll set a guard," Heyoka said. He started to order Naxk to stay with Kei, but hrinnti females and males were not comfortable working together, another cultural snag. "Two at a time, and we'll leave a com down here. Kei, take the first watch. If Bey makes it through from the other end, tell him to stand watch with you and send the rest of the squad back to camp. We'll post your relief in four hours. Naxk returns with Mitsu and me."

Kei flicked an ear in answer, but Naxk saluted crisply. "Yes, sir."

Heyoka picked up one of the coldlanterns. "Move it, Corporal," he said. "You look done in, which is exactly what you deserve. Let's get back to camp and have a med check you out."

"I'm fine," she said, but then moved too fast and sucked in her breath at a sudden jab of pain.

"Yeah," he said. "I can tell."

When the news reached the *Marion* up in orbit, Major Erek Dennehy didn't know whether to curse or order champagne. This was going to throw his hrinnti training schedule all to blazes. Experts from every corner of the Confederation would be popping out of the proverbial woodwork to crawl all over those caves.

And who knew if this was the only find they'd make? That cave system could run on for miles under those mountains and even richer discoveries might be waiting for them farther in.

Ancient crystals, Blackeagle had said. Twenty times the size of the ones destroyed on Anktan last year, and *active*. If Confederation experts could figure out how they worked, they might even be able to trace them back to the original flek home world, which had never been identified. What a boon that would be! They might at last be able to carry the war to its source.

But such an intensive search was sure to disrupt the laka's quiet life again, and they were only now making a comeback after nearly being exterminated during the last occupation. According to reports, it was difficult for them to achieve viable population numbers because they were such a complicated species. They seemed to be divided into innumerable castes, each possessing a unique body configuration and speaking a separate dialect. One form apparently existed solely to translate among the rest. Because of this, human linguists had never made much headway communicating with them and laka were singularly uncooperative. It was going to be harder than all get-out to explain any of this to them.

But we have to try, he thought, and he still had to salvage what he could out of the training exercise. He'd better go on down there and see to the details himself.

Blackeagle had requested medical assistance; he had a man down. Dennehy checked the duty roster, then assigned Med-Tech Brascelli to meet him in the shuttle bay in fifteen minutes.

Heyoka dragged Mitsu out for the med's inspection as soon as the tiny, ten-man shuttle landed. She'd made herself scarce when they'd returned to camp and he had to pry her out of the supply tent over severe

protests. He supposed she'd developed an aversion to
doctors over the past year, which was natural, given what
she'd been through.

"Two cracked ribs and a nasty cut on the back of the
head," Brascelli announced, after checking the readout
on her portable scanner. She was a tall, angular woman
and towered over Mitsu. "No concussion, fortunately.
I'll have to clean the cut, then seal it. The ribs will take
several hours of deep stim to knit. She can be fit again
by morning."

Mitsu looked as though she might bolt, but Heyoka
nodded. "I'll check back later."

All around him, the small camp bristled with energy.
Everyone was energized by the discovery and eager to
go down and see the crystals. Well, he thought, they
would all get their turn. It was going to take the entire
squad to set a proper watch until a qualified assessment
team arrived.

Unfortunately, Bey had not been able to find an
outside entrance into the cave system, so the only
access at the moment was through the hole Mitsu
had "discovered." They were going to have to work
their way out from the crystal chamber.

He took Montrose and Naxk back with him to the
site, intending to post them as the next watch.
Major Dennehy had already gone ahead with Fletcher,
a stolid human trainee with a knack for electronics
and demolitions.

Dennehy turned to him as Heyoka entered the
chamber. The blue lights rippled over his face. "It's
incredible!"

Heyoka caught Kei's eye. "Has there been any sign
of activity, Private?"

Kei hunkered down on his heels and stared moodily
into the gleaming crystalline columns. "No."

"Good," Heyoka said. "Montrose and Naxk are

waiting topside to relieve you. Send them down, then return to camp and find some dinner."

Kei made a vague salute. Heyoka hoped the major was too absorbed in examining the crystals to notice, but Dennehy shook his head after the hrinn had gone.

"You're going to have trouble with that one," he said. "He's too headstrong."

"I know," Heyoka said, "but he's also a natural leader."

"And a born warrior, as are all of your hrinnti recruits." Dennehy sighed. "I've read the reports of his actions on Anktan with you last year, but he's been in training for months now and you still haven't eliminated that sizable chip on his shoulder. I suspect he's just too mature to change his ways. We'll have to recruit younger hrinn in the future, if we continue to recruit at all."

"He's impatient to fight the flek." Heyoka brushed against the slick white wall and shuddered. It smelled faintly of flek. "They all are. They've left their world and their people, everything they've ever known, to come out here and stop the flek. They aren't human and they're never going to respond exactly like human soldiers, but they are still an asset."

"Not if they don't follow orders," Dennehy said. "Private Kei looks like he wants to tear your throat out."

Very perceptive, Heyoka thought. No doubt, Kei did want to tear his throat out, just the savage *other* within him ached to return the favor every time those potent fight pheromone molecules danced through his brain. It was the way evolution had made them, the way their brains were wired, as much a part of them as their fur. "I'll—work on it, sir," he said. "We'll get it straightened out, or I will send him back to Anktan."

"See that you do, Sergeant," Dennehy said.

Footsteps echoed in the passageway, then Montrose

and Naxk entered the crystal chamber. Seeing them together brought home to Heyoka how short the hrinnti female was for her kind, barely taller than Montrose.

"Reporting as ordered, sir," Montrose said with a salute.

Naxk also saluted, without hesitation or challenge, Heyoka noted.

"At ease," he said. "You've got the watch and Montrose is senior. If you see the least variation in color or hear any unusual sound, contact us immediately. Otherwise, you'll be relieved in four hours."

The two took up position on opposite sides of the crystals, bodies stiff, hands locked behind their backs. The blue light bathed their serious faces, one furred and tawny, the other shaven and dark, so different from each other.

"Lord, it's hard to tear myself away," Major Dennehy said. He pinched the bridge of his nose. "It's like finding the Holy Grail. We've been searching for something like this for as long as I've been in the service."

"Same here." Heyoka gestured at the passageway. "At any rate, let's go back to camp and plan. I had a thought that perhaps, after the team gets here, you could drop the squad over on the other side of the island and let us finish the exercise."

"That might work," Dennehy said. "You certainly can't continue over here. This place will be crawling with experts."

They worked their way back through the labyrinthine cave in the chill circle of light from the coldlantern, climbed the rope ladder that had been left in place, and returned to camp.

The med's fingers were gentle on the back of Mitsu's aching head, but she hated to be touched. "Are you almost done?"

"No, I need to put you out for the stim," the med, Brascelli, said, capping the tube of the pungent sealant in her hand and repacking it into her kit. "Lie down here on the cot."

"Forget it!" Mitsu scrambled to her feet, then hunched over against the jolt of pain in her ribs.

"The bones have to remain perfectly aligned while you're under stim," the med said, "and conscious people can't be still that long. Lie down."

"I just need a day or two," Mitsu said. "I'll be fine."

"Even if I strapped those ribs, you could puncture a lung if you weren't careful," Brascelli said. "I certainly can't certify you to return to duty if you refuse treatment."

Then they would send her back to the ship, Mitsu thought. What little chance she had to shake this everpresent fear would be lost. No other unit would have her; she was damaged goods.

"Lie down," the med said. "You'll sleep like a baby."

That was the worst of it, the promise of sleep. Sleep always brought dreams these days, and, in her dreams, she was always back there on Anktan, with the flek. *In the white room.*

Trembling, she stretched out on the canvas cot and closed her eyes. The med pressed something cool and metallic to her upper arm and then she was floating. The clatter of the camp faded, the pressure of the cot beneath her back, the pain stitched across her ribs with every shallow breath. It was almost pleasant, to drift so . . . .

The immense grid on the plain beyond the mountains was filled with coruscating lights, bizarre pinks and purples, electric blues. The sound began again, shrill and agonizing, climbing quickly toward unbearable. She stood beside the crystals in the heart of the grid and fought to save the irreplaceable facility from terrible hair-covered, verminous beasts who meant to destroy it.

One, blacker than the rest, raced toward her, visible one moment, gone the next, as though he were a poor holo image, winking in and out. She raised her laser-stick and took aim. She would kill him first, the rest later. She raised her weapon and fired.

Chapter Four

A blood-curdling scream broke Heyoka out of a sound sleep. He leaped to his feet, rifle already in hand, ducking under the tent flap before he had come fully awake. He paused outside, the camp coming alive around him. The night was warm, the scent of night-blooming flowers strong in the air. His heart lurched into high gear as the two sentries, Visht and Onopa, darted into view.

Before he could question them, a second scream split the night. It was coming from Mitsu's tent, he realized, and peeled the flap back. Inside, Mitsu sat bolt upright on the cot, head clasped in her hands. "They're in my mind!" she said, her voice cracking. Tears streamed down her cheeks. "They won't leave me alone!"

Med-Tech Brascelli knelt beside her, scanner already at work. "She should be fine," she said in a daze. "I gave her a sedative to keep her down and let the stim knit her ribs. She should be out like a light until morning."

Heyoka waved a hand before Mitsu's staring eyes.

45

"I think she still is," he said quietly. "She—had a bad time back on Anktan. The flek worked her over. There are memories buried in her subconscious that no one, human or hrinn, should ever have to experience. The sedative must have kept her under when she would normally have woken."

"Damn!" Brascelli took Mitsu's shaking shoulders and eased her back against the cot. "It's all right," she said to the unresponsive woman. "You're on Oleaaka with your squad. The flek are light-years away. It was just a bad dream."

Anger surged through Heyoka. "This isn't a field hospital! You should have checked her records back up on the ship before you treated her." Mitsu was mumbling now, but he couldn't make out the words.

"Her ribs are almost healed, at any rate," the med said. "I'll sit with her for a while. I could give her something else, but at this point, I think it's safer just to wait until she comes out of it. She'll be okay."

Dennehy squeezed into the small tent and stared down at Mitsu, whose eyes had now closed, though her lips still moved. "I want a full report when we get back to the ship."

"And you'll get it, sir," Brascelli said, her face flushed, "but if this soldier has such special medical needs, why is she training with a combat unit?"

And that, Heyoka thought, was yet another problem that traced back only to him.

Montrose studied the young hrinn across the cave as they guarded the great crystalline columns. Her fur was a rich golden brown shading to black on ears, muzzle, hands, and legs, very striking. She was barely taller than his six-foot-five frame, though, quite short for one of them.

"Tell me about your home," he said to pass the time.

They had turned their coldlanterns off to conserve the energy packs and the rippling blue glow filled the chamber like an exotic gas.

"Anktan is no longer my home," the hrinn said. "I left all that behind when I joined the Corps."

Montrose prided himself on doing his homework and he'd always been intrigued by nonhostile aliens. He'd studied hrinnti culture after he'd gotten this posting and found the hrinn a fascinating species. "I've done a lot of reading about Anktan," he said. "Aren't there five Lines in your region?"

She fixed him with a heart-stopping black-eyed stare that made him look away. "Once there were six, then for a time, only five Lines continued. Now, since the Black/on/black came among us, there are six once more."

"'Black/on/black,'" he repeated. "That's your name for Sergeant Blackeagle, isn't it?"

"It is more than a name," she said, and he thought she bristled a bit. "It's who, and what, he is. We would all be dead now, if it were not for him. He found the center of the emerging *pattern/in/progress* and cleared the flek from our world."

That term had religious significance, he remembered, and decided to steer clear of the subject. "Which Line did you come from?" he said and shifted position to keep his circulation going. The cave was cool, the air much drier than outside. "Vvok? Jhii?"

"I was born of Kendd," she said, "but at the Final Gleaning, I was designated a late cull."

"Oh," he said, trying to remember what he'd read in the sociological notes about "culls." "Is that bad?"

Her ears flattened and a snarl rattled low in her throat. Bad choice of words, he told himself. "Hey, I was kicked out of two schools before I got my act together. I set fires, stole airhoppers. Worst kid in three districts,' they said. My dad had to send me to military school."

"The male who sired you?" she said. "Why was he consulted?"

"Human fathers live with their families a good deal of the time," he said. "He was trying to train me up right, so, of course, he wanted me to behave."

Her ears pricked forward. "Did he beat you?"

"I got my share of drubbings," he said. "And you?"

Naxk parted the tawny fur on her throat with both hands. A fearsome jagged scar twisted from her left ear down across her throat. "I once lived through a beating from Yikan herself, Line Mother to all Kendd." Her muzzle rose proudly. "She nearly changed her mind about culling me. Few Kendd culls have ever been able to say that."

"I—see." The Adam's apple in his throat bobbed as he swallowed. "And how did you come to be recruited by Master Sergeant Blackeagle?"

Her black nose wrinkled and he glimpsed the wicked double rows of teeth. "I survived."

The light playing through the massive columns flickered, then rippled faster, as though the frequency had suddenly increased. Naxk pinned her ears back. "The sound has changed."

"I don't hear anything beyond a faint background hum," Montrose said. He snatched up his rifle from where he had propped it against the cavern wall. Across the chamber, the blue light bathed Naxk's tawny face so that she seemed to be standing underwater.

The hrinn backed away from the crystals, shaking her head. "The pitch is rising! Did you touch something?"

"No." He couldn't actually hear it, but he could *feel* the resonance in the bones of his inner ear. Though the frequency was too high for humans, hrinn, with their much more sensitive hearing, evidently detected it.

Naxk snarled and her wicked claws sprang free. She stared at him wildly. "Turn it off!"

"We can't!" Montrose said. "We don't dare touch anything." He fumbled for his com unit. "We have to report."

But no one answered, despite repeated attempts on his part. The grid must be interfering with transmissions. He turned back to Naxk, who was huddled against the wall, hands over her large, mobile ears. "Get back to camp!" he told her, shouting to make himself understood over noise he couldn't even hear. "Tell Blackeagle to send reinforcements, but no hrinn!"

She scrambled to her feet, swaying, her black eyes crazed.

"Do you understand me? Tell the hrinn not to come back down here!" He activated a coldlantern and pushed it into her hands.

Shaking, she fled the chamber, back toward the rope ladder and freedom from pain. He took up his stance braced against the wall, as far from the crystals as he could manage, rifle in hand, and grimly watched as the strobing effect of the bright blue light continued to quicken.

It seemed Heyoka had just settled back down to grab a few winks, as humans said, when more commotion disturbed the camp. He heard Onopa, the human sentry, call out in challenge. A hrinnti voice answered, and he thought he recognized Naxk.

Why had she left her post? He rolled back onto his feet, fumbled for his boots. His orders had been very specific and she wasn't due to be relieved for several more hours. Of course, measured time had always proved a tenuous concept for hrinn. He'd had more than one problem with that already.

He sealed the front of his shirt and ducked back out

into the heavy, scented air. Insects sang in the night and the breeze soughed through the surrounding trees. It seemed very peaceful—everywhere else. "Private Naxk," he said testily, "who gave you permission to leave your post?"

The hrinnti female was wild-eyed, her fur standing on end. "It was the noise!" she cried. "A terrible hum! My ears were going to burst! I couldn't stay!" She fought for breath. Obviously, she'd half-killed herself to get here this quickly.

"What noise?" His ears flattened. "Where's Montrose?"

"Back in the cave." She leaned her head back, panting away the excess heat.

Major Dennehy and Med-Tech Brascelli appeared, their faces concerned. "What's going on?" Dennehy demanded.

"The crystals—started making a noise," Naxk said. "So loud, I thought my skull would explode!"

Cold fear washed over Heyoka. His handclaws flexed. "Did the lights change?"

"They got—" She snarled in frustration, searching for the right word in Standard, then switched to hrinnti. "—faster, like water rushing downhill, and there was a piercing, high-pitched noise!"

Heyoka's ears flattened. "Why didn't you call on the com?"

"Private Montrose tried, but it wouldn't function anymore. He said it was interference." She dropped her gaze. "He told me not to send any hrinn back down there."

But he had to go, Heyoka thought grimly. If the crystals had been reactivated after all these years, then the flek might indeed be coming through again. He had to inspect the installation for himself and then mount a defense.

"Ishara, Riordan, with me," he said. "The rest of you,

stay with the camp and the major. See if you can raise the ship, while I'm gone. Tell them what's happening."

"Hold on, Blackeagle!" Dennehy said. "According to the private here, you won't be any use down there. I'll go."

"I'll bring ear protectors," Heyoka said. "I always carry a pair in my kit." He pulled on his combat vest, picked up a coil of synthetic fiber rope.

Dennehy blocked his path, head and shoulders shorter. "Stand down, mister, and that's an order."

A snarl rose in Heyoka's throat, but he managed to choke it back. *Tear his audacious throat out*, urged his savage *other. He has not proven his right to rule over you!* He fought to draw an even breath. "Major," he said as reasonably as he could manage under the circumstances, "this is my command."

"Not anymore," Dennehy said. "As of now, I'm taking over."

Angry voices rose and fell, rose again, outside Mitsu's tent. She sat up, then hunched over, holding her whirling head, which seemed about to float away. Had she tied one on last night, even on this All-Father-forsaken island? Evidently so. She and Blackeagle and the rest of the unit must have been celebrating something. She wondered blearily just exactly what it had been.

She swung her legs off the rickety cot, but it took two attempts before she found her balance and stood. In the dimness, she seemed to be still wearing her tan fatigues. She fingered the light weave. A bit ripe. A bath was in order, or maybe she should just soak her head, in cold water, if at all possible.

Running her fingers through her close cropped black hair, she pushed through the tent flaps out into the night air. Two of the squad were kitting up as though it was muster and paid her no attention. She squinted at them, trying to focus.

"What's the hurry?" she said. "Has Blackeagle called nighttime maneuvers?"

A red-haired kid, Riordan, she thought was his name, glanced up at her. "It's the flek crystals," he said briefly. "They've gone active."

It all came back, Kei leaving camp, her following, the ignominious fall into the cave. She turned back to her tent. "Wait!" she called over her shoulder. "I'm coming too!"

"No, you're not," Blackeagle said, looming tall and black suddenly at her side. "You're going to stay here until the med certifies you fit for duty. Where is Brascelli anyway? She was supposed to keep watch over you the rest of the night."

She glared up at him. "I'm fine!"

"And you'll stay fine, right here in camp," he said.

"You don't trust me," she said and thought she would burst if she weren't allowed to do her job. "You think I'll go flek again, given half a chance!"

"What I know is that you were injured today and need more rest before you return to duty," he said. "Anything else is just your imagination working overtime."

Her hands were clenched at her sides. She felt as though she couldn't move, as though her enduring humiliation were written across her face for everyone to see. "Did you ever think," she said slowly, "that it might have been better just to let me die back there on Anktan?"

"Yes," he said in his usual enigmatic fashion. His black eyes gleamed down at her, his massive frame outlined in starlight. "Now, get back to bed, and that's an order."

She managed the few steps back into her tent and then collapsed onto the cot, head spinning. Brascelli, carrying a coldlantern, eased in and raised an eyebrow. "I just stepped out for a few minutes." She gave Mitsu an appraising look. "You okay now?"

"Fine." Mitsu bit her lip and gazed down at her feet.

"Good." Brascelli pulled a medscanner out of her vest pocket and switched it on, then studied the readings. "You just had a bad reaction to the sedative, I guess. It happens once in a while, nothing to worry about."

"No problem," said Mitsu.

The med changed the settings, squinted at the readouts, then clicked the scanner off. "Looks okay to me, for now. I'll check you again in a few hours." She withdrew, presumably to do something more productive than baby-sit a crazed corporal.

Mitsu stared down at the dim whiteness of her hands in the gloom. Well, if she was going to lose her mind again, it would be nice to get it over with. One more trip to those crystals ought to tell the tale, one way or another. She picked up her holstered pistol, then her laser rifle, loosened the bottom of her tent and crawled out into the night.

Ninth Translator-at-large woke Fourteenth Coordinator before dawn. The other members of the coordinator's retinue roused from their floorbeds and reacted to this intrusion with shock.

"The breeders are extremely agitated," the translator said. "They insist they are being called!" Her forearms wove a pattern of distress. "They are singing their most violent songs and won't desist. Eldest Coordinator says we may have to put them down early this season."

"Before the Feast of Leavetaking?" Fourteenth Coordinator stiffened at the thought. Ritual soothed rougher transitions like Leavetaking and all the castes of course looked forward to playing their traditional roles. She sat up from her slingbed. "Should we perhaps move Leavetaking forward a few days?" she asked. "Would that take care of it?"

"No, you don't understand!" Ninth Translator danced

before the shallow niche in her trepidation. "They have left their nest and gone to the heights—to that—place!" She broke off and turned her head aside, unable to bring herself to actually say its rightful name.

"They cannot have gone there!" Fourteenth Coordinator sat back, her hands opening in astonishment.

"Yes." Ninth's voice was a strangled whisper. "They pushed me aside and stampeded out into the night. No matter how I pleaded, I could not reason with them. It was like the old stories, from before."

"But they can't actually accomplish anything up there," Fourteenth Coordinator said. She felt a dithering fool. She should have anticipated something of this sort. That was her function, to weave the lives of the colony together into a harmonious whole. "The entrance was buried long ago. Nothing is left."

"It does not matter. Their bodies remember the way, and, if they keep themselves stirred up like this, they might also remember what they once were, what we all were," Ninth said. "Once that happens, they will no longer be satisfied with what little they are permitted now."

Heyoka checked on Mitsu after Dennehy left and found her missing—again, along with her rifle. Her scent still hung in the tent, mingled with canvas and plastic and the acrylic fibers of the cot. She couldn't have left more than a few minutes ago. He barked orders over his shoulder for Fletcher to take charge and call the ship every five minutes. Its orbit had taken it out of range for the moment, but it would be back in position soon.

He set off after his partner through the tangle of vines and trees, over scattered rocks. She was moving more slowly than he might have predicted and he thought she must be still groggy. He caught the scent of her hand on trunks and boulders more and more often as she steadied herself.

She should have stayed behind with the meds back on Emsell, he thought. They'd tried to tell him she wasn't ready and he saw that now, but he'd wanted so badly to believe she could recover. He would always feel what had happened to her on Anktan was his fault. She wouldn't have been there at all, except to cover his back.

Of course, she wouldn't have fallen into the hands of the damned flek, if she'd obeyed orders then either. Doing what she had been told had never been her strong suit, but she'd been a good enough soldier to make up for that. He grimaced and quickened his pace, using his hrinnti night sight to navigate where a human would have tripped and fallen a dozen times over.

He found her, flat on her face, breathing hard, close to the cave opening in the side of the hill. Her rifle lay beside her.

"Going somewhere?" He squatted beside her and his nose wrinkled at the coppery tang of human blood.

She heaved over on her back and cradled skinned hands against her chest. Her breathing was labored. "Crazy, I guess."

The fur on the back of his neck bristled. "That's not funny."

"Nothing is," she said. "That's the problem. I can't go anywhere, do anything, without everyone looking at me like I might break."

"When you pull stunts like this, it's no wonder!" He switched on his coldlantern. Her face was alabaster pale and her blue eyes stood out like sapphires.

"I just wanted to see them again, to find out if I could stand it." She sat up and rested her forehead on bent knees.

"The crystals?" he said.

"Yeah." She looked at the hole in the black rock with its rope ladder extending down into the darkness. "If I can't hold onto myself down there, then wash me out." She closed her eyes. "I don't want to endanger my squad."

"This isn't about you!" He stood up, threw back his head and loomed over her. "There's a war going on. We've got boots to train and you're lying out here, AWOL, feeling sorry for yourself!"

"But you don't know," she said.

"Don't know what?"

"What's inside my head," she said. "Despite everything, they're still there and it's all I can do to hold them back."

The flek, he thought numbly.

The small black com unit on his belt beeped. He punched it on. "Yes?"

"Dennehy here, down in the cave," it said, though the signal was thick with interference. *"I escaped, then got far enough from the crystals to use the com, but the rest of the squad is pinned down by locals, at least five that I could see. They need evac, unless you want them to fight their way through a bunch of unarmed civilians."*

"Locals—you mean laka?"

"Affirmative," said the major.

"Can you make it back to the ladder?"

Mitsu scrambled to her feet.

"I can, but the rest are trapped with no egress."

"Meet us above then," Heyoka said. "The laka have never been hostile, but I'll gather the rest of the squad and escort the rest out."

"Negative!" Dennehy barked. *"The crystals are still activated. They're reached the point where even humans can hear them now. Montrose was right. A hrinn couldn't function down here."*

"I'll go." Mitsu was breathing hard and her face looked gray. "I'm the ranking human in the squad. It has to be me."

Chapter Five

Montrose had seen holos of native Oleaakans, of course, in preparation for the training exercises, but hadn't quite taken in their scale until the sudden appearance of these five out of the side passage. They were so—big. The laka stood now shoulder to shoulder in front of the crystals as though to protect them. Their gleaming bodies, tinted in various pastel shades, were head and shoulders taller than a man, and their shell-pink eyes peered down at the human soldiers with unnerving directness.

In the center of the chamber, the crystal matrix kept up its shrill keening, now audible in the human range. Montrose was having trouble concentrating.

Riordan edged along the slick white wall, rifle at the ready. "Should we blast our way out?"

Montrose shook his head. "No, they're not armed. Wait, unless they charge. Maybe they'll back off, or at least communicate what they want."

"According to the briefings—" Steve Ishara, a big, bluff man, hunkered down and studied the natives

57

through narrowed eyes. "—the laka are a 'peaceful, retiring species.'"

Onopa gripped her rifle with both hands. Her sun-bronzed face was grim. "They don't look so all-fired retiring to me."

"We'll split up," Montrose said. "Ishara, take Riordan and Niels. Try to break past them and make it back to the ladder. The major headed that way and so far they haven't gone after him. I'll take Onopa and try the other tunnel. With luck, they'll be confused and won't follow either party."

Ishara looked dubious. "Blackeagle sent a hrinn to scout for an outside entrance into the cave, but it didn't find one."

Montrose grimaced. "*He* didn't find one—not 'it,' and, if you ask me, we could use a few of those hrinn at our backs right about now."

"Yeah, sure," Ishara said. "Anyway, you don't know where that passage leads. It could be a dead end. You and Onopa might wander around down here in the dark for days."

The crystals' wail revved up another notch. The natives tensed and Montrose felt as though the sound was sautéing his brain. "There has to be a way in from outside, or these guys wouldn't be here now. Anyway, if we don't find the exit, we'll come back." He checked his rifle, then switched on his coldlantern. "On my mark—go!"

The other three darted past the natives into the side tunnel. Montrose ducked his head and dashed into the far passageway. He kept moving, listening for sounds of pursuit. The cave twisted, opened out into an unoccupied chamber, then doubled back on itself. It was dark and claustrophobic, stuffy. He felt like he was running in place, not getting anywhere. Onopa dogged his heels, uncomplaining and silent as a shadow.

Finally, he signalled a halt and stood with his spine pressed to the stone so he could catch his breath. By the coldlantern, he could see roots penetrating down through cracks in the ceiling rock overhead. They must be close to the surface.

Breathing hard, Onopa reached up and ran her fingers over the black stone. "I think this may be a lava tube, left over from the island's origin. It could go on for miles, maybe even lead down to the sea."

Something brushed the cavern wall in the impenetrable darkness behind the bright circle of light. The hairs stirred on the back of his neck. "Keep moving," he whispered hoarsely and motioned her on.

Onopa, who had already seen action on three worlds, before applying for specialized Ranger training, nodded and slipped into the darkness ahead, activating her own coldlantern. Montrose followed at a trot, his heart racing.

The noise came again, more of a scrape this time. Voices rose and fell. Not human. Not hrinnti either. "Faster!"

Onopa ran, her light bobbing with each stride. Their footsteps echoed and again they seemed to be running through an endless night.

Then he glimpsed a patch of gray-black beyond Onopa, only slightly less dark than the cave, but peppered with stars. He redoubled his pace and caught up just as the floor curved upward. They climbed hand over hand, feet struggling for footholds. Montrose slipped, then caught himself on an outcropping of jagged rock. Pain shot through his hands and he could tell by their slipperiness that he was bleeding.

Onopa reached down and hauled him by his belt up into the sweet-scented Oleaakan night. He sprawled at her feet and took in great lungfuls of fresh night air. The breeze sighed against his face, filled with the tang of the not-too-distant sea. Tiny night flyers fluttered overhead, black against the green-black sky.

Out of the darkness, a wall of four-armed, four-legged bodies surged forward to surround them.

Montrose heaved onto his feet, while Onopa swept her light over the natives and swore.

"You're not going anywhere, but back to camp!" Heyoka informed Mitsu. He didn't like that overbright gleam in her eyes, reminiscent of a feverish child who refuses to be put to bed. She needed to be back under the watchful eye of the med.

Mitsu wiped her scraped hands on her thighs, leaving smears of blood that looked black in the starlight. "I can slip in, flank the natives, get the drop on them—"

Dennehy's grizzled gray head appeared as he struggled up the rope ladder. The older man was breathing hard as he pulled himself out onto the vine-covered ground. The vines slithered fastidiously out of reach. "They weren't armed, but they blocked us, when we tried to leave, and made no effort to communicate."

"That's strange," Heyoka said. "According to reports, they usually avoid ruins on the surface."

"I think it's safe to say they don't feel any aversion to these." Dennehy mopped his overheated face. The night was sweltering and the breeze seemed only to move the thick, humid air around, rather than cool. "We're going to have to take stiff security measures when the assessment team arrives. We can't have them barging in like this."

Mitsu peered down into the cave, then met Dennehy's eyes. "Let me go down there, Major, and assess the situation," she said reasonably. "I'll report back as soon as I know what's up."

"No!" Heyoka said, before Dennehy could answer. "Hell, I'm in charge here." The major's brow wrinkled like an old pit bull's. "Why not, if she's fit for duty? *You* certainly can't go. Those crystals would burst your eardrums."

In his haste to catch up to Mitsu, he'd left the damn ear protectors back at camp and it was too late to go back for them now.

Mitsu sat very still, her back straight. Though her eyes were huge in her haunted face, she looked more like her old self than she had in quite a while, he thought, more like a Ranger in the field and eager for action. If he insisted she go back to camp now, he'd have to explain to the major, and that information would probably wash her out of the military for good.

"All right," he said gruffly. "Take your rifle, as well as your sidearm, and don't waste time trying to be a hero. Just take one quick look and report back. Don't open fire unless your life is in danger. I'll decide what, if any, our response will be."

"Yes, sir!" Mitsu saluted, but her blue eyes twinkled. Heyoka knew that look. She'd put one over on him. In the old days, there'd been absolutely nothing she liked better. She slung the rifle over her shoulder and climbed lightly back down the ladder—as though her hands weren't scraped raw and she hadn't broken two ribs earlier in the day.

As though she were in her right mind, which Heyoka very much doubted.

Second Breeder stalked about the underground chamber, beating his second-hands against his flanks in a restless chant of disapproval. He turned his face this way and that, taking in the eerie blue beauty. Songs he had never sung, concepts that lurked deep within his cells and had never made themselves known, quivered now almost within reach.

How dare those squalid creatures defile this place!

True, he and the other breeders were only short-lived males, fit for little except procreation, but even they understood its power when it called out to them. Once, long ago, important things had happened here, momentous things of which the other castes would no longer speak. It was rumored, though, that *drones* had done these things. He shivered at the thought.

The great crystal trees in the center of the room *sang*, such a pale word for the incredible rush of sound and sensation and resonance. That was how he and the other breeders had known they must come. Its call had penetrated the night and jolted them out of their bored stupor.

It hinted at power and must truly have some immense meaning, but he and his fellows were too low-bred to understand. A translator might have been able to decipher it, but translators were female, and females, with their intense need for cooperation at all levels of laka society, did not approve of power.

Second Breeder let the song reverberate through his body. Some of the others had chased after the intruders, but that was pointless. What could any of them do, except block the aliens' path, should they attempt to come back? A very unsatisfactory alternative, he thought. There ought to be more one could do, even a useless drone like himself.

He scratched an itch just behind his first-shoulder and let his mind roam. Somehow, some way, there ought to be something . . .

It appeared to be either the same group of natives who had cornered them back in the cave, or another very much like it. Was there another way out? Montrose reached for his pistol and clicked the safety off.

Onopa gave him a sideways glance, her broad face impassive. He felt a burst of irritation. He'd had trouble reading her ever since she'd joined the squad five months ago. She never gave him any clues. In combat, it cost lives if you didn't know what your partner was going do without being told.

"Let's try to give them the slip," she said in a husky whisper, gazing purposefully into the darkness as though the natives weren't there. "They're not armed, so we don't want to fire on them if we can help it. We can keep this from turning into a diplomatic incident, if we can lose them in the brush and then head back to camp."

Of course, just where camp was, in relation to their current position, Montrose was not sure. He supposed they could at least head for higher ground and then hole up until daylight. And, once they got away from here, they could check in. The coms should work up here, away from the interference.

"All right," he said. "You go left. I'll take right. We'll rendezvous up beyond that outcropping of rock." He motioned toward the hills.

Onopa nodded, switched off her light, then edged left, putting more distance between herself and the nearest native. It hesitated, then reached for the tall woman. She ducked its grasp and plunged into the darkness, leaving swaying bushes in her wake. The native darted after her.

At the same moment, Montrose dove right as two more laka closed on him. Their scent was thick and musky, laced with a sickly sweet base note. Despite their size, they were faster than he'd anticipated and one snagged his sleeve. He dug in his feet and broke free, then scrambled up the dark hillside on lacerated hands and knees.

They followed, climbing relentlessly, and seized his ankle. He slid backwards, dropped his pistol and fumbled desperately to retrieve it with one hand, clawing for a handhold with the other. His fingers found the pistol, so he turned over and tried to take aim. The native snatched the sidearm out of his hand with surprising ease.

Peaceful and retiring! he thought angrily. They should have had better intel than this, even for a training exercise. What kind of situation had they blundered into?

The native swayed above him, chanting in a surprisingly melodious voice. He wrenched at his ankle, but the creature tightened its grip and wrung a yelp out of him. He swore under his breath and hammered at it with his fist.

Another set of inhumanly strong hands seized him from behind and, then holding him aloft, bore him away into the overheated Oleaakan night.

Mitsu ran into Ishara, Riordan, and Niels just as the three stumbled up to the rope ladder. They were out of breath and tense, glancing back over their shoulders.

"Don't go down there!" Riordan, a chunky red-haired youth, wiped his perspiring forehead. "The locals have staked out the crystals and they don't look friendly. We were lucky to escape without having to take any of them out."

Mitsu hopped down from the ladder. "Did they attack?"

"No, we split up before they made a move," Niels said. He had the white hair and pale skin of a colonist from Brae's World, which had fallen to the flek three years ago. "Montrose and Onopa ducked out the other way. We're supposed to rendezvous back at camp."

Mitsu stepped away from the ladder and nodded. "The major sent me to check the situation," she said. "He and Sergeant Blackeagle are waiting above right now. Go up and report. I'll be back in a few minutes."

"That's stupid," Niels blurted and looked back into the darkness. "They could be right behind us."

"I have my orders, mister," she said, "and so do you."

"Yes, sir," Niels said. He gave her a sour look that clearly said she was off her rocker. Ishara stared instead at his boots.

She had to put some distance between herself and Heyoka before they reached the top and he called her back, so she plunged into the darkness. The coldlantern cast its cone of light before her as she oriented herself with one hand on the cool wall. She was so tired of everyone waiting for her to go off the deep end and do something crazy.

Even though she tried to be quiet, the sound of her footsteps echoed. Her heart leaped into overdrive. They would hear her coming!

But these were only laka, the rational part of her brain insisted, civilians. They were supposed to be peaceful to a fault, so unable or unwilling to defend themselves, they'd let the flek nearly wipe them out. Whatever their reasons for coming down here tonight, most likely it wasn't to hurt anyone.

It was just like the brass to get all excited over a few harmless gawkers. Even Heyoka was getting delusions of grandeur, now that he had his own command and oversight of the hrinnti training program. He didn't need a partner anymore, he needed subordinates. If she kicked this fear, she would probably have to find a new partner, someone who had his mind on the here and now.

She felt vibration in the wall beneath her palm. That night on Anktan swept back over her—*the grid fully functional at last, the crystals shrilling, the lights tinting the attacking hrinnti faces pink and purple*. She had been a stranger then, someone else entirely.

Sweat soaked her forehead, her shoulders, her back. This was stupid! she told herself fiercely. The grid had been inactive for decades. Nothing and no one was coming through, or they would have done it a long time ago!

It was odd that the flek had secreted their chamber down here in such a small space. The configuration of this matrix was almost as big as the one the flek had grown back on Anktan, but that facility had been constructed to transport hundreds of flek warriors at a time. This one could not handle more than thirty at the most.

She rounded another bend and glimpsed the faint blue glow up ahead. The rifle was a comforting weight looped over her shoulder. She raised her pistol and clicked the safety off. It had warmed to the touch, as though now part of her.

She eased forward, shoulder sliding along the wall. Her hand carrying the pistol looked dead-white in the eerie blue shimmer. Flek warrior-drones were that shade of white, with vicious red eyes. Before Anktan, she'd encountered flek in battle, of course, but either dead or at a distance. Once she had come face to face with them, it was apparent holos did not do them justice.

But she'd become accustomed to them, during her captivity, far too accustomed to them. Sometimes she still thought she remembered what it was like to have four arms. Guilt oozed through her mind, white-hot and amazingly fresh. How could she have been so gullible?

It wasn't her fault, the meds and therapists had told her over and over. The flek possessed mind-control techniques far superior to anything humanity had ever developed or condoned, and had honed them to perfection during centuries of slaving. They could literally make you believe anything. And so she had.

One last curve and then the crystal chamber was before her. The white walls reflected the blue glow and magnified it a hundred times. Her ribs ached and she braced them with her free hand. The bones had knit, but the muscles and tendons were still strained from the fall.

The sound emitted by the crystals had altered, much more audible to human ears now, and harder to bear. A hrinn would indeed have been in agony down here.

The scintillating blue light had reached a blinding intensity and she glimpsed a four-armed shape pacing around the matrix. *Flek!* her reflexes insisted and she dropped into a firing crouch.

No, it was most likely only an Oleaakan native, her rational mind said. The flek had left this world long ago and the laka's similarity in basic body type had been noted before. It had even been postulated as one of the reasons the natives had been allowed to survive. She hesitated, pistol ready.

There was no sign of Montrose or anyone else. Perhaps they had escaped through the side passage, she thought. Or perhaps the natives had proved dangerous after all and their torn bodies lay strewn across the cavern floor just out of sight. After all, no one had ever suspected the flek had dug in back on Anktan either until it was almost too late.

The hum was overwhelming this close. Even her bones vibrated with it. She huddled against the wall, teeth clenched, trying to decide what to do. If she dropped this native in its tracks, she could get past and find Montrose and the rest of the squad. But Dennehy had ordered her to scope out the situation and then report back, nothing more.

If she did, then maybe Blackeagle would back off and not look at her all the time like she was going to explode. The figure hesitated, then turned toward her. The light pulsed so brightly that its every movement seemed abrupt. It was still little more than a backlit outline to her light-dazzled eyes. She held her breath, body flattened against the wall just beyond the last curve. If it saw her, she might have to defend herself, despite the major's orders.

The native craned its head, atop that woefully spindly neck, as though searching for something. Was its sense of smell so keen that, like the hrinn, it could smell her out? She tightened her grip on the pistol and shaded her eyes with her free hand.

It hesitated and she eased back into the cave. She should leave, she thought, but she wanted to pick up useful intel. What little she had acquired so far would be of almost no help.

She withdrew further into the shadows. The figure stood framed in the pulsing blue light, like a living beacon, then turned back, so that for a second she got a good look at its characteristic smushed-in face. She froze, unable to move or think.

It was a *flek*, undersized and probably immature, certainly not a grown warrior-drone, but a flek all the same. The enemy was here.

Chapter Six

Mitsu's next coherent thought, after recognizing the flek, was that more of them would come through, or perhaps had already, and were skulking about in the shadows beyond this chamber. These caverns could already be teeming with them. She had to destroy the grid before this world was overrun. Then she had to notify Heyoka and Dennehy.

Flash. Already, the strobing light was burned into her optic nerves so that she saw it even with her eyes closed. Something seemed to lurk in the spaces between each burst, sinister and fierce, waiting to pounce. *Flash.*

Ears ringing from the ever-rising hum, she glided forward, pistol trained on the flek. She had trouble following the creature's movements between one flare and the next. *Flash.* It was like seeing a holo with strips cut out of each scene so that a portion of the visual information was missing. As far as she could tell, though, the flek wasn't armed. She should take it captive after she'd destroyed the grid. *Flash.*

No, kill it! her mind insisted. There's no point in

hauling it back to the surface. Flek never talk! They just turn themselves off, when they're captured, so all you have left is a corpse! It's not worth the risk!

She fired. *Flash.* Melted compound burst from the wall to the right; she'd missed, and badly. Her target jerked back, then disappeared into the passage beyond. She would have to go in after it.

Flash. Her heart thudded against her chest and she felt sick. Finish the job, she told herself and willed her hands to stop shaking. Blast the crystals, then take care of the flek. There was no time to go back and receive orders. *Flash.* No time.

She leveled the pistol, tried to squeeze the trigger, but could not. Had the safety reengaged? She checked. *Flash.* The indicator light glimmered green: Safety off. She raised the pistol and sighted in on one of the shimmering columns. It was so beautiful, like a shaft of living blue light, flowing from the floor almost all the way up to the ceiling. *Flash.* What right had something so menacing to also be beautiful? The breath rasped in and out of her straining lungs; her throat constricted and her vision tunneled in. She braced her firing hand with the other, which shook just as badly. It doesn't have to be neat, she told herself. Just do it!

The pistol bucked and she stumbled back. *Flash.* A puddle of slag appeared in the white building compound of the opposite wall, far to the left of the crystalline column at which she'd been aiming. She stared down at her hand. She was an expert marksman, ranked close to the top in her training class. True, she'd been out of action for most of the past year, but even a two-year-old couldn't have missed at that range!

Flash. She raised her hand and fired again. Her arm swung wide and the shot melted the cave floor, sending drops of molten stone flying. She threw the pistol away and sank to her knees, head spinning.

This was her worst nightmare. She wasn't in control. Something lurking deep inside would not let her do this, some part she thought she'd eradicated through months of excruciating therapy. They insisted she'd plumbed the depths of what the flek had done to her, but it had all been a lie. *Flash.* She was never going to be her old self again, never wear a Ranger uniform and return to battle alongside her mates. She was damaged goods, tainted, unfit for human or hrinnti company, unable even to trust herself.

Flash. She glanced over at the tunnel where the enemy had fled. At least she could track the bastards and ascertain if Montrose and Onopa were still alive. Even if she was unable to kill flek, she might be able to do that much.

Her useless sidearm lay on the floor, the metal shimmering in the fierce blueness. She stowed it in her holster so that she could pass it on to someone who still had all her marbles, someone who would be able to use it to annihilate flek as it was intended.

Heyoka guarded the cavern entrance after Dennehy and the three human recruits returned to base camp. The heat settled around him like a smothering blanket, so that his fur seemed thick with it, while, overhead, unfamiliar stars paraded slowly across the green-black sky. A night creature squalled in the nearby rain forest and he shivered.

This world was far from Old Earth, where he'd been raised, and even farther from Anktan. He thought of the ongoing battle that raged out there in the depths of space where night always prevailed, the alien worlds transformed beyond all recognition because flek preferred their planets blistering hot, their atmosphere toxic and laced with heavy metals.

Kei had every right to resent being kept out of that

battle. He resented it himself. Too much was at stake for the hrinn to go on playing at war. They were extraordinary warriors, when you took into consideration their obvious physical advantages combined with the ability to blueshift. Humanity should accept them as they were, and not insist on pointless rules and military courtesies, but he could see now he was never going to convince High Command of that.

He bent forward and sampled the air emerging from the vine-obscured hole. The vines quivered at his nearness. Mitsu's scent lingered, along with the rest, but it was all stale. Something must have gone wrong. No matter what it might have cost, he should never have let her go down there alone. Being a civilian was far better than being dead.

He keyed her com code, but there was no answer. The night breeze, redolent of the sea, blew his ruff back the wrong way as he got to his feet and paced, trying to work out his next move. Even though the noise would make it hellish for a hrinn down there, he couldn't wait for the investigative team to arrive. By the time they got here, nothing would be left to find but her dead body.

His com crackled. *"Blackeagle?"*

"Yes?"

"Dennehy here. I just had an update from the ship. The front at Bala Cithni has collapsed. The Fourth Fleet has received orders to fall back to Sigur Prime."

"But—" Heyoka's mind whirled with the implications. "That would leave Aldus and Maennar Three unprotected, as well as—"

"Oleaaka," Dennehy finished. *"The shuttle crew is going through their preflight checks. We have to be ready to evacuate in two hours in order to board the* Marion *before it leaves orbit."*

Heyoka threw back his head, stared up at the stars. It would take him at least thirty minutes to make his way back to camp from this point. That left very little time to find his squad.

"*Any sign of your people?*"

"No, sir," Heyoka said. "I'm going in after them."

"*Permission denied!*" Dennehy barked. "*I'm not losing you too. Return to camp. We'll make every effort to contact them. If we can't, they'll have to survive on their own until we can swing back this way.*"

That meant his troops would be trapped behind the lines, Heyoka thought numbly. As Rangers, they were trained to make the best of a situation like this, but the last time the flek had held this world, they'd set their environmental engines into action and wreaked havoc upon the local ecology. Five of the six islands still were uninhabitable, even after all these years. If the flek came back and tried again, this time they would most likely succeed.

"Yes, sir, I'll find them," he said into the com, as though reception had been poor and he'd misunderstood, then switched off. Even so, he could almost hear Dennehy's splutter of indignation at the other end.

No matter. He wasn't about to desert his troops. He'd rather die first. The fierce hrinnti *other* inside his head approved. *They were huntmates. Such could never be abandoned without losing honor.* But then, he thought, it was always on the side of action over prudent restraint. Perhaps he should listen to it more often.

He climbed down the ladder and headed into the tunnel. They might all get out of here in one piece, if he hurried.

Aliki Onopa scrambled higher and higher up the loose rock of a cliff face until her pursuers fell back. The laka were of a burly body type, their trunks reminiscent of a chunky pony still bred on her home world, Kalana Colony, though the ponies, of course, lacked the four arms. They couldn't have negotiated this type of terrain either.

After she ascended out of reach, they milled around below at the foot of the cliff and watched her with those unnerving pale eyes. Climbing, apparently, was not one of their skills. Unfortunately, they had caught up with Montrose, though she had hopes that he was still alive; she'd heard him swearing a blue streak as they'd carried him off.

At the top, she pulled herself up onto the long, wiry grass, then sat on her heels. A strand of her long black hair came loose in the breeze and played around her face. She brushed it back impatiently. The night was longer on this world than Kalana. According to her internal clock, it felt close to dawn, but that was still at least a good six hours off. She keyed her com to ask for orders. It crackled ominously. Perhaps the satellite was down, or perhaps it would function if she put more distance between herself and the flek grid.

She weighed her options—return to camp and report to Blackeagle, or follow Montrose, either to release him, if opportunity arose, or pinpoint his location for later retrieval. Both options had strengths and weaknesses. After a moment's reflection, she decided to track Montrose. It might be difficult to find him later, and the natives were obviously not as harmless as everyone had supposed. After all, they had routed the flek all those years ago. There might just be more to them than HQ realized.

According to the briefings, the sole laka habitation on this island lay northwest of the flek ruins. She slipped into the trees, knife drawn, using the scant starlight to navigate around the cliff and work her way back down. The dark spine of the mountains loomed behind her, while before her the moon-silvered sea glittered an opalescent blue-white all the way to the horizon.

Unfamiliar night-blooming flowers had opened fleshy white petals and were emitting a cloying sweet scent.

Onopa wiped at her eyes, which were beginning to tear. She must be allergic to this stuff. She detoured around another bed, then spotted a faint trail which led in the right direction. Perhaps the laka and Montrose had already come this way. She—

A bright light flared less than twenty feet away, and she thought for a moment she had found the rest of the squad. But this light was an intense emerald green, where coldlanterns would have been white, and this was brighter than a hundred coldlanterns anyway. She shaded her dazzled eyes. "Blackeagle?"

A hand reached out of the light and seized her left wrist. She slashed at it with her knife, but then another hand grabbed her and squeezed hard enough to make her drop the weapon. "Who are you?" She had an impression of pink eyes watching her from a mauve face. "I just want my companion back," she said. "Then we'll leave. We don't want to hurt anyone."

The light, she saw, now that her eyes were adjusting, was cast by a huge tree. Tiny ovals of green light shifted with the breeze. Had they hung lanterns of some sort? If so, why so many and how had they lit them all at once? This world had no tech. She squinted, trying to make out the source.

A soft alien voice murmured. Another answered, its tone sharp, as though the two argued. Sweat rolled down Onopa's back. She wrenched at her imprisoned wrists. If she could just reach her holstered pistol. Damn! She could have used a translator unit at the moment, but this had been just a training exercise, and the laka were supposed to be reclusive.

She dropped to her knees in the sandy grass to make herself as unthreatening as possible. The imprisoning hands held on, but she could see a bit more through the glare now, enough to know that it was the leaves themselves which were emitting the light, not lanterns or candles. "Montrose?"

"Onop—" His answer was abruptly cut off.

She struggled back onto her feet and was jerked forward, into the light and a warm tangle of laka bodies. They had a distinctive odor, not unpleasant, but she knew she would never forget it after this night. "Let me go!" she said as they hustled her into the trees. "No one will—"

She tripped on something and hit her head against an unseen trunk. The blow stunned her and she sagged in her captors' grip. They didn't even seem to notice and Onopa lapsed into foggy semiconsciousness as they dragged her away.

Mitsu emerged up out of the cavern entrance onto the side of a hill. The air was deliciously fresh after the dry staleness of the cave. Black rocks tumbled about made it all the harder to see, but it was obvious this had been recently excavated. None of the squad were in evidence. If they'd come through here, they must have gone back to camp.

As she probably should. There was little she could accomplish by herself now, except recon. But then the flek who had come through the grid would be free to lose themselves in the dense forest and mountains. On Anktan, she had been duped into fighting for them. At least this time she could lay down her life trying to prevent the loss of this world.

She swept the loose dirt around the rocks with her coldlantern and found it had been literally trampled, both by human boots and nonhuman feet. Clever bastards! They must have surprised Montrose and Onopa just outside the cave, overcome them and then dragged the bodies off, though there was no sign of blood. She stared off into the darkness, where green-black sky met the solid onyx of mountains at the horizon. The tracks leading away were quite clear. They obviously thought so little of their enemy they weren't even trying to hide.

Maybe the flek thought they had overcome all resistance in this area and were just doing a quick reconnoiter before returning through the grid. If that were true, then her best course would be to wait here for them to come back.

But the very thought of passively skulking on the hillside made her break out in a cold sweat. She had to do something, anything, follow them and kill their prisoners with her own gun before the enemy had the chance to go to work on them. They would be far better off dead. What the flek did to their captives was unspeakable.

When Heyoka knew, he would go after them too, she thought. He would never stop until he roasted them all to ashes, then counted the bodies twice. The memory of her abortive attempt to destroy the crystals flashed through her mind and she flinched. Don't think about that! she told herself. If you do, you won't be able to do what has to be done.

She set off into the darkness, pausing every few steps to check with the coldlantern and make sure she didn't lose the trail.

Fifteen minutes later, she glimpsed a blaze of light on the hillside, above and to the right of her. She crept forward, using stands of trees for cover. Her head ached, where she'd laid it open earlier, and her ribs protested at being abused again so soon.

Voices rose and fell, pitched too low for humans. She couldn't make out the words, but the cadence sounded flekish all right. She knew High-Flek only too well. It seemed to have been burned into her brain. She eased through the shadows, hoping her quarry didn't have better night vision than humans.

A human voice broke into the stream of alien words. Her heart raced. So at least one of the squad was still alive. She eased her pistol into her right hand, unslung her rifle from her shoulder and carried it in her left.

The timbre of the voices shifted, higher, more agitated. She fired a green laser bolt into the sky, low enough to show them that she meant business. "You are without function or purpose!" she called out in High-Flek. "Destroy yourselves immediately!" Then she changed position to prevent them from pinpointing her location.

The voices cut off so that she could hear the distant roar of the sea and nothing more. The green light, which seemed to be emanating from a large tree, faded abruptly, and she was left in total darkness.

This was stupid. She needed backup. She keyed her com. "Heyoka?" A muted crackle was all that answered.

"Dammit!" She wriggled into a better position, trying to get some idea of where the flek had gone. "Heyoka! I've found them!"

"*Mitsu?*" the com said faintly in Heyoka's voice.

"Get a fix on me," she said. "The flek have come through and taken Montrose and Onopa. I tracked them this far, but I'll have to wait for dawn to do anymore."

"*Flek? Are you sure?*" he said. "*You've actually seen them?*"

"Damn straight!"

"*But I went down in the cave long enough to check the grid myself,*" he said. "*I nearly burst my eardrums, but I didn't see anyone or anything.*"

She swallowed hard. "Look, I know a flek when I see one."

"*It doesn't matter,*" he said. "*I'm up here just outside the original entrance now, waiting, and we've all been ordered back to the ship. We have less than an hour before the shuttle lifts.*"

"I can't go back," she said, "not with flek here. You get someone down there to destroy those crystals before a whole flek division comes through."

The front has shifted. Flek are sweeping back this way, Heyoka said and she heard the urgency in his voice. *Down here or up there in orbit, it doesn't make any difference now. They're going to be all over the place. We have to evacuate. Return to camp and that's an order!*

"What about Montrose and Onopa?"

I'll handle it, he said. And then she knew, from the telltale catch in his voice, the second of hesitation. He had no intention of being on that shuttle himself. He would never abandon his command.

"Okay, then," she said and stared up at the night sky, the pinprick stars, indifferent and remote. "I'll head back, but don't wait for me."

Mitsu, he said, *I want you on that shuttle!*

"I know." She removed the com button from her collar and stuffed it into her pocket. Heart racing, she pulled her knees up under her chin, braced her back against a tree trunk, and settled in to wait for dawn.

Night climbers chittered softly in the surrounding trees, and as always, in the background, was the insistent voice of the distant sea. The ground was damp and the smell of rain rode on the wind.

She had wanted things, herself, lots of times over the years, and hardly any of them ever came to pass. Life, it seemed, was shot through with disappointment. No one ever got her way. She understood that now.

Out of boredom, Kei was wrestling with Bey, human-style, just outside the camp when Major Dennehy came and stood over them. Kei looked up from the ground where he had his huntmate pinned. Bey stiffened with Kei's unsheathed claws pricking at his throat.

"Attention!" Dennehy was in no mood for horseplay.

The two hrinn untangled themselves and regained their feet, both saluting, Bey more quickly than Kei.

"The Confederation front at Bala Cithni has collapsed." Dennehy's hands were locked behind his back. "The flek have broken through and are sweeping this way."

An eager snarl escaped Kei. "Good! The pattern is making itself known. We will finally get to fight!"

"I don't know anything about so-called 'patterns,'" Dennehy said. "But when you get to fight, it won't be here. We don't have enough men or equipment to make any sort of stand. We're evacuating in an hour. Private Bey, you will be in charge of the packing detail. Gather up the tents and foodstuffs so we'll be ready when the shuttle lands. It's best for the laka if we don't leave anything behind to make it look as though they collaborated with us."

Kei's ears flattened. "I am Leader!"

"No, what you are is insubordinate!" The gray-haired, stocky human whirled upon him, staring dangerously directly into his eyes. "You don't have the self-discipline to be a leader of any sort! Put yourself on report, then get busy and break down this camp!"

For a breath, Dennehy's life hung in the balance. Kei's claws ached to rip the human officer's throat out. He was short and soft, as well as old and slow. On Anktan, the old always fell to the young and fit, once superior experience no longer outweighed strength, and this would be the work of but a moment. Then the man turned and stalked away. Kei snarled with frustration.

Bey's ears flattened. "I will never understand humans. The enemy is coming here—to us—and they want to run away?"

"They do fight sometimes," Kei said. "I have seen the recordings and the Black/on/black has related many tales of battle."

Two of the humans, as well as Mitsu, were still down in the tunnels. The other three had come back with Dennehy. Besides them, only the six hrinnti trainees, the med, and the major were left in camp.

"Find Naxk, Visht, and the others," Kei said, assuming leadership, because, no matter what the major said, he was still biggest and strongest. He would be Leader until one of the others Challenged and bested him. "Have them pack up the camp, as ordered." He swiveled his head, sampling the Oleaakan wind. "I will find the Black/on/black and reason with him. He must make the major understand. Why should we leave this world when the time to fight has finally arrived?"

Chapter Seven

Heyoka raced back through the tunnel, knowing he had to get to Mitsu, but dreading the crystal chamber. If only he had brought his ear protectors, this would have been easier. As it was, the terrible shrill assaulted him as soon as he even neared the chamber. He slowed and clamped his hands over his ears in a vain attempt to protect them, wanting to roar with the pain. He'd known it would be bad, but remembering, and experiencing, were two altogether different things.

He edged into a universe of scintillating, pulsating, overwhelming *blue*, now laced with bursts of *pink* and *green* and *purple*. The crystals, at least two dozen strong, were irregularly spaced about the grid. They waxed and waned, the crest of each pulse so bright, his overstressed retinas could make out little in the relative dimness in between. He reeled against the white wall and tried to think. Obviously, whatever mechanism was activating the grid hadn't backed off one iota.

The chamber smelled of human and hrinn, as well as something else unidentifiable, but definitely not flek.

That species had an acrid odor, unmistakable once encountered. Even human soldiers complained of their reek. He would have known at once if flek had been down here in the last few weeks, much less hours, and they had not. Mitsu must have had a flashback from Anktan.

He drew his laser pistol. His orders had been to preserve the grid intact for study, but that was before the flek had swept through Confederation defenses and headed this way. They could not afford to leave the crystals now. He fired a coherent beam of sizzling green light which struck the nearest pillar dead-on and then ricochetted back at him. Pain seared the tip of his right ear and combat reflexes took over. He found himself on the floor, head ringing. The pistol went sliding across the rock floor.

The crystals in the matrix back on Anktan had been fragile, fairy-tale constructions, but these, far older, must be solid enough to support a building. Breathing hard, he got his knees under him, then reached out and touched the glassy smoothness of the pillar he'd fired upon. The light's modulation slowed, as if in response to his touch, and a tone resonated so loudly inside his head that even his teeth vibrated with it. He jerked his hand away.

Over the many years these crystals had been growing, they must have become too dense to be destroyed by ordinary means. This job would require heavy ordnance, and they had brought none to this world.

He retrieved his sidearm, then ducked into the side passage that had to lead to the surface, following the scent of human and that strange unidentifiable one, which logic said must be laka, since Montrose had reported seeing them in the caverns too.

If Mitsu were headed back to camp, as she'd said, this would be the shortest path. He might meet her down here, but he knew from her voice, she wasn't coming back. She thought she'd seen a flek and she was no longer answering her com.

The passage ended finally in a steep climb over tumbled boulders to a newly excavated hole in the hillside. He had to climb to reach it and the scent of both human and laka was very strong here.

Outside, the night air was heady, filled with the green scent of unfamiliar plants and the distant salt of the sea. He examined the ground and found tracks. Mitsu's scent was scattered about here too. He tried his com. "Mitsu?"

No answer. The wind sighed against his face. He tried again twice more, before giving up and trying another code. "Montrose?"

"Sarge, is that you?" a voice asked softly.

"It's me," he said. "Are you all right?"

"Yeah," the voice said, *"except Onopa and I have been shanghaied by locals. They don't seem angry, exactly, but I can't make out what they want."*

"What about Jensen?"

"I don't know, Sarge. I heard shots a little while ago though."

Alien voices murmured in the background, rising and falling, as though they were arguing about something, although he knew better than to attribute human emotions to an alien species. "Can you give them the slip? We have orders to evacuate and the shuttle is going to lift in less than thirty minutes."

"Onopa's down, Sarge, groggy and confused with a knot on her head."

She needed a med, then. Damn! Heyoka fingered his singed ear and stifled a snarl. "Then make her comfortable, if they'll let you, and give me directions to your location."

"West, southwest of the tunnel opening, sir. Look for

*a green light. They have this tree that they turn on—
sometimes, anyway. Not at the moment, though."*

"A tree?"

"Yeah, I know it sounds weird."

If he went after them, there was no way he could
be back in time to make the shuttle and that would
put him in direct violation of orders. An incident like
that could kill a career. No more advancement or funding
for his hrinnti training program. But it was Mitsu out
there, as well as Montrose and Onopa, all three under
his command, his responsibility.

"Okay, I'm on my way," he told Montrose.

Mitsu could hear Montrose somewhere in the darkness,
but not clearly enough to make out more than one word
in five. He was still alive though. That was something.
She checked her pistol. She didn't think she would be
able to fire upon a flek, but they didn't know that. She
might be able to pin them down long enough for their
prisoners to escape.

"Montrose?" she shouted into the night, then
scrambled to a new position twenty feet to the right
behind a stand of spiky red-topped bushes.

"Jensen?" The voice came from about thirty yards
to her left.

"How many flek are there?" Head down, she moved
again, working her way closer. Several black outlines,
too big to be human, moved with her in a parallel
course and she wondered uneasily about flek night
sight.

"These aren't flek," he called. "They're laka and
unarmed. Don't fire upon them."

She dropped flat onto the warm damp ground,
breathing hard. Montrose had seen combat; all the
human recruits on this training exercise were seasoned
troops. They should know a flek when they saw one.

It was obvious the enemy had already started meddling with his mind. She felt sickened at the thought.

For the moment, he believed these flek were just harmless laka. Soon he would think he was a flek himself. It was so easy for them to turn a person's mind inside out. So damn easy. She pressed her cheek to the dirt, breathed in the rich, earthy scent, trying to stop shaking. Sweat soaked through the back of her shirt, rolled down her temples.

"Corporal?" Montrose called. "The sergeant called and said the shuttle is lifting soon. We have orders to report back to camp on the double!"

Something rustled in the darkness a scant ten feet away. She tightened her fingers on the laser pistol. She could turn it upon herself, if nothing else. Nobody was ever going to pick her mind apart again, then put it back together cross-eyed. She might not be able to burn them all into ashes, as they deserved, but she could at least die human.

A tree in the center of the clearing blazed into light again, a great green brightness against the night sky. Dazzled, she reeled back and covered her eyes with one hand as the dark forms rushed her. She got off a single shot and the green beam pierced the night. A voice screamed, not the least bit human, then something pinned her arms.

Flek! her mind screamed and she fought like a cornered hrinn, but the iron grip did not give and she could find no purchase to wedge her way out. She had the impression of smooth chitin, punched-in-looking faces. Her heart raced so that she could not distinguish between the beats. She would not be taken! Not again! Never again! She went on fighting as the implacable hold tightened and tightened, until, unable to breathe, she passed out.

❖   ❖   ❖

Bey went through the camp and assigned the hrinn, male and female, to load ordnance and sealed packets of foodstuffs on the shuttle. They would leave the unwieldy com for last. He still found it strange to work with unrelated females. Back in the secret mountain hold of Levv, both sexes had lived and toiled together, but that had been a social aberration, born of necessity. After the great battle down on the plains, when the honor of Levv had been restored, most of the surviving Levv males had applied for membership in traditional males' houses.

Kei and Bey and five other Levv males, however, had elected to follow the Black/on/black into the Confederation armed forces instead. There, they were expected to work with both hrinnti males and females, as well as humans. It had been a difficult adjustment.

He found Naxk, her gear already stowed in her pack, taking down tents. She was sturdy and sleek, her ears large, and her fur tawny with marvelous black points. Bey had practiced hand-to-hand combat with her enough to admit she fought well, but she was a cull, after all, and therefore inherently inferior.

"Leave the tents to me," he said gruffly. "You take care of the foodstuffs."

She bristled. "You are not Squad Leader."

He raised his muzzle, let his unbound mane show to its best advantage. The Rangers had insisted he crop it, upon enlisting, but it was already growing back out. "Kei has gone after the Black/on/black and Skal is not here, so for the moment I am biggest."

Her handclaws sprang free. "The Black/on/black says size does not matter. You are not my superior!"

His hackles raised and a fierce joy surged through him. After all this playing at war, it was wonderful to have someone confront him, almost like being on Anktan again. "I am Leader now!"

Her ears were flattened, her claws fully extended. She was shedding anger-scent so thickly, it was all he could do not to strike her.

"The Black/on/black has forbidden this," she said and her throat was tight with fury. "We are not to waste our strength fighting one another, otherwise how will we ever defeat the flek?"

"What flek?" He gestured at the mountains and snarled contemptuously. "Have you seen any flek on this soft, pretty world? I see only humans babbling about flek, dashing about, playing at younglings' hunting games. There have been no flek here until now, and we are supposed to close our eyes and just run away at the first hint of a fight!"

"Private Bey!"

The voice came from behind and Bey realized Major Dennehy had approached from downwind.

"Stand down, and that's an order!" The major had a pistol in his hand. Bey was experienced enough now to see that the safety was off. "There will be no fighting in the ranks."

Naxk turned her eyes aside in submission and retracted her claws.

Bey glanced angrily from her to the human. "We are warriors! We cannot go on like this, never drawing blood, never making a kill, not even to eat fresh meat!"

"I see," Dennehy said. He lowered the pistol, but did not put it back in the holster. "Well, I suspected you were not Ranger material from the first."

Naxk caught his eye. "But the Black/on/black—"

"Blackeagle was an aberration," he said. "A one-time happening born of unique circumstances. We won't see another like him, and it's too bad. We could use a whole regiment. And Blackeagle made a very strong case for the hrinn's inclusion in Confederation forces. I was willing to be proved wrong. However, when we get back to headquarters, my recommendation will be to terminate this project and return you people to your homes."

"This is my home!" Naxk's chest heaved with indignation. "You are my Line! I have no other!"

"Don't be ridiculous," Dennehy said. "We'll just send you to your own world. You can take up your normal way of life. Not everyone is cut out for the armed forces, but there's no shame in that."

But Bey understood the desperation in Naxk's black eyes and the cant of her ears. She was a cull. Kendd would not welcome her, if she returned, nor of course would any other Line. If she had remained on Anktan, she would have been a highly positioned servant, but now, after renouncing her Line, there would never be a place for her.

"I will not go!" Naxk spat. She was breathing hard and her eyes were shining dangerously. "I will stay here and fight the flek, as I was promised!" She snatched up her pack and weapon and prowled off into the darkness.

Dennehy stared after her, his mouth agape. The sparse iron-gray fur atop his head stirred in the breeze. He waved a hand. "Never mind," he said. "Blackeagle can deal with that one. We have to get the rest of you hrinn on the shuttle."

Bey's ears twitched. This major intended to allow both the Black/on/black and Naxk to stay behind and confront the flek, but force the rest of them to return to Anktan and admit they had never been allowed anywhere near the war? His claws sprang free and he snarled.

"I don't like your attitude," Dennehy said. "Get hold of yourself, Private."

The wind ruffled Bey's mane. He was not well marked, being only an unexceptional brown/on/buff, nor, despite his size, was he a particularly renowned fighter among his own kind. He had hoped to remedy that through Ranger training. The Black/on/black was not bigger than other males, yet in the great battle down on the plains he had fought with a strength and purity that was already legend.

He pictured himself making application to a males' house, any of the males' houses along the Mish River Valley for that matter, and being chased away, perhaps even killed for his presumption. If he were not good enough to fight alongside a bunch of soft-skinned, dead-smelling humans, his own kind would reject him without a second thought.

"I will not go either," he said, and felt a fierce exultation at the decision. "I will stay and fight at the Black/on/black's side!"

"No one is staying, if I can help it!" Dennehy's face reddened. "It's bad enough we may have to rendezvous without a sizable portion of Blackeagle's squad, including Blackeagle himself. I'm not throwing away any additional lives!" He glanced at the silver-gray sweep of the shuttle just visible against the night sky a quarter of a mile away. "In fact, forget the packing and go strap yourself in on the shuttle. I'll collect the rest of the hrinn. We don't want to cut the deadline too close." He holstered the pistol and turned away.

Bey threw back his head and roared. "I *will* fight at the Black/on/black's side! We will drench our claws in our enemies' blood until they flee at the very sound of our names!"

Shocked, Dennehy gripped his pistol, but Bey reached for the power buried deep in his body and went into blueshift. The tents, the stubby human male before him, the gun, all became *electric blue*. Now Dennehy moved so slowly, it was child's play to reach out and snatch the weapon from his nearly motionless hands.

Then, with skill born of long practice, Bey dropped back into normal speed and snarled in the shorter human's face, though the telltale weariness brought on by blueshift without preparation already dragged at him.

Dennehy staggered back and stared at him with unbelieving eyes. Bey realized this particular human must never have seen a hrinn blueshift before.

"We will not flee this world when it is finally—*finally*—time to fight!" Bey said as Visht, Kika, and Skal, the three remaining hrinn in camp, sprinted up, eyes aglint at the thought of a good brawl. "This is what we were bred for, what we have trained for since we left Anktan. We would shred both duty and honor, if we ran away merely to preserve our hides, and a hrinn has nothing else of value."

"I'm—going to the shuttle now," Dennehy said. "If you have any sense, you will go with me so we can all live to fight another day."

Bey understood then that this human feared they would prevent him from leaving. "Go," he said. "We will not stop you."

"A dead hrinn brings no honor to his people." Dennehy wet his lips and glanced behind. "Even Blackeagle understands that."

"Does he?" Bey said. His blood sang with anticipation. "Then why isn't he here, preparing to flee with you like a frightened *zzil*?"

Visht snarled softly. "I weary of all this prattle," the big yellow/on/white said. "Where are the flek? When do we get to fight?"

"Soon," Bey said. "I think very soon."

The four of them watched as the major turned his back and started down the path to the waiting shuttle. They could smell the acridness of his fear on the breeze.

Kei tracked the Black/on/black back to the tunnel opening on the hillside. He squatted there as the vines shifted out of his path, bristling at the thought of entering that terrible chamber again, with the crystals wailing like a *dako* with its tail caught in the rocks. But that was where the Black/on/black had gone, so that was where he must follow.

The Black/on/black had spared Kei's life upon so many occasions there was almost a Sponsorship between them. Kei had never been Sponsored, but he had heard tales of how such relationships were forged and he thought this must be very close.

When they had first met, the Black/on/black himself had been under the prestigious Sponsorship of a leader of a highly ranked males' house. All the older males of Levv had been killed by the flek when Kei was still young, and of course at that point Levv had been outcast, despised. No reputable males' house would have accepted cublings born of that supposedly tainted Line, had they dared to apply.

As it was, they had dared nothing, except to hide in the mountains and keep the existence of the remnants of their persecuted Line a secret, until the Black/on/black had sniffed out the truth and restored their honor. Kei would never hide again, nor turn away from danger.

He descended the rope ladder into the darkness, then used his nose, rather than a coldlantern, to follow the Black/on/black. He ran one hand lightly over the stone to guide him. The teeth-gnashing wail of the crystalline matrix made itself felt long before he could detect the blue glow.

He pressed his shoulder to the wall and edged closer. The crystals' frequency climbed higher and higher, the pulsating flashes accelerated until they were a wave of blue highlighted with incandescent pinks and greens and purples. His head felt as though it would fly apart. His vision blurred and he realized he had to get out of here, but his legs wouldn't move. He tasted the flatness of blood on the back of his throat and it was hard to make his thoughts hunt together.

The wail ascended even higher. The light flashed a lambent green-white and then he could see nothing. There was a great inrush of hot, foul-smelling air. He fell to his knees, jaws agape, and pressed his hands uselessly to his ears.

Something—or someone—had arrived.

Chapter Eight

Though it was quite late, the laka compound had never properly settled for the night. The great, towering barrier trees, which marked out the common area and held back the rain forest, were still open, the leaves unfurled, and there was a general air of anxiety. Luminaries had been stimulated so that light still flooded where there should have been only soothing darkness. Immature laka huddled here and there in small groups according to caste. The breeders' ill-advised rampage had required all adults to go out and search, and the keepers had not come back to dispatch the youngest to their nests.

Something stirred in the surrounding damp darkness of the rain forest. Heads swiveled, thinking perhaps the rebellious breeders had returned, then Third Gleaner emerged with a limp body and laid it sorrowfully on the grass. Everyone gathered round. It was one of the strangers-from-beyond, a "human." It lay, quiet and pale, making not a single sound, its energies apparently quite disrupted. All were horrified, cultivators, coordinators, translators, and scouts alike.

Ninth Translator-at-large, just returned from searching for the breeders down among the rocks by the sea, worked her way to the forefront of the crowd, especially dismayed. Beginnings were critical. All relationships were set with the utterance of the first few words, the first carefully thought-out gesture. This set of strangers-from-beyond had not yet come into the compound to establish essential harmonies, and this was a most inauspicious way to begin.

It had been some time since the last set had visited this world and, though she possessed body-memories of other occasions, she had never personally seen one of this species. She directed a callow young cultivator to stimulate a pair of nearby luminaries, then leaned forward to examine the still face by their shimmering green light.

The head was elegantly sculptured and covered with fine black filaments. Each strand was like polished onyx, she thought, like the bowl of the night sky itself when both moons had dipped below the horizon.

She turned back to Third Gleaner. "It is not dead?" she asked in the stilted gleaner syntax.

The gleaner hesitated, obviously distraught. "No," she said, "I felt it move, when I set it down."

"What is wrong with it then?" she said.

Third Gleaner turned her head aside and closed her eyes. "I held it too tightly," she said. "It was trying to escape and I did not know it was so fragile."

"*You* injured it?" Ninth Translator was incredulous. First the breeders, and now this. Laka society was experiencing critical discontinuities.

"I only meant to restrain it," Third Gleaner said. "I thought to bring the creature here so it could be dissuaded from running wild with the breeders like its companions."

Ninth sat back on her haunches. And so it always went, she thought, when a caste tried to perform outside its carefully proscribed parameters. They could have expected no less. It was, after all, the bred-in function of gleaners to gather things and bring them back to the compound, and so she had found this alien and brought it here. "Where did you come upon it?" she asked.

"In the ceremonial arena," the gleaner said, "near the tallest luminary." Her first-hands dithered about each other in a telltale dance of distress. "Sixth and Second Gleaner encountered the runaway breeders along with a pair of these creatures, but they were strangers-from-beyond-the-sky and we could not reason with them."

"And this one?" she prompted.

The small form stirred, then sat up, put a slender forearm to its head, looked about in what seemed like uncertainty.

"It was hiding in the dark, calling to its companions, one of which was apparently struggling to free itself. Perhaps it wished to leave the breeders, who have been so insolent tonight."

The small creature struggled onto its two feet, though it still appeared dazed. It was amazing how it could stand at all, since it lacked back-legs for balance. The very sight of its graceful form made Ninth Translator feel dull and stumpy. Imagine having such exquisite coordination.

"And where are the other two?" She folded her first-hands in a gesture of forbearance. It never did to rush gleaners. They were linear thinkers, always having to put one foot down solidly before moving the other three.

"They are still back at the ceremonial arena," Third Gleaner said. "Should we have brought them too?"

Ninth Translator shuddered. It was very bad form to impose one's will upon any other sentient, but most especially this species. They thought so differently and carried such terrible weapons. One never knew how they might take even the suggestion of violence. Harmony had to be established at all cost so that the two species could honor the sacred spark of consciousness that bound them as one. She would have quite properly sacrificed her own life, rather than distress them, but gleaners were too unimaginative to understand that.

This incident brought to mind the terrible stories of those days, so long ago, when the unharmonious ones had nearly destroyed both this world and the laka. The ancient records said they had actually *struck down* any who opposed them, had tampered with the atmosphere itself, instead of adjusting their own metabolisms to take advantage of the chemistries of this world.

The diminutive stranger edged closer to Ninth Translator, spoke in a quick, fluting voice. It seemed agitated and drew a weapon out of a cunning pocket fastened at its waist. Ninth Translator stood very still, not wishing to further alarm it.

"Are you quite undamaged?" she asked in her best approximation of its dialect based on body-memories.

It answered, but the sounds ran together. She concentrated, accessing the specialized areas of her brain meant for translation. With a few more exchanges, she would be able to speak some rudimentary phrases. "The gleaner did not mean you harm," she said. "Might you do her the honor of overlooking her transgression?"

It backed away, then turned and stumbled off into the night. Third Gleaner twitched.

"Do not go after it," Ninth Translator said.

The gleaner sat on her back-legs and picked at a molting patch on her carapace with quivering fingers. "You could not communicate with it?"

Ninth walked over to one of the luminaries and stroked its sensor knot so that it ceased to glow. "Not yet."

The other went rigid with grief. "But I wished to beg its forgiveness!"

"I asked for you, but I do not think it understood,"

Ninth Translator said, turning to the second luminary.
"It will be necessary for you to live with the shame for
now."

"But," Third Gleaner said disconsolately, "I cannot!"

"You do not have permission to remove yourself from
the colony," Ninth said hastily and wished a more
experienced head were present. She was not qualified
to counsel a lower caste on such matters.

Third Gleaner folded in upon herself, hiding her face
with all four hands in a gesture of misery. "I shall stay
here and petition the coordinators for Leavetaking at
first light."

Linear thinking again. Ninth Translator knew better
than to say more. Gleaner logic had led to this blind
conclusion and it would take a better translator than
she to guide her out again.

Heyoka snarled as the shuttle trailed orange-red fire
across the night sky; perhaps, he thought, the portent
of what was to come. If the flek were on their way back
to this world, the sky would soon be full of such
comings and goings.

He sagged back on the rocks and shook his head.
Now he was marooned here, as well as AWOL. Even
if he made it back home at some point, his career as
a Ranger was over. At least, with any luck, all of his
hrinnti recruits and most of the humans were on that
flight, stranding only Mitsu, Onopa, Montrose, and
himself. Having grown up on Earth, he understood
humans far better than hrinn. If he had to be stuck
here, it was probably better this way.

At any rate, he had to catch up with the others
before the flek made landfall on this world. Then the
four of them could hide up in the green mountains,
live off the land, perhaps even commit the odd moment
of mayhem now and then against the flek. That at least

would be of some service, unless, or until, they were caught.

The fiery afterimage of the shuttle's ascent still hung before his eyes when he caught another glow, low on the horizon, bright green, ghostly. The lighted "tree" Montrose had mentioned?

He risked a call on his com, but Montrose didn't respond this time. That didn't bode well. It was about five hours before local dawn and he felt the lack of sleep pulling upon him. He hadn't been on active duty since Enjas Two. No matter that he had worked out during training, it was hardly the same thing.

Rising, he shook himself, then sampled the breeze. As usual, it blew from the windward side of the island, carrying the rich scent of unfamiliar plants, rocks, the brininess of the sea, and . . .

His ears waggled. There was an unfamiliar element in the melange tonight, the same scent he'd encountered down in the cave, most likely the laka, since they were out and about. What had provoked that? he wondered. Traumatized by their near extinction, the peaceful laka normally went out of their way to avoid humans. Yet tonight, they had been downright aggressive.

Was it their intrusion on the crystals, or perhaps just the presence of the hrinn? They had encountered humans before, but they had never seen one of his kind.

He bent lower, scouting for human spore. The ground sloped down here, littered with black, volcanic rock and covered with vines and bushes. After a moment, he picked up Mitsu's scent amidst the sharp greenness of the vegetation. Another snarl escaped him. Damnation! She *had* come this way. He'd been hoping against hope she had obeyed orders and circled back to base camp. Then she would have made it off-world on that shuttle.

Her scent grew stronger, though he picked up almost nothing from Montrose and Onopa, as though they were being carried, so that their feet rarely touched the ground. Montrose had mentioned that Onopa was injured. Now that the shuttle was gone, there would be no med for her. He bristled. His fault. His responsibility. He should have foreseen this possibility. The laka had survived the flek, after all. It was altogether conceivable they weren't as mild mannered as they had led the Confederation to believe.

Mitsu's trail was leading to the blaze of green light, as Montrose had said. He realized that, if the laka had any sort of decent night sight at all, his tan uniform was going to be highly visible, so he stripped off his shirt and stashed it behind some rocks. His black fur would blend in with the night. He paused at a small mountain stream to drink deeply. The swift water was cool with a faint aftertaste of several minerals—iron, perhaps, and zinc. There was no point in worrying about local contaminants now. If he were going to react, he might as well get it over with. He doubted Dennehy had left them a five-year supply of water.

Mitsu's scent was very clear now. Once he got his hands on his partner, he was going to shake some sense into her. This had as much to do with her former recklessness coming back into play as what the flek had done to her. She was young, and the young thought they'd live forever.

The light radiated down from the center of a clearing ringed by a large grove. Unlike most of the rain forest, the trees here had leathery leaves that whispered against each other like mice brushing against a wall. His hackles rose. He caught a stronger trace of Montrose's scent, then Onopa's.

The grove itself smelled dark and earthy, wet. Perhaps there was a marsh within, or a bog. He circled, careful to remain downwind. Shapes moved, dark outlines silhouetted against the almost phosphorescent green radiance. The light seemed to be emanating from the leaves of a single tree so its outline was brilliant in the night.

One of the shadows turned just so and his reflexes screamed *flek!* for a heart-stopping instant, but the shapes did not reek as flek did and he forced himself to remain calm.

He strained his ears to pick up some scrap of human conversation. The few words he caught were laka and he could make nothing out.

Finally, he decided to risk a direct approach. He was armed, after all, and the laka had always tolerated the presence of Confederation forces in the past. Most likely, he just needed to sort out the misunderstanding that had resulted in the confinement of his personnel.

He stepped into the eerie green light and held up empty hands, though his rifle was slung on his shoulder and his pistol was still snug in its holster. "I won't hurt you," he said slowly. "I just want my people back."

Three of the closest laka froze.

"Sergeant Blackeagle!" Montrose called out of the darkness back inside the grove. "Over here!"

The three laka glanced over their shoulders, then blocked him shoulder to shoulder like a living wall. This felt wrong, Heyoka thought, like they were angry, like they had a reason for holding the humans.

"Is Corporal Jensen with you?" He forced his voice to remain calm.

"No," Montrose said. "Onopa is, though. We're all right."

He turned back to three laka. Even though these specimens were smaller than some holos he'd seen of the species, they were still impressive this close up. Four arms and four legs, sinuous necks, carapaces. Their pink eyes reflected green in this light. "I'm going to get my people," he said, hoping at least his manner would reassure. "Then we'll leave."

He edged around the three, but they darted back in front of him. Damnation. He stood in place and waited to see what they would do. After a moment, they began to wail in high-pitched voices that set his teeth on edge.

This was getting him nowhere. He was tired and worried and out of patience. "Okay, okay," he said, though he knew they might understand no more than the tone of his voice, if even that much. He turned away, gazed at the ground, as though he were leaving, and wandered in a large careful circle that gave him the angle to enter the grove.

When he thought the laka had relaxed their guard a bit, he lowered his head and sprinted toward where he had last heard Montrose's voice. This was where the ability to blueshift would have come in really handy, he thought regretfully.

The laka intercepted him before he'd gone twenty paces, much quicker than they looked. They lined up shoulder to shoulder again and blocked his path. With a snarl, he leaped on the closest. It went down with an agonized cry. His *other* surfaced and he had to force himself not to tear at the tender neck skin with teeth and claws.

It was not a flek! he told his violent *other* as he rolled away. This was not Anktan or Enjas Two or any of a dozen planets where he'd been in hand-to-hand combat with the enemy. This was just a misguided laka. It only needed to be intimated.

He came up to his knees. The laka he'd attacked was still down a few feet away, keening, as though it were hurt. One of its forelegs was twisted at what looked to be an unnatural angle. The other two laka were frozen, then as one, they tackled Heyoka and knocked him to the ground.

His head hit hard and rang like a bell. Dazed, he

fought with both tooth and claw now, drawing sour laka blood. In another moment, the rest joined in, and he was smothered by a veritable mountain of laka flesh.

The agonizing high-pitched wail of the transfer chamber continued to mount. Kei's teeth throbbed and he thought his ears would rupture. Blood trickled from his nose. If he didn't get away, he realized he might actually die in this stinking flek warren without ever striking a single blow. He dug his claws into the rock and pulled himself onto his feet, galled that the human major had been right. This was no place for hrinn.

If the Black/on/black had been caught in there, he was surely dead now, either in glorious battle, or because his body had been turned inside out by that unbearable noise. Kei wondered how many flek their leader had killed and what sort of tales might be told about this night.

None, he told himself angrily, if he didn't make it back to Anktan to tell the first. Choked by the nose-burning reek, he pulled himself along, step by step, back through the darkness toward the hole in the hillside and the rope ladder.

The agony lessened with each bend in the tunnel until he was able to think again, able to draw a breath without fighting for air. Then he heard oddly rhythmic footsteps behind. He pressed his back to the rock, drew the laser pistol, and waited.

A flek strode around the last turn, visible by the red patterns painted on its chitinous white body. It had evidently been treated with a luminous compound for just these circumstances. Kei raised his laser pistol and shot it point-blank as he had in so many simulations.

The beam bounced off and was absorbed by the cavern rock. A bubble of red-hot slag appeared overhead and Kei felt the heat on his muzzle. The flek raised its own weapon, a slim white tube, and fired. Kei was already moving as its arm came up, but even so the beam brushed his ribs as he ducked and the stink of his singed fur filled the stale air.

His head was whirling. He had forgotten about flekish armor, though he'd never heard it to be this effective. All the same, there should be vulnerable points, but he would have to aim more carefully. *Stand and fight!* his instincts insisted. *This is the enemy and the time is now!*

But the wisdom of the Black/on/black was strong in his memory. When the Black/on/black had first found the flek entrenched on a great plain on Anktan and known them for the enemy they were, he had traveled with Kei back across the mountains to assemble a hrinnti and human force that ultimately defeated the invaders. He had not thrown his life away in a valorous, but unwinnable battle against overwhelming odds, but smelled out a different *pattern/in/progress*, then used it to rid Anktan of flek forever.

Kei reached for the power that lay hidden in his body and blueshifted. The flek seemed to stand still as he snatched the tube from the flek's paw, then tried to use it himself. There were no visible controls though and he could not figure it out.

And there was the very real possibility that, even if he spent enough time to puzzle the workings out, the beam would bounce as harmlessly off the flek's coated hide as his own weapon had.

Maybe if he had studied harder back at the training base, paid more attention, he would know what to do now. He had been so certain though that all which was required to defeat flek was a laser pistol, claws, fangs, and an undauntable heart. Snarling, he whirled and fled back toward the rope ladder and the clean outside air.

Chapter Nine

After her escape, Mitsu found a depression that had once been a pond in the forest and huddled there, rocking, in the grips of a rage so white-hot, it seemed a nova had exploded behind her eyes. The flek had put their filthy hands on her!

The Oleaakan night, though hot as bath water, seemed cold and threatening. The wind from the sea increased until it whistled through the trees looming overhead. Intertwined limbs tossed and cracked against each other and the smell of rain rode in the air. Out at sea, a storm was brewing.

She closed her eyes and bent forward, pressed her face to her knees, trying not to scream. *That terrible white room, the conditioning that sent her spinning farther and farther from reality, her growing tolerance, then acceptance of flek tastes and songs and customs.*

The only thing which had sustained her down through the long months in Rehab was her determination never to fall victim to the flek again. She had sworn an oath to die first, and now she had just strolled into their trap like an idiot and let them carry her off!

Did some warped part of her still believe she was flek? That farce down in the cave had revealed a lot about what was lurking in her subconscious. Perhaps she had even betrayed herself into their hands on purpose. If so, she might as well go and throw herself in the sea, for all the help she was going to be in recovering Montrose and Onopa. She'd be of more use to Heyoka if she returned to the ship and locked herself up.

She glanced up at the shifting canopy of leaves overhead. Neither the mountains or the sea were visible from here. Face it, she told herself. She had no idea where she was. That flek had carried her off; then, when she'd come to in the middle of a nest, she'd run off in a blind panic without even taking stock of the surroundings.

One of the first tenets of Ranger training was to know the terrain and where you were at all times. Instead, she was lost, and would continue to be, until the sun came up and she could get her bearings. Unless . . . her hand strayed to the com on her belt. She keyed it on.

"Blackeagle?" Her voice sounded tinny and lost in the night.

No answer.

He was probably out of range, or even dead. The bloody flek had probably killed him, killed them all, while she was unconscious. *After the white room . . . she had fought even her partner . . . she heard the ear-splitting squeal of the transfer grid on that night, saw herself run through the installation, rallying the confused flek who were on the point of losing the battle—*

She had been weak and there was no way she could make up for that. The enemy had broken her and the crimes she had subsequently committed could never be put right. Kei was right to look upon her with so much hatred. What he didn't understand was that she hated herself more.

She tried the com again. "Blackeagle?"

It crackled, then fell silent.

Too much interference. She had to get to higher ground, at the very least out of these trees. Then perhaps she could find out if she were the only sentient left on this sodding world besides the flek.

When the breeders untangled themselves from the great pile they had made with their bodies, Twenty-fourth's foreleg was damaged beyond repair. The chitin was quite shattered. Second Breeder stood over his fellow as he lay keening, pale blood soaking into the earth, while the others milled about the ceremonial clearing.

Once before, in the interval since Second had emerged from the sac, a young male, not yet officially released from the nest, had wandered off a cliff and broken his body upon the rocks below. The adult females had been indifferent, saying he had obviously been too foolish to breed and there were more than enough drones as it was. It would have been necessary to discard some anyway. The young of all castes had been anxious and more circumspect in the days to follow.

Second Breeder judged this incident to be quite different though. The first had been caused by an error in judgement, while this injury had been inflicted purposefully.

The alien beast's action had been so overt, so forceful. Second Breeder felt his mind brimming with intriguing possibilities. A strident new song burned just below the level of his awareness, intoxicating and different. He remembered how he and the other breeders had acted in concert, actually leaped upon the savage alien, borne it to the ground and pinned it. Such a feeling of power and purpose! He thought he might well burst from it.

The beast regained its feet, its fur tinged with green by the light of the immense luminary. Its claws were no longer visible, and it looked harmless enough for the moment. It snarled and they all retreated a bit. In the background, Twenty-Fourth Breeder continued to keen.

"It's like *them*," Sixth Breeder's awed voice said, "the unharmonious ones, who took whatever they wanted and then spoiled what was left. We are doomed!"

"Don't be ridiculous. It doesn't look a bit like them," Second said. "My body-memories say they were shaped more like us, like real people, with four arms and legs, smooth, hard bodies, and one head."

"It has only one head!" Sixth Breeder craned his neck as he studied the hulking black-furred stranger as it paced back and forth.

"And that's as far as the resemblance goes," Second said. "Can you think of any creature, significant or not, which does not have but a single head?"

Sixth lowered his gaze in shame. "I am so utterly ignorant," he said. "I will never be able to sort out things half so well as you."

"Perhaps not," Second said. And he did feel an unaccustomed largeness within, a sense that he might well be more than others.

The beast limped a bit, seeming to regard them warily, but was otherwise undamaged, which was more than could be said for Twenty-fourth, whose cries were weakening. Second felt that sense of largeness swell inside him again——*pride*, it was called. They, he and the other breeders, had brought a dangerous, clawed alien down all by themselves!

Eighth Breeder approached. He had always been a nervous individual and now both pairs of his hands waved uselessly. He glanced at the beast, then flinched and looked away. "Shouldn't we go back? The night is almost over and the coordinators will be here as soon as it's light. They will be very sharp with us, I fear, for opening the forbidden place."

The coordinators would scold, and the keepers would scold as well. He could hear them now: he and the others were simply drones, useful for but one day of their entire lives, and far more in number than were actually needed. Some of them would be dispatched without ever being allowed to perform their sole function in life.

He had always pondered the strangeness, that the other castes should be so much more useful to the colony, while drones had but a single moment of service. They should be allowed to do more, see more, perhaps even *learn* something.

The new song, hovering at the edge of his awareness all night, seemed closer than ever. Second closed his eyes, feeling a strange, sweet ache for something unnameable, then let the song burst into his mouth. He had heard its beginnings in the voice of the marvelous crystal forest, when it summoned them from their nest. It was wild and riotous, something entirely unimagined, forthright, even brash.

The others joined in, their voices tentative at first, until they caught its rhythm, then louder and more enthusiastic. There was emotion in that song, exuberant and charismatic. He felt wide as the sea itself, as he sang it, as though he could march across the island and—

What?

He faltered. It was as though there was something immense he was supposed to do, perhaps even somewhere he should go, but he had no idea what it might be.

The beast growled again, a rattling, deep-throated sound that skirled at the edges of Second's mind. Sixth edged closer until his side scraped against Second, though he was shorter by a head. "Shall we jump on it again?" he said, and his voice quivered with an excitement Second had never heard before.

"Perhaps," Second said and he felt very eager himself. This was a new thing, never thought before, that they should—should—

He groped for a word that would say what he felt, how they should watch the alien and make sure no other laka were injured. There should be a word that made clear all of that. It must be secreted down there, deep in his cells, with all the other body-memories that refused to make themselves known. In the old days, though, terrible things had been done, although breeders were never told exactly what. Surely the laka had needed such a word then.

"If the keepers come to fetch us back, how shall we bring the alien with us then?" Sixth asked. "We do not speak its language so we cannot ask it to come."

It had been so heady, being out on their own, singing any song they chose, going wherever they might. Second realized he did not want to go back, ever. The thought of having to return to the colony was like being stuffed back into the sac, after hatching. He was simply too large for that now.

"If the keepers come," he said boldly, "we will tell them to go away. We wish to remain here. This will be our colony."

Eighth's hands froze in a gesture of shock. "But how will we eat?" he said. "Where will we sleep? How will we ever know what to do or when to do it?"

"Those are foolish questions, fit only for hatchlings," Second said. "When we need something, we will find it. Perhaps even the songs will tell us what we need to know."

The beast edged toward the trees and Second could

see it was going to try to escape again. "Surround it!" he cried. "Don't let it get away!"

His fellow breeders circled the black-furred alien, shoulder to shoulder, and settled in to keep watch. Second felt a wave of anticipation. The beast strode about the circle, quite agitated, and would most likely try to force its will upon them again. When it did, they would have to respond. How wonderful, he thought. How fascinating and utterly glorious. He could hardly wait.

At first light, Kei stalked through the abandoned Ranger camp, so miserable he could hardly lift his ears. His first encounter with a flek as a Ranger, and he'd run without even drawing blood. It was unbearable. He didn't know what to do with himself. He could never show his face to the Black/on/black again, never return to the world of his birth.

He'd heard the shuttle leave during the night, some hours before, as humans counted time. That was bizarre anyway, chopping up time into tiny bits, like breaking up a log, then counting the pieces. Humans were obsessed by numbers.

Nutrapaks lay scattered about and his stomach insisted food would be welcome right about now. He started to open one as the wind whistled against the tents, then threw the plas package aside. He was a hrinn. He needed fresh meat and grains, not this overprocessed grit. He would hunt for himself, now that there was no one to stop him.

Beneath the murmur of the wind, he heard fur brush against fabric. He looked up, bristling. Kika's pale-gray silhouette stood before the farthest tent. Her unbound mane whipped in the wind and she had discarded her uniform shirt.

He tensed, always uncomfortable conversing with

females who were not Levv. Bey had reported that she had been Jhii, but disgraced in some way, and had barely escaped Anktan with her life. "I thought you left with the others on the shuttle."

Kika snarled. "We had no desire to leave just as the enemy arrived!"

The rest came into view then: tawny, undersized Naxk; enigmatic Visht, who rarely spoke more than two words at a time; piebald Skal, bad-tempered and hulking even for a mature male, though not so tall as Kei; and his huntmate, sturdy, faithful Bey. "All of you are here then," he said in Hrinnti.

"Except the Black/on/black," Naxk said. "We scouted half the night, but could not find him."

"I tracked him back into the cave," Kei said, "before the flek came. I do not know if he closed with them in a fight or not."

Naxk's tawny ears pricked with interest. "You saw them—the flek?"

Kei stiffened. The breeze teased at an errant strand of his mane. He raked it aside savagely. "One."

"Where is the carcass?" Bey asked, eagerness written into every line of his body. His black eyes were aglint with joy. "I want to see it!"

Naxk and Kika rumbled approvingly.

"I—did not kill it." Kei felt his heart shrivel with shame.

Skal pushed forward. He alone of the six still wore his tan Ranger shirt. It had come loose at the neck and hung open so that his black and white markings were clearly visible. His lips wrinkled back from his teeth in a fierce grimace. "It ran away?"

"No." Kei stood very still, thinking of the excruciating noise, of how his brain had threatened to boil out through his ears, the way his vision had wavered and he'd been almost blind from the pain, how the air itself refused to enter his chest. But those were only excuses. There could be no acceptable reason for allowing his enemy to escape.

They looked away, unable to process the enormity of what he had done. The biggest among them, Squad Leader by right, *had turned aside from first blood*.

Finally, Bey turned to Skal, next biggest among them, as well as the oldest, a seasoned fighter. The rest turned also. Skal's distinctive scent filled the air as he realized what was coming. Kei had a flash of white-hot anger. Skal was big, but nothing more, not fierce, nor clever, nor especially fast. He couldn't even hold blueshift for more than a handful of breaths. This was not the *pattern/in/progress* they had been seeking. They could not put themselves beneath the claws of such an inferior leader.

Skal threw his head back and roared. The sound echoed against the green-carpeted mountains above, then out across the aquamarine sea. For a breath, Kei hovered on the edge of Challenge. Hot desire for cleansing combat beat through his blood. He could defeat Skal, who was slow and had not absorbed the hand-to-hand Ranger techniques as well. He was still biggest.

Then he saw the cant of the others' ears, the disapproving set of their shoulders. He had disgraced himself and they would not follow him now, no matter how well he fought. If he disputed Skal, they would turn and tear his throat out on the spot. And he found it tempting to force them to end his shame. One snarl, one sweep of his claws, and it would be all over.

Then he remembered how it had been back on Anktan. The Black/on/black had convinced them that no one could hunt the flek alone. They had been forced to put Line politics aside, as well as the traditional divisions between male and female, and bind themselves together into a single massive hunt, strength multiplied by strength, to sweep the flek from the plains and take back their world.

Now that the shuttle was gone, along with the human Rangers, they were few and the flek were here. They could not spare one even so unworthy as himself. He lowered both eyes and ears, and positioned himself at the rear of the pack.

The tree flickered out about an hour after Heyoka found himself trapped by the laka. He spent the rest of the night in darkness, unable to find a way out without injuring another native. As good as hrinnti night sight was, the natives' seemed even better. Every time he'd so much as flicked an ear, they were all over him. Montrose had not called out again and he was hopeful the two humans had escaped in the confusion of his capture.

When dawn finally brightened the sky, he made out the mountains first, off to the left, rugged and green, sweeping above the horizon. Several large six-legged avians soared overhead on their way to the restless sea. The air was humid and sweet, the clouds so low upon the trees, they seemed to be growing out of them.

His shoulder ached where he'd hit it in that earlier, ill-advised fracas. The laka he'd taken down last night lay unmoving on the ground, probably dead. None of the rest had made any move to aid or comfort it, or take it back to the village for help. They still surrounded him, a multicolored lot, their pink eyes brilliant with the rising sun. He prowled back and forth across the grass, assessing their strength, looking for weak spots.

His savage *other* raged within at the delay in finding his people, but he subdued it with an effort. He had given in to it earlier, but attacking had been a big mistake. It seemed to have triggered a primal response in the natives, clumsy, to be sure, but unmistakably aggressive. He should have known better.

Way to go, Blackeagle, he told himself. You managed to make a bunch of pacifists hot for your blood. He should have kept his mind on persuading the laka to provide shelter and supplies, and perhaps even defending their homes and themselves against the flek, but instead, like an idiot, he'd antagonized them.

He still had his laser rifle, but he needed to conserve the charge for real battle. If he couldn't get out of this without drawing further blood, he didn't deserve to be a Ranger.

Now that there was enough light to see clearly, it was time to try diplomacy again. "Look," he said and held up empty hands. "I don't want to hurt anyone else."

The natives stirred, moved in closer. Each one was a different pastel color: pink, blue, green, yellow, mauve, purple, as though they were a bunch of terran flowers. They had been "singing" off and on all night, a chorus of odd atonal buzzing that set his fur on end. They often moved in unison too, like a bizarre dance, though there was nothing particularly rhythmic or graceful about it.

Their scent was strong, but not unpleasant, a bit like the greenery of this island, which no doubt comprised much of their diet. They watched him carefully, seeming to wait for something.

"I'm sorry about last night," he said. He had no sense they understood anything he said, not even the tone of his voice. "We'll make reparations for your loss, I promise."

Their eyes, large in their oval faces, did not blink, did not even seem to have lids. Their hands, four each, were poised, ready, for—something.

Heyoka felt the *other*'s dangerous impatience rising

again. "Look, we can't just sit here all day. Either kill me or let me go!"

Silence. All eyes on him. Stillness. What did they want?

He fingered the stock of his laser rifle, then slung it onto his back. If they were so eager for him to make the first move, then he would. He couldn't stand this waiting anymore. "I'm leaving," he said, "but we must do this again sometime."

Suddenly their gaze shifted to something beyond him. He turned and found himself confronted by dozens more laka outside the circle, every one of them bigger than these who had held him prisoner all night.

Chapter Ten

After Sergeant Blackeagle tracked them back to the lighted tree, the laka dragged both Montrose and Onopa into the dark recesses of the surrounding grove. Shoved down between the gnarled roots of an old giant, Montrose could still hear the peculiar "singing" the laka seemed to go in for and Blackeagle's occasional snarl, but could tell little about what was going on.

It was dark and quiet, though enough ghostly green filtered through the trees to cast pools of light on the forest floor. The smell of stagnant water arose close by, reminding him that he was monstrously thirsty. His captors, however, wouldn't release his arms so he could access the canteen agonizingly just inches away on his belt.

Onopa, lying beside him, seemed more alert and spoke to him through the darkness occasionally, but in the end fell silent. He hoped she had just drifted off to sleep instead of succumbing to her head wound.

At some point, he must have slept himself, despite the discomfort of his cramped position, because suddenly he jerked awake without knowing what had woken him. He blinked. The rose of early dawn had crept into the eastern sky and Mitsu Jensen was standing in front of him, her face and uniform artfully smudged with dirt, a sonic blade humming in her hand.

The head of a dead laka lay against his foot, bleeding pungent ivory blood into the earth. His mouth dropped open and he realized the three-fingered hands had slipped from his arms. He stumbled up onto his feet and away from the headless corpse, heart pounding. What—?"

"You okay?" Jensen whispered, then slid around the tree without waiting for an answer. The second laka thrust Onopa toward her as though trading for its life. Jensen severed its neck with an expert stroke. The head dropped to the ground and rolled until it came to rest at the base of a tree.

"You're in luck," she said. "I was having trouble down in the cave a little while back, but apparently I can still use a knife." Her face was sober, her tone offhand. "Of course, you have to catch them right at the neck joint, otherwise the knife just slides off."

Montrose could have sworn the poor laka looked surprised. He made a grab for her knife hand, but he was stiff and sore and she easily dodged him. "Stop that!" he whispered fiercely.

"Stop what, junior?" She stepped back, thumbed the knife off, and resheathed it in her boot. The green afterimage danced in front of his eyes.

"Stop killing *laka*, goddammit! They just roughed us up a little, nothing life-threatening. That's not a license for you to wipe them all out."

"These are flek, junior, not laka." Her face was unconcerned. "You'd better learn the difference, if you ever want to see home again. Now, take your partner here and return to camp." She bent down and brushed back Onopa's black hair to examine the bruise on her forehead. "It doesn't look bad, but you should get it checked. I'm going to find Blackeagle."

She disappeared into the trees, and so help him, God, he was reluctant to go after her. She was even colder-blooded than the hrinn, and that was saying something. How could she go after civilians like that without a second thought?

He levered Onopa onto her feet. The tall Kalanan swayed, but then found her balance.

"I'll be all right," she said and pulled her arm free, "but I think our Corporal Jensen has lost it."

"You may be right." He did some quick calculating, based on the position of the sun, then set out for the base camp back up on the mountain, which rose above the forest. They could hear laka off to the east, making some kind of commotion, and steered clear, though it meant they had to wade through a blasted swamp.

Maybe Blackeagle could handle Jensen. At any rate, the sooner they all got off-world, the better.

Fourteenth Coordinator positioned her retinue well back, then sat on her haunches and considered the bizarre scene before her. After cavorting all night, the errant breeders had now assembled in the ceremonial area. Their postures were quite disturbing, many of them not the least bit deferential or uncertain, despite their shocking aberrant behavior.

One of the furred aliens stood inside their circle, no doubt inciting them to even more unacceptable behavior. This whole train of events was probably its fault. The colony had not experienced anything so disruptive for many generations. She turned to her personal translator, designated Fourteenth, of course, like herself.

"Direct them to return to their nest," she said. "They must be both tired and hungry. Tell them the keepers are waiting to feed and groom them, and afterwards we will discuss their disgraceful actions."

Fourteenth Translator, a lovely, lithe individual tinted a delicate orange, bent her head and spoke to the breeders in the simple, truncated grammar that was all their limited minds could process.

At first, they made no answer. Instead, they milled about with quick jerks, quite unlike their normally playful gestures, and looked to one another for guidance, rather than herself. She found that quite disturbing.

Then, when one finally did speak, the reply was abrupt, his tone actually defiant. The translator, quivering with disapproval, turned back to Fourteenth Coordinator. "They say they will not go. This is their colony now and they want no other." She ducked her elegant head in shame for having been the vehicle of so rude a message.

"Their colony?" Fourteenth Coordinator backed away in shock. "Do they think to build shelters for themselves, gather food, perhaps even whelp their own young?" Each of those ideas was more ridiculous than the last.

The translator began to speak, but at that point the furred alien ducked out of the circle of breeders and ran toward the cliffs leading down to the sea. To Fourteenth Coordinator's dismay, four of the sturdier breeders actually pursued it, leaped and brought it down in the grass before it had taken more than a few steps. It struggled beneath their weight, snarling and snapping.

"Let it go!" Fourteenth Coordinator cried and dimly realized the faithful translator was already relaying her words before she'd finished. "You know aggression is not permitted! Release it!"

The four breeders glanced up at her from the ground, but did not comply. Their eyes glittered strangely in the rising sun.

This was what came of aliens mingling freely among

them. Fourteenth Coordinator reeled from the shock
of it. If drones were allowed to behave so, the terrible
times would return. The colony would degenerate into
violence once again and they would lose all they had
worked so hard to build.

Those four would have to be put down early. There
was even the possibility none of this hatching were fit
to breed. Perhaps something had gone wrong in the
brooding tower, the temperature had been too high or
low, the gene charts misread. Better to forego progeny
this cycle and thin the ranks than to breed vicious,
unnatural savages.

She turned to her retinue and summoned her personal
messenger. Small and unobtrusive with a lovely pale-
green sheen to its carapace, it crept forward, obviously
unnerved by this outlandish situation. "Summon the rest
of the coordinators," she said in messenger dialect. "We
must discuss what will be done."

The furred alien was still struggling to free itself. She
walked closer, the translator at her shoulder, trying to
stare down the wayward breeders who were pinning the
creature. Its teeth and claws were extracting a heavy
toll, but they did not seem to care. "Let that poor beast
go," she said. "This crude conduct is doing great damage
to your harmony, to all of us, in fact. Laka do not
behave like this."

The translator relayed her words. The breeders
answered quite forcefully.

"'This is a good thing.'" The translator's voice was
strained and faint. She closed her eyes, obviously appalled.
"'A right thing. This beast damaged one of us and we
will damage it!'"

Fourteenth Coordinator was horror-struck. They must
be put down immediately, as soon as the keepers could
be summoned. She saw that now and she was quite
certain her sister coordinators would concur. Such

depravity! Any hesitation would only allow the outrageous behavior to spread further.

An alien voice rang out from the grove, shrill and demanding. The words, although not laka, were tantalizingly familiar. She had the feeling that she could make sense of them, if only the creature would speak again.

The breeders, along with her retinue, searched for its source up in the trees. The voice called out again, then a beam of hot green light pierced the morning air and struck one of the drones pinning the alien. He screamed and rolled away, all four legs thrumming against the ground, his sleek blue carapace badly scorched.

The shot had angled down from the treetops, Fourteenth Coordinator noticed. Off to the side, the alien beast used teeth and claws to free itself from the remaining breeders. It leaped to its feet, leaving a trail of injured males in its wake, and called out to the shooter.

A second beam of light raked a nearby breeder and the remaining laka scattered. The injured one fell to the ground and lay moaning. The others stared dumbly at his twitching body from a prudent distance away.

Not since a generation born so long ago that only body-memories remained, had such violence been perpetrated among them. Fourteenth Coordinator stumbled toward the safety of the trees on the far side of the clearing, urging her retinue before her. Terrible! her mind wailed. Terrible, terrible! What were they to do now, with such wickedness awakened within them? How could they ever achieve anything approaching consonance again?

Mitsu gunned down a third screaming laka before Heyoka was able to climb high enough to stop her. She had concealed herself in a clever blind made of slender boughs bound with grass, high up in the tallest tree.

Had she been there all night, watching his farcical attempts below to free himself?

He grabbed the laser rifle and pushed it aside just as she fired again. The laser bolt sizzled through the leaf canopy and set fire to a limb. "I said—stop it!" He wrenched the barrel free of her hands and tucked it underneath his arm. "What do you think you're doing?"

She was pale, her blue eyes standing out huge in her drawn face. "They're just flek!" she said, her hands clenched around a limb. "I know we can't get them all, before they get us, but we can damn well go down fighting!"

"Mitsu, take another look. Those are *laka*." Heyoka sagged back against the trunk and let his weariness wash through him. "Noncombatants, as well as possible allies, at least they were until you started skewering them!" The wind was stronger up here, full of a thousand new scents, shifting the leaves so that shadows played across their faces.

"You've been out of combat too long, furface," she said. He saw that she'd smudged her cheeks and forehead with mud, as well as camouflaged her uniform. Her fingers played with the sonic blade sheathed just inside her boot. "Don't you know a flek anymore when you see one?"

"As a matter of fact, I do." He searched her eyes. As before, they were too bright, too eager. "How about you?"

"I couldn't do it before, down in the cave," she said, the words tumbling out. "But I'm okay now. They're going to pay for what they did to me, each and every one!"

The fur on his back stood up. "Do what?"

"Destroy the crystal power matrix for the grid," she said. Her eyes would not meet his. "I tried, but my arm wouldn't aim straight."

It was a form of shell shock, he thought. She was still suffering from the aftereffects of Anktan. "We talked about this before," he said steadily, "how the laka bear a superficial resemblance to the flek, but it's no deeper than that of humans to other humanoid alien races, a certain symmetry of form arising out of similar function. Laka don't really look that much like flek, and they certainly don't smell like them, which indicates an entirely different body chemistry. Stop for a moment and think!"

Her ribs heaved, as though she'd run a race. "Admit it, furface. They had you down," she said. "I saved your life—again."

"Yes," he said, deciding not to debate the laka's intent, "you did."

She smiled and, though it was a pale imitation of former smiles, he realized how long it'd been since he'd seen one on her face. "So, we're even." She sat down on the branch and peered through the leaves at the scene below.

The laka had scattered, leaving behind three either dead or dying bodies. They didn't seem to have any concern for their injured, he realized. That much, at least, they had in common with flek. "Have you seen Montrose or Onopa?" he said.

She raked her fingers back through her disarrayed hair. "I released them a few minutes ago. Onopa was a little unsteady; she'd taken a knock on the head, but I got the jump on the flek who were holding them, then sent them on ahead back to camp."

There were more bodies then, he thought, probably hidden back in the trees. They were never going to be able to repair the already tenuous relations with the laka after this. The bark bit into his back and he shifted position.

"There is no camp," he said, "or at least there's no

one back at what's left of camp now. Didn't you hear the shuttle? We'd better collect Montrose and Onopa, then head for the mountains and hide out. The front is moving this way."

"Hell, the front is already here." She drew the knife from the sheath in her boot and thumbed it on. The green blade thrummed at full charge. "Take a look around. This place is crawling with flek."

"Right," he said, at a loss on how to deal with her delusion for the moment. "Let's go back to camp, then we'll decide our next move."

She gazed at him with perfect clarity, more at ease than he'd seen her since she'd been released from treatment. "You want to take the point?"

"Yes," he said, "so let me hang onto the rifle. Mine is down there somewhere. I lost it in that last go-round."

"No problem," she said. "I've still got my pistol."

After the breeders drifted down to the sea, Second Breeder reclined on the warm, black-sand beach and admitted to himself that he *was* both hungry and tired, as the coordinator had suggested. The air reeked of salt down here, which was corrosive to carapaces and not at all to his liking. The shoreline was barren of anything but sand and rocks and slimy sea wrack, and he had no idea where food might be obtained, other than back at the nest. Gleaners were a lowly caste and he had never paid their activities much mind. Breeders had a much higher purpose, the continuation of the colony. Still . . . he gazed wistfully out over the pale blue-green water . . . it would have been nice to have a ripe shellfruit right about now.

It had been a glorious night, filled with freedom and action and singing, but now it was over. The alien beast had escaped, though Second had picked up the stick it had dropped: a long, slender, black tube with a strangely curved grip at one end. This stick had purpose, he was sure of it, like a gleaner's scythe or a cultivator's hoe. It was the tool of some unknown caste.

Tenth Breeder came over and settled beside him. His brow ridges had been singed by the green fire back in the clearing. Despite the pain, he was clearly in good spirits. "Come with me back to the cave," he said.

"It was a very exciting song," Second Breeder said glumly, "but we can't live on songs and, anyway, the cave has stopped singing."

The waves threw themselves onto the shore, washing fractionally higher each time, making them edge back. The sun glimmered fat and orange-red as it slowly climbed. "It was more than just a song," Tenth said. "The trees of the crystal forest in that chamber were set into a particular order. I've been trying to remember where I'd seen it before and now I know: it is the same as my mark."

"What mark?" Second Breeder felt very dull, even though the light was increasing. Just a short time ago, he'd seemed on the edge of a vast new understanding. Now he felt like a foolish hatchling again.

"The mark on my back." Tenth craned his head around to look. "See?"

"Oh, that." Second Breeder glanced over at the dark blue pigmentation and was not impressed. All breeders bore such blemishes; just like cultivators and translators, messengers and scouts, every individual of every caste bore a mark somewhere on its body. It was just a chance of birth.

"It matches the placement of the crystal trees!" Tenth was almost beside himself, trying to make Second understand. "See? Three blotches here, two there, seven on the other side? It means something!"

Second roused himself to look closer. The scattered

streaks did look something like the distribution of crystals down in the cave chamber, but that could be said of many marks, he thought, if you looked at them long enough.

"When I was down there and gazed upon them," Tenth continued, "it was as though I remembered something I'd never been told. My body was telling me that the lightning should go first *here*, then *there*, and *there*."

Second regained his feet and distastefully retreated again from the rising morning tide. Back in the forest, he could hear cheerful avians croaking. "What lightning?"

"The lightning that makes them sing." Tenth was fairly dancing now in his agitation. He'd always been smaller than Second, but now he seemed almost large.

"But they're not singing anymore," Second said. "For all we know, they will never sing again."

"That's why I have to go back. If they do sing again, I might remember even more."

"I don't want to go," Second said. "I'm tired, and besides, the alien beast might come back searching for its stick and then I could hurt it."

"How would you hurt it?" Tenth asked. "You don't have claws or sharp teeth like it does."

"I—" Second began, but couldn't finish. What could he do? There must be something.

"And anyway you have a mark too," Tenth said. "Don't you understand? If mine means something, then yours does too. Everyone's does."

If his mark did have significance, it didn't concern crystals buried down in boring caves, Second thought. It had to do with acting as one pleased, going places, saying whatever one liked, taking, leaping . . . none of those words seemed quite right. As before, he was certain the words he wanted existed somewhere, if only he could reach them. Once learned, he was positive they would never be lost again.

"Come with me!" Tenth urged. "Don't wait here for the keepers to scold you back into the nest."

Second heaved onto his four weary feet and followed Tenth up the sandy slope and toward the hills. His former exhilaration had faded, but perhaps, if he did go, the cave would sing and he would feel those strange stirrings again. Then he would know what the missing words were, what the mark on his own back meant, what more there might be for a breeder to accomplish in the short time that was given to him. Everything.

The flek reached the abandoned camp just after sunrise. Kei's hackles rose as he spied them from his vantage point, a mountain ledge high above their former camp. The flek were as white and gaunt as the ones Kei had fought on Anktan, and, even at this distance, there could be no mistaking that acrid smell. Most of these were smaller than the warrior-drones he'd fought before, though, and only a few carried laser-sticks.

Little was left down there but tents, sleeping mats, a bulky com unit, and some scattered food packages. The wind tumbled discarded blue-and-white wrappers through the rocks. The hrinnti Rangers, under Skal's direction, had stripped what ordnance Dennehy had abandoned, though they were by no means proficient at all of its many forms.

So far, the flek were few, not more than twenty in the detachment swarming over the deserted camp. The crystals had been deactivated, for whatever flekish reason. Their nerve-wracking screech had cut off abruptly sometime before dawn. Naxk and Bey had been all for going back down to see what had happened, but Skal had led them up into the mountains instead.

That had been good strategy, Kei acknowledged. The new Leader had not allowed hot-blooded desire for battle to cloud his reason. Perhaps this particular hunt was better off for not being under Kei's claws.

And that was a very bitter thought indeed.

Chapter Eleven

When the antiquated grid had been inexplicably activated from the other side, Transfer Tech-Drone 4129 had been summoned from the city to examine it. He had waited up there on the hill to see if anyone came through, but though the grid generated the proper frequencies and stood quite ready, no one transferred.

At length, he was ordered to go through with a minimal team, including guards, and search the immediate area on the other side. No Maker had breathed on that misbegotten world since its far-side grid had been abandoned, many cycles ago, but obviously something or someone was tampering with it.

It was apparent as soon as he came through the grid that the air was too cold and thin for any sort of comfort. Makers could survive in such unwholesome conditions, but no breeding project would ever be successful on this world unless the atmosphere were drastically improved.

The work to do just that had been initiated long ago, but the project had been terminated short of completion and he did not know if it would ever be feasible to take it up again, perhaps only when the Makers ran short of proper worlds to sculpt. World-architecture was the ultimate art form, more beautiful and beguiling than any other, but selection was the province of the long-range planners, and he didn't pretend to understand their reasoning.

A hulking, fur-covered beast poked its nose into the transfer chamber just after he arrived. He followed it back through the tunnel to a primitive fiber ladder that led up to a hole in the mountainside. It fired an energy weapon, then somehow, without seeming to move, disarmed him and escaped.

4129 knew himself to be a bit slow these days. His tenure was almost up, and he was due to surrender his body for consumption by his replacement shortly. He might have been injured and thereby spoiled the planned transfer of memory if his body had not been sprayed with a sealant of his own devising against passage through this outdated and untended grid. Even protected, his side felt scorched.

The animal must possess at least a rudimentary level of sentience and so its presence here was at odds with what was known about this world. Since the Makers had abandoned the site, it was listed as unoccupied, except for those few left behind at the time. They had been a disturbed minority, produced by a faulty hatching and tainted with bizarre personality quirks that had actually proved transmittable to other Makers. The Deciders deemed them extinct by now. No one could be that insane and prosper.

The foliage around the exit hole, mostly sickly looking green ground-vines, had been thoroughly trampled. The vines flinched out of his way, as he climbed up, silvery sap still oozing here and there. He left his three tuners back in the transfer chamber to ready the grid for their return, but directed the rest of his team to follow the tracks and broken stems back up the slope to a series of temporary shelters, now deserted. Six full-grown and armed warrior-drones set a perimeter and kept watch over the company.

Agents of the Enemy had been here, and recently. Packages with a military insignia familiar to all Makers were still scattered about the hillside rocks, although nothing of value, as nearly as he could tell. He was, however, just a grid specialist, dispatched because of a familiarity with outdated systems, not a xenologician. It was not for him to make sense of these random bits and shards.

He leaned over and picked at a broken piece of white sheeting that protruded from the dirt. His team could carry out a superficial analysis, but more knowledgeable experts would have to be sent through to do a full scan.

If this particular grid even continued to function, that is. Its frequencies had skewed badly during the years of untended crystal growth. It was just chance it had been activated when someone was around to notice.

He turned to a bandy-legged investigator. "Conclusions?"

Highly specialized, the investigator was but half the size of a full tech. Its sight organs had been purposefully stunted to devote additional cortical tissue to its remaining senses, which were exquisitely acute. It swung its head to sample the air for analysis in its specially adapted lungs, retaining a minute amount in a side membrane for later examination, then rubbed a tattered piece of cloth between its chemo-sensitive forehands. "Artificially produced. Crude workmanship. Probably human."

The animal he had encountered down in the cave was definitely not human, but the weapon it fired might well have been of human manufacture. Imagine taking up with something so primitive! Humans were notoriously indiscriminate in their choice of allies, while Makers had no need of other species to augment their ranks.

If they required some ability not currently within their gene pool, they simply designed it into the next generation of warriors, techs, or deciders. So much more efficient that way, so pure.

Other species of course did have their uses, especially as fodder for slave markets. Many of the galaxy's more advanced races disdained trade in less technologically sophisticated goods, but would purchase exotic slaves or pets. If this world had become infested with furred primitives, the Makers could always use another shipment of unique slaves.

Transfer Tech-Drone 4129 waited as his team probed and dug and sniffed and pried until they had extracted every bit of information available at this level of investigation. Then, when he was about to summon them back to the grid, two bipeds approached the abandoned camp from a lower elevation. It had been so long since he'd seen one of these, it took a moment for him to recognize them as human.

His investigators froze, then formed ranks. They had no skill with weapons, but knew how to use their bodies to advantage in a skirmish. The warrior-drones stepped forward in a precise formation bred into them, raised their laser sticks and fired.

"Holy Mother of God!" Montrose dove for cover, pulling Onopa with him. The two of them hit the ground rolling as laser bolts sizzled into the dirt and blasted the raw rock beneath into slag. He sidled desperately on bruised knees and elbows, keeping low. Of all the things they'd expected to find in camp, flek were not even on the list.

He took a glancing burn to the right leg, protected to some degree by his thermoinsular uniform, then found cover behind a drooping tree insufficient for the purpose. He propped his back against the trunk, tried to control his ragged breathing. The injured leg throbbed like a sonuvabitch. Onopa had gone the other way, instinctively splitting the enemy's fire.

By God, Jensen had been right. There were flek on Oleaaka. He'd thought she was around the bend, as crazy as the day Blackeagle had rescued her back on Anktan. If they ever got out of this mess, he owed her a drink. Hell, he owed her a whole bar.

The flek chittered among themselves, high and screechy. Sweat ran down his face, soaked his back. The material over the burned leg looked charred. His vision wavered and it seemed he was at the bottom of a deep dark well with only a circle of light above.

"Montrose?" Onopa called from that circle. "You all right?"

A laser blast answered and she didn't speak again, either dead or wiser, he didn't know which.

From the bottom of his well, he heard rustling in the grass, or was it just the leaves of the tree overhead? He squinted, but couldn't tell. His rifle lay inert in his hands and he wasn't sure he had the strength to lift it, even if something were coming. If *flek* were coming, he corrected himself. Not something, *flek*!

The rustling was louder now, like dozens of small feet creeping toward him. His mouth and his hands were numb; his eyes seemed only to be able to stare straight ahead and he was so frigging cold. *Shock, stupid,* some still functioning portion of his brain told him. *Get up, move!*

But where would he go? He closed his fingers around the rifle stock, marshalled all his strength to steady the butt against his chest. Even that slight movement made his leg throb, as though it had grown five sizes too large, and he had to clamp his jaws to keep from crying out.

"Montrose?" The voice was closer now, a whisper beside his ear. "Montrose, dammit, answer me!" Fingers

fumbled at his belt, pulled off his medkit, applied it
to the bare skin inside his arm.

Coolness flooded through him as the kit went to
work analyzing his injury, then released appropriate
meds. "W-what?" he said, unable to turn his head.

"You have to stand up," Onopa said. Her voice was
strained as her fingers took his upper arm and pulled.
"We've got to get out of here. Give me the rifle."

The pain retreated a bit, but he felt muzzy, confused,
distant. "No!" he said. "The flek!"

"You're just going to shoot your own foot off," she
said. "Put the safety on and give me that thing." She drew
it from his nerveless fingers and he couldn't resist.
"Now stand up."

He got his good leg underneath him and let her take
his weight. Fortunately, she was almost as tall as he was
and sturdily built. The mountainside seemed to swirl
around him in great dizzying loops. He closed his eyes
and let her guide him. The tree's long trailing fronds
brushed his face as they passed beneath them and then
he could smell the sea in the distance. "Where's
Blackeagle?" he said with great difficulty.

"Hell if I know!" She was breathing hard. "Now,
come on!"

She smelled good, he thought fuzzily, between throbs
of pain so intense, despite the meds, they blotted out
all thought. She was redolent of soap and sweat and
leather, like the barracks, like home: good clean smells.

"I counted six warrior-drones," she said, looping his
arm over her shoulder, "and they're all on the small side.
The rest are just dinky little techs of some variety I've
never seen before. I took a couple out and they've
pulled back for the moment. At any rate, if we can avoid
the big ones, I can take the rest."

"How—many?"

"Twenty—twenty-five, maybe. I couldn't get a good

count crawling around on my belly." She studied the terrain, then started downhill.

He followed her lead as best he could, hopping on one leg, though his sight was distorted. After half an hour of stomach-wrenching sliding and stumbling down uneven terrain, she eased him to the ground and looked around, hands on her hips. Her chest heaved and her uniform was soaked with sweat. She blotted her forehead with the back of her wrist. "I can't believe it. There's no sign of them now."

His head spun and he felt far too cold for this tropical climate. Somewhere high above them on the mountain, he heard something small scream and die in the claws of a predator. "They must be up to something," he said as a relentless ink-black tide encroached upon his vision. "They're probably following us, hoping we'll lead them back to the rest of the squad. They wouldn't lose us that easily, not flek."

"Maybe they had orders," she said. "They could have had a time limit and had to return through the grid."

"If so," he said, "they'll be back."

He felt her knife cutting away his pants leg, then the air assaulted his raw burned flesh. His fingers clawed the moist earth, then a spinning darkness swept him away.

Heyoka kept a close eye on Mitsu as they worked their way up from the lowlands to the abandoned camp. The sun beat down and he felt utterly lifeless under its glare, but she kept pace, looking more fit and confident than he'd seen her since before Anktan. He wondered if she had regressed to an earlier time when flek were just the enemy, abstract and unknown, and she had never betrayed him or the Confederation or herself.

It was by no means certain the flek would sweep back over this world, once Confederation forces pulled out of their current position, but she had to come off it, in case they did. She was a danger to herself and everyone else, including the timid laka, in this condition.

He led her away from their former route, keeping well clear of the recently unearthed entrance to the cave. No point in stoking her delusions, he thought. The wind had switched at dawn and now bore the mysterious, wet smells of the rain forest that blanketed this side of the mountains.

"We'll collect Montrose and Onopa," he said as they skirted a mountain stream rushing over stair-step rocks on its way down to the sea. "Then we'll establish a camp higher on the mountain, somewhere we can set up a base station to communicate with any Confederation ships that come in range. The *Marion* is probably long gone by now, but sooner or later, someone will come back, even if just to gather data." They paused for a cool drink. Kneeling, she bathed her smudged face in the stream, while he poured water on his head and tried not to think about internal parasites.

Her black hair kept straying into her eyes and she tore a strip for a headband out of the tail of her shirt. "What about the flek?" she asked. "You don't think they're just going to sit on their so-called hands while we four play Ranger up in the heights?"

His ears flattened. "We'll worry about that *if*, and *when*, they land."

She examined a long thin scratch on her arm. Her mouth quirked. "They're already here, furface."

"Those were laka." A muscle jumped in his jaw. "Not flek."

"They were flek," she said stolidly. "Even if I didn't know one from the other, which I do, I read the reports back at base. Laka don't attack, not even with provocation. Their brains aren't wired for it. They let the flek nearly wipe them out once before and never raised a feeler!"

"They don't have feelers," he said, feeling desperate. "And that whole mess was my fault. They kept blocking me when I was trying to reach Montrose, so I finally lost my temper and jumped one, injured it badly too, I'm afraid. I seemed to have triggered some sort of mildly aggressive response, but even that was ineffective."

She fell silent, staring off up at the riot of green that covered the low mountains, then grinned. "You're so full of it, Blackeagle! You almost had me going there for a moment."

Let it go, he counseled himself. Maybe later, she'd be ready to listen. He'd try again in a few hours. For now, she was just too caught up in her delusions.

Above them on the hillside, Heyoka caught a flash—the metal barrel of a rifle, perhaps? The wind was in his face, but he couldn't detect any familiar scents. It had to be Montrose or Onopa, though. Who else would be lurking up there armed?

"Did you see that?" He pointed out the flash to Mitsu. She snatched the rifle out of his hand, dropped to one knee and sighted in. "No, it's Montrose!" he said in alarm. "Don't fire!"

She squinted, held her breath, then he took the rifle back and toggled the safety on. "There are no flek!" He gripped her shoulder with his free hand and flexed his claws through her uniform. She flinched and tried to pull away, but he held on and stared down into her ice-blue eyes.

"I know what happened to you on Anktan was worse than anything I can imagine, but you have to move on. This is Oleaaka. The flek may be on their way, but they're not here yet!"

She dropped out from under his grip, whirled and took up a fighting stance. She was breathing hard and two bright red patches surfaced in her cheeks. "Don't ever do that again!"

"Mitsu—"

"I'm not crazy!" She backed away. "I know what I saw, and you should trust me enough to believe me. They were flek!"

He stared at her in silence. If she bolted, either now or later, it might take days to find her. She was an expert, trained in both sabotage and losing herself in rugged terrain. Even a nose like his might have a hard time if she got a proper head start. Once she started stalking the defenseless laka, they wouldn't have a chance. Given enough time, she could easily exterminate the entire population of this island by herself.

"Okay," he said. The wind down from the mountains ruffled his fur the wrong way, a prickly sensation. "I believe you."

Her eyes darted around, as though seeking an escape route.

"Let's find Montrose and Onopa before the flek do," he said. "Then we'll draw up a strategy for doing the most harm with what little resources we have."

"I want my rifle," she said, still unmoving.

He tossed it to her and hoped he didn't regret it before the end of the day. Her mouth tightened and she flipped the safety off.

Kei dug his claws into crevices in the crumbly black rock and climbed straight back up the cliff, a feat that taxed even his powerful frame. There, he reported to Skal about the flek and the two Rangers.

The Leader prowled back and forth beneath thick overhanging greenery, considering, while Naxk and Bey snarled with eagerness. "There is a pattern here," Skal said. "Perhaps *storm/against/stone*, or *undue/transformations*."

"Whatever this pattern is," Kei burst out, "we don't have the time to sniff it out! Our enemy waits below!"

Skal leaped at Kei with open claws and the big black ducked, his own handclaws springing free. The two squared off and regarded each other with foolhardy directness, while the other four stepped back and looked on in silence.

The blood thrummed in Kei's ears, whispered of power, chances to be taken, honor to be regained. He could take Skal. The certainty beat through him. The big black and white was a careless fighter. He had seen that over and over in training.

"You were not so eager for battle down in the cave when you encountered the flek," Skal said, his tone caustic.

Shame flooded through Kei and he was forced to look away. He had run back in the cave, and it did not matter that he'd thought he had no choice. He had lost his honor in that moment, and until he found a way to regain it, he did not deserve to lead. He had no right to Challenge Skal or anyone else now.

Without another word, the black-and-white Leader picked up his rifle, specially adapted for hrinnti double-thumbed hands, and led the five of them back down the hillside, his ears canted forward.

Kei stationed himself at the rear of the pack, puzzled that any humans had remained behind on this world. During his relatively short contact with the species, he'd found them to be sticklers for human patterns like *orders*, *chain of command*, and *regulations*, and the major had commanded everyone to be on that shuttle.

They entered the camp, bristling with anticipation of a fight, but found it empty, both of humans and flek. The pervasive stink of their enemy was everywhere though, and the trail led downhill toward the sea. Human spoor ran in the same direction, overlaid by the flek.

Kika looked up from examining the ground. "They're

tracking the Rangers." As always, the pale-gray female ran slightly apart from the others, a peculiar preference that had marked her out for scorn back in training.

At the head of the pack, tawny Naxk froze, her ears flattened, then gave the familiar spread-fingered hunt gesture for them to disperse. She had evidently detected recent tracks. "This way," she said in a rattling whisper that was half snarl and the others automatically spread out, filtering down through the gullies and ravines, leaving no route unexplored.

Kei unslung his rifle from his shoulder and chose his footing carefully. A set of boulders loomed, half buried in the rich black earth and he passed them on his right. The scent was very fresh here, both flek and human, very intense. Then a human head, topped with black hair, popped up from behind the rocks. "Kei!" An arm waved.

He started to respond, then heard the whisper of feet, many feet, in the long grass. He leaped forward and flushed three diminutive flek from a weedy clump. Unarmed, they scuttled away in a panic, as though fleeing an overturned rock. Kei forgot the rifle and raked the nearest with bared claws.

It hit the boulders with a sharp clack and slid to the ground, legs kicking. The other two got away, but he heard Naxk snarling with eagerness. At least one had crossed her path.

Onopa scrambled out from behind the rocks and fired at the injured flek at close range. It emitted a single high-pitched squeal, then lay dead and smoking.

How strange. When he'd fired upon the one in the tunnel, the beam had just ricochetted without doing the enemy any damage. Onopa was already on the move, quartering the immediate area, trying to surprise more of the enemy. Kei searched himself and found Montrose unconscious, one of his legs laser-burned.

Then he was as good as dead, he thought dispassionately, staring down at the human. He'd certainly never run again with a leg that badly damaged, and they had no restorers to even attempt to mend the injury. As for human doctors, well, he'd seen the mess they'd made of the Black/on/black's leg after he'd been injured by flek fire and even humans thought there was no place in war for a cripple. He rubbed the ropy scar across his own muzzle, remembering. He'd run afoul of a flek weapon himself as a youth.

Up ahead, Kika squalled as a wave of the smaller flek swarmed her. Kei signaled Bey and they charged as the team they'd always been until earlier today, converging from opposite directions.

He heard something hard scrape against rock from higher up on the hill and whirled, ears flattened. A green laser bolt seared the spot where he had been standing. The scent of earth and melted rock permeated the air and a thick, red rage exploded behind his eyes. He surged up the hillside, sending clods flying. It was the marked flek he'd seen in the tunnel. This close, though, it was obviously undersized. Its stink filled his nostrils and he threw aside the rifle, remembering how this one had taken a direct hit down in the tunnels to no avail.

He leaped and it collapsed beneath his weight, squealing, its four hands flailing. He raised his claws to slash its throat, but that area was protected by the same special coating and resisted his claws.

Onopa's head appeared above the rocks. "Stand aside!" she called.

Kei threw back his head and roared. "This kill is mine!"

"Stand aside, dammit!" She had a bloody welt across her face and her black hair flowed loose across her shoulders like a mane. "It took down Montrose!"

"The rifle won't work," he said. "I fired on it in the cave and the beam just bounced off!"

The flek convulsed into a quivering hard ball, legs and arms in the middle, head ducked against its chest, eyes closed. Kei tried his claws on it again, but the protective coating was too tough. With a snarl, he kicked it away in disgust.

As soon as she had a clear shot, Onopa fired upon it. The beam bounced off and melted a furrow in a nearby boulder. She stood staring, eyes wild, chest heaving.

Kika, Visht, Bey, and Skal climbed into view a moment later, rifles in hand, then Naxk approached from above. They gazed down at the enemy they had crossed light-years to find, an enemy who destroyed worlds with the same casualness that a hrinn might crush a tiny black nit, an enemy who, apparently, could no longer be killed by ordinary means.

Chapter Twelve

Ninth Translator-at-large directed the sanitizers to clear away the dead drones and deposit their bodies in the compost pit outside the compound. Sanitizers were simple creatures without much ability to adapt and they had not been able to work out for themselves what needed to be done. This situation was unprecedented in their lifetimes.

Fortunately, Ninth thought, the loss of a number of males before breeding was not critical; there were, after all, many more than were needed in every hatching, but the disharmony engendered by their night of bravado and subsequent violent deaths would persist among the populace for some time to come.

A sturdy sanitizer passed, bearing a decapitated carcass. Several of the drones, in fact, were similarly mutilated. Ninth turned her face away, quite ill at the level of violence indicated. Such depravity, right here in their colony!

Fourteenth Coordinator entered the ceremonial clearing with her customary retinue of translator, messenger, and scout. She was well beyond her callow youth and so quite lovely, all pale blue tinged with rose at her joints. Ninth suddenly felt shy and ducked her head.

Fourteenth's translator, both smaller and younger than Ninth, stopped well back, a courteous acknowledgment of Ninth's senior status and experience.

"Where are the survivors?" Fourteenth Coordinator asked.

"They fled to the beach," Ninth answered with a pang. "Though the keepers report five of them left afterward and were last seen climbing back up to—" She could not bring herself to finish.

"*That* place?" Fourteenth Coordinator was rigid with disapproval.

Ninth could have collapsed with shame. "I could not reason with them, though I tried."

"Someone is at fault here," Fourteenth Coordinator said sternly. "Our males are designed to be as tender as the new grass and as biddable as ivy in the spring. Laka have not bred such willful drones within living memory!"

"If you wish, I will question the keepers again," Ninth said, "although they maintain it was the activation of the crystals in that—place—which skewed the breeders' energies toward violence."

"That cavern should have been destroyed," Fourteenth Coordinator said grimly. "We have done our best to obliterate all traces of those before-times, but we should have tried harder." She stared off toward the sea which sparkled under the midmorning sun. "Have the keepers fetch the rest of the breeders back," she said finally. "They are to have all the help necessary, even from the gleaners and cultivators, if needed. As for the missing five . . ." She stared out over the cliffs down toward the pale sea.

Ninth waited.

". . . they must be put down immediately. When the keepers finish ministering to those on the beach, dispatch

them to the cavern. They are to do it there, out of sight.
We'll have no more upset."

Not in the ceremonial arena, with the luminaries
ablaze and all the colony in attendance, giving homage
for their sacrifice? Ninth stiffened. "It will be—very
hard," Ninth said cautiously, already trying to think how
best to phrase this unprecedented instruction to the
tenderhearted keepers. It would have to be circuitous,
leading them through several sequential conclusions so
they came to the necessary decision on their own.

"Not as hard as putting down a whole generation,
regardless of caste." Fourteenth Coordinator's gaze was
hard.

"That would never happen!" Ninth was aghast.

"It did happen—often—in the first days of the
colony." Fourteenth Coordinator bent her neck a bit,
beckoning Ninth closer and signifying the intimacy of
the moment. "And not just with breeders either. With
sanitizers and cultivators, even gleaners, though they
were named differently then. Madness was rampant and
we had to sacrifice much to cut it out."

Ninth was quivering. "I did not know."

"You could not have known," Fourteenth Coordinator
said. "It is an ancient secret, remembered by the bodies
of only a few in each generation against the danger that
we might inadvertently come around to those days again
in the great cycle."

The air seemed suddenly colder. Ninth did not know
where to look, what to do with any of her hands or feet.
"Were even translators so afflicted?"

"There were no translators then, child," Fourteenth
Coordinator said. "In fact, those wicked days were the
reason for the development of translators, so caste could
be divided from caste and the madness therefore
segregated. It was felt that if the castes could not
communicate with one another, then the madness

could not spread and be therefore more easily rooted out. New languages were developed, ones that fit the function of each caste, a simple and direct tongue for gleaners, a quiet and peaceful one for breeders. Each was given only what it needed."

"I have always known what we translators do is important," Ninth said, "but never suspected it meant the colony's very survival."

"You are the best of us," Fourteenth Coordinator said. "The days to come may be very terrible and you may see almost unendurable things before we pass through this side of the cycle, but you must never forget how much we depend upon you."

Ninth was galvanized. "I will work harder," she said. "I will find more and better words to make the breeders listen and smooth the way with the keepers."

"I know you will, child," Fourteenth Coordinator said. "I only hope it will be enough."

When Heyoka and Mitsu reached the base camp at midmorning, they found trampled tents, scattered shipping crates, and a few broken cots. The rising wind shrieked through the tent frames and the hillside rocks, kicking up swirls of dust. Heyoka sniffed out the truth immediately.

"Flek!" His lips drew back in a soundless snarl. They *had* either landed or come through the transfer grid after all. Mitsu wasn't as far off as she'd sounded, but how could she have known? Those had been laka last night. He'd swear on it.

"Where?" She had her rifle at the ready, her grip so tight, her knuckles shone white through the skin of her hands.

"Here," he said, "and recently." Fur bristled across his shoulders and his *other* wanted to roar with eagerness.

She took cover behind the towering tree, pressed her

back to the trunk, and scanned the empty camp with a practiced eye. A windswept wrapper caught on a branch close to her face. She flinched and swore. "Montrose and Onopa?"

He sampled the air, then padded over to the tree and knelt. "They were here too," he said, "along with the flek. Montrose was down." He could smell the length of Montrose's body where he had fallen on the grass and the stink of scorched clothing as plainly as if a picture had been etched into the earth. "There was a fire fight. He took a bolt, in the leg, I'm guessing."

Mitsu drew her sonic knife with her free hand and thumbed the blade on. "We have to find them!" A note of panic had crept into her voice. "You know what the flek do to their prisoners!"

"I have some idea," he said. His ears flattened as he remembered her pinched, crazed face, the alien wildness in her eyes. It had taken days for her to be able to speak even a few words of Standard again instead of High-Flek, weeks for her to understand who she was. "We'll find them."

He wished now he'd searched harder for his rifle. One of the laka had probably picked it up without knowing what it was. But Mitsu had been so efficiently on the rampage, confusing laka with flek, he had decided to let it go and slip back later, once they'd located their personnel.

They finished checking the camp. In spite of the hasty departure, little of value had been left beyond a few foodpaks and a com unit far too big to haul up to the mountains. He stuffed his pockets full and saw to it that Mitsu ate the contents of one, then stowed as many as she could carry too. She was pacing back and forth, in a fever to be after the flek, and after ten more minutes of useless reconnoitering, he agreed.

Again, he took the point; his hrinnti nose had the

advantage over her human senses. Twenty feet outside camp, he had another startled realization. Kei and Bey, Skal, Visht, Kika and Naxk, every one of his hrinnti recruits were tracking the flek too. None of them had caught that damned shuttle.

"Bloody independent to the last!" he muttered under his breath. This whole project was pointless. How could he have been so dense? Hrinn didn't take orders because they couldn't even conceive of what an order was or a human who had the right to give one. On Anktan, no hrinn obeyed anyone who hadn't demonstrated the ability to tear his or her throat out. They were never going to function inside human command structures because their brains just didn't work that way. He, and the Rangers, had been fooling themselves. Despite the potential of his people as superb warriors, this hodge-podge of human and hrinn was never going to work.

Mitsu brought up the rear, slipping every now and then as weariness weighed upon her. Like him, she'd been on her feet all night, except for when she'd climbed that damned tree and constructed a firing blind. It was catching up with both of them. They were going to have to find some time to sleep.

Sure, he told himself, they would do just that, as soon as the flek called the war off. Then he wondered at himself. That was almost a joke, and here folks thought hrinn had no sense of humor.

After about an hour, he tracked their quarry to a rocky cliff overlooking the rain forest. The grass had been heavily trampled and the scent record was thick. The sun was high overhead, beating down on his black fur and he regretted leaving behind his shirt. He and Mitsu checked the area and found one boulder which bore a slag mark where it had been struck by laser fire.

"They *were* here." Mitsu looked around, her eyes

darting. Her face was wan and her blue eyes stood out dark against translucent skin.

He sank to his heels, then caught a strong jolt of flek rankness. "What—?" He prowled over to the cliff's edge. Clawed and laser-burned flek bodies had been cast into the scree below. He counted at least eight in just the top layer. Mitsu stood beside him, staring down, not blinking.

"Those aren't warriors," he said. "They're too small and they look specialized, some kind of techs, maybe."

"A scouting party?" she said. "Perhaps they came through to find out who tripped the grid."

He turned back and quartered the area more thoroughly, reading the scent signatures like a book. "It looks like the hrinn ran the flek down here. I don't think anyone besides Montrose was wounded." He paused besides a clump of spiky grass. "Onopa's scent is here, along with the rest. They're all headed downhill."

Mitsu clambered down the unstable slope to have a better look at the carcasses. "The entrance to the cave isn't that far from here," she said over her shoulder. "I bet they're headed that way."

He read the trail further, flattened his ears at what he found, then joined her on the slope. She was staring fixedly at the pile of corpses and her grip on the laser pistol was overtight.

The flek were already beginning to reek in the strong sun and his eyes watered. They needed to move on. "One more thing," he said. "They're still traveling with at least one flek, and I can't tell if our missing Rangers are its prisoner, or it's theirs."

The miserable flek would not walk! Kei was ready to tear it apart in frustration, except that his claws could not make any impression on its reinforced hide. He and Bey were forced to carry it between them and such close proximity to flek stink was almost more than the sane mind could tolerate.

He sneezed, then sneezed again, felt disgusted, soiled. His claws would never be free of the taint! Kika gave him a quick glance, but remained otherwise inscrutable, which was all he expected of females anyway. Who ever knew what they were thinking?

Naxk and yellow/on/white Visht kept well ahead and upwind, an odd pairing, though they seemed to tolerate each other. Skal prowled just in front, bearing the injured human on his shoulder with less than stoic patience. The other human, the sound one, kept pace, but was clearly struggling to do so.

Softskins! Kei wanted to spit with frustration. Why had he ever followed the Black/on/black across the skies to their sprawling holds that reeked of dead metal, concrete, and plas? They talked and talked and never once used their noses to smell out what was right before them. No wonder they were losing the war. They spent more time yammering than fighting!

The truth was that, after the destruction of the flek grid on the plains, he had felt caught up in the newly named pattern, *stars/over/stars*, which was so large and lengthy, no one could say precisely where it had begun or when, if ever, it would be complete. For himself, he had felt certain its shape wasn't fully known yet. He had something important left to do, and that thing, whatever it was, would only make itself known if he stayed at the side of the legendary Black/on/black.

At the training base, though, he had seen what humans had made of the Black/on/black. There, this hrinn-among-hrinn, was called by the human name of Blackeagle and considered nothing more than a common *soldier*, as humans named such things, an interchangeable unit, valued only when it did as it was told and trained others to do the same.

It was true Rangers knew many exotic, innovative ways to fight and many more ways to destroy, all of them fascinating and quickly lethal. On the battlefield, in case they were ever actually let near one, a hrinn so trained might truly make his enemies quail.

But these Rangers had bizarre ideas: Enlisted hrinn should not fight among each other, even though there was no other way to establish dominance, and males should live with females, should train and eat in mixed company, as well as fight together. Though he had lived his early life under similar circumstances at Levv, it was an aberration and they'd had no choice. And even so, male and female had kept apart as much as possible. He could not imagine living an entire lifetime in such unnatural circumstances. Conventional hrinnti wisdom dictated that male and female were meant to come together only in the time of Gathering. Additional contact resulted in disaster.

Up ahead, Skal halted beneath a copse of swaying frond-trees and eased the wounded Montrose off his massive shoulders. A flight of tiny brown six-legged avians burst from cover at the noise and the human groaned. He should be left in peace to die, Kei thought resentfully, or have his throat torn out, to send him cleanly through the Gates of Death. This hauling about of dying meat was pointless.

He and Bey deposited the inert flek a few steps away as Kika caught sight of a handful of small, six-legged animals, shaped much like the jits of his home world, only furred and flightless. Pale-gray Kika immediately plunged after them and was gone. Naxk, no doubt just as hungry, whirled and followed.

Kei sat close to Bey. His former huntmate did not acknowledge him, but did not move away either.

Onopa settled on the ground beside Montrose, raked her long black hair back from her face, then opened her canteen and gave the wounded man some water. Montrose's eyes opened. He stared about wildly and then choked. "Drink it, damn you!" Onopa said and tried again.

Montrose lifted his head long enough to swallow, then fell back, limp and spent by even that small effort.

"That one will die," Kei said, "and, even if he doesn't, he will never be whole enough again to fight. You dishonor him by hesitating. You should cut his throat before he weakens further."

Onopa flushed. The bones of her face stood out in the sunlight. Her eyes went fierce and narrow as though she would attack. "Humans take care of their wounded," she said.

His ears flattened. "Like you took care of the Black/on/black? I saw his leg before the healers restored him. He could barely walk!"

"I don't know anything about that," she said, "but we don't believe in mercy killing."

The word "mercy" was one he'd heard used before, but never fully grasped. Deep-sleep language studies imparted vocabulary along with basic concepts that had reasonable cognates in both species. The explanations provided for "mercy" had made no more sense than the ones for "kindness" or "gentleness." The Black/on/black had tried to fill in, but Kei had never made the least bit of sense out of any of them.

Montrose's dark-haired head tossed on the grass and he groaned. His face was creased with pain. Onopa gave him a second drink from the canteen, then took one herself. She mopped at her golden-tan skin with the back of a sleeve. "Back off," she said. "I'll decide what to do."

Kei's lips wrinkled away from his teeth in a soundless snarl and he stalked away. As if he would dirty his claws on a moaning, soft-skinned Outsider! If she wanted that one dispatched, she would have to do it herself.

A few paces away, the flek was still curled up into a tight white ball. He gave it an experimental rake with bared claws. They screeched harmlessly across the tough surface. It was like scratching steel. What had the flek come up with? None of the warriors he'd encountered during the invasion of Anktan had been similarly armored.

Kika and Naxk trotted back into the shifting shade, each bearing the results of a successful hunt. Kika had two small carcasses over her shoulder and Naxk, always eager to prove herself, carried four. The scent of fresh blood overrode flek stink for the moment and he felt his own hollowness, though the meat had an unfamiliar tang. He remembered Mitsu, just the day before, counseling him against eating off-world game.

The beasts were delicate and small, apparently built for tree-climbing and hardly more than a few mouthfuls apiece. Kika handed him one, while Naxk apportioned hers out. There was no question, of course, of wasting one on the wounded Montrose. Even if he had been in any condition to eat, food could not be cast away on one who could not fight.

That still put the kill one portion short. Naxk was down to the final carcass before she came to Onopa and turned aside to tear off a mouthful for herself. Kei knew she could not share; it was, after all, her kill. No one else had any right to it, and it was a point of honor that a hrinn always fed from her own kill.

Onopa looked away, and Kei read the expression on her face. He had seen it hundreds of times during training. *Hrinn were only savages*, it said. *They could not be expected to act any better.*

With a growl, he tore his own share in two and thrust a gory half at her. The blood spattered on his uniform and had a strange yellowish tint. It smelled even more alien than the meat and his nose twitched. Onopa sat rigid and silent, then took the bloody leg and gave a small jerk of a nod. "Thank you."

Kei raised his muzzle to the wind. He had learned the appropriate human protocol for this situation, but this was not Confederation territory and they might never see another human. Here, finally, it was acceptable for him to be a hrinn again. He saw no point in muttering the meaningless ritual phrase "You're welcome."

Skal glanced sideways, threw down his unfinished meal. "It's gone!"

Kei lurched to his feet and pushed through the others. The patch of grass where he and Bey had left the flek was deserted. Their supposedly traumatized enemy had taken advantage of their inattention, unrolled itself, and fled.

Chapter Thirteen

Mitsu was in a fever to catch up, but Heyoka set the pace. They had to be cautious, in case their squadmates were captives of the flek, rather than the other way round. Avians were thick along the edge of the forest and curious, often following them short distances and creating a disturbance that might mark their presence to anyone who was paying attention.

The Oleaakan sun beat down from the blue-green sky, taxing both his endurance and hers. He tried his com repeatedly, but no one answered. Twice, they stopped to catch their breath and drink from one of the tumbling mountain streams. Each time, Mitsu threw her head back and pressed her hands over her eyes, looking on the thin edge of exhaustion.

"I think they're heading back to the cave's lower entrance," he said as they worked their way down-hill along the stream. The ground was soft and spongy, due to the daily quota of rain. The smell of sun-heated mud filled the air. "Maybe we should go back to where you fell through, and slip up on them, just until we know what the situation is."

Her face was set and white. He could see memories flickering in her eyes, what she had done back on Anktan, what she had been.

"You know you can't go down there," she said. "Not if the crystals are activated. They'll burst your eardrums."

He didn't look at her. "I got through it before. I can again if I have to."

She whirled to face him and nearly lost her footing on the soft bank. One boot slipped into the water. "You don't think I can do it by myself!"

"I think we're a team," he said. "We work better together."

"We didn't at Anktan," she said, "and it almost cost your life."

"Anktan was not your fault," he said. "You can't blame yourself for that."

She didn't answer, just pushed herself harder, pacing impatiently each time he had to smell out the next turn in their quarry's trail, then leaping ahead, running when possible, climbing, sliding, a small determined engine in perpetual motion.

They reached a thick stand of trees so dark green, they were almost black. His nose twitched as he smelled blood, though it was neither human nor hrinnti. He examined the ground and found dirt heaped where bones had been buried to avoid drawing scavengers. "Someone made a kill here," he said.

Her face was pale, strained. Her haunted eyes flickered from point to point to point, as though every tree, every bush held a potential enemy. "Flek don't hunt and they sure as hell aren't neat."

"No." He cast about for the trail. "So that must mean the hrinn aren't prisoners. I can't imagine a flek allowing them to chase after local game."

Her body sagged and she leaned against the dark-green tree, eyes closed.

"They're okay," he said, "and not too far ahead. We'll catch up soon."

"Do they still have that flek with them?" she asked.

The stink was unmistakable. "Yes."

"I don't understand," she said. "Why don't they just kill the damn thing? There's no point in interrogating it. Flek never talk when they're captured, no matter what you do to them, and they couldn't understand it anyway, even if it would talk. Why are they hauling it along with them?"

"You can ask them in a few minutes," he said. "They can't be much ahead of us now."

Mitsu pushed off from the tree and fell in behind him, her steps dogged and her face determined. He had seen that same ragged look on men and women who had been out for days under constant fire, he thought. She was running on raw nerve.

When they reached the recently excavated cavern entrance, Aliki Onopa appeared from behind a stand of bushes and waved. "Over here, Sergeant!"

They found Montrose stretched out on the ground, his leg laser-burned and his dark face ashen. He opened his eyes at the sound of their voices, but did not seem to see them.

"Do you have any meds?" Onopa asked. "I've already exhausted my kit and his too."

Mitsu pulled the standard medkit off her belt and handed over the thin black rectangle. Onopa knelt and applied it to the feverish skin on Montrose's upper arm. The unit whirred into action and she sat back, shaking her head. Loose black hair tumbled around her face. "I don't know why he isn't already dead from shock."

"Why didn't you answer your com?" he said, checking Montrose's pulse. It was thready and fast.

Her eyes darted to her pocket. "Oh," she said. "I shut them both off when we were hiding. I didn't want the flek to hear it."

"So what happened?" Heyoka said. Mitsu retreated to the cavern entrance and peered down inside, too wired to stand still, and that made him even more nervous.

"Evidently a group of flek came through the grid," she said. "They caught us up by the base camp and took down Montrose, but then let us go. I think they wanted us to lead them to the rest of the Rangers on this world."

"They couldn't know it was just a training exercise," he said. "They probably figured we had a real base."

"When the hrinn caught up with us, the flek attacked, and all of them were killed except the one who must be the leader. At least, it's biggest, though not near the size of a full warrior-drone." She glanced over at the tunnel entrance and Mitsu. "Unlike even the warrior-drones, it's armored somehow and nothing touches it, not laser rifles or claws or blades. We were distracted for a moment and it got away again. The hrinn tracked it here and went in after it. I said I'd stay out here with Montrose. I—" She stopped and stared down at her clenched hands. "I didn't want him to die alone."

Heyoka nodded.

"What about the grid?" he said. "How are they going to get past the noise?"

"I don't think they were even considering that," she said. "They just wanted to bring down that damn flek before it went back through the grid and reported our presence."

"We'll go after them," he said, "then come back for you once the situation is resolved."

Onopa nodded. "When Montrose—if he doesn't need me anymore, I'll join you."

He left her half of his remaining foodpaks, then trotted over to Mitsu and took her by the arm. She looked up sharply from the cave's entrance. "I want your promise you won't kill any more laka," he said.

She blinked at him and jerked away. Her face was white with strain. "They were flek, goddammit. They were *all* flek! I wouldn't hurt a civilian!"

This wasn't going to work, he realized. "Give me the rifle then."

With a practiced move, she drew the sonic blade with her left hand and thumbed it on. She was as proficient with the left as the right, and he had good cause to know it. "You think I'm still working for them!"

"No," he said and spread his empty hands out. "But there were laka down there before and I don't want any more mistakes."

"I'll show you!" she said. "I'll kill that damn flek myself and bring back the body!"

He made a grab for her, but his fingers closed on empty air. She ducked, whirled, and scrambled into the entrance. He followed, but had to navigate the loose dirt and rocks inside and she was much more agile. If only he could have blueshifted, he would have been upon her before she had time to react.

Sure, as his adoptive father, Ben Blackeagle, used to say, and if wishes were rifles, the Oglala would never have lost their land.

By the time he made it inside, Mitsu was gone. He set out after her.

Kei blueshifted and surged ahead of his huntmates to enter the crystal chamber well before them. He hadn't drawn power; indeed, as far as he knew, there were no thermal pools on this world where one could do so, making blueshift a risky move. He could easily deplete his energies and pass out, but they had to stop the nit-eaten thing. According to the stories he'd heard, once the flek knew the Confederation held this world, warrior-drones would flood through the grid by the thousands.

The cave did not appear the telltale *blue* of blueshift in the dark, but as soon as he entered the primary transport chamber, he recognized the blueness that stained everything so that the garish pinks and greens of before were washed away and the blue was twice as intense. The sound was not nearly as bad, though, in blueshift, becoming attenuated, slowed down, lowered, more of a thunderous rumbling than a bone-shattering shrill.

Three tiny flek were cowering in the center of the grid, while his former captive, limping badly, stroked the crystals, touching one here, another there, using all four hands at once. Sometimes, one or two hands lingered in a long stroke, sometimes using only light, staccato flicks. The vibrations altered with each touch. Kei could tell that much even in blueshift. His vision wavered and he had a pang of sudden ravenous hunger. He couldn't hold this much longer. He ran to the flek, took hold of two of its spindly forearms and thrust it back against the wall.

The world snapped back to normality and the terrible keening of the crystals assaulted him like an electric shock. He snarled with pain and fought to keep his feet.

The flek struggled, bracing itself with all four legs, but could not break his grip. The three smaller flek swarmed over him. He had to release the larger one to peel them off and fling them one by one against the wall. They each hit with a satisfying crack and slid down to the floor to twitch. He turned back to the larger flek and thrust it away from the crystals, but his movements were slow, his coordination off. He should not have risked blueshift, he thought.

Then the two females staggered into the chamber. In the lead, Kika's jaws were agape, her black eyes glazed. She spotted him struggling with the flek, turned as though to attack, then went down as surely as if she'd been struck, pawing at her ears.

Naxk leaped over her, but the flek fired its laser stick with a free hand and she squalled with pain. The stench of burned fur mingled with the hated stink of flek.

Kei closed upon the flek again and held on with the grim certainty that, if he let go, he would be crisped in the next breath. The agonizing, teeth-grinding sound of the grid resonated inside his skull. The rippling lights increased in frequency, faster, faster, so that the modulations came one upon the next.

Out of the corner of his eye, he saw Bey and Visht enter, running as though they had been paired all their lives. Quite properly, they then split up to attack the flek from opposite sides, so that it was forced to pick only one to fire upon. Its bolt caught Bey, the faster of the two, square in the chest, and Kei thought he would hear his huntmate's anguished shriek even after he himself was long past the Gates of Death.

Visht's massive shoulder knocked both the flek and Kei against the wall. Kei's skull struck hard. His claws loosened and his thoughts dissolved into white static . . .

. . . He could hear again before he could see. He was lying on the cavern floor, which was rock, unlike the wall, and very rough. His muzzle was jammed uncomfortably against something and one arm twisted painfully behind his back. The noise had incredibly risen yet another octave and his brain threatened to boil out through his ears. Deep within, he felt the familiar gnawing emptiness that blueshift drain created.

He knew by its familiar scent that the body lying on top of him was Bey, and that he was dead. Laser fire crackled again. The acrid aftermath filled the air along with the stench of scorched meat and hide. He heard Visht roar with pain.

Cold. He was savagely, thoroughly cold, as though an icy predator were eating him from the inside out. He blinked furiously, willing his dazed eyes to see, even one finger to move. He could not make sense of this. They were *losing*. There was only one flek left, not even a full-sized one at that, and six grown, Ranger-trained hrinn could not bring it down!

He smelled Skal as the Leader broached the chamber. Where had he been? Skal should have led the attack, for the honor of his position in the hunt, if not his gender, and yet he had allowed two females to precede him.

Kei struggled up onto his hands and knees, levered himself out from under Bey's corpse. His huntmate was still warm, the muscles limp. The familiar smell of his fur, the scent marker for Levv, their maternal Line, was strong. Kei realized that he might never smell that scent again.

The whiteness before his eyes contained small prickles of blue and green now. He pressed his palms to the smooth wall and felt his way up. The crystals wound on and on, a terrible, wrenching sound. He wanted to throw back his head and howl with pain.

Skal was strangely silent and he felt the flek brush past him unhindered. Why did the other not attack? "Skal?" Kei said, but could not hear his own voice above the shrill. "Tell me where it is and I will distract it while you attack!"

"Shut up, mush-for-brains!" Skal called. "*I* will say when we hunt and how, and I say the time is not now. Let the earless thing go back where it came from. What do we care?"

"No!" Kei felt his way along the wall in the direction

of Skal's voice. "You can't let it escape! The Black/on/black has said it will bring back thousands—"

"The Black/on/black!" Skal said. "Who is Leader now? Do you see him here?"

The sound emanating from the crystals was so high, so shrill, the very cave itself vibrated. Soon the whole structure would come tumbling down and bury them all.

Kei heard feet scrape, smelled the lessening of Skal's scent. Was the other *leaving*?

Then he detected another scent, human—Mitsu. She came bursting into the chamber, yelling words that were unintelligible over the crystalline wail. Skal answered, then roared.

Kei rubbed desperately at his eyes. If only he could see!

The pink-green-blue sparkles intensified. He could almost make out shapes within them. He pressed his back to the wall and let it guide him toward the two mingled scents, hrinnti and human. The flek was behind him, moving about, busy.

He pushed away from the wall and his flailing hand brushed one of the crystal pillars. Energy surged through him as though he had touched a live wire in some human contraption. A note more piercing than any yet stood his hair on end. Air whooshed out of his chest and he fell to his knees, but in that split second, he had *seen* clearly. Skal's black-and-white form had retreated to the far side of the chamber, well back in the tunnel. Mitsu had her knife out and was hurling herself at the flek.

Then his vision went white again and he could make out only random sparkles zigzagging before him like excited molecules. The crystals ascended another agonizing note, then a green so intense, that even he could see it, flashed over into white—

He found himself on his back, head throbbing,

tongue lolling. The smell of burned fur and ozone and flek filled the air as the noise spiralled down to a low, teeth-rattling hum.

The flek positioned itself in the middle of the crystalline matrix. Mitsu had just enough time to fling herself at it when the light went green, then a pure, incandescent white. The cavern twisted inside out. The air flashed colder than ice-melt and she was *falling*.

Her arms flailed for support which was no longer there. Her stomach cramped and *up* switched suddenly to *down*, then *up* again. The technician had triggered the transfer, she thought numbly. It was traveling home via the grid and she, with it, no doubt back to one of the numerous flek hellworlds they had crafted from lovely green jewels like Oleaaka.

Abruptly, she was *elsewhere*, facedown against a hot, slick surface. She inhaled reflexively, then fumbled at her shoulder for her rifle. Damn, it was gone, no doubt lying on the floor back in the cave. The air stank of sulphur, brass, synthetics, and a thousand other particularly flekish scents. Unbidden, memories surfaced like air bubbles from the bottom of a dank and noxious marsh. The flek breeding chambers had smelled like this on Anktan, and the chambers for growing the edible fungi that they consumed, and *the white room*.

She coughed, then coughed again. Her eyes burned. Tests had proven that mammals could survive for a number of days breathing the noisome mixture that fleks preferred, but in the end, they always died, and in the meantime, it was never pleasant.

A hazy, mustard-colored sky arched overhead like a poisonous dome. She was outside, on top of a rise with a partial view of the surrounding area. A large transfer grid lay several miles away, recognizable by its five irregular towers. It was not lit though, and she saw no other flek.

In the opposite direction spread the patchwork of a vast flek city: large, oddly shaped, white buildings without doors or windows, typical flekish design. They used porosity generators to pass through walls. She had worn one on her belt once.

Trembling, she scrambled to her knees and looked for the knife. Just seconds ago, it had been in her hand. It lay a few inches away, still activated and humming. She snatched it up and glanced around. Her heart was racing a million light-years a second as the noise generated by the matrix wound down into silence and she was left alone with the sound of the flek's breathing, soft and sibilant.

Though it had been seemingly stunned by the transport, the flek now began darting about, fussing with the crystals. She ducked behind a crystalline pillar. This set of power crystals was large too, but not nearly as massive as the one in the cave.

She should kill this flek before it reported to the hive, but first, if she had any hope of returning, she had to reset the grid. And to do that, she would have to question this technician.

In High-Flek.

The very thought made her sick. Cold sweat trickled down her back and her hand shook so badly she had to grasp the knife with both hands to keep from dropping it. Every time she talked to a flek, it meant accessing the part of her mind that had been duped into believing she was one of these creatures back on Anktan and that way skirted madness. It had taken months to dig her way out of what had happened in that white room. She could never give in to it again!

Heart pounding, she crab-walked off the grid's central

platform. The flek made a few more adjustments, its four hands deft and sure. The strobing pinks and greens and blues flickered, faded, so that the only light left was what little filtered down through the yellow haze.

The flek touched a tiny crystal embedded in its right forewrist and the gem pulsed an intense pink. "Replacements required," it said. "Loss of all tuners, warriors, and investigative crew on Planet 873." It touched the gem a second time, and the light winked out.

Kill it! her mind insisted. As soon as it reports to its hivemates about what it found, warrior-drones will flood through here and exterminate everyone back on Oleaaka!

But she didn't want to die, and she most especially didn't want to die here, where the air reeked of flek and their concerns and the white room seemed so close. She wanted to live, and that surprised her.

If you're going to go back, she told herself, then you have to make it talk.

The flek scuttled forward, evidently drawn by the inadvertent scrape of her boot. "Designation?" it said in pure High-Flek.

All-Father blast it! Appropriate answers rose up in her mind and she shivered, despite the heat. She had spoken to the flek back on Oleaaka, but just a few words, skimming over the surface of all those horrific memories. She didn't want to dig deeper after working so hard to banish everything flek from her mind.

It edged closer, craning its spindly neck, seeking the source of the noise. It stepped into view and blinked at her. "Purpose for being in this restricted place?"

Chapter Fourteen

Heyoka skidded to a stop in the crystal chamber as the pulsing of the light began to slow. There was no sign of Mitsu, but he'd encountered Skal lurking in the tunnel just short of the entrance. Their eyes had met, then the big black-and-white male had followed him in without a word, head lowered, glowering.

In the waning blue light, he saw hrinnti bodies scattered along the wall around the grid. The sound had already subsided to a bearable level. Fur bristled down his back; the peculiar flatness of *death* mingled with the lingering stink of flek hung in the air. Whatever had happened, he was too late. The flek seemed to have escaped, and Mitsu was nowhere to be seen.

Kika lay closest, her pale fur luminous in the fading light. She was groaning, both hands clasped over her head. Red-orange hrinnti blood stained the fur around her ears. He bent over and touched her shoulder. She flinched violently. "It's Blackeagle," he said in hrinnti, not sure she could hear him, then reached down and detached the med unit from her belt.

The versions carried by the hrinn were especially configured for hrinnti bodies, which metabolized drugs differently than humans. He applied it to the hollow between neck and shoulder where the fur thinned out a bit. It whirred, then the green treatment light flashed. "Where's Mitsu?" he asked. "Did you see her?"

Kika did not respond, so he motioned to Skal who was making no effort to help. "Check the other tunnel and see if she's down there."

He pulled a coldlantern off his belt and activated it before the crystals failed completely. On the far side of the chamber, Bey's honest dark-brown face gaped blankly at the ceiling. A terrible laser burn seared his chest and abdomen. His legs were limp and twisted at unnatural angles. Heyoka knew that vacant look well; he was dead. Ten feet away, within reach of one of the massive transport crystals, Kei sprawled on his back, tongue out, struggling to breathe in great, shuddering gasps.

He set the coldlantern on the floor and knelt beside Naxk. Like Bey, she'd taken a direct hit. Heyoka unhooked the med unit from her belt and set it against her neck. Naxk shuddered, then the tension melted from her body and he knew the med had dealt with her pain, at least for the moment.

They were unseasoned troops, he thought, and that factor was partially responsible for this utter failure, but worse than that, they had made contact with the flek without the voice of experience, without his supervision. If he had been here, he would have directed them to be cautious, use the pillars for cover, creep up on the enemy, but instead, they had reverted to a classic hrinnti assault, dashing in, depending on intimidation, pitting teeth and claws against a laser.

And what in the devil had happened to Mitsu? There was no sign of her dead or wounded body, thank goodness, but she should be here somewhere, unless she'd gone on through to the tunnel on the other side, or—

She'd transported with the flek.

He looked up. Skal hadn't moved. "I told you to check the tunnel!"

Skal scratched a patch of white fur on his shoulder and gazed brazenly into Heyoka's eyes. "If she's down there," he said, "she'll come back. If she's dead, there is nothing to do."

Heyoka leaped to his feet, his murderous *other* lusting for blood. His handclaws sprang free. "Rangers take care of their own! If you've learned nothing else over these past months, you should have at least learned that!"

Skal flicked a dismissive ear, but every line in his powerful body denoted belligerence. "The weak fall, the strong live to hunt another day."

Challenge. Heyoka understood the nature of the moment now. Skal had chosen this particular bit of chaos to make his move. "You think you smell a pattern here, don't you?" He strode over to Visht and bent down to check the big yellow male's pulse. He was still alive, his heartbeat strong. He'd taken a glancing laser bolt across the top of one shoulder and hit his head on the wall. Unclipping the medkit, Heyoka applied it to Visht's neck without looking up. His own pulse pounded. "You think this is *undue/transformations* or *stealth/in/intent* or something equally deep and meaningful."

The mention of the sacred *patterns/in/progress* galvanized Skal. He shook himself and snarled. His own particular musk, fraught with fight pheromones, flooded the chamber. Provocative scent molecules danced through Heyoka's head, setting into primal links, and he felt how his *other* longed to match teeth against teeth, claws against claws in the oldest and best of ways.

"There is a pattern here all right." He straightened,

ears flattened to his skull. "It's called Chain of Command, but I don't have to name the damn thing to know the first time you come against me, I'll whip your sorry tail from one end of this planet to the other!"

Skal's coal-black eyes blinked. "Hrinn do not have tails."

Heyoka's claws retracted a bit. Gods, that was funny, almost worthy of a human. Hrinn did not possess a laugh reflex, but he felt an almost human response to that non sequitur way down deep, in his most secret places where his human upbringing had insured he would never be fully hrinnti.

His violent *other* fumed, but the moment had been defused and he could think clearly enough to choose his plan of action now. He didn't have to tear Skal's throat out, not today, anyway.

"You don't deserve a tail," he said and gestured at Naxk. "Take her outside to Onopa, then come back and help Visht. I don't want anyone left in here in case the grid activates again."

Skal glared at him with hot black eyes that knew nothing of humor or military niceties, and most certainly nothing of mercy. He glowered back, willing himself to remain cool and not let Skal provoke him into a pointless fight. They were so few, they couldn't afford to lose anyone else. As it was, Bey's death was a terrible blow to their tiny force. Somehow with only five hrinn and two humans, most of them injured, he had to hold this gate against the flek.

Finally, Skal dropped his eyes. "I will take Visht."

"No," Heyoka said, looping Kika's limp arm over his shoulder. "Take Naxk. She's the worst injured."

"But she is female!" The wrinkle of the other's nose said he was insulted at the very thought.

"You noticed," Heyoka said. "Very good. I wasn't sure you could tell the difference."

"Males do not touch females out of season!"

"Don't worry," Heyoka said. "She's in no shape to make advances."

Skal snarled, snatched up Naxk's unresponsive form, and disappeared into the dark tunnel that led back to the surface.

Heyoka struggled to pick up Kika. Unlike diminutive Naxk, Kika was a mature, rangy female, almost as tall as himself, and he was very tired. Her nostrils flared and she stirred against his chest. "Don't struggle," he said. "I'm going to take you back to the surface."

She murmured something unintelligible that trailed off after the first few words. He shifted her weight to his shoulder and set out through the dark tunnel after Skal, leaving the coldlantern behind for the rest of the survivors. His mind raced ahead, trying to plan, salvage some sort of opportunity out of what seemed to be nothing but disaster. And, once he'd gotten his personnel to safety, he had to figure out what the devil had become of Mitsu.

He had a sinking feeling he already knew.

"Purpose for being in this restricted place?" the tech-drone repeated. It crept forward to peer around the crystal pillar at Mitsu, then scuttled back to pick up its discarded laser stick. It brandished the weapon at her. "Surrender, Despised Agent of the Enemy!"

Her face blazed hotter than the blood-orange sun beating down through the haze. She thumbed the sonic blade off, slid it back into the sheath in her boot, then slowly stood. She should have killed the tech while she had the chance, then taken out as many flek as possible before she died.

With only a sodding knife? some incredulous part of her brain asked. She would never have gotten within reach. Though this was just a tech, she had seen it fire at the hrinn back in the cave without hesitation. The situation had gone beyond knives and stealth. She had to think of something else.

A memory surfaced. *The white room. A lesson, one of many imparted there.* Her fingers twitched, then beat out a flekish song for Safe Arrival. She lacked the chitin necessary to make the beats resonate as they ought, but, despite the length of time since she'd learned it, got the rhythm right. Rhythm was all important, she knew, to the songful flek.

The tech-drone raised its own hands and joined in, accompanying her song through to the end. Its clicks sounded clearly and she was taken back for a heart-wrenching second to Anktan, *the lowly flek worker assigned to instruct her, the sense of accomplishment when she had mastered the complex and alien rhythms, the white room ... always and forever would she be imprisoned in that white room ...*

The flek cocked its head, fixed her with scarlet eyes. "Purpose for being here?"

She blanched. "To report," she said in High-Flek, her mouth very dry. It was so hot, so damn hot, and her throat was already raw from the sulphur fumes. All the knowledge of the flek and their ways she had been force-fed bubbled up through her subconscious, white-hot and dangerous, an unknown sea where she could lose herself forever. She had to stare out over the flek's back, not focus on its alien face, or she knew she would scream.

"Designation?"

"Spy-Drone 87650," she said, the classification she had received from the flek on Anktan. Her hands were sweating. Her stomach cramped. All-Father, she couldn't do this. She felt twisted inside out; she couldn't go back in her mind, remember what she had been and thought and done during those terrible days. Why not just attack it and be finished with this whole miserable screw-up?

"You were assigned to the world linked to this grid?" Its off-balance posture communicated disbelief.

Don't look at its eyes, she told herself. Don't think about what it really is. "Yes."

It sat back on its haunches and processed what she had said. It was only a tech-drone, not qualified to make important decisions concerning anything but its assigned grid. She was gambling that it had little specific knowledge beyond crystals and mechanisms and adjustments.

Over on the city side of the rise, a thin white line of flek emerged from a low building on the outskirts, too small for her to make out their type. She felt an additional stab of panic.

"That world has lain fallow for many units," the tech-drone said. "You were in residence during the entire time period?"

"Yes," she said, speculating that an ordinary drone would know nothing of human biology or potential lifespan. "This body is quite durable, though I shall be gratified to leave it behind."

"We have no facilities for xeno-information processing." Its first-hands hesitated and it looked forlorn. "This world, though very beautifully rendered, has been classified as Failed and supports only a single garrison. Due to certain environmental irregularities, optimum parameters could not be maintained. No breeding has been carried out here for over two hundred units. It shall be necessary for you to travel to at least a tertiary nexus."

"I see." She did not, however, have the slightest idea what it was talking about. "I will—have to go back, then, to the abandoned world, to pick up some—information I left behind. After that, I can go to the tertiary nexus."

The flek marching from the city complex started up the transfer grid's rise, single file. She could see now that they were small, less than knee-high, and of two distinct types. The first she had encountered before, back at the transfer grid on Anktan, although she had never been told their function. They had long, delicate arms, completely out of proportion with their dwarfed height, and double-jointed fingers on all four hands.

The second type were even stranger, possessing only vestigial eyes and bizarre raised pads that spread like blisters across the palms of their foreheads. She shuddered.

"Further access will require input of a Decider," the tech said placidly, and stood aside for the arriving workers.

"I have to return *now*," Mitsu said, her heart racing. "The inhabitants there cannot be trusted to leave my information cache intact and I have gathered news of the Enemy."

The flek was thoughtful. "I am sure the Deciders will be interested in your findings. They have always been reluctant to part with that particular world. The Makers came close to crafting something very beautiful there."

"You must send me back now!" Mitsu insisted.

The small workers sorted themselves out, the nearly blind ones positioning themselves well back and waiting, while the others each embraced a different crystalline pillar. Soft pinks and blues and greens sprang into life at their touch. A faint hum became audible.

"This grid must be retuned," the tech said. It passed among the smaller flek, adjusting the lie of a finger on this pillar, the bend of a hand on the next. "Units of untended growth skewed the harmonics of the abandoned grid and have in turn skewed this one to a lesser degree. Transfer grids of this old design must be constantly recalibrated. The one you came through no longer accesses anywhere but here."

"How—long before it is ready?" Mitsu was trembling.

"These tuners are quite adept," it said. "They were
bred especially for this outdated grid's specifications.
They will signal when the matrix is primed." It settled
back to wait, forelimbs crossed, hands resting on its
chest.

Mitsu was familiar with that position. Once, on
Anktan, it had meant her captors would leave her alone
for a while. The tech had gone dormant, a state not
quite the same as sleep, as a human would recognize
it, since it could go on indefinitely, but the tech would
not stir again until needed.

So, now what was she supposed to do? Deciders were
much cannier than drones and techs, and doubtless
knew enough of the Enemy to recognize her sham for
what it was. She couldn't risk running into one of them.
Whatever happened, she had to avoid the flek city.

After the furred aliens had ferried the last of their
dead and wounded out of the cave, Second Breeder
coaxed his four fellow breeders out of the rear tunnel,
where they had concealed themselves, back into the
spacious main chamber.

The acrid taste of the blue light lingered in the air.
Subtly different from the scent of the light which had
killed their fellows at the ceremonial grounds, it conjured
images in Second's mind, dimly seen shapes that were
almost like memories.

The crystal trees stood in the center, growing from
the floor in a pattern which did mimic the mark on
Tenth's back. Thick and glassy, they only flickered now,
just the palest imitations of their colorful magnificence
a short time before. They were still humming, but so
softly, the sound was barely audible, even to their keen
laka ears. Before, when they had been in full soaring
voice, Second Breeder had wondered if it were possible
to die of joy.

And that white creature who had stood against all the
off-worlders—it had looked like a real person, except
for certain odd proportions of leg and arm, neck and
head, along with its lack of tint and piercing red eyes.
Second couldn't get over how attractive it had been,
compact and yet graceful. It had been a drone like himself, but so competent, so functional. Obviously, it
understood the crystal trees growing down here in the
dark, what they were for and, best of all, how they could
be persuaded to sing.

They arranged themselves in a half circle and let the
last of the light play over their wondering faces. "Perhaps
the stranger will come back," Second said. He had
propped the firing stick, lost by the alien back in the
ceremonial arena, against the wall. It was wider at one
end than the other, and a mechanism of some sort was
built into it.

"This can be our colony," Tenth said. He was large
for a breeder, his carapace a mottled blue, except at
his joints, which shaded to a sallow and disappointing
white. "Then we could always have such exciting songs."

Sixteenth Breeder indicated doubtfulness with the
cant of his head. "There is nothing to eat here," he said.

It was true the want of food was making itself very
much known. Second was feeling decidedly slow-witted.
"We must find a gleaner," he said, "and make her bring
food down here."

"How will you make her?" Sixteenth said. "I have
never yet heard a gleaner speak a single intelligible
word."

Second mulled this over. "Then we must secure a
translator too."

"Translators never listen to breeders," Tenth said.
"They only tell you when to eat and where to sleep and
all the things you should not do." He reached out and
touched a wondering first-hand to the translucent length

of the nearest crystal. Its hum modulated to a slightly higher register. He snatched his hand back and stared. "I could feel—that tree is not—right, not where it should be."

"Where else should it be, except here where it started?" Second said, testy with hunger. "Do you want it to sprout legs and walk outside?" He drummed both pairs of hands on his sides with impatience. Words hovered at the edge of being spoken, ideas glimmered just out of reach—forceful, brave, clever ideas, all of which, of course, were far beyond the capability of a mere breeder.

Tenth stroked the crystal tree again, longer this time and with all four hands. The light phased from pink to blue to purple to green, rippling faster. The hum changed pitch as he touched it high, then low. "That is somehow—better," he said finally. "I don't know why, but it feels more—complete."

"Bah! Playing with these glass trees is for hatchlings! At some point, the keepers will come and make us go back to the colony. That's what we should be thinking about." Second stalked to the edge of the chamber where he had left the alien's stick propped against the curving white wall.

"They won't come down here," Tenth said. "They say it's a bad place, that terrible things happened here and could happen again, if laka ever forget."

Second snatched the stick up, turned it over in his first-hands while his second-hands probed each swell and protuberance. The highly polished surface felt cool and sleek, welcoming to the touch. He thought again of the furred alien, how it had leaped upon the breeders, how in turn they had leaped upon it and then pinned the wretched beast to the ground.

That was what a breeder ought to be doing, taking real action, doing something beyond waiting for the

opportunity to breed, an opportunity which might not
ever come. A breeder should . . . at . . . tack. *Attack*. That
was the word he had been seeking as a keeper seeks
an errant hatchling. When someone *attacked* the colony,
you should *attack* back!

How wonderful! It was as though the right word had
opened up entire new vistas inside his head. He saw
hints of other things one might do, other ways to live
and found himself dancing with joy.

"What's the matter with you?" Tenth demanded.

"I understand!" Second could not be still. He spun
around, flung out his arm and pointed the stick as the
alien had. "I understand now what I am supposed to
do! When something *attacks* the colony, I am supposed
to *attack* back!"

"What does that mean?" Tenth sounded quite sullen.

Second's fingers played over the stick, pressing each
knob in turn. One of them close to the wide end gave
with a slight click. A tiny spot of green bloomed like
an exotic flower. "It means that, when the off-worlders
hurt us, we don't have to stand back and let them."

"Get in their way?" Tenth looked at Sixteenth, then
back to Second. "We tried that. It didn't work."

"No," Second said. "We make them get out of *our*
way!" His probing fingers touched the same lever as
before, but this time, it yielded to pressure. Bright green
fire splashed across the room. Sixteenth cried out, then
collapsed, his off-shoulder a black smoking ruin.

Chapter Fifteen

Kei's vision cleared by midafternoon, except for a lingering bit of static. The terrible drain of blueshift was still upon him so that his muscles twitched, and his right palm had been burned in that brief contact with the crystal. At the moment, he could not hold his rifle to fire it, but he still had his claws, if it came to a fight, and, by the Voice, he wished it would. He craved an entire horde of the enemy upon whom he could vent his rage and frustration.

Bey's seared body lay twenty paces uphill, hidden behind a rock formation. Kei had trailed along as best he could, his vision phasing in and out, when Onopa and the Black/on/black carried it up there. It troubled him to abandon Bey as though he were some cast-off carcass. The dead should be given honorably to the sky, though perhaps this sky on this alien world would not receive him.

From his earliest memories, Bey's dark-brown form had been with him, in the stark, cold cave that was all the nursery Levv could give its cublings, when the flek attacked the mountains of his home and scarred his muzzle, and then later on the plains, when, following the fabled Black/on/black, they had finally defeated the invaders.

Bey, who had been always at his side, deferring to his Leadership, until today. A low-throated snarl escaped his throat. His lifelong huntmate had died knowing he had fled the flek in the cave and it was more than Kei could bear. Even if his brains had boiled out through his ears, he should have stayed down there, fought to a clean and honorable death as Bey had. Now, if he killed every flek in the entire universe, it would not be enough to reclaim his honor.

Kika looked up, then left Naxk's prostrate body to walk unsteadily to the mountain stream just at the forest's tangled edge. A covey of scarlet avians cried out, then burst away at her approach. Her ears never twitched.

She had recovered consciousness fairly soon after being removed from the cave, but her damaged ears still leaked blood. Her balance was off and her hearing severely impaired. Whether the effects were temporary or permanent remained still to be seen.

The pale-gray female dipped a strip of cloth torn from her uniform in the rushing water, then returned to Naxk, who had suffered a bad burn across her chest and was fighting for every breath. Kika lifted the smaller female's head and squeezed the cloth so that water dripped into her panting mouth. Naxk snarled and pushed feebly at Kika's pale-gray hand. Kika held her more firmly and forced her to drink.

On the other side of the clearing, Visht sat hunched over, head in hands, staring at his feet with pain-glazed eyes. He had also been burned, but not as badly as Naxk. Aliki Onopa had tried to speak to him earlier, but he refused to answer.

Kei could almost read his thoughts. They had trained hard to fight the flek and had been so foolishly certain none of it was necessary, that with tooth and claw and a laser rifle, they were more than the equal of any ordinary Confederation soldier. They would succeed where humans had not. At the first opportunity, they would drive the flek before them like frightened yirn back on their home world.

But then one undersized flek, not even a warrior-drone according to the Black/on/black, had defeated them. They had all lost their honor today. Only Bey, who had died, had preserved his intact.

A hrinn had but two legs, several males who had long ago trained Kei had been fond of saying: Duty and Honor. Honor had fled. All that was left now for them was Duty.

Montrose was soaking his burned leg in the stream and seemed more alert. His uniform had protected him to some extent, being specially treated to resist laser fire, and the medkit had worked against swelling, shock, and pain. The Black/on/black was sitting on his heels beside him now, discussing something.

The tall female, Onopa, had disappeared into the rain forest, probably to forage. Food . . . Another snarl rattled in his throat. He felt the urgent need to replenish what he had fruitlessly spent in blueshift earlier.

The Black/on/black gripped Montrose's shoulder, then rose to walk back across the clearing to Kei. He stood over him, blocking the sun. "How is your hand?"

Kei snorted. "It does not matter."

The Black/on/black gazed down at him. He had shed his shirt somewhere in the last day and his black fur gleamed in the sun, not a single off-color hair anywhere, the ancient legend come to life. His mane had come unbound and whipped in the breeze. His eyes smoldered like black flame. Kei looked away, ashamed to be in his presence.

"We were whipped," the Black/on/black said, and though his voice was low, it carried across the makeshift camp.

Kika followed him with her eyes, though Kei doubted she could hear him. Visht struggled to his feet. Montrose swung his burned leg out of the stream and turned around to listen.

"And we'll be whipped again and again, if we survive," the Black/on/black said. "That's just part of being a Ranger."

Visht looked doubtful, while Kei flattened his ears.

The Black/on/black sighed. "Think of it as the *something/in/motion* which rules all soldiers. What makes this pattern special is that, when you get the stuffing knocked out, you pick yourself up, go back and make the enemy pay!"

Visht's ears pricked forward and there was a hopeful gleam in his eyes.

Montrose cleared his throat. "What about Jensen, sir? Did the flek take her prisoner?"

The Black/on/black raised his nose into the wind as though seeking her scent. "I don't know. I got there too late."

"She fought well," Kei said gruffly. "After I hit my head, I could see only a little, but she was charging the flek, knife drawn, just as the grid flashed white. Then they were gone."

"If she was far enough inside the platform not to be vaporized, then she must have transported." The Black/on/black's tone was bleak. He closed his eyes, pulled his lips back, as though in pain. "I hope she took out a hundred of the bastards when she got to the other side."

Even the traitor had fought with more honor than he had, Kei thought wearily. He should have thrown himself through the grid with her, whether he could

see or not, brought down as many flek as claws and
teeth could manage before he passed through the Gates
of Death.

He could stand it no longer and lurched to his feet,
stiff and sore from nose to claws. "I must tend to Bey,"
he said gruffly.

Visht stood too, ears drooping. "I will go with you."

"No!" Kei bristled. "He was my huntmate!"

"We are Rangers," the Black/on/black said. "That
makes us all huntmates, human and hrinn alike."

"Yes," Montrose said. His dark face was lined with
pain. "I'll go too. What can we use for shovels?"

The Black/on/black shook his head, a particularly
human gesture which always looked odd to Kei. "Hrinn
do not bury their dead. They are 'given to the sky.'"

Kika was looking from one face to another, unable to
hear what they were talking about. The Black/on/black
put one hand on her shoulder. "Bey," he said loudly and
jerked his head upward. "He must enter the sky."

Understanding dawned in Kika's black eyes. She
glanced up at the rugged green mountains that formed
the backbone of the island. Clouds were scudding across
the peaks and accumulating in dark patches as though
it might rain soon.

"There is no place for that here," she said.

"We will make one," the Black/on/black said. "A
Ranger place." He turned to Montrose. "It has to be
high up, where the clouds touch the peaks. I don't think
you could make it with that leg, and besides someone
needs to stay with Naxk and Kika until Onopa gets
back."

Montrose bowed his head.

Kei could see he did not want to stay, an almost
hrinnti response to the situation.

"What about Skal?" Montrose said finally and looked
around. "Couldn't he stay?"

"That's a good question," the Black/on/black said grimly. "I haven't seen him since we evacuated the cave. Has anyone else?"

The survivors looked at each other, but no one remembered seeing the Squad Leader since he'd carried Naxk out and deposited her unconscious on the grass.

"He'll be back," the Black/on/black said, "and then he's going to have a lot of explaining to do."

Mitsu was limp from the intense heat by the time dusk fell on the flek world. The brash red sun, diffused by the thick atmosphere, slipped toward the horizon with agonizing slowness. Her uniform was plastered to her body by sweat. Her throat burned and the effort it took not to cough was draining what little reserves she had left. If this took much longer, she wouldn't have the strength to enter the grid.

The tuner-drones went about their work with dogged persistence, ignoring her. The tech remained off to one side, dormant, and she could see silvery splotches across its smushed-in face now. It was old. They must be hard-up indeed for techs on this so-called "failed world," she thought. She had not seen one half so old on Anktan. The flek prized efficiency above all else. Most were sacrificed long before achieving this age and then consumed by their successors in order to pass along crucial memory engrams.

She fingered the foil of the only remaining foodpak in her pocket, but put off eating it just yet. She was merely ravenous and thirsty for the moment. If she didn't get off this world soon, she would need it much worse later, as well as a decent water source, if there was such a thing on this world.

The lights down in the flek city were easier to see as the sun faded: typically flekish pinks, blues, and greens, along with the occasional purple. How many of

the flek down there were warrior-drones? She ought
to go, she told herself, and find out. If she ever made
it back through the grid, that kind of knowledge could
be invaluable intel.

The very thought of venturing into a viable flek hive
made her ill though. No one would expect it of her,
after what she had been through. She paced around the
grid platform, wondering if these misbegotten tuners
would ever be done. Perhaps the tech was just toying
with her. Maybe they all knew she was an imposter and
were just waiting for her to make a move. That might
even be what passed for flekish humor.

Finally, as the shadows lengthened, a pink sphere
detached itself from the city and drifted toward the grid.
She watched it with sick fascination. It was moving too
fast to be a worker on foot.

The tech stirred, then checked the tuners, making
minute adjustments here and there. She watched the
approaching sphere nervously, dizzy with the heat, but
unable to stand still. "Is the grid ready?" she asked.

"Not yet. It is antiquated," the tech said, "very
delicate, and these tuners are inexperienced. The
last set died on the previous world and these had
no opportunity to ingest their knowledge, although I
will attempt to retrieve at least one of the bodies
for that purpose when you return."

The pink sphere reached the bottom of the rise and
then winked out. A large flek unfolded itself and ambled
up the hill toward the transfer grid.

Mitsu was frozen. There was no place to hide,
and, if she did run, they would know she was an
imposter for sure, if they didn't already. She had to
bluff it out.

This flek did not seem to be a warrior-drone, but
that gave her little relief. Though much larger than the
tech, it was not a Decider either. She had seen several

back on Anktan and they were at least twice the size of a tech with overlarge heads and stunted arms.

The flek stopped at the edge of the crystal matrix and studied her, its red eyes glittering in the sunset. It wore a belt around its gleaming white middle, fitted with several devices, of which she recognized only one, a porosity generator for entering buildings. "Designation?" it said crisply.

"Spy-Drone 87650," she said, her mouth dry. "Your designation?"

"World-Architect 549." It canted its head. "We had not received word of a spy-drone left in place on Planet 873."

"I—was trapped there," she said, "for a very long time, until this tech opened the grid and brought me back through."

What in the name of the Thirty-Nine Systems was a "world-architect," she wondered. She'd never heard of that caste before.

The flek architect was watching her closely.

"I left an information cache behind," she said. "This tech is going to effect my temporary return, then send me on to a tertiary nexus for information processing."

"The Primary Decider will confer with you," the architect said. "You are directed to accompany me to the Integrating Chamber for inquiry."

"The grid is almost tuned," she said. Panic ricochetted through her. She gripped her sweating hands together to keep them from trembling. "I must return as soon as possible. Delay might impair any chance of retrieving the records. I can report to the Decider, when I return."

"This tech reported contact with the Enemy on Planet 873," the architect said, "which supersedes all other priorities. The Primary Decider will evaluate the details you supply so response can be planned."

She would have to go with it for now, then give it the slip as soon as they reached the city and circle back here. Refusing in front of the tech would only give her away.

Heart pounding, mouth dry as the desert back on Anktan, Mitsu followed the architect down the slope. It paused at the foot, while she gazed out over the flek city. More spheres were visible among the buildings and broad walkways, some larger, others smaller, pink and blue and purple. She had a flashback of the grid on Anktan. *Beautiful under the night sky, like a wonderland of fairy lights, and so big, large enough to transport thousands of warrior-drones.*

With an almost subliminal hum, a field of pink light enveloped both herself and the drone. She put out a finger and touched the shimmering pink skin. It tingled and hummed more loudly, but did not give to the pressure as they lifted into the air and floated toward the city. She withdrew her finger and watched through the field of translucent pink. The city grew nearer with surprising speed and the architect did not appear to be controlling their progress in any way. Their "vehicle" must be managed from some central area. Since she was supposed to be a flek spy, familiar with this, she did not dare ask how it worked.

She would get away, she told herself over and over. They would not flay her mind open this time. She would die first, and as many as she could reach would die with her.

White, irregularly-spaced towers passed below, some low and stubby, others almost ethereal, rising high into the murky yellow twilight. And everywhere, she saw flek, striding purposefully with that terrible single-mindedness only their species had perfected. The entire city was alive with them. There had to be a million at least, she thought, all of them poised to invade Oleaaka.

❖   ❖   ❖

Heyoka would have liked to wrap the corpse for its last journey, but they had nothing suitable, so in the end, he took the shoulders, leaving Visht and Kei to carry the legs and they climbed toward the rugged center of the island. The afternoon was waning, but it was still devilishly hot and they were all three panting before they had gone a few hundred feet.

The clouds gathered above, ever more dark and ominous. The humidity seemed only to increase and it was soon obvious why hrinn were never meant for a tropical climate.

The wind streamed against their faces, filled with alien green scents, and, beneath that, the salt of the sea at their backs. Because of his burned hand, Kei could only carry left-handed and did not speak at all. Visht, silent by nature, said nothing either, but it was Kei that concerned him.

Something had happened, during the battle perhaps, or earlier during the day, which had affected him. Even the way he carried himself was different, and the fact the others deferred to Skal now, instead of Kei, spoke volumes. Dominance had shifted, which ordinarily never happened among hrinn without Challenge. Had Skal and Kei fought? Skal had appeared to be the only uninjured survivor of the battle, and he did not believe the black-and-white's fighting skills were good enough to come away from an encounter with Kei unmarked. Heyoka could not make sense of it.

They stopped to rest, easing Bey's poor body to the rocks, then gazing back down the slope at the island spread out below. Green sward, just subtly darker than the greens of Earth, covered broad terraces to the east, while the green tangle of rain forest dominated the rocky slopes. The wind gusted and a ripple of silver undersides flashed like slow lightning. It was a lovely land, with its black sand beaches and lush vegetation. If Oleaaka were not already inhabited, humans would gladly have colonized.

Without a word, Kei picked up Bey's leg and stood waiting to continue. Heyoka resumed his place at the shoulders and Visht joined them. They needed a high place, open to the sky. Heyoka remembered that much from Anktan. When he had recovered enough of his strength, after the final battle, they had taken him to the peaks, at his insistence, and shown him the dead.

He had known there would be casualties, but, despite their victory, the numbers were staggering, all placed on the highest summits, where the fierce wind and sun desiccated the corpses in short order and predators did the rest. The humans of course had asked for plots of land to bury their dead, mightily shocking the hrinn, who found the practice barbarous.

The light ebbed as they climbed until, high up, on a rocky ledge, Visht slipped on loose scree, breaking open the wound on his shoulder. He sprawled on the slope, ears flattened, eyes narrow with pain. Heyoka set his burden down, then reached to help him up. Visht struck at him with bared claws.

He drew back and waited while Visht collected himself. Kei had tactfully averted his eyes, and Heyoka now realized he should have done the same. It was difficult to avoid giving insult when you had not been raised in a culture. A portion of his mind was hard-wired with hrinnti instincts, but even those had by necessity been dulled by years of living with humans.

"Why did Skal leave the squad?" he asked Kei, while they were waiting.

Kei bristled. "He is Leader now, so he goes when he pleases. No one can question his right."

"When did he become Leader?"

The wind gusted, rattling the leaves of a stunted tree

growing at an angle out of the rock. Kei snarled, but would say no more.

"He should be here," Heyoka said, "helping us, honoring his huntmate for the last time."

Kei turned on him, teeth bared, claws flashing. He looked altogether unsoldierlike, savage. "He is hrinnti, not human, and he will never fit into your hidebound human patterns! Whatever is at work here is much larger than anything a human has ever named!"

"This is not just a *pattern/in/progress!*" Heyoka was breathing hard and the blood was surging in his ears. His savage *other* strained to break free. *This could not be settled with words,* it insisted. *Only teeth and claws and blood could resolve this matter.* With an effort, he turned away from its seductive whisper. "This is a combat situation! If hrinn are ever going to have a chance to make a contribution to this war, we have to maintain order and discipline, the chain of command!"

"Those are patterns fit only for softskins!" A voice rang down from above.

Heyoka, Kei, and Visht looked up the slope. Skal's black-and-white form stood on a rocky point, legs braced apart, unbound mane flowing in the wind. "Your pattern is finished, Black/on/black, just like you! Everyone knows you're a burnt-out wreck now. You should have stayed on Anktan, listening to the stories the old Tellers spin for cublings about you. This is a new place and needs fresh eyes and ears. We will make our own pattern here!"

"Like you did down in the cave when you hung back?" Heyoka threw back. "That didn't look the least bit new to me. I would have called that fiasco *death/ in/longing*, wouldn't you?"

With a snarl, Skal disappeared.

Heyoka just had time to realize Skal had entered blueshift before the fight was upon him.

Chapter Sixteen

Skal's leap blind-sided him; no one could see a hrinn moving in blueshift, except another hrinn doing the same. Heyoka rolled with his attacker, then used the momentum to regain his feet. Skal was momentarily visible, off-balance, his black-and-white face reminiscent of a human-style harlequin mask, then he disappeared again and Heyoka was reeling from a dozen unanswered claw marks.

His savage *other* roared at the pain, and then he was no longer thinking at all, just reacting in a white-hot fury. How dare this upstart Challenge him when so much was at stake! He would tear Skal's worthless ears off and feed them to him an inch at a time!

Off to one side, Visht and Kei guarded Bey's lifeless body, black eyes unreadable. This was a *pattern/in/ progress* they all understood, one that could only be settled between him and Skal. No one would interfere. Hrinn always respected Challenge.

A spatter of cold rain struck his muzzle. He shook

it off and circled warily, waiting for the next strike. One slash across his chest was particularly deep and the hot scent of blood filled the air as it soaked into his fur. He caught a whiff of Skal, too, rancid with fight pheromones, then; without warning, he was falling back. His head cracked on the rocks. His ears rang, and Skal was tearing at his throat. He threw an arm up to fend him off, then saw an opening and buried his own teeth in Skal's shoulder.

His opponent threw himself backwards, roaring with shock. Heyoka pursued, but a buzzing whiteness obscured his vision and his legs gave way. Skal's blood was hot and sweet in his mouth as he struggled to rise. How strange, he found himself thinking. He had never tasted hrinnti blood before. Who would have thought it would be sweet?

He floundered, groping for Skal. His fingers brushed against fur, then lost contact. He whirled, cursing himself. He had to finish this now. A hrinn who lived to fight another day would take down his enemy, sooner or later. He had to find—

His vision cleared just as Skal came at him again. He caught tiny flashes of black-and-white fur as the other dropped in and out of blueshift, creating a series of startling static images. He was playing with him, Heyoka realized, as he struck uselessly at empty air where Skal had just been again and again. Skal could finish him off anytime he chose. This was a chump's game, what humans called "shooting fish in a barrel."

He leaped at a half-seen blur of white and again his claws closed on nothing. Overbalanced, he fell, then Skal was upon him, fingers knotted in his mane, yanking his head back, exposing his throat for a final, fatal slash.

His fierce *other* reached deep within, where Heyoka could have sworn there was nothing left. For an instant, less than the wink of an eye, the familiar stain of blueshift colored the sky, the mountaintop, his opponent's face. Time slowed to a crawl and he was alone with Skal in a chill universe of crystalline blue. Moving too fast for Skal to see, he broke his hold and scrambled away.

Normal colors burst back into his vision. He sprawled nose-first on the ground, so exhausted, he could barely flick an ear. Drawing upon cellular energy without preparation could be fatal, his former sponsor, Nisk, had always warned, and he'd found that to be true, to his regret. Ignorant of ancient techniques for supercharging cells, he had often been careless back on Anktan, but he had never expected to be able to draw power again and certainly hadn't expected to face Challenge up here.

Skal was slowing down too, though obviously he'd found some way to prepare for this fight. The big male dropped out of blueshift and regarded him with savage black eyes.

"This is pointless!" Heyoka said, struggling to get up. He got one leg underneath him, but the other would not support his weight. Rain began in earnest, the large drops close together and cold. Thunder cracked on the other side of the valley below. He dug his claws into the rock and tried harder. "Our enemy is the flek, not each other! If either one of us dies here, that just makes one less to hold the grid and we are far too few as it is!"

"Weakling!" Skal threw back, but he was panting heavily and his ears were askant. "You are not fit to lead!"

"I am the only one fit!" Mustering the dregs of his strength, he heaved to his feet. The scene before him wavered, as though he were viewing it underwater. "You're a Ranger now. Think back on your training, all you've learned these last months. You know what we have to do here, how important it is!"

Skal disappeared into blueshift. Heyoka whirled,

claws bared, but it was no use. He would not see his opponent until it was too late. How ironic that the Black/on/black, whose body supposedly contained the highest number of power receptor cells of all hrinn, should die in a pointless blueshift brawl with a third-rate punk like Skal.

He could retreat, the human-educated part of his brain whispered, and live to fight another day.

His savage *other* roared in outrage. Honorable hrinn did not run from Challenge! It was unheard of, unthinkable! Such cravenness would shred his honor! Better to die cleanly!

He felt the edge of the ledge behind him, as well as the wind of Skal's approach. He ducked an invisible blow as unseen claws grazed his neck. Certain death was at his throat. He could do as his *other* demanded, accept it and die, or—

Without thinking further, he turned and plunged over the ledge, arms flailing at the distant canopy of the forest below.

A coughing fit overtook Mitsu in the travel sphere and she could not stop. She knotted her fists and leaned against the spongy covering, holding her breath. This toxic atmosphere would kill her, probably sooner rather than later, and permanent lung damage would no doubt set in even before that. Her tearing eyes burned and she had difficulty swallowing.

World-Architect 549 regarded her with indifference. "Are you damaged?"

"This—shell—is not suited for these conditions," she said hoarsely. "I must either abandon it soon or return to Planet 873."

On Anktan, to her everlasting shame, the flek had made her believe such a thing was possible, that a flek could be altered to pass as human, though, as far as

Confederation scientists could tell, it was not. Every flek spy ever unmasked had turned out to be a mind-twisted human. She herself had been betrayed into enemy hands by just such a person. He'd died in Heyoka's raid believing he was a flek trapped in a human body and she'd come very close to sharing the same fate.

The pink sphere dissolved and she blinked at the scene before her—a dazzling white concourse suspended amidst at least twenty more, all looping over and under and even through one another without guardrails or supports of any kind. Flek of dozens of body types she'd never seen before thronged the broad surfaces. They were all the same dead-white with demon-red eyes. A flekish song of joyous service was being broadcast and the chittering of the thousands singing along filled the hazy air.

She felt closed in, though they were out in the open air, trapped and claustrophobic. The flek city vibrated around her, alive with multitudes of the enemy. Her heartbeat pounded in her ears. I can't do this, she thought. She felt dizzy and her chest hurt. I can't be that person, the spy-drone clothed in human flesh. I can't go that close to madness again.

Another coughing fit overwhelmed her. She hunched over, braced herself as she fought to control it. Cough-tears streamed down her grimy face. "Water!" she finally croaked to the waiting architect. "This shell cannot function efficiently without water."

The architect diverted a small round courier. It paused for instructions, then scurried away, rejoining the service song. The scrabble of its feet on the gleaming white concourse made her skin crawl.

Her guide started off and she had to follow or be left behind. It strode purposefully ahead of her with its four long legs, much faster than she could manage. She hung back at its heels, trying not to breathe too deeply and trigger the coughing again.

The courier returned and scuttled along at her side, matching her pace, handing up a half-moon carafe filled with water. It was stale and bitter, left over, she suspected, from some sort of cleaning job, but she let it trickle down her parched and aching throat, then felt moderately better.

She passed back the carafe. The courier snatched it out of her hand and turned away, both sets of shoulders hunched. It thinks I'm disgusting, she thought, and remembered how she too had once found herself so, had longed to shed her loathsome pink skin and regain the sleek purity of flek chitin.

They entered an open chamber thronging with the caste known as Deciders. Pink and yellow globules of light danced over their heads. Huge, irregular-shaped screens formed the three walls, each displaying different scenes or marching lines of statistics. The architect continued on to the far side, but Mitsu found she had stopped without meaning to. Her legs simply would take her no closer.

A Decider turned its heavy carnelian gaze on her and she felt it could see right through her shabby deception. "Spy-Drone 87650."

Her fingers danced over one another and she realized she was beating out the flek service song with her inadequate fingers. Cold fear raced through her nerves and she made herself lower her hands to her sides. "That is my designation."

"We had not retained notice of your deployment on Planet 873," the Decider said.

"Preparations were hasty," she said. "There was little time when I was assigned."

"Your original phalanx?"

All-Father, she had no idea what that term meant. Her hand itched to draw the sonic knife from her boot and bury the shimmering green blade in the hulking

Decider's chest. And what good would that do? the rational part of her mind asked. You should have killed that grid-tech when you had the chance. Now they know everything it knows.

"Your phalanx?" the Decider repeated. The hot red eyes bore down on her like the visual components of some terrible, sentient machine.

"Dead," she said, for lack of anything better to say.

"On Planet 873?"

"Yes." Sweat soaked her uniform, plastered her hair to her head. The scene before her winked in and out. Everything seemed far away and the rotten-eggs reek of sulphur was overwhelming. Heatstroke, she thought fuzzily, was becoming a real possibility.

"How?"

How—what? She had lost track of the conversation. She blinked unsteadily at the Decider.

"How did your phalanx die?" it said. "Did the Enemy sweep back over Planet 873, after the Makers retreated, or did the perverted ones kill them?"

The laka? "Yes," she said, for lack of anything better to say, "they killed them."

The Decider fell back into a contemplative posture, arms bent, oversized head lowered to prevent distraction. "We had hoped, if we withdrew our forces, the Enemy could be enticed to overrun Planet 873," it said finally. "Once they had eliminated the perverted ones, we would return and exterminate them in turn, which is much easier. Then we could finish the needed atmospheric adjustments to transform the planet according to the architectural style of that period."

They were afraid of the laka. How strange. Mitsu was fast losing her grip on reality, but she filed that tidbit away for later examination. Humanity had fought the flek for generations, in varying degrees of intensity, and more often than not, they were the ones losing territory. How had the gentle laka managed to frighten flek off their world?

Sweat ran down her back, pooled at the base of her spine. She felt cold and hot at the same time. "I have gathered information on the perverted ones, as well as the Enemy," she said, "which is hidden on Planet 873. I must go back and retrieve it."

"The grid-tech spoke of furred animals who fought with manufactured energy weapons," the Decider said.

"Yes," Mitsu said, "but they were very primitive. One tech and a few warrior-drones were more than a match for them."

"True," the Decider said. "However, you will be accompanied by a full phalanx of warrior-drones, when you return. They will be responsible for the recovery of the information, as well as the procurement of at least one specimen of this new species for our records."

Mitsu's knees wobbled. She forced herself to straighten, though black dots shivered like dancing molecules behind her eyes. "And the perverted ones?"

"Kill all who come . . . reach of . . . weapons. Under no circumstances, listen . . . thing they . . . or sing . . ."

The voice had gone tinny and flat, far away. She knew she should focus, that her very survival, as well as those back on Oleaaka, depended on it, but the hot, thick air closed in on her and it was so difficult to breathe. She felt herself falling, and too late, put out her hands. The hot floor seemed to rise up and strike her. Her lungs strained, as a fierce red tide rolled in and swept her thoughts away.

It took Sixteenth Breeder some time to die. He thrashed about between the crystalline columns in agony, his shoulder burned to blackness, pleading with his nestbrothers for release.

Second told him to go ahead and die, if he wished,

but Sixteenth didn't appear to understand. His screams should have been disturbing. Certainly, Second Breeder's three remaining companions found them sufficiently so that they left the cavern in search of their own gleaner and translator, as planned. But, for some reason, Second was intrigued. The cries of pain summoned pictures in his mind that hinted at great doings, brave accomplishments, wildly satisfying pleasures. He could not tear himself away until Sixteenth finally uttered a long, sibilant sigh and died.

It had been reminiscent of a Night of Leavetaking, Second reflected, though vastly more exciting. Deaths on those occasions were abrupt and unexceptional, each one inevitably brief and the same as the last. He had attended five of the annual ceremonies during his short life, though of course this season would have finally brought his turn to participate.

The thought of the Leavetaking made him hungrier than ever. If one of the utilitarian laborers had been at hand to prepare Sixteenth's body, he and the other hungry breeders could have at least eaten *that*. As he recalled from previous ceremonies, processed properly, discarded breeders were quite tasty. Well, when their new colony was established, he would see to it that they had a plentiful supply of laborers.

He hoisted the stiffening corpse between his two sets of shoulders and carried it through the tunnels to the surface. If they acquired a translator before the body spoiled, they could still prepare a feast of their own.

Outside, the light had dwindled to faint rose on the western horizon. The clouds overhead were low and black and the sweet scent of rain hung heavy in the air. It would rain soon, and long too. He deposited the body close to the cavern entrance.

Shortly thereafter, his companions returned, dragging along a delicate translator. All three breeders were beating out Second's forceful new song on their second-hands and the rhythm was quite stimulating, though the translator appeared distraught. Her color had faded to a pasty white-green and she had actually cracked her carapace trying to escape. Tenth Breeder had a firm grip on one of her forearms and was dancing about, looking quite pleased with himself.

"You cannot do this!" the translator cried. "You must all return to the colony at once!"

"*This* is our colony," Second said boldly, "and you are now our translator."

"We could not find a gleaner," Tenth said and released the translator. She scuttled out of reach and then cowered. "They have all returned to the compound for the night."

Another dismal night without foodstuffs. Second contemplated that prospect and felt quite displeased. He turned to the frightened translator. "Are you familiar with the preparation for the Feast of Leavetaking?"

Her face paled beneath its green tint. "No, of course not," she said, clearly aghast. "That is the responsibility of the keepers."

"But you have seen it," Second persisted. "Translators go everywhere, talk to everyone, or else nothing would get done."

"It has been my privilege to be a translator-at-large the last two seasons," she said and averted her eyes.

"Then you know what to do." Second studied her closely.

"That is not my function!" She was trembling now. "And it is not yours either!"

"'Each to her own function,'" Second said testily, quoting the keepers.

"That is the true and proven way of things," the translator said. Her voice was shaded with misery. "All else is madness!"

"We will make a new way," Second said. He dashed

forward and twisted her arm. "We are hungry. Prepare that body for consumption."

Obviously, she had not noticed Sixteenth's charred form before, because now she stiffened and then folded in upon herself.

"This is useless!" Tenth said in disgust. "She won't perform any tasks outside her caste. None of them will."

Second glared down at her trembling form. "Then we will eat *her*!"

"How?" Tenth said.

He did not know. In fact, he knew nothing at all of any real use, Second realized. He was just a mouth to feed, a body waiting to breed and then be sacrificed in the annual Leavetaking, useful for one brief moment in an entire lifetime.

The only time he had felt large and important was back in the ceremonial arena when the furred alien had stood against them and he had . . . had . . . *fought*. Yes, that was the word he'd been searching for all of last night and most of today. When he'd *fought*, and then later again, when he had watched the gleaming white stranger *fight* the furred ones down in the cave, everything had seemed possible.

"Never mind," he said, and realized he truly didn't care anymore about eating. His hunger was growing familiar, like an everpresent shadow with a mean little edge to it, and he found he liked that, the meanness, the sense of sharpness. "Detain her," he said. "When it is light, I shall go to the compound and fetch back both a laborer and a gleaner."

Heyoka's claws shredded the forest's top layer of leaves as he fell. His scrabbling right hand gained purchase on a slender limb for a second, then slipped, and he plunged through the emerald shade again. Desperate, he used both hand- and footclaws on the bark of a forest giant. He scored the soft wood, almost arrested his fall, but then the tree contracted, as though in pain, and threw him off.

He hit the fork of the next tree over, bounced, then dug his claws in again. This time, they held and he found himself clinging to a massive trunk at least two hundred feet in the air. His heart raced and the breath rasped in and out of his straining lungs. The tree quaked beneath him and he quickly retracted his claws, clinging instead with his arms and pulling himself up to a more secure seat.

The tree still trembled, and he began to climb down, hand over hand. This species must have at least a rudimentary nervous system, he told himself. It flinched when he paused, then shuddered violently. He cursed and slipped a good fifty feet before he was able to stop this time, and took a solid blow to the ribs.

He'd be damned lucky if he hadn't broken something, he thought, then eased himself down as fast as possible. The tree swayed, seeming uneasy, and he thought what his adoptive father, Ben Blackeagle, might have made out of this encounter. *Everything is related,* he had always said, *the plants and the earth and the animals and the stars. They are all your relatives.*

The tree spasmed and then he was free-falling, arms and legs windmilling until he landed, spread-eagled, in a stand of dense, prickly bushes. He lay there, stunned, scratched and bruised from end to end. These were no relatives of his and this was certainly no place for a hrinn.

The brush rustled, then parted. A startled lavender face peered out at him with pale-pink eyes.

Chapter Seventeen

World Architect 549 stood by as the Deciders consulted the records. The small figure on the floor had not moved since collapsing. Whether that was normal for the species or not, the architect did not know. It might just be a dormancy cycle, but he had little interest in Enemy physiology, or anything else beyond his inbred fascination with world-sculpting.

When word had spread that a grid-tech had reported advertent transport of a Maker spy back from the prohibited world, he had been mildly curious. What was Planet 873 like now? Had the Makers' aborted conversion process persisted to any degree? For most of his adult life, he had been posted on this failed world, trying to reverse the chemical disunity which made breeding impossible. The exquisitely sculpted landscapes here included sector-wide renowned sulphur flats and possessed many other singular beauties, but he was stultified by his failure to find effective remedies.

Planet 873, though, was rich with possibilities. Others had failed there long ago, not his particular generation of architects, and the failure had been of a more extreme nature, having nothing to do with the chemical limitations on the site. If only they would let him assess the landscape, something lovely still might be accomplished.

"It speaks pure High-Maker," said the largest of the Deciders, the Venerable Seven herself. "It must have been conditioned by our own hands. The Enemy has never displayed any ability on its own to acquire our tongue to that degree."

"But there is no record of a turned Enemy spy assigned there," a younger Decider said. "And that world has lain fallow since the monstrous perversion. The Enemy was not there then. How could one such as this have been assigned since?"

Architect 549 bowed his head and edged forward, signalling his desire to speak before this august company.

Decider Seven raised her forearms in aggravation. "You are not needed here until we make a decision," she said severely. "Go back to concocting your atmospheric potions, impotent though they are."

"I had a thought, unworthy for your consideration, I am quite certain." He waited, neck twitching. A Decider's displeasure was usually, and swiftly, fatal.

The Decider sat back on her haunches, folded both sets of arms across her chestplate. Pinks and greens glinted off her highly polished chitin so that she appeared to glow. She did not go so far as to give her assent, but neither did she kill him for his impunity.

Emboldened, he continued. "Send this creature to Planet 873 and assign me to accompany it. I will assess the conditions there and report back with the cache of information it mentions."

"We cannot be certain it is as it claims to be," Decider Seven said. "Even if it is our creation, better to kill it out of hand than take risks."

"But it speaks so well!" he blurted, before he could stop himself, foolish in his youthful eagerness. "What are the odds that an unturned Enemy could present itself this elegantly? Has one ever done so before?"

"True." The Decider rose and walked over to the crumpled form. Its breathing was quite ragged now, its thoracic cavity heaving. "We have not had information on the perverted ones since abandoning 873, but the transfer-tech did not encounter any sign of them. Perhaps it is time to have a more thorough look. That world may yet be salvageable."

The architect was already planning which hatching of investigators to take, which line of searchers would give the most accurate readings. He had recently heard of a promising genetic offshoot of the standard type which could interpret wavelengths of up to—

"Remember." The Decider prowled over to him and stood breathing through her spicules on his unprotected back. "Fifty phalanxes had to be terminated upon our initial withdrawal from that planet. Should you become tainted by the perverted mind-set, we will sacrifice your worthless life immediately upon your return, as well as that of your entire hatching."

A dire threat indeed. Such a drastic action would indicate to all extant hives that the genome which had engendered his branch of architects was faulty and therefore not worthy of continuance. He would have to be very vigilant.

"I wish only to be of service," he said humbly.

"Very well, then," she said. "Revive this pathetic shell, if it is not already too late."

The disgusting creature had called for water earlier, so the architect sent another courier for more, then directed it to pour some upon the creature's mouth in hopes that it might swallow.

✧   ✧   ✧

Coolness bathed Mitsu's face, drawing her out of the steaming red dark. Water trickled down her nose. She sputtered, coughed. Her hand flailed weakly at her cheek and came away wet. She could not think where she was, or how she'd come to be here. It was so hot, so sodding, sodding hot, and her lungs strained to inhale.

She sat up, ran trembling fingers back through her soaked hair, cracked her eyes open. Garish flek pinks and purples and greens assaulted her and the smell of sulphur was overwhelming. She wrapped her arms around her chest and rocked. She had dreamed this repeatedly on Anktan, that she had returned to the flek, and now had to fight her way back to sanity all over again. Only, this time, it was real.

Her hands trembled and she struggled not to be sick. She was still in the Deciders' chamber, seated on the slick white floor, surrounded by screens with filled with incomprehensible scenes. One of the small flek couriers stood a few feet away, holding an empty container.

"This Enemy shell is weak," the Decider said in lilting High-Flek. Disgust colored its tone.

"I—regret its inadequacy," Mitsu said.

"You must return," the Decider said, "before the shell expires. There, you will retrieve the information you collected on the perverted ones and bring it back here for our evaluation." It beckoned to a row of waiting warrior-drones. "These shall accompany you, along with the world-architect, who wishes to take readings at the site of the abandoned environmental engines."

She counted over thirty warriors, far too many to deal with herself, without even taking into account the blasted architect. Her heart sank. They must suspect her story, and no wonder. It was utterly lame. If she could get back to the grid without collapsing again, perhaps she could disable it from this side. Every breath now was more difficult than the last. Her time was growing short. If she died here, without closing the grid, Oleaaka would fall again to the flek, and Heyoka and his hrinn along with it.

There had to be a way.

The architect loomed over her, almost bumbling for a flek. She shuddered and tried not to look at its eager, smashed-in face. "I am ready," she said, and set off at its side down the broad white sweep of the concourse. The city was broadcasting a unity song now and she could hear thousands of synchronized feet walking in time on the plazas.

The phalanx of warrior-drones followed.

Ninth-Translator-at-large cowered outside the cavern entrance. She was surrounded by out-of-control breeders. She had always been warned breeders were unstable, that one had to maintain constant vigilance, lest they veer away from communal harmony and the old horror sweep back again, but she had never before seen any evidence that such cautions were valid.

She saw it now. The miscreants had taken hold of her, actually dragged her here, so close to this site of ancient troubles. On the way, Tenth Breeder had thrust her into a rock wall when she struggled and cracked her side. She trembled at the memory, sickened. It was all true, the old stories of violence and strife, folly and hatred. She realized she had never really believed them, not in the same sense that one trusted one's own day-to-day sense memories.

They had to be put down, as Fourteenth Coordinator had ordered back in the ceremonial arena, and, now that she was damaged, her own time of service was over. She would never be whole again. At the first sign of dysfunction, she would be put down herself as well.

The light was fading. Soon it would be dark. She should be back in the compound with the other translators, sharing everything that had been seen and said and done this day among the laka, comparing notes, deciding how to serve the colony even better.

Miserable and shaken, she crept a single step closer to the trees, whenever her captors were not watching her. The foolish breeders boasted among themselves, strutted about singing songs she had never heard before, forceful chants with strong, bold rhythms. Where was their concern for the needs of the community, she wondered. How could they be so misguided?

A low hum sprang up, traveling through earth and rock as much as the air. Tenth Breeder's head swiveled and his pink eyes gleamed with eagerness. "It returns!"

Second Breeder, the most vulgarly aggressive of the lot, beat his hands more loudly against his sides, so that his wicked song of *fighting* echoed throughout the clearing.

The sound was coming from the recently reopened cave, she realized and shuddered. Down there was the most forbidden place on the entire island, worse even than the ruins in the forest, and they were ghastly. She could not go down there. If necessary, she would struggle until they killed her, but she could not bear to be in the presence of such bitter wrongness.

She edged closer to the tree line, closer. The wall of silver-green leaves stirred in the breeze, promising concealment. Two of the four breeders had disappeared into the cave by the time Second Breeder glanced her way and realized what she was doing.

"Stop!" he cried in the simple breeder dialect.

Instead, she bolted into the dark pool of shadows, keeping her head down, going always toward the most tangled vines, the slimmest opening, the deepest cover.

Behind her, the terrible hum which had presaged all this grew louder, more shrill. She could feel her pursuer's dilemma. Breeders found that sound exciting;

it seemed to mean something to them. Now, he had to decide whether to ignore it and chase after her, or return to the depths and bask. She pressed on, weaving through protruding roots, squeezing between trees, climbing outcroppings of rock.

She ran and ran, going always uphill, away from the colony, since he would not expect that, until abruptly, she was alone with the screams of disturbed avians, the scuttle of minuscule feet fleeing her approach, the whisper of leaves in the breeze.

He had given up the chase.

Heyoka realized the creature was laka. He extracted himself from the prickly bush, leaving a good deal of black fur behind, and stood slowly. Rain pattered down through the dense leaves and dripped off the native's head as it studied him. The figure was smaller than the specimens he'd seen back at the grove, though sturdily made, graceful in its quick, precise movements.

"I'm sorry," he said in Standard. "I didn't mean to frighten you."

The native scuttled backwards at the sound of his voice. A basket full of pale green melons was strapped across its back; it had probably been gathering wild fruit up here on the slopes.

The insistent rain trickled down branches and trunks, pooled on leaves, then overflowed and soaked into the already soft ground. The sharp green scent of the forest intensified with each passing moment. He spread his hands, careful to keep his claws retracted. "I won't hurt you."

It froze, obviously terrified.

He pressed his hands over his eyes, wishing it would just go away. His head was spinning with weariness and there was no way to communicate with it. No one had bothered with even rudimentary laka language tapes on the trip over. Little progress had been made in deciphering the language over the years. A successful translation of laka would have required at least one laka to speak to on a consistent basis, and the natives were notoriously shy, avoiding Confederation forces on all occasions possible.

At any rate, he didn't have time to attempt contact now. He needed to get back down the mountain to Onopa and Montrose before Skal returned. He didn't know how the new Leader felt about working with humans, but he suspected a break was planned, perhaps even a fatal one.

To his relief, the laka lowered its head and melted into the underbrush. He pushed a handful of wet mane out of his face, leaned back against the nearest trunk and took stock. The aching drain of blueshift still pulled at him and he was far colder than the temperature warranted.

Anger simmered beneath that exhaustion though. He stared back up at the looming gray mountain with its verdant greenery and his savage *other* looked with him, snarling in the recesses of his mind. He'd never lost a fight to anyone but his sponsor, wily old Nisk, and he had been a worthy opponent, respected by hrinn all up and down the Mish River Valley. Skal, on the other hand, was only an ignorant brawler. He should have been able to disable him with both hands tied behind his back and not even breathing hard. Maybe Skal was right, though; a hrinn who couldn't hold blueshift wasn't fit to lead. The rest of the hrinn would follow Skal now, until one of them successfully Challenged him, or Heyoka found some way to do it himself.

He made his wobbly legs carry him to a clearing and then tried to get his bearings. The sun had almost set, but he noted its position, dimly visible just below the clouds, as well as the downward slope that led eventually to the sea, and calculated roughly where he was. The base camp must be off to the east, probably a good hour's hike or more. The lower cave entrance itself was less than a half mile down the side of the mountain.

Priorities, he counseled himself. Skal, Kei, and Visht did not have much farther to go to place Bey's body close to the sky, then they would be coming back. He had to locate his human personnel and move them to safety, though he didn't know how he was going to do that without laying a trail Skal could easily follow.

One hand braced on his aching ribs, he started working his way downhill. Motile silver-green vines snared his feet, slithering as often into his path as out of it. The air was thick and humid, the forest claustrophobic and dark and dripping with the persistent rain. Although hrinnti night sight was better than a human's, he still needed a bit of light to see by, and, between the clouds and the dense canopy, little penetrated.

Panting, he stopped at a rushing mountain stream and drank his fill. He waded into the shallows and dribbled a handful over his head and ears, closed his eyes, thought again about the fight up on the ledge. He'd gotten his tail thoroughly whipped, there was no doubt about that. But he *had* blueshifted, there at the end, just for a second.

It had taken weeks, after he'd overextended himself during that last battle on Anktan, before he'd been able to see normal colors again, longer before everything didn't taste and smell of ashes. Nisk had said he'd burned himself out and would never be able to draw power again.

This was the first indication he'd had that perhaps Nisk was mistaken, he might be able to use metabolic overdrive again, at least to a limited degree. If only there were a thermal pool somewhere he could soak in to recharge his cells and find out.

Then he snorted. Get real. There was no time for soaking in pools at the moment or for anything else. He had to find Onopa and Montrose, then come up with some clue as to what the devil had become of Mitsu. He feared she was dead on some flek hellworld. And, if she weren't dead, then she was a prisoner again, a scenario far worse.

He took one last drink, then plodded on through the dim, sweltering forest, paralleling the stream, the sultry air thick enough to ladle. After a few minutes, though, he became aware of a definite throbbing presence, more of a sensation than a sound, rumbling up through the earth.

It was the grid. Someone had set the crystals off again as Kei and Mitsu had inadvertently done the day before. Perhaps the laka had gone back down there for their own inscrutable reasons.

On the other hand, it could be the first wave of a flek occupation force coming through. Damnation! If only he had some demolitions! He would have to sweep back by the abandoned base camp at some point and see if Dennehy had left any behind. That cave needed to be collapsed, no matter how disappointed Confederation scientists would be later on.

For now, he had to get down there and see who, or what, was coming through that grid. He climbed a half-fallen snag and took his bearings again to make sure he wasn't walking in circles.

Something stirred in the underbrush on the opposite stream bank. He caught the scent of laka and pinned his ears back. He didn't have time for more of their bizarre fun and games.

Claws bared, he eased into the stream, up the far

bank, tracked the telltale movement in the vegetation for a few strides, and pounced. He brought down a warm, thrashing body and pinned it on the mossy ground with one knee. He raised his handclaws, threatening to strike. "Be still!"

The terrified laka squalled, then went limp. Its pink eyes were fixed and staring, and he could see each beat of its blood beneath the pale-green skin of its delicate neck.

"I won't hurt you, if you don't fight me." He eased the pressure. "What are you doing here?"

It spoke in a soft hurried voice in its sibilant tongue. He did not understand a single word.

"Were you going down into the cave?" He pantomimed "down," pointing to the earth.

It shuddered and struggled to regain its feet.

"So you do understand that much." He pulled it up, keeping an iron grip on the closest of its four wrists. Its sides heaved, as though with emotion, and it braced both pairs of legs. Four arms and four legs, he thought with a prickle of disgust. Even though the pigmentation and proportions were wrong, its body had a distinctly flekish cast. "Is that how you survived all those years ago?" he asked. "Because you look like them?"

The vibrations from the grid increased. At this distance, it was merely annoying, like the whine of a mosquito in his ear. Down in the cave, though, it would be brain-rattling. He looked at the trembling laka. Now that he could see its other side, it was obviously injured. Green had pooled below a cracked body plate like a bruise.

Killing it was out of the question. The natives were civilians and relations were already precarious at best, but he couldn't just release the damn thing either. If it fetched its fellows while he was busy checking out the grid, their sheer numbers could overwhelm him.

"So," he said, more to himself than the laka, "you'll have to come with me."

It didn't understand at first, but when he dragged it downhill in the direction of the cave, it suddenly reared back and struggled anew to free itself.

It realized where they were going and was terrified. He shook it into submission, then wondered what it knew that he didn't.

Chapter Eighteen

The acrid yellow haze seemed thicker than before, when Mitsu stepped out of the travel sphere. The phalanx of warrior-drones, world-architect, and transfer-tech, along with Mitsu, could just fit onto the transport pad of the grid, and she had to squeeze through the flek who had arrived before her. The sickening touch of slick white chitin against her bare skin brought back even more unwelcome memories.

Off to one side, the tech had itself sprayed with a nacreous substance by one of its small assistants, then entered the grid and made final adjustments on the power matrix. She tried to note what it did, but it was hard to make out much between fits of coughing and through tearing eyes. Her throat was raw and an ominous rattle filled her lungs.

Once again, the grid's sound wound up and up, quickly reaching the level of unlubricated machine parts grinding each other to metallic dust. She gasped and covered her ears. The pulsing lights quickened. The air crackled with energy, as though something alive were holding them in its mouth. The temperature dropped, and she was *falling*.

She fought to make her shocked lungs breathe. The sky switched places with the floor, then righted itself with a stomach-churning wrench. Spent, she opened her eyes and sagged against the warrior-drone on her right. It bore her weight without even seeming to notice. Multicolored lights writhed over the pure white walls: magenta, teal, azure, violet. They had arrived once again in the underground chamber.

At least, she thought it was the same chamber. Her heart pounded. Perhaps many flek transit points looked alike. What if they had changed their minds and taken her somewhere else?

The transfer-tech bustled about, dampening the crystals with furtive little strokes, so that the screech subsided to a mere teeth-rattling hum. The warriors, laser-sticks in hand, spread out with typical flekish efficiency and searched both tunnels leading out of the main chamber. She could hear their sides scraping against the walls.

There was no sign of Heyoka or the rest of the squad. If this was the right place, then at least one of them must have survived, or there would have been a heap of bloated hrinnti corpses down here.

"Where is the cache you spoke of?" the architect asked her. "You must return with it as soon as the grid is reset. The Deciders are most eager to examine your information."

"It's outside—hidden in the forest." This was Oleaaka then. A tremendous sense of relief ran through her. She tried to remember which passage led out, but she was so tired and her head seemed to be filled with the poisonous yellow atmosphere of the world they had just left behind. The room slid sideways She braced her hands on her thighs, even more disoriented than when she had gone through the grid before. Perhaps the effects were cumulative, she thought, or perhaps the toxicity of the flek atmosphere would take time to wear off, if indeed it ever did.

She glanced around surreptitiously for her lost rifle, but it was nowhere in sight. Whoever had removed the bodies must have taken it too. She only hoped it had been Heyoka.

The warriors returned from searching the back tunnel and presented themselves for instructions. Their eyes gleamed fiery red in the flickering lights, as though rubies had been set deep into the sockets. "We must go to the surface," the architect told them.

"Position yourself in the middle of our formation," one of the drones ordered. "We can protect you there. Above all else, do not converse with, or listen to, the perverted ones. Any sign of contamination will result in immediate termination."

She fell into the indicated position as they entered the other tunnel, but there was only room in the twisting passageway for them to proceed single file. Flek hemmed her in, fore and aft, inundating her with their acrid odor in the confined space. She had been in battle against them many times, seen them sweep down a beach or a plain or a field. It felt bizarre to be on the other side, protected by them, rather than at their nonexistent mercy. Sweat rolled down her neck and back and the breath still rasped in her lungs. There was a tinny ringing in her ears that had nothing to do with the grid. She plodded on, one foot in front of the other.

When they finally reached the narrow hole that led out onto the mountainside, the warriors in front scrambled up and wedged themselves through. The fresh air revived her slightly and she quickened her pace. Once outside, she would give these flek the slip, then double back and find a way to destroy the grid. Heyoka and the others, if there were any hrinn or humans left, would have to take care of the warrior-drones. The grid had priority.

The crisp sizzle of a laser-stick came from outside and her heart raced. Heyoka? She lurched forward, pulling herself up over the tumbled rocks hand over hand. Another bolt was fired and panic made her desperate to find out what was happening.

She dug her fingers into the black earth and pulled herself out. The cool night air, freshened by a recent rain, was like an exotic perfume, and, for the first time, she felt like she might really escape with her life. She heard the gurgle of a stream nearby. The darkening sky held a few glimmering stars out over the sea, while overhead, clouds obscured the view. The forest stretched around her on three sides of the horizon, a solid black outline against the lighter twilight. She couldn't see anyone but her flekish escort.

Flek had better night sight than humans, so obviously they were seeing something she couldn't. She gathered her energy to dash for the safety of the trees, then one of the drones caught her by the arm. "This way," it said flatly.

Its grip was painfully tight, and, if she struggled, she would give herself away. She had to play along for the moment. "What were you firing at?" she asked breathlessly, fighting not to cough.

"A perverted one was lurking," it said. "But we fired upon it and it has fled."

Heyoka had time to think *Mitsu is still alive*, before a laser bolt boiled the mud just short of his boot. Startled, he let the laka twist free. It turned and fled back across the stream.

Mitsu's pale face gazed out from behind a wall of white flek bodies. At this distance, and without light, he couldn't tell if there was any sanity left in her eyes. They hadn't restrained her, though, and actually seemed to be protecting her. There was only one reason why the flek would ever bring her back to this world. They must have turned her again. It had probably been easier the second time, since the groundwork was already laid.

The nose-burning stink of flek filled the air. He shuddered and then dashed after the laka, following it into the hot, sticky closeness of the rain forest. It seemed to have some idea of where it was going, and since he didn't, its path was as good as any.

The flek showed no sign of coming after them, so he finally stopped and listened. He didn't want to get too far from the cave. Mitsu would rather be dead than be controlled by the flek again. Of that, he was certain. He had to do what he could for her, even if all he could manage was to release her from her misery.

Leaves rustled upwind and the fur across his shoulders bristled. A silent snarl bared his teeth. His handclaws sprang free and he readied himself to spring.

The foliage parted and he smelled the distinctive musk of *laka* before he saw the same hesitant green-tinted native. He couldn't afford to waste time trying to keep it from giving him away. "What do you want?" he said roughly, hoping at least it would understand his tone of voice. "It's not safe here. Go back to your village."

It gripped its front two hands together in a curiously human gesture, like a child caught misbehaving, met his eyes, looked away. "Badt," it said in heavily accented Standard. "Very, very badt."

"Wha—?" His ears drooped with surprise.

"Badt!" it said again. "Run now."

"I can't run," he said slowly. "I have to go back for my friend."

"Not know 'friend' word," it said. "Just 'badt.' One musted run."

"You run," he said. "There's no reason for you to stay. I must go back to help my friend."

"Very oldt ones," it said. "No talk. Run."

Evidently some of the attempts to communicate with the laka had gone far better than Confederation linguists and officials had ever known. The laka must possess at least a rudimentary understanding of Standard; they just didn't want to talk to humans. Or hrinn, for that matter. Without mirrors and other hrinn around to remind him, he kept forgetting which he really was. "Go back," he said. "I will stay."

"You stay—this one stay," the laka said. "Speak for you."

"Not to the damned flek, you won't," he said. "I don't want to talk to them anyway. I want to tear their sodding heads off!"

The laka turned its face aside and cringed. He felt irritated with it for being so fastidious, and irritated with himself for being so blunt. Rangers worked with the indigenous population, whenever possible. Such alliances multiplied their strengths, and he might be stuck here for a very long time. Local support could mean all the difference. "They will kill you," he said, "without hesitation. Go back and I will handle this."

"No kill." It turned back to him. "No back. Talk. Sing. Make listen."

"Talk won't do any good here," he said, "or songs. I don't speak High-Flek anyway, so we can't talk." Though Mitsu did speak excellent High-Flek, he thought with a pang.

"Talk is life."

Yeah, right, he thought. Typical pacifist palaver. It was amazing the flek hadn't wiped out the laka forty-eight years ago when they had the chance. From where he stood, the job looked all too easy.

"Look," he said, "I don't care what you do, as long

as you stay out of the way and don't attract their attention. I have to shadow them and find out what they're up to."

The laka regarded him with an uncomprehending stare. He shook his head and then plunged into the undergrowth. The flek couldn't have gotten far.

By the time Aliki Onopa found her way back to the makeshift camp, dusk had fallen and a stiff salt-tanged breeze was blowing inland from the sea. This sea smelled subtly different from the ones of her home world, Kalana Colony. Different chemistries, she thought wearily, unshouldering her sling woven of dead vines, but this world seemed to be harmonious with most human needs.

Montrose was asleep off to one side. On the other, Kika rose and shook herself, a looming pale-gray shape in the deepening dark. Naxk was still stretched out on the ground and Aliki could hear the rasp of her breathing.

"How is she?" She gestured at the injured hrinn.

Kika rubbed at her ear with a fretful hand. "My hearing is still bad," she said. "Talk louder."

"How is Naxk?" Aliki said at the top of her voice. A flight of startled avians burst from a nearby tree and veered toward the mountains.

Kika's nose wrinkled. "Weak."

Aliki picked through what she'd gathered, including several small furred game animals she had brought down with her laser pistol, and handed Kika one. "Do you think she could eat something? That might help."

Kika tore off a haunch and sniffed. Her ears flattened. "Poison."

"You can tell just by the smell?" Aliki took the haunch herself and sniffed. It smelled gamey, a bit rank, but no worse than many cuts of fresh meat. She laid it aside and selected an orange and green furred avian instead. "How about this?"

Kika examined the small corpse. "Yes," she said, with typical hrinnti brusqueness. "This is safe." She ripped the carcass in two, then bent to wake Naxk.

The smaller hrinn jerked up, claws bared, snarling. Kika put a hand on her shoulder. "You must eat," she said in Standard and pushed the raw meat into her flailing hand.

Naxk stared wildly around. "I am not hungry," she said. Her black eyes were huge in the starlight.

"Your body needs to repair itself," Kika said, even though Aliki did not see how, with her damaged hearing, she could have understood. "You must eat."

"There are no restorers here to repair my body," Naxk said, "so it does not matter if I eat. I will die, but it was a good hunt."

Kika settled beside Naxk with her nose in the wind. Her mane, now unbound, whipped around her head.

Aliki looked from one furred face to the other and exasperation welled up. "You will not die," she said, "because that would be giving up, and Rangers do not give up! This is a fight, like any other, and you aren't allowed to quit!"

Naxk lay back against the ground and snarled weakly.

"Eat!" Aliki shoved the other half of the still-warm carcass at Naxk. "Eat, or I'll shove it down your throat!"

Naxk bristled. "You are not big enough to shove anything down my throat!"

"Try me!" Naxk was probably right, but Aliki felt desperate enough to make the attempt anyway. They were so few, they could not afford to lose any more. "Sergeant Blackeagle was wounded by flek fire too, year before last. Do you think he just lay down to die, when it happened? And where would you be now, if he had?"

"Yes, the Black/on/black," Naxk said, reverence in her voice. "He brought his own pattern."

"The Black/on/black would never give up." Aliki took Naxk's large hand, trying not to think of the three-inch claws concealed there, and wrapped the hrinn's fingers around the carcass. "It's not that much. Just eat a few bites."

With difficulty, Naxk raised the meat to her muzzle and tore off a mouthful. The effort exhausted her, but she chewed with grim determination.

Aliki was able to encourage her through two more bites, then Naxk fell into an uneasy, twitching sleep. She really was very beautiful, Aliki realized, gazing down at her. Hrinn were obviously made for fighting, with their double rows of teeth and claws, but beyond that, they were elegant, muscled and tall with that plush two-toned fur. It was as though she had never taken time to really look at one before.

Kika came up behind her and stared down. "You were firm with her, like a hold-sister, or even a blood-cousin."

"Rangers are family," Aliki said loudly enough to carry to Kika's damaged ears. "We leave everything and everyone else behind to fight the flek, so we take care of each other."

"She will die anyway," Kika said. "Her wounds are too severe."

Aliki grimaced. "I won't let her die!"

Kika regarded her with those space-black eyes that seemed deeper than even the night around them. Her nose twitched, as though an unfamiliar scent filled the air. "There is *something/in/motion* here, very large and powerful. I thought we had left all such behind on Anktan. The Line Mother warned, when she drove me away, that I would be forever outside all patterns, but tonight I feel this one strongly. I must think about it, whether I have ever heard its name, whether something so broad and encompassing can even be named by one as lowly as me."

Aliki had been told a little about hrinnti *patterns/ in/ progress* during training, how hrinn believed great unseen forces governed all of life so that the trick was figuring which one was arising at any given moment in order to anticipate events. "I'll name this one," she said. "It's called Recovery. It starts with us pulling Naxk and Montrose through, no matter what it takes, then reorganizing, and kicking those damn flek off this world!"

Kika's ears flattened, and for a moment, Aliki thought she had gone too far. "If so, maybe we are still in the midst of *stars/over/stars*," she said. "That one is said to be powerful and far-reaching enough to stretch even between worlds."

"Yeah," Aliki said, baffled, but willing to play along. "That must be it, *stars/over/stars*."

"Then extraordinary measures must be undertaken," Kika said. "Things never before attempted, impossible tasks. We must be ready for anything."

"All right by me," said Aliki.

"I must prepare," Kika said, then disappeared into the night.

Aliki stared after the form, wondering what exactly she had set in motion.

Skal did not offer to help carry Bey's body, but stalked stiffly along behind as Visht and Kei bore it ever upwards toward the velvet night sky until the ancient rock crumbled beneath their boots at every step, and they could climb no higher. The big Leader had raged for some time after the Black/on/black had thrown himself over the cliff and escaped honorable death at Skal's claws. They could not be certain what had become of him, but it was always a bad portent when an enemy did not die before one's eyes. Kei did not envy anyone who had the Black/on/black as his enemy.

The wind raged against their faces up this high, filled with the verdant greenness of the rain forest below, and always, as base note, the alien tang of the sea. Kei positioned Bey's body carefully, face-up, so the stars and sky could look upon him, as he and his fellow cublings had been taught all too young back in Levv's disgraced days.

It was difficult to leave him here, decent, honest Bey, who had always hung back, letting others take the lead, but never stinted to give his all. Kei would miss his support, as well as his sober, steadying influence. Bey had been a thinker, a rarity among hrinn. He resolved to cultivate more of that quality in himself as a memorial to his lifelong huntmate.

"Enough!" Skal spat.

Visht, who had been leaning silently against a rock shelf, lurched upright. The fur across the top of his right shoulder had been singed away. Exhaustion and pain were written into every line of his body and Kei did not know how the big yellow was going to make it back down the mountain without rest.

"We should sit with Bey," Visht said stolidly, "until either the Voice speaks his name one last time or dawn comes. That is only proper."

"Don't tell me that you are one of those earless priests! I thought we had left all that behind!" Skal bared his claws.

Visht tensed, a pale outline against the onyx night sky. The clouds parted and a few stars appeared. His breathing was hard and fast.

"Only a priest would be stupid enough to listen for the Voice in an alien place like this!" Skal said.

The Black/on/black did not believe in the great Voice who had spoken hrinn into existence, or in priests, yet he would never have behaved to those who did with such disrespect, Kei thought. He, himself, was currently undecided. He had doubted before the arrival of the Black/on/black on Anktan, but was no longer certain such things did not possess meaning.

He glanced down at Bey's limp body. The wind ruffled the dark-brown fur, revealing the lighter buff undercoat. He smelled like Levv, like home. Abruptly, Kei sat beside him and leaned his head back to stare up at the stars, listening with all his might.

Visht sat too, nose into the wind. "We are being silent as Uwn First-Male taught us," he said, "if someone wishes to speak."

That had the ring of ritual, though Kei was unfamiliar with the words. Behind his left shoulder, Skal gave a low, rattling snarl and Kei's hackles rose. He was Leader, Kei thought, and had every right to strike them down for their insubordination, but if he did, who would he lead? The two injured females waiting back down the mountain? The Black/on/black who, if he wasn't dead, was no doubt plotting at this very moment to tear Skal's throat out? That pair of soft-skinned humans?

Like it or not, he and Visht were all Skal had left.

Chapter Nineteen

The phalanx leader-drone insisted their time on this failed world was limited. It was cold and the air was miserably thin. Mitsu was to retrieve her cache of information on the Enemy and perverted ones immediately so they could return through the grid.

The rain forest stretched around them to the west, an impenetrable dark mass, rich with sound even at night. It smelled glorious, after the sere poison of the flek world, wet and green, brimming with compatible life. She started to speak, then broke off in a fit of coughing, her breathing passages still irritated. She hunched over and closed her eyes, fighting to control the spasm.

About thirty feet away, a small stream cascaded down the mountain and over rocks. She lurched to her feet, thinking a drink would help her abused throat. Even this unexpected movement alarmed her warrior escort and they enclosed her with their towering white bodies. This close, she could smell their distinctive odor and remembered how the hrinn hated it.

"I need—water," she choked out. "Let me pass!"

The ones between her and the stream parted just enough for her to squeeze by. She knelt on the wet bank and scooped up a double handful. After the bitter flatness of the water earlier, this was cool and soothing. She let it trickle down her tortured throat, then bathed her face.

"We must go," the phalanx leader said behind her back. Its voice was harsh with disapproval.

"This shell does not have good night sight. It cannot find the cache in the dark," she said without turning around. The forest began about ten paces beyond the stream. The breeze stirred a strip of low bushes and she could smell their fragrance. So close. If only she could lose herself in there, hide out until dawn, then search for her lost squadmates. Perhaps they had gone back to the base camp. Once reunited, she and Heyoka would form a battle plan, destroy the grid and drive these sodding flek into the sea.

"We can guide you," the phalanx leader said stubbornly.

And they could. Like hrinn, flek had superior night sight. Flek technology employed light for other things, transport among them. They did not require artificial light in order to see at night. "No," she said. "We will wait for dawn. It won't be long, and when it's light, I'll be able to find it quite easily. This shell must rest until then. You will keep watch."

She bathed her face again, then stretched out on the mossy bank. The damp earth beneath her cheek smelled wonderful. She dug in her wet fingers and felt the mat of tiny living roots beneath.

The quick, precise four-beat rhythm of flek steps surrounded her as they set up their perimeter, two of them even splashing across the stream to the opposite bank. Damn. She closed her eyes, trailed one hand in the water, and waited for them to grow careless.

❖   ❖   ❖

When Heyoka located Mitsu and the flek again, they had not moved from the cavern entrance. Were they guarding the grid? He watched from the trees as she discussed something with one of the warriors, then dispersed them to stand guard while she lay down to sleep.

Since she wasn't bound, or agitated, or resisting them in any way, it was quite clear she'd gone over again. The realization hit him like a blow. He hadn't really believed it before. It wasn't her fault, anymore than if she'd taken a laser bolt to the head. He knew that, but he still felt sick. He had put her in danger's path. If it was the last thing he ever did, he would see her free of them.

He made a quick count. At least thirty, a full fighting unit, and more might be stationed out of sight or back inside. An additional undersized drone with an unfamiliar body configuration moved into his line of sight, some variety of tech perhaps. It carried an array of instruments and busied itself taking readings of the soil, water, and air. He didn't like the looks of that. Flek had attempted at least once to make this world over, and, even though they'd failed, five of its six islands were still poisoned ruins.

Perhaps the great chemical engines that were to have transformed this island had malfunctioned, or the laka would have died too. Flek technology had no doubt improved over the last forty-eight years. If they were set to try again, they might well succeed this time.

Mitsu was surrounded on three sides by warrior-drones and several more had crossed the stream. They were all armed and he'd never get at her with any kind of direct assault. He cudgeled his weary brain for a solution. If he went back for Onopa and Montrose, the flek would probably move on by the time he returned, and Montrose was injured anyway. This might well be his best chance to rescue her.

Ears flattened, he ghosted through the vines and trees, huge patches of fernlike plants, relying on his nose for guidance as much as his eyes. Thunder rumbled overhead; a storm seemed to be moving down the mountain. He could smell the rising humidity.

He climbed upstream until the flek were well out of sight and earshot, then broke cover and crossed to the stream. The rushing water glimmered white over the rocks at the fall line as he slipped into the current.

It was only chest-deep, so he waded out to the middle, then immersed himself, leaving only his nose and eyes exposed, and let the current take him. A series of low falls lay between him and Mitsu, tricky to negotiate, but the flek would not expect infiltration from that direction. He rolled over on his back, aimed his feet at the V of rushing white water, as he had been trained, and approached the first set of boulders.

His right shoulder took a glancing blow as he plunged over and he bit off a curse. The water smoothed out into a pool, then picked up speed and careened toward the next falls. He could see two V's between the submerged rocks this time and had to guess which was the safest. He aimed for the one on the right, but raked his ankle on a sharp edge and drew blood.

At this rate, he'd be in pieces by the time he got there, he told himself. Some Ranger he was these days. He tightened his muscles as the third and last falls loomed.

This one had a steeper drop, which was to his advantage, if he could keep from braining himself on the rocks. Once he was over, he would dive to the bottom, then surface beside Mitsu.

And once you have her, he asked himself, what are you going to do? She's gone flek again. She'll fight you

tooth and nail, just like she did on Anktan and she's
ferociously efficient for her size.

Well, there were methods of keeping a captive quiet.
Rangers were schooled in those too. Once she realized
who he was and that she was safe, she might well snap
out of it again.

But would he and the rest ever be able to trust her
again at their backs?

The gentle susurration of water over the rocks
soothed Mitsu to the point where she wasn't quite
asleep, but drifting a bit, almost dreaming. Sleep
dragged at her, a deep midnight blue, so tempting, but
she couldn't let go. The sun would be up soon and she
had to make her escape before then. It would be much
harder to elude flek in full daylight.

The island breeze sighed against her hair, warm and
languid. She was so tired, a weariness that saturated
both head and limbs, reaching all the way back to
Anktan. How long had it been since she felt both safe
and sane? She couldn't rememb—

A powerful hand seized her wrist, and, with a quick
jerk, tumbled her into the stream. Her mouth opened
reflexively to cry out and she inhaled a shocking lungful
of water. Choking, she thrashed and opened her eyes,
but saw only liquid blackness.

Laser bolts sizzled through the water and she felt the
heat of them on her face. The imprisoning hand drew
her deeper. She reached down to the knife hidden in her
boot. A second hand came out of the darkness to pin her
free wrist and draw her onward through the water. Her
lungs burned with the need to breathe and the bubbling
stream sounds were fading. She could make out nothing
beyond the terrible ringing in her ears.

She kicked out, made contact with a body less than
a foot away. She fought to kick it again, but was flipped

over and held tightly so that was impossible too. Who would want to drown her like this? Not the flek, she thought. They were putting her to use. Kei, perhaps? The laka?

The water picked up speed. She twisted, trying with the last of her strength to free herself. Everything was receding. Or maybe she was receding, sliding along a dark tunnel, toward another place, black as onyx, silent and isolated, another reality.

In the darkness, her head struck something immense and solid. She cried out with the last of her air as night closed around her like a great cold fist.

At the first red-orange hint of dawn, Kei and Visht shook the stiffness out of their backs and stood. The rain-laden wind buffeted their faces, blew their fur back the wrong way, and yet Kei felt strangely at peace. He had not heard the Voice in the depths of the night, and he had not really expected to, but Bey would remain up here on the peak, close to sky and stars and clouds, as was proper. Wherever and whatever the big brown/on/buff was hunting now, he had died with honor and that would have been of paramount importance to him.

"Now," Kei said, looking askant at Skal, who perched glowering on a boulder a body length above, "we must find the others and see if the flek have returned. They could already be in the middle of a fight without us."

"Who are you to say what we must do, rag-ear?" Skal rose bristling to his full height, His handclaws sprang free; he was clearly spoiling for another fight. "I am strongest! I say what we do, and I have not yet decided!"

"This cannot wait," Kei said, his own shoulders bristling in response to Skal's abrasive scent. "Flek invaded Anktan once before and they may return, if we show weakness. After all this time, we have a chance to finally draw blood and our huntmates below may already be dying!"

Skal prowled back and forth on the narrow ledge, but there was an acrid undercurrent of nervousness in his scent that had not been there before. "The flek fled to its own world. It saw how many we were. It won't come back."

"That's not what the Black/on/black said!"

"I have no interest in that cull-face's useless words!" Skal's handclaws gleamed red in the raw morning light. "Like the humans he's so fond of, he talks and talks, but words do not win fights! He's a burnt-out toothless wonder, fit only to be a doddering old Teller entertaining nurselings! He looks like us on the outside, but inside he's a soft-skinned human. He has no idea what it really means to be hrinn!"

Long simmering anger surged through Kei. His ears flattened. "You hung back," he said, "in the cave, when you should have taken the lead. I asked you for help, but you said to let the flek escape! No wonder you were the only one uninjured."

"I was trying to read the arising *pattern/in/progress*," Skal said sullenly. "You saw what happened to all those who rushed in. There was no point in acting until I sniffed out its shape."

"You want to know what pattern rises around us?" Kei met his eyes with brash disrespect. "I think I caught a whiff of *fire/in/water*."

Skal snarled at the naming of the notorious hrinnti pattern of bitter deception.

"As Leader, you should have been first into that chamber, before all other males, and certainly before any female! Instead, you let a young cull like Naxk take the lead while you watched your huntmates bare their throats to death and did nothing!" He had lost the right to Challenge, but he knew suddenly that he could no longer just turn his eyes away and follow this one.

Humans did not always select the biggest or strongest

of their kind to lead. The Black/on/black had explained this repeatedly during training back at the base. They believed that experience, temperament, and intelligence counted at least as much as strength and size and speed.

Without warning, Skal blueshifted and was upon Kei. He stumbled backwards beneath both their weight, struck his head on the rock ledge and felt unconsciousness snarling like a huge black beast at his throat. He struggled to tear his way out of the encroaching darkness. Though he had been unworthy to offer Challenge himself, Skal had attacked first, as was his right. Kei was now fully justified in responding.

The joy of battle sang in his ears, or perhaps it was only the pounding of his blood, but it sounded and felt like pure joy. *This*, unlike all the drilling and following of pointless orders, *this*, he knew how to do. *This* was what all hrinn were meant for, from the day they first fought their way out of the nursery. He shook his head until his ears flapped, fought to see, all the while raking Skal's body with feet and handclaws.

The other bellowed with pain. The weight on his chest eased. Kei lurched onto his feet and blinked furiously. The air seemed hazy and he could only make out vague forms. Where was his opponent? He lashed out in wide arcs, unable to make solid contact.

A boot scraped to his left, toward the rock. He whirled and his foot caught on something heavy and limp—Bey's lifeless body. He stumbled, then, before he could recover his balance, Skal leaped on him again from above.

His opponent's teeth slashed at his throat. He felt the hot gush of his own blood soak his fur. Beaten again, he thought numbly, as he had been so many times at the claws of the Black/on/black. Clearly, whatever the name of this pattern, it did not mean for him to lead. Perhaps it was better to die honorably, so that others, more capable than he, could blaze the difficult trail before them. This war was so important. It was only a matter of time before the flek swept back over Anktan again. He felt it in his teeth and claws.

Then he heard Skal's sneering voice again in his mind. *"I say when we hunt and how, and the time is not now. Let the flek go back where it came from."* Skal wasn't the one to lead either. He probably wouldn't know this pattern if it bit him!

With a roar, he broke free and threw Skal off. The black-and-white rolled away, snarling, came up into a fighting crouch. His black eyes glittered at Kei in the dim morning light.

"If the time to hunt is not now," Kei said, "when will it be? Tomorrow? The next day? Or perhaps never?"

"We were few!" Skal skulked just out of reach. "The flek was armed. It had already cut everyone else down! Someone had to keep his head!"

"*We* were few?" Blood soaked Kei's neck and matted his fur. The hot, rich smell of it enraged him further. "It was only *one*, but now it will come back and bring thousands more! We could have stopped it before, but how will we now fight thousands? Did you understand nothing of what happened on Anktan? These are not honorable enemies who fight one to one. They war ship to ship, world to world!"

Skal charged Kei again, but this time Kei wrenched himself into blueshift. He had made no preparations, and was injured and exhausted. He would pay for it, he knew, was already paying for it, with the fearsome drain of cellular energy. The rocks and the sky and Bey's corpse were stained a shimmering deep blue and he was shockingly, dangerously cold. Skal's movements s l o w e d. Time stretched out. From his chill, blue perspective, he watched Skal's claws inch toward his neck and considered. He could duck aside, slash Skal's throat, shove him over the cliff or break his neck where he stood, but Skal's death would only reduce their numbers even further.

If you would be Leader, then lead! he told himself. He dropped back out of blueshift, sidestepped Skal and used the momentum of his charge to throw him, a Ranger trick, which did not require that one be tall or fast or brimming with energy.

Skal thudded heavily to the rock and Kei pressed bared teeth to the tender throbbing vein in the neck where the blood sang close to the surface. His black eyes held Skal's from above. "Yield," he said hoarsely, "or I will end this here and now!"

"I am Leader!" Skal struggled, but stopped when Kei slashed just deep enough to nick the vein. "You dishonored yourself, when you ran away! You saw how the squad turned away from you afterwards! They'll never follow you!"

Dishonor. He would never escape the taint. It would always be with him. He did not deserve to win. For a breath, he almost backed off, then an image rose up in his mind: *Kei, as he would have been, honorably dead in the cave at the flek's feet. No subsequent warning would have been given to the rest of the Rangers above. No Kei would have fought alongside the Black/on/black and Visht and Kika and Naxk. First Oleaaka, then perhaps Anktan would have been overrun.*

At last, he understood the choice he had made back there. "If I had stood and fought in the cave, when the flek first came through, I would have died honorably, just like Bey," Kei said. "Instead, I lived to fight another day and make the flek pay. Do you wish to do the same, or shall I grant you a thoroughly honorable death?"

Skal stilled beneath him. His breathing was ragged, the smell of his seeping blood overpowering. Kei had all he could do to stay his claws.

The former Leader turned his eyes away in the traditional gesture of surrender.

After Second Breeder lost the captured translator in the forest, he wandered about in the cool night shadows for a good long while, hoping to come across her cowering somewhere. She was damaged, after all, and probably in pain. How far could she go? Instead, he found nothing of interest except the other three errant breeders.

"Why didn't you go back into the cave?" he asked. "The crystal trees were singing again and it was bound to be glorious down there. Perhaps the colorless one even returned and would have told his secrets!"

Tenth Breeder looked to the other two. They dropped their dispirited gaze. Their hands drooped. Their shoulders were downcast. "We were afraid," Tenth said. "After what happened to Sixteenth, this isn't amusing anymore."

Thunder cracked. Dark, brooding clouds had drifted over the mountains and blotted out the nascent dawn. Second beat his forehands restlessly against his sides. "What happened to Sixteenth is not important," he said. "Like all of us, he would have been put down anyway, after the Feast of Leavetaking. What matters is that, by leaving, we finally have the chance to think exciting new thoughts, choose our own actions."

"I'm so hungry," Eighth said glumly. "I don't care about new things anymore. I just want to go back to the compound and eat."

"Then go!" Second brandished his alien light-stick, though he prudently kept his fingers off the protruding knobs that had activated it before. "I want to sing that new song I remembered, and make more songs! I want to . . . to . . . *attack* someone!" He savored the feel of that lovely new word.

He broke into his new song with its delightful bold

rhythms. After a moment's hesitation, the other three sang with him, and by the end, he could see their shoulders lifting.

"Now," he said, feeling larger and braver than ever before, "let's go back to the compound and take as much food as we like."

"Take food?" Tenth said.

"All the melons and shellfruits we want," cried Second, "as well as a gleaner and a translator to talk only for us! Then we'll go back down into the cave, wait for it to sing, and do whatever we like."

"I do want to touch the crystal trees again," said Tenth. "I could feel the life brimming in them. They spoke to me. I just don't understand yet what they are saying."

"You will," Second said solemnly, "just as I am remembering more of what we used to be with every step. I don't care what the keepers say. My body-memories make me think drones were not always the timid creatures we are today, and very soon we will find our true voices. The laka will have to listen to us then."

Chapter Twenty

A faint green-tinted light penetrated the forest canopy, though the morning clouds hung low and thick. Ninth Translator thought it would rain soon. Her cracked carapace throbbed with each step, but she did not spare herself. The violent ones had returned! No wonder the breeders were so disgusting and bold. In the space of a single night, all the laka's worst fears had sprung back to life.

And that furred one was hardly any better, with its brash manner, vicious teeth and claws. It had made the situation worse back at the ceremonial arena in that unseemly brawl with the runaway breeders. They had obviously been roused enough by its aggression to access some of their deeply buried body-memories passed down from long-ago progenitors. The cycle had begun again and there was only one place it could end, if the coordinators and translators did not act.

The colony had prevailed before, she kept telling herself, as she struggled down the winding gleaning trail. But the truth was, the ones who had been so clever were long dead. No one living had resolved these things, and, though all laka possessed relevant body-memories of that period, so did breeders. It worked both ways.

Low-hanging spikeleaves brushed her face, surrounding her with their cool spice, which usually would have given her pleasure. Now they only made her shake her head and chafe at the delay. The smell of imminent rain intensified, as though the air were about to overflow. Hurry. Hurry. She must summon the castes and organize what must be done. Everyone must act in concert before it was too late. Everyone!

The land dropped steadily; she was descending into the main bowl of the colony with its broad, moss-covered sweep and hatching tower at the center. Her heart swelled at the familiar sight. Gentle home, where everyone had her function and no one ever presumed to want more than she was given. How much longer would it survive?

Five small rose-colored builders, specialized for housing repairs, bustled toward her on their way to the forest to gather raw materials. She stopped and spoke to them in the preemptory mode. "Go back to the builder nests and summon your fellows to the communal area," she told them. "I have something important to say and it cannot wait."

They turned and each headed off in a different direction, having sorted out their destinations through subtle nuances of gesture anyone but a translator might have missed. She hurried on to intercept a trio of gleaners just leaving with woven baskets on their shoulders and directed them to spread the word among their own.

Each new caste she encountered turned aside from its current task and complied with her directives. By the time she reached the communal area with its great luminary trees, her side ached so that she could barely walk. One of her sister translators, Third, spotted her

distress and supported her until she had settled in a
shady hollow dug out of the earth. A processor brought
her a container of restorative nectar and a wedge of
sweetcane.

She ate slowly, letting the needed energy kindle within
as she waited for the colony to gather. Her mind roiled
with all she must relate. It was agonizing to be the source
of such terrible news, and yet they had to know.

What they would think, once they were told, she
could not even begin to say.

When Heyoka hauled Mitsu's limp body out of the
water, for a heart-stopping instant, he thought she was
dead. Her skin was cold and alabaster-pale, her lips
bloodless. He tilted her head back, brushed the wet hair
back out of her eyes, checked her pupils, her pulse.
She jerked, gulped in a ragged breath, then coughed
up so much water, he felt ill with guilt. His probing
fingers found a knot behind her ear that would have
rivaled an ostrich egg.

But she was alive. He held onto that.

Mindful of the flek, who must be pursuing, he carried
her into the deep silver-green of the rain forest, forcing
his way through thick stands of bushes and sapling trees
that grew close together until he found a secluded dell.
Unlike hrinn, flek were sight-hunters. Warrior-drones
didn't have an acute sense of smell, though they could
detect heat signatures. This spot dipped below the forest
floor though, and he doubted the two of them would
stand out to flek senses. They should be safe for a short
time.

Supporting her head, he eased her back onto a layer
of damp leaf mold, then parted her black hair to
examine the lump again. The swelling was receding,
slowly. Her pupils seemed equal though. He checked
her belt for the medkit, but it was nowhere in sight.

Nonregulation equipment for a flek, he supposed. They'd probably confiscated it, or perhaps she'd even cast it aside herself.

Wind whipped through the trees, tangled his mane over his eyes. Thunder rumbled, once, twice, then again. He gazed up through the tossing leaves. It was going to rain, definitely. He tied his mane back with a tuft of grass to keep it out of his face. His lips pulled back in a soundless snarl. Damnation. He hated getting wet.

Hunched under the dubious shelter of a tree that trembled when he touched its mottled bark, he retrieved the com from his own belt and keyed in a command code. "Montrose?"

A few feet away, Mitsu groaned. The fingers of one pale hand twitched.

He studied her still face, the dark lashes contrasted against her translucent skin, remembering that sobering day on Anktan when they had finally brought her to see him after the conclusive battle. He had been confined to a thermal pool, critically weak, suffering from blue-shift burnout, but she had been so thin, he'd thought he could see the cavern wall through her pitiful frame.

Her head turned. She murmured an indistinguishable word, then another. His heart raced. He prepared for the struggle that was bound to come when she covered consciousness, but then she quieted.

A dark-green vine slithered over his hand and he jerked away, cursing. The vine continued on, oblivious of his reaction. He turned his attention back to the com. Perhaps the elevation here was too low. The system should still be working through a tiny satellite they'd released upon arrival in the system from the ship, but if the flek fleet had made orbit, the satellite was probably history.

He might have to switch to the com's secondary terrestrial mode and then climb one of these sodding overgrown trees, not an enticing prospect, especially when they were prone to buck one off. He tried again. "Montrose? It's Blackeagle."

"Sarge?" Montrose's voice was faint and filled with static. *"We expected you guys back hours ago. Are you all right?"*

"Still kicking," Heyoka said. "Has Kei come back yet?"

"No." Montrose sounded worried. *"Isn't he with you?"*

"Long story," Heyoka said. He batted a tiny four-legged flyer out of his face. "I won't get into it right now, but I have retrieved Mitsu."

"Then she didn't go through the grid after all," Montrose said. Relief colored his voice.

"Unfortunately, I think she did, but she's back, along with at least a full unit of flek." He let Montrose digest that tidbit. "Move camp immediately and don't leave any trace behind. Find safer, less exposed ground."

"What about Kika?" Montrose said. *"She left camp about an hour ago. There's just Onopa and Naxk and me left, and Naxk is too bad off to move under her own power."*

"Kika can find you, wherever you go. Trust me on that. As for Naxk . . ." Heyoka hesitated. Humans always underestimated hrinnti stamina. "If she's still breathing, she can walk. You only have to ask her."

"Where should we hook up?" Montrose said. *"The beach, maybe, or somewhere in the forest?"*

Heyoka considered. "No," he said as the rain finally pelted against the leaves overhead, "meet us at the laka village."

A chill, driving rain made the climb back down the mountain torturous. Kei, favoring his burned palm, kept having to catch himself one-handed whenever he slipped, while Visht's shoulder made him stiff and prone to stumble. Lightning flashed a river of molten white fire across the brooding sky, and though he had never before been cold on this too-warm world, Kei was now. He ducked his head to keep the rain out of his eyes and thought longingly of Anktan's arid climate.

By the time they reached the cover of the trees below, their fur was sodden. Kei stalked along in front, feeling the other two behind. Visht remained as silent as ever, while Skal was a skulking, malevolent presence. Even the sound of his breathing infuriated Kei and he longed to whirl and rip the black-and-white's throat out, but Skal had yielded, and, for now, their numbers were too few for him to indulge in such a frivolous luxury. Maybe later, when they returned to Anktan . . .

By the time they reached the streamside clearing where they had left the others, he was longing for a fire. One flavored with gynth leaves, he thought sourly, though he'd smelled nothing the least bit like gynth on this world. At the very least, perhaps Kika or Onopa had hunted, and fresh game would be waiting.

The grass was trampled, but otherwise he saw no sign their fellow Rangers had ever been here. His ears flattened. Had they been captured or driven away?

Visht looked to him with expectant black eyes and he realized he was Leader now. He must decide what they would do next. "The com," he said and fished his unit out of his pocket. Onopa's code? He wracked his brain. The rain streamed down and he felt like a fool, standing there, trying to remember something as stupid as a string of numbers.

"Over here," Visht said suddenly. "I've found their trail, though it's almost washed out. They've taken a lot of care to erase their tracks."

"Any sign of flek?"

"No," Visht said. His yellow mane clung to his neck. He looked like a half-drowned cubling.

Kei joined him and cast about for spoor himself. "Did they all leave together?"

Nose twitching, Visht quartered the verge. "All but Kika. She left sometime earlier. Her trail is even more faint and heads down toward the sea."

"Stupid female!" Skal threw back his head and snorted his dismissal.

Kei whirled and, open-clawed, struck him to the muddy bank. "She is your huntmate now, and a fellow Ranger. You will give her your respect!"

Red-orange blood welled in the claw marks across Skal's neck, then washed away in the rain. He snarled, but did not lift his eyes. Visht stood back impassively, gazing over both their heads, studying the trees beyond the stream as though they were brimming with game.

"We must catch up," Kei said, "and find out what they know. They may have had word from the Black/ on/black, or perhaps the ship has come back." He swiveled his head. "Is there any sign of him?"

"No," Visht said, "only his trail from when he left with us."

Skal pushed himself up from the mud. His handclaws were flexed and Kei could smell his eagerness to fight. Kei loomed above him. "Do not even consider it," he said. "We cannot afford the time it would take for me to spare your life—again. This time, if you come at me, I'll rip out your throat and leave your bones for the scavengers."

Skal did not meet his eyes, but defiance was obvious in every rigid line of his body.

"Why did you come here?" Kei asked suddenly. He clenched his hands to keep from striking Skal again. "Why did you join the Rangers, if you had no wish to follow the Black/on/black and honor his ways? We knew it would be strange and difficult, but most of us fought at his side on Anktan. We had smelled the flek and knew they were real, that the pattern which had brought him back to us was huge and all-pervading, so no one was outside its influence. But your males' house did not answer the Black/on/black's call. You weren't there with us on the plains that night, so I do not understand why you volunteered."

Skal did not answer.

"He was cast out," Visht said, his voice unexpected in the silence.

"What?" Even wet, the fur bristled along Kei's neck.

"For random killing," Visht said. "They said he craved the smell of blood—hrinnti blood."

Skal lunged to his feet and stood, head hanging, sides heaving with emotion.

"How do you know this?" Kei asked slowly.

"As a Priest of the Voice," Visht said, "I visited many of the males' houses along the river valley that summer before the Black/on/black returned from the stars. My fellow priests, scattered throughout the valley, thought *something/in/motion* was in the first stages of pulling itself together, something vast and powerful. Many hrinn felt it and I was trying to learn its name before it was upon us."

Skal lowered his ears and the look in his eyes was haunted.

"At the Vandd Peak Males' House, there was much talk of a young black-and-white who had killed twice without any hint of Challenge." Visht's eyes glinted. "He had been chased away and would have been slaughtered on sight had he ever dared return. I heard similar tales at the next two males' houses. A rogue, they called him, throwback to the days of chaos, totally without honor."

"Then why didn't you tell the Black/on/black?" Kei said. "Why let him go off-world with us?"

"Many are marked with black and white. I had no proof," Visht said, "only suspicions, until now."

Visht hadn't revealed himself either, Kei realized with a start. The Black/on/black was not overly fond of priests, having been forced to Challenge and kill one before the Council would listen to his request to join him in fighting the flek.

He looked at Skal. His wet fur was plastered to his body, so that he looked much smaller. Kei tried to decide what he felt about this shocking new bit of information. Anktan was far away. He himself had been raised outside of many hrinnti conventions, and none among them could be spared, if he could be put to use.

"It doesn't matter what you did before," he said finally to Skal. "Humans don't care about the same things important to hrinn. This is an entirely new pattern and all that counts is what you do from now on. Just keep your head down and follow orders!"

Skal flicked an ear, signifying he had heard. Satisfied, Kei waded across the stream and followed his fellow squadmates' trail into the forest.

Kika finally found an outcropping of rock overlooking the black sand beach that would suit her purpose. She had known from earliest memory that she possessed the potential for healing. Restorers cropped up in the Jhii Lineage from time to time, as they did in all Lines, but Jhii had always considered them self-indulgent failures, contributing nothing to the continuation and improvement of the Line.

The first time she had produced a fat blue spark at the end of one claw, she had still been in the nursery. It had seemed a marvel to her, something wonderful and alive, all her own. Upon learning of it though, the current Line Mother, old Menn, had ordered her beaten until she couldn't move. As she lay bleeding at the Line Mother's feet, she was told Jhii did not breed cublings only to have them stolen by the Restorers.

She had come very close to dying that day and her ribs still bore the scars. Even now, she trembled at the memory. In order to survive, she'd learned to suppress any hint of the ability to accumulate power, though it had been difficult to ignore the energy simmering through her nerves whenever she had been out too long hunting in the sun on a torrid day.

Then last year, on one such day, she had been unwary enough to lose control after an exhausting hunt and loose a spark in the presence of two of her huntmates. As dutiful daughters of Jhii, they had told the new Line Mother, and she, in a fit of white-hot rage, had gone after Kika herself. The thought of being Challenged by the Line Mother was so stunning that she had given too much ground and not fought well. Only the intervention of the Black/on/black, who had been there recruiting for the Rangers, had preserved her life.

But this was another place, another time, and there was no one else here, human or hrinn, who could do what must be done. As Onopa had pointed out, events now unfolding were undoubtedly part of *stars/over/stars* and new things must be attempted. She had left Jhii and crossed the stars. Now Naxk and Onopa, and even Kei, Visht, and Skal were her Line. If Naxk died, it would be her fault. Though she had no training, she had seen this done upon more than one occasion when Restorers had treated residents of Jhii. She must at least try.

First, she had to draw power. The best source would have been a thermal spring, but this was an alien world with a very different geology, and she had seen no such spring here. The next best source was the sun, and it would shine again today. She was sure of that. Though it rained often here, since they arrived, it never went on for long. Already, the downpour seemed to be fading into mere drizzle. If she waited, the sunlight would blaze down again, feeding the special cells in her body.

She would absorb as much as she could, then go back and see what could be done for young Naxk.

Second Breeder led the other three until they found a lone gleaner working in a grove close to the compound. Her carapace was dull orange, quite unremarkable, and she was undersized as well. He rushed forward to block her path. She hesitated, a stalk of sweetcane, green outside, white within, held in one hand. Her placid pink eyes flickered from his face to those behind him, but she did not speak.

The reasons gleaners did not use the same dialect as breeders, Second decided suddenly, was that they were too stupid. Breeders were obviously much the superior caste. He darted forward and seized the sweetcane out of her hand. She cried out, then fell back, shaken.

He bit off a chunk, then passed it to Tenth Breeder. It tasted glorious, much better than anything he'd ever eaten. Tenth ate a bite, then gave the rest to the other two. They squabbled over it, each demanding to be first, and that was almost better than the food.

The gleaner tried to creep away, but Second charged and bowled her over. The blood sang through his head as she lay on her side, crying out, legs and arms waving in distress.

"How silly," said Tenth, who was growing more bold. He edged closer and peered down at her. "Why doesn't she just get up?"

"She's afraid," said Sixteenth. Green sweetcane juice dribbled from his jaws. "She thinks we'll hurt her."

"Well, I certainly will!" said Second. "I'll *attack* her, if she gets up again!"

"But she has to get up, if she's going to bring us food," said Tenth. "I'm still hungry. What else does she have in her basket?"

Eighth and Twenty-seventh crowded the trembling gleaner and sorted through the basket's contents, which yielded several small shellfruits and a bluemelon. Second snatched the melon and let the others divide the rest. They complained, but ate their share anyway.

"Now," said Second to the mewling gleaner, "I've changed my mind. You can get up and find us some more food."

Instead, she closed her eyes and buried her face in her forearms.

"I don't think she understands," said Eighth. "She still believes you're going to hurt her."

"I will, if she doesn't find us some food!" He picked up a sharp-edged rock. The weight of it felt wonderful in his hand and he lobbed it at her shoulder. It only bounced off, so he bent to sort through the undergrowth and find a larger one.

"Wait," said Twenty-seventh. "Right now we only need a translator. If you damage her, then we'll still have to find both another gleaner and a translator."

That made sense. As diverting as *attacking* was, Second was forced to be practical. "All right. Stay here and watch this gleaner. Do not let her return to the colony. I will move in closer to the compound, hide, and secure a translator as soon as one happens by. Then we'll have everything we need."

"This is one of the main trails into the compound," said Eighth. "If we stay here, someone is sure to come along, maybe even a keeper. Then we'll have to go back."

"All right," Second said. "Take her to the ruins in the forest then. They aren't far away. I'll meet you there."

Chapter Twenty-One

Water dripped, dripped, dripped onto her face. Mitsu brushed at it with the back of her hand, but the irritating trickle continued. She was hot and sticky, as well as soaked, and lying on the ground, she realized. Had she bunked down in a damn creek bed?

Her eyes flew open and she stared bewilderedly up at silver-backed leaves and tightly interwoven limbs shifting in the wind. The air was redolent with mud and leaf mold and rotting wood, which struck her as wonderful for some reason. Rain pattered against the leafy canopy above and a small percentage of the errant drops were working their way through and hitting her in the face. She turned her head away and tried to think. This was obviously a forest, so she must be in the field somewhere on patrol. But on what world? The air didn't smell like Earth or Anktan or Enjas Two. And where was furface?

When she raised up on her elbows to look, blinding pain stabbed through her head and she slumped back to the waterlogged ground with a strangled moan. Heyoka's face swam into her field of vision.

"Lie still," he said in that familiar rumbly voice of his. "You took in some water when I snatched you from the flek, and then there was this rock—"

The flek? She massaged her aching forehead, trying to think.

"Can you still speak Standard?" His voice sounded strained. "You were entrenched with a flek unit just outside the cave, speaking High-Flek again like a native."

"Flek?" She couldn't make it come together. "Come off it. What would I be saying to a stupid flek?"

"You tell me."

"I—" She had an intense flash of a poisonous yellow sky, the everpresent stink of sulphur, a relentless red sun. Her heart lurched into overdrive as memory flooded back. "I went through the grid after that tech," she said in surprise. Why hadn't she killed it on the other side? She massaged her throbbing temples. Surely she'd meant to take it out.

His black eyes were enigmatic, but she thought she read worry in them, or perhaps even fear. "What happened?" he said. "How did you persuade it to transport you back here?"

The oddly shaped pieces were jumbled inside her head and some of them seemed to be missing altogether. "I lost my rifle," she said. She remembered being so afraid, she couldn't breathe, the bitter flatness of the water they'd provided in the flek city, how the Decider had looked at her. Had it known she was faking? Why hadn't it just done away with her on the spot? A great shudder wracked her body and for a second she was trapped in that white room again, and trapped as well in a human body. She stretched a trembling hand out to touch the wall and it faded.

"I realize it's not your fault, but I have to know," Heyoka said. "What did you tell them? Do they know how few we are here?"

The shattered pieces of her memory drifted just out of reach, refusing to assume their correct shape. "Where are we?" She didn't seem to be able to make linear connections between his questions and the proper answers, as though all her thoughts were being rerouted along safer passages and she had to arrive at the desired information by circuitous means.

"We're in the rain forest halfway up the mountain, close to the laka village," he said. He took her face between his hands and tried to make her meet his fathomless onyx gaze.

The silkiness of his fur against her skin was startling. For a moment, she recoiled. *Flek didn't touch each other that way*, her traitorous subconscious whispered. But she wasn't flek, she told herself. She didn't have to abide by flek rules.

"What did you tell them?"

She jerked free, then struggled up to her hands and knees. All-Father, but her head ached! "How did I get here?"

"I told you—I stole you out from under their noses," he said. "Look, we don't have time for this. I've designated the village as our rally point, so we can rendezvous with Montrose, Onopa, and Naxk, but before we go, I need as much information as possible so I can plan. What do the flek want here? Why have they come back after all this time? Are they going to reoccupy Oleaaka?"

"They came because of me," she said. Rain dripped down her neck and she shivered, even though the forest was a steam bath. "I told them I had hidden information here, so we came back for it."

A silent snarl wrinkled his forehead. "What information?"

"There—isn't any."

"Right," he said. "You brought them all the way back here for information that doesn't exist."

"I made it up," she said unsteadily. "I could, because I didn't lose myself this time."

"Sure," he said and pulled her to her feet. Her knees buckled and he took her weight. "Come on. You can rest, once we get to the village, then maybe you'll be able to make more sense."

"The laka village?" Pinwheels of light were bursting behind her eyes like fireworks—red and green and *white*. Like the *room* on Anktan. She flinched. "They won't go there, the flek. They're—"

"What?" His black eyes pierced her soul.

"They're afraid of them," she said unsteadily. Her stomach was on the point of rebelling. She felt so sick, she could hardly see. She blotted the cold sweat on her forehead with the back of her sleeve. "The flek think they're 'perverted.' They're afraid to talk to them or even listen to anything they say."

"Why?" Heyoka bent down to maintain eye contact. "Mitsu, this is important! You've got to remember!"

"I—don't—know why," she said. The trees spun and she pressed the heels of her hands over her eyes. So dizzy.

Heyoka picked her up. He'd lost his shirt somewhere in the last day and her cheek was pressed to the familiar musk of his fur. "I didn't lose myself," she whispered into the plush blackness. "I held on this time."

"It doesn't matter," he said, but his voice was fading. "Just tell me what . . ."

But it was too late. She couldn't hear him anymore. For such a long time back in Rehab, she would have given anything to hear his voice again, but now it was just too bloody late.

The warrior-drones remained quite agitated after the furred beast abducted the Enemy-born spy. World-Architect 549 had stood back as six of them plunged into the cold water and attempted to retrieve it. The current was swift, though, and the stream bed studded with rocks. Two of the largest warriors were swept into boulders at the fall line and damaged themselves going over. The rest detoured around and swarmed down the cliff.

The architect had followed at a safe distance, curious to see if they would recover the creature. By the time they reached the pool below, though, both the furred one and the Enemy had disappeared into the forest.

Warrior-Drone 21487, who had been assigned command of this phalanx, was furious enough to tear off the head of the unfortunate drone who was closest at that point. The neck joints gave with a dreadful snap, then he cast the skull into the water and watched it bob downstream out of sight. The headless body fell to the bank and spasmed.

The architect sat back on his haunches, mildly disapproving. Wasteful of their limited resources, he thought. That drone might have proved useful later on. 21487 should have been practical and killed one of the damaged ones instead. "Before we return, I must take readings at the former site of the environmental engines," he said.

"No!" 21487 said. His red eyes had a terrible, wild look. "I cannot spare an escort. We must recover the spy unit!"

The architect took care to remain well out of reach. "I believe the Deciders may be quite pleased with my findings, upon our return, and therefore with you too. With what I've already recorded, my preliminary readings suggest it may be possible to tip the balance here in our favor with less commitment of resources than previously calculated."

"And what will you do if the perverted ones approach?" the warrior said.

"Only one has presented itself so far," the architect said. "And it ran away without attempting to speak. Much time has passed since Makers walked this world. Perhaps *they* are afraid of *us* now."

The warrior hesitated, and the architect turned his head away, giving the commander a chance to work through the variables. It was a well-known fact that warriors, bred for fighting, were poor at making decisions outside of combat conditions. And that was as it should be. Decision-making was, of course, the province of Deciders. Architects, however, were bred with a fair amount of leeway in their mental parameters. Creative world design required unfettered thinking and an eye for possibilities. His kind had to be able to see beyond the moment and manipulate abstractions, as well as project viable alternatives.

"The Deciders will be displeased, if you do not recover the spy," said the architect, "but they might be persuaded to overlook the loss, if I have more interesting matters for them to consider. And, if we return later in force, the spy might be recovered more easily then."

The warrior-drone's front hands clenched. It squared up both pairs of shoulders. "Take ten drones as your escort. The rest will search with me for the spy. We will meet back at the transfer grid, when all objectives have been achieved."

That might be a very long time, in the case of the departed spy, the architect thought, though he prudently did not voice this. Ten of the guards fell in as he headed downstream.

Ninth Translator, waiting beneath a luminary tree in the compound's center, heard numerous reports of the approaching aliens before she actually saw them. Fortunately, there were only two, returning scouts said. They were of widely divergent somatic types, both very strange. She wondered if this meant the aliens had finally succeeded in differentiating their body types. That would signal a marked step forward in their social development. They might actually become civilized.

The gentle rain filtering through the great tree's leaves was soothing, but her side ached so that she could hardly remain still. Longing for the moment she could lay down her life, she had to concentrate to turn her attention from her fear of the violent ones and focus on this new development.

One of the aliens was quite tall, covered with luxurious black fur, walking on two legs, rather than four. It carried in its arms a second alien, small and delicate, nearly as devoid of hair as a laka, but as soft of skin and defenseless as a hatchling. As the two drew closer, she realized she had encountered them both before, though separately.

The entire colony was gathering, waiting for what she had to say. Cultivators and gleaners scattered out of the furred one's path as it descended into the communal area. Why had it come here, she wondered numbly. Why didn't it just go back to its own world? Didn't they have enough problems as it was?

It laid its burden down beside her, arranging the head and limbs with what seemed to be great care, almost with the tenderness of a keeper, she thought.

"Why come?" she asked, using her limited command of its language.

It regarded her with glittering black eyes, then spoke. Most of the sound combinations it used were unfamiliar, but she did extract one bit of meaning out of the vocal stream—"help."

Did it want laka help? Or was it offering to "help" them? From what she had seen already, its notion of "help" would doubtless be forceful and violent, and that would be of no use at all. The breeders needed to be soothed, not encouraged in their current path. And as for the disharmonious ones, violence would not work there either.

"We must handle this ourselves," she said in laka. "You cannot do what must be done. Only we can."

It shook its head.

"No help," she told it in what little she had of its language. "Go back. We help."

It spoke again, but she understood nothing. This was getting them nowhere and she had so little strength left, she needed to save it for what lay ahead.

The smaller one stirred, dragged an arm over its face and sat up. Its eyes weren't black, like its companion's, but a startling combination of blue nested within white. It seemed weak, though there were no overt cracks in what she could see of its outer covering. Perhaps its injuries weren't serious.

Everyone was watching Ninth Translator-at-large now, sanitizers and coordinators, gleaners and scouts, keepers and even a few of the rounded-up breeders. She gazed out at the sea of bodies and faces. They were so beautiful, she thought, each giving her or his best to the colony, never asking for more. In a way, they were like a song, each caste contributing its particular note. The laka could not give up what they had worked so hard to establish on this gentle world. Somehow in the past, they had made the violent ones listen before. They must do it again.

"Wise ones," she said, speaking first in the coordinators' dialect, "the disharmonious invaders have returned. I have seen them myself."

A wave of disquiet ran through the assembled coordinators. The other castes waited patiently. They would be told all they needed to know when the moment was right.

Fourteenth Coordinator pushed forward, accompanied

by her full retinue. Both pairs of her shoulders were set with determination. "Then the proper songs must be sung at once."

"Yes," Ninth said. "And the breeders should be shut away, lest they become further agitated."

"Have they all been brought in?" Fourteenth Coordinator asked.

"No," Ninth said. "One small group is still at large. They dragged me away and held me against my will for a short time, though I was able to escape. I fear the four of them have veered too far out of synchronization and will have to be put down as soon as they can be located."

"That must wait," Fourteenth Coordinator said. "First we will attend to the violent ones. Then we must find some way to destroy that wretched cave. We gave up before and sealed it from without. We should have made sure there was no way they could ever come back."

"But who knows the songs?" Ninth asked wearily. She stared out at the gathered multitude of simple workers. Their pastel sides shimmered in the rain and they gazed back, as yet uncomprehending. "Which of those among us can we ask to go to these creatures?"

"You will go, child," Fourteenth Coordinator said, "as will I; we all will, coordinators, gleaners, sanitizers, scouts. This song is woven through our very blood and it will come to you at the proper moment."

"You must be mistaken," Ninth said, trembling. "I know every dialect of the colony, but I do not remember any such song."

"Your body remembers," Fourteenth said. "When the time comes, you will know what to sing."

The knowledge was hidden within body-memories then. Ninth hung her head and tried not to think about how very tired she was, how her cracked side ached and life fluids were hemorrhaging beneath her carapace. It was strange how one might contain things never suspected in the mundanities of day to day life, how one might well be larger than she ever suspected.

"Instruct the keepers to seclude the breeders," said Fourteenth Coordinator. "Then we will go to the cave."

Several of her sister translators took up Fourteenth Coordinator's instructions, repeating them first in the gleaners' dialect, then in all the others, one by one. With a sigh, Ninth gathered her feet beneath her and went to the keepers, who were doing their best to restrain the headstrong breeders.

"Rest now," she told them as their pink eyes rolled and their feet shifted restlessly. "You had a long, tiring night without food. Stay here with your keepers, feast on bluemelon, and all will be well."

A chunky young breeder with a carapace of such a dark pink, it was almost red, advanced upon her with far too much assurance in the jaunty set of his head. "We refuse to be shut away in the darkness anymore. We want to run through the forest on our own, go wherever we will!" Several more breeders crowded in behind him and pressed close upon Ninth. "There are things," he said importantly, "that we were meant to do."

Appalled, she backed up, as the dismayed keepers surged forward to deal with their unruly charges. "I—

Behind her, the shorter alien cried out in surprise, then turned to the furred one and rattled something off in their own choppy language. Ninth could not separate out more than one or two words—something about "speaking" and "Flek," whatever that meant.

The furred one snarled.

Mitsu was flushed. "It's speaking flek, I tell you!"

Heyoka felt the fur bristle across his shoulders. Could she possibly be right, or, more likely, was she just disoriented, as when she'd fired upon defenseless civilians?

The sea of laka swung their gaze to him, to both of them, and he realized a snarl had escaped his throat. He forced his *other* to quiet. "Are you sure?" he said as evenly as he could manage.

"Damn right I'm sure!" Mitsu darted forward, then swayed and had to catch herself on the tree trunk. Her face went pale as watered milk. He could see cold sweat on her brow. "And I was right the first time back there in the grove too! They *are* flek!"

"We've been over this before," he said. "They *resemble* flek, just like some alien sentients are humanoid, but not human. Form follows function and all that."

"And I'm telling you that laka just spoke High-Flek!" She was breathing too fast, perhaps having another breakdown right before his eyes. Two hectic spots of red bloomed in her cheeks.

"All right," he said, desperate to divert her attention. "Calm down. I believe you."

"You do?"

"Sure, shortstuff." He gestured at her as the sun broke out from behind the clouds and the rain drizzled a last, few rainbow-tinted drops. "Now sit down, before you fall down, and stop frightening the locals."

"We have to get off this world," she said, "and report back to Command. This planet is crawling with flek, and has been for years!"

"Yeah," he said, "we'll do that." And all the while, he was trying to decide what to do. She'd obviously flipped out again. Being wrenched through the grid, then trapped on a flek world, for heaven's sake, would make anyone crazy. If she hadn't been over the edge before, she certainly was now.

"We have to rendezvous with Montrose and Onopa," he said. "Let's pick a point out in the forest and meet there."

"No," she said, "you already said they were coming

to the village. Besides, I want to question the laka and find out why they never told the Confederation anthropologists they were really flek."

"Not now!" he said. Her right hand twitched downward and he eyed her boot sheath with worry. She'd lost her rifle somewhere along the way, but she probably still had that damn knife. If so, with her experience and training, she could carve up half this village and never break a sweat.

"Yes, *now*." She released the tree and tottered toward the pale-green individual who'd spoken to them earlier.

The laka looked up and he realized this was the same one he'd met in the forest.

Mitsu started to speak, but he took her arm and jerked her back. "Don't tip our hand!" he said in a low urgent voice before she could protest. "Think! They've been covering for the flek for years and we're stranded behind enemy lines. Don't blow what little advantage we have."

She blinked, seeming to consider what he was saying, as though it made sense. "I—"

A green bolt of laser fire sizzled through the air, scalding the edge of Heyoka's boot and carving a deep fissure in the towering tree. The trunk convulsed as he and Mitsu both dove for cover, but the laka just stood there, frozen, uncomprehending. A familiar, telltale nose-burning stink permeated the air and his hands itched for a weapon.

"Get down!" he called, even though he doubted the laka understood. He groped for the com unit on his belt and punched in Montrose's code.

"*Sarge?*" Montrose's voice said. "*We're almost within sight of the village, but I thought I heard laser fire just a minute ago. Are you all right?*"

"Take every precaution on your approach," Heyoka said. "We're pinned down by flek fire."

Chapter Twenty-Two

Kei took the point as they entered the rain forest and the three of them matched one another stride for stride in silence. High overhead, wind whispered through the leaves, laden with exotic scents that had no analogs in their homeland. Except for that and the sultriness of the air, Kei mused they might have been hunting in a wooded area back on Anktan, each reading the body language of the others, for once in perfect accord.

Visht had assumed the second position, backup to the Leader, while Skal, bleeding and chastened, brought up the rear. Yet that position was important, Kei thought, ducking a low-hanging limb, as were all the elements of any successful hunt. None of those selected could afford to be weak, and certainly none could be spared.

Occasionally, something slithered out of their path into the dark-green brush as they approached. At first, Kei had thought these to be small animals, but upon closer examination, the source usually turned out to be plants, either scurrying or creeping aside, another indication this was not home. His hackles rose. Very strange.

His com unit buzzed and he realized he'd thrust it into a pocket while they were up on the mountain, sitting vigil for Bey. His heart leaped. He stopped and dug it out, then keyed it on. "Black/on/black?"

"No, it's me, Montrose," a human voice answered. *"I've heard from Blackeagle though. Is this Kei?"*

"Yes." Kei's ears flattened. He had never much liked talking into these foolish mechanical devices. It felt too much like conversing with a piece of wood or rock for his taste.

"Where are you?"

"We're in the forest, following your trail," Kei said. He gestured at Visht and Skal to come closer and listen.

"Then you can't be far." Montrose hesitated. *"Black-eagle and Corporal Jensen are pinned down by flek fire at the laka village. Can you hear anything from your position?"*

Then the flek had already come back. Kei swiveled his ears and listened hard. The rain had eased, and, above the whisper of the wind, the susurration of leaf against leaf, it seemed he did hear a distant crackle. "Yes," he said, "but it's very faint."

"Move up and join us from the north," Montrose said. *"Then we'll go in together and relieve Blackeagle."*

Kei's lips wrinkled back in an automatic snarl. He was Leader! He would decide what was to be done!

But then he caught himself. They couldn't afford to settle matters of dominance now. Too much was at stake. Whoever was to be Leader, they were all Rangers and the Black/on/black was under attack. "Yes," he said shortly. "Give me your position."

"We're in a low marshy area by a pond at the far end of the village," Montrose said. *"From here, we can see a ring of those big trees with the leathery leaves*

*that glow at night rising up out of a clearing. We'll sit
tight and wait for you. Naxk can't move that fast anyway, and neither can I. Just follow our trail."*

Kei switched the com unit off. He could hear the
sizzle of laser fire more clearly now. They had to hurry.
"This way," he said to the other two and crashed
through the undergrowth.

Kika sat on the rock, fur plastered to her body by the
rain, staring out at the restless aquamarine ocean. It was
always in motion, like something alive and stalking its
prey. The white-frothed waves rolled in and in and in.
She could hear them only faintly with her damaged ears,
but the rhythm possessed an enormously soothing quality.

When the rain finally stopped, she raised her head
to the thinning gray clouds, then stripped off the rest
of the confining wet uniform and laid it aside. Yes, she
thought as the first rays of the yellow sun broke through
and warmed her soaked fur. The welcome heat tingled
through her, down into the smallest spaces between,
where she was ordinarily never warm. The glorious
sensation built, fierce and exciting at the same time,
as though a wondrous flame were being kindled within
her core.

She tilted her head back, closed her eyes, let the sun
pour down on her, panting excess heat away as it built
up. There had been days, running between the House
of one Line and the next to carry messages, when she
could not avoid the sun's effect. Power had simmered
along her nerves and through her muscles, until it
seemed she would burst trying to contain it. But she had
never mentioned it, never let anyone see the faintest
manifestation of it again, after that first nearly fatal
incident in her cubhood until that last fateful day.

Well-being surged through her now. She felt more
whole than she had ever felt in her entire life. The pain

of her bruises faded from her consciousness, her wrenched leg, the ache in her ears. She was drifting along in a river of molten sunshine—

Her com unit buzzed. Not now, she thought. Not when the sun was pouring down over her back and shoulders, filling her to the brim. The warmth was tingling, electric, driving out the lingering physical misery of the last few days.

The link buzzed again, and she realized with a start that she could *hear* it, not faintly, as though muffled with layers of cloth, but clear and sharp. She put a wondering hand to her ear, then picked up the soggy uniform pants and extracted the com unit button from their pocket. "Yes?"

"Kika? Blackeagle and Jensen are under attack in the laka village." It was Montrose's husky voice.

Her ears pricked and she stared back over her shoulder at the trees. "On my way!"

"We've moved from the camp by the stream into the forest," Montrose said. *"Let me give you directions to our current position and we'll rendezvous."*

"There is no need," she said, bundling the wet clothing underneath one arm. "Unless you flew, I will find you."

There was great consternation on the seaward side of the compound, so Second Breeder circled around and approached from the opposite direction, using first the vine corral, then the shellfruit arbor to screen his path. The mottled-green vines shifted restlessly as he passed, but no one else seemed to pay him any heed at all.

As he entered the concentric circles of thatched nests, bolts of the alien's marvelous green fire sizzled through the air. He heard cries of pain, saw gleaners and builders dashing back and forth without the sense to *take cover*.

Someone was *attacking*! How delightful! He still had the alien's deadly stick and wondered if perhaps it would allow him to *attack* too. Rising from the deepest recesses of his mind, he had fleeting images of other *battles*, they were called, other *wars*. This was evidently what breeders had been allowed to do in earlier times, not merely sit about the compound, complacently eating and growing, waiting for that final day when they would finally be allowed to fertilize a selection of viable egg sacs. They were supposed to fire *weapons*, kill *enemies*, *rend* heads from bodies! Long buried concepts and words flooded into his consciousness and he felt *armed* and ready for anything.

He quivered as he edged forward, straining to see the source of the brief flashes of electric green *fire*. White chitin glimmered in the sun. It was the others, he realized, the ones who had long ago made the crystal forest in the cave. By their scent, they were all male, like himself, but so forceful, so potent. He could not wait to tell his fellow breeders back at the ruins about this!

Then he thought of his *mission*—to *capture* a translator, so that they could speak through her to their gleaner and complete their plans for a new colony. What a perfect time to *steal* one. The compound was in complete disorder. The coordinators hadn't reached consensus evidently, so the other castes were milling without direction. The keepers kept trying to herd the young males back into the nests, but their charges were resisting and he was certain, in the midst of this disorder, no one would pay much attention to yet another stray breeder.

Second slipped through hysterical knots of sanitizers and cultivators, keeping his gaze down, affecting to be frightened. He wasn't afraid though; he was stimulated. This was exhilarating, wondrous. He'd never felt so utterly present and involved in his entire life.

The translators were busy directing the colony's evacuation in the absence of coordinator instructions, and he could find none who were alone. The *weapons fire* was fiercest towards the compound's center, so he worked his way in that direction, using nest walls for *cover*, avoiding the *line of fire*. He gripped his *weapon* stick with great care, considered adding his contribution to the melee, but, as exciting as that would have been, it would also have drawn attention, and he was not ready for that yet.

The furred alien, who had shown itself back at the ceremonial arena to be quite good at *combat*, had taken to the moss-covered ground and was now crawling toward the nearest circle of nests. With that move, the *angle* of the *cross fire* which had it pinned down was much less efficient. Second Breeder caught himself watching the *tactics* of the two forces with admiration, when he should have been working toward his *objective*.

The other alien, the smaller one with only a bit of dark fur on its head, had gone to ground too and was heading in the opposite direction. Something long and metallic caught the sunlight and glinted in its hand. The two of them were going to *flank* the *enemy*, Second realized with delight.

Beneath the leaf shadow of a tall luminary lay a single translator, head back, eyes closed, gasping with the effort to breathe. She was an odd shade of pale green and the plate on her side was damaged. He looked closer; his fellow breeders had cracked that carapace only the day before! Second regarded the injury with a fond sense of recognition.

The two aliens *drew* most of the *incoming fire*, and by watching the patterns carefully, Second was able to advance step by step, always keeping to *cover*, once even using the smoking carcass of a scout. It was so exciting, he had all he could do to make himself stop, once he'd reached his goal.

The translator did not open her eyes as he approached, not even when he hunkered down beside her, watching the surrounding trees and the deadly rain of green *fire*. Smoke and the stench of burned bodies permeated the air. He leaned over and prodded her with his alien stick. "Get up!"

"No," she said wearily, still not opening her eyes, "do not attempt to move me. This position should prove safe enough."

"I don't care about 'safe'!" Second Breeder reared back, swung the *weapon* and struck her injured side. Flecks of shattered green carapace flaked off in a very satisfactory fashion at the blow. She squalled with shock and pain.

"Get up!" he said.

Her eyes flew open and she shrank at the sight of him.

He loomed over her, relishing the sensation. "If you don't get up, I will *strike* you again!"

Her pink eyes swirled with fear. "I cannot!" she said hoarsely. "I am injured and will die, if I move!"

"I think you can," he said. "And I don't care if you die."

She trembled. "Where do you want me to go?"

"Away from here," he said, "so we breeders can start our own colony."

"But, *this* is our colony." Her head swiveled as she gazed around at the familiar surroundings, the luminaries, the circular rows of nests, the carefully tended berry arbors and shellfruit patches, the vine corral. "There is no other."

"Now there will be." He gave her first-arm a savage jerk and her jaws gaped at his daring. "This one no longer suits us."

She nervously eyed his *weapon*. "But breeders have the best food, the softest, quietest nests. You do no work and are served by all. One entire caste devotes their lives to your welfare. What more could you want?"

"We don't know yet," he said, "but we are going to find out. Get up, or I will *hurt* you again!" He found himself hoping she would refuse just so he could *strike* her one more time.

Evidently reading his intention, she shuddered and managed to lurch to her feet.

The *firing* seemed to have shifted away from this end of the village for the moment. He calculated the best *escape route*. "This way!" He pulled her roughly by the arm toward the far end of the compound.

"I don't understand," she whispered, more to herself than him, as they wove through the abandoned dwellings. "What could you want out there on your own? What could you do?"

He did not answer. He was too busy thinking about all the delicious possibilities this experience had opened up in his mind. More deeply buried body-memories were surfacing with every breath.

He wasn't sure what they wanted in the end, but they would begin by taking whatever, and whomever, they wished.

Green death blazed through the air in a wide arc from the east. Heyoka recognized the standard star firing pattern; he'd encountered it a thousand times on other worlds, other battlefields. But in those distant places, the flek had been pitted against seasoned soldiers. Here, there were only himself and Mitsu, both unarmed, except for knives, and the clueless laka who were being cut down in droves.

The smell of scorched flesh and burning thatched walls was overpowering. He kept his head down and

crawled across the moss, seeking better cover. Mitsu had
dived in the other direction, properly dividing the flek
fire just as she had been trained, strange behavior for
one who had just been through the flek mill again and
had to be thoroughly brainwashed.

According to Montrose, the rest of the squad was
rallying at his current location in the forest. Though
some of them were injured, most still had laser rifles,
but it would take time for them to arrive. By then,
it would probably be too late, for him and Mitsu, and
for the village. He had to take action now, but he
needed a weapon. For the hundredth time that day,
he cursed himself for being careless enough to lose
his.

A laser bolt caught another helpless laka and it went
down a few feet from him, screaming and clawing at
its burned shoulder. He flinched, remembering what
it was like to take the full brunt of a flek bolt. He had
been wounded in a battle on Enjas Two last year, taking
a serious burn to the knee and leg. He'd endured
months of rehabilitation afterward, and even that had
proved insufficient until he'd received a unique restorative
treatment from his own species.

He used the screeching laka for cover and hitched
on his elbows until he reached the nearest hut. It was
a conical structure, made entirely of thatching bound to
limber posts set in the ground. He parted the aromatic
hay and scanned the interior. Circular pits had been
dug into the floor and filled with cream-colored down
of some sort. Knots of fresh herbs hung from the ceiling
and scented the air with a dry tang. It was soothing
and cool and quite useless for protection. He pushed
through and stood up in the dimness.

More screams filled the air outside. The laka didn't
even seem to know they should hide or run away. Some
of the largest were just standing there, staring at the

flek with horrified pink eyes as though they couldn't conceive of what to do next.

Damnation! His ears flattened with rage. He had to do something, anything! He couldn't just hide in here until relief arrived. By then, the village would be reduced to a scorched ruin, the laka a pile of smoldering corpses, and Oleaaka overrun once again with flek.

He stalked around the hut, his empty hands clenched. Just one weapon, even a—

The supports for the hut jumped out of shadows at him, slender saplings bent into arches, long and supple and strong. He wrenched one out of the earth and tested its tensile strength. Not the best homemade weapon he'd ever seen, but something solid at least to wield against the flek.

He flattened himself against the wall and dug a hole in the thatching to peer out. Across the cleared circle of earth, a warrior-drone spotted him and fired at the hut. The thatch wall burst into flames. He jerked back, cursing as smoke curled through the air.

Snarling, he ducked back to the rear of the hut, but flek had already swept past and surrounded him. The smoke thickened and burned his nose. He was going to have to get out of here, surrounded or not, if he was to avoid being suffocated or burned alive.

He thought he heard his name; the voice sounded like Mitsu. He keyed his com unit to hers. "What's your position?"

"I made a break for it into the next ring of huts," she said. *"I'm clear for the moment. How about you?"*

"I thought you lost your com," he said suspiciously. "I didn't see it back in the forest."

"I put it in my boot. I didn't want the flek to find it."

A bright orange curl of flame appeared overhead and ate down through the roof. He could feel the heat on his ears.

"Where are you?" she said. *"I'll come and bust you loose."*

But could he trust her? He didn't know. She sounded like her old self, but the director at the research station had too, back on Anktan, and all the while he'd believed he was a flek transferred into human flesh, Maybe they'd been able to finish the job they'd started on Mitsu this time and she was just waiting for her chance to betray him and everyone else she knew.

The com unit crackled. *"Furface, where the hell are you?"*

He shut it off and shoved it back into his pocket. Better not to involve her, crazy or not. He'd make a break for it himself.

Edging toward the low doorway, he peered out again. No flek in sight. Perhaps they had moved on, counting on the fire to do him in.

Or just waiting to pick him off, once he bolted, the savage *other* inside his head suggested.

He'd go out trying, then. Damned if he was going to squat here in the shadows and wait for death. Gripping his makeshift staff, he darted out into the sunlight. The air was filled with the cries of injured laka and the acrid stink of the approaching flek.

Then he saw them, a pair of warrior-drones who had taken up positions at forty-five-degree angles to catch him in a cross fire. They had a dead center bead on him. It was too late to go back, too late for—

The first shot caught him on the upper arm. Reflexively, he twisted away from it and then watched, dumbfounded, as the electric-green bolt passed in its straight-line trajectory. His arm was singed, but not toasted. He stared down at his fur in amazement and realized it had gone *blue.* Everything was *blue,* the huts and the rocks, the ground, the laka and the flek. He'd fallen into blueshift.

The other flek's hand inched toward the firing stud. He studied the angle for a second, then sidestepped the bolt before it fired. The cold of blueshift drained at his limited reserves. It was almost silent, all sounds slowed down to the point of incomprehensibility.

Blueshift transformed the landscape and had a fascination all its own, beautiful and quite deadly as it spent his life. He shook himself. There was no telling how long he could hold this accelerated state, certainly nothing like the hours that had once been possible. He had to attack now, before he lost what little advantage he'd gained.

The flek seemed frozen in the dappled shade where they were just emerging from the trees. Laka had gathered at the far end of the village, instead of fleeing, as common sense would seem to dictate. He reached for the savage *other* he always carried within, bared his claws and raced toward his enemy.

Chapter Twenty-Three

This was it, Mitsu told herself, as she dodged from tree to tree in the village. One screaming laka went down after another and the air was choked with black, roiling smoke as the rows of huts caught fire. A laser bolt sang past her cheek. She dropped without thinking and felt the heat trail expand above her like a deadly flower.

This was all her fault. She had convinced the flek to bring her back here just to save her own worthless hide. Why hadn't she found some way to destroy that damned transfer grid when she'd had the chance? Maybe she *was* still suffering from the aftereffects of the conditioning, like everyone thought. Why else was she pulling such stupid grunt-level stunts?

And where was Heyoka? She tucked her head, eased belly-down along the rain-saturated ground, but saw no sign of him anywhere. She wiped a hand over her face and felt the cool smear of mud left behind. Then, on the perimeter of the village, the firing slowed to a crawl and stopped. She hazarded another glance. Two charred laka lay ahead of her, their carapaces still smoking and blocking part of her view. Beyond them, three downed flek sprawled, their red eyes staring up sightlessly at the sky.

But she hadn't taken them out, and Heyoka, who'd also lost his rifle at some point, certainly couldn't have done in three at once either. The laka, then? She turned her head and gazed back across the village. The natives had coalesced into a frazzled rainbow knot down at the far end and were staring in this direction with frightened pink eyes, no more help in a fight than a herd of stupid cows.

She risked getting up to her hands and knees. Her head throbbed, but the knife felt good in her hand, like a trusted old friend who would not let her down. The village thrummed with dread and she sat back on her heels. Where were they? At least twenty more flek warriors were out there somewhere. Why had they stopped firing? It could just be a trap, to lure her and Heyoka out of cover so they could be picked off.

Warily, she regained her feet and gazed around, still damnably dizzy. Maybe Heyoka was injured, or even . . . dead. No. She would find him. It was just going to take some time.

Unseen silk brushed her face, and then, between one blink and the next, Heyoka's seven-foot frame appeared on his knees, head bowed, tongue lolling, panting as though he'd just completed a twenty-mile quick march.

"Are you all right?" She sheathed her knife, then took his arm.

"I could ask—the same about—you." His breath was coming in shuddering gasps. He closed his black eyes, shivering as though he were in the depths of winter.

"Never mind that," she said, trying to lever him onto his feet. "I only counted three flek down. Let's get under cover before the rest find their nerve and swing this way."

"Oh, they'll be back," he said. "I took out as many as I could, before I lost blueshift, but it wasn't nearly enough."

"You blueshifted?" she said, then grunted as he lurched onto his feet and she took his full weight. The throb in her head intensified and bright specks of red and gold danced before her eyes. She blinked hard. "I didn't think you could do that anymore."

"Neither did I," he said. "Guess we both screwed up."

"That was almost funny," she said. "You go on like this and you'll have your own stand-up routine in some space station bar."

"Don't be insulting." He pushed away from her and straightened. "Did the laka get out okay?"

"No, they're having some kind of convention," she said, "over there on the far side of the village."

"Idiots! Why didn't they just scatter into the forest?" Heyoka shook his head. "They have to know this island inside out. They could have dispersed and run rings around the flek."

"Because they *are* flek," she said. "Or at least they speak flek. The warriors who came back with me through the grid were deathly afraid of them, kept calling them 'the perverted ones.' I told you that before. Why don't you believe me?"

"Because it doesn't make sense," he said grimly. "That knock on the head cross-circuited your brain. You just think they're speaking flek."

"Come on, then," she said. "I'll show you." She set off toward the milling laka. Heyoka made a grab for her arm, but she slipped out of reach.

The laka ignored her as she approached. One of the more hulking specimens was sorting them into groups. What had seemed like chaos a moment ago had become purposeful orchestration. She stopped before a small lavender one who was standing apart, speaking to another of approximately the same size. It still sounded like flek-speak to her, though oddly accented. Her skin crawled. For all the superficial differences in body structure and the oddball pastel coloration, these creatures *were* flek. It was obvious. "Why didn't you run away?" she asked it in High-Flek.

The two of them stared at her. Then the closest craned its neck as though seeing her for the first time. "You address me, a lowly breeder?" it said finally.

"Why not? You speak the language of the Makers," she said, while Heyoka looked on in amazement.

"I speak the breeders' dialect," it said, "which is given only to us, the keepers, and translators. How is it that you, an alien, speak it too?"

"This is the language of the ones who attacked your . . . facility," she said, not having ever encountered a flek word for "home." "I learned it on another world."

"The forceful ones, yes," it said, and she thought a tinge of longing colored that statement. "They have come back."

"You have heard of them before?" She was aware that Heyoka hovered just behind her shoulder now.

"They do what they want," it said, "take anything they want, and it is rumored they are all male!" It turned its lavender face toward the other side of the village, where the flek had emerged from the forest. "I would like to see such creatures close-up just once before the Feast of Leavetaking."

A larger laka, its carapace a breathtaking blue that shaded to midnight along its joints, stepped between her and the smaller ones. It spoke to her sharply, but Mitsu could not understand. She answered in High-Flek. "I do not understand."

"Do not further agitate the breeders," it replied, switching to flek as though it were the most natural thing in the world. "We shall be days singing them down as it is."

"How is it that you speak the language of the Makers?" Mitsu asked.

The laka seemed to fold in upon itself and turned its head aside. "Do not name them so!"

"Why not?"

"They do not 'make' anything," it said. "They destroy! Look at our compound, our poor builders and sanitizers. The shellfruit arbor is in ruins and half the vines have fled. We shall have to use gleaners to clean up the mess and they will find that very upsetting. The terrible ones 'make' nothing except death and destruction!"

Heyoka took her shoulder and pulled her around. His black eyes bore into her. "Did you really understand any of that?"

"I told you before—they're speaking flek." Her heart raced. "They *are* flek."

He stared at the grouping and she could see the wheels rolling in his head as he tried to make sense of this bizarre set of facts.

She turned back to the laka. "The Makers were here, on Oleaaka, before, many units ago. They tried to change this world, but in the end they gave up and abandoned it. Do you know why?"

The laka started to speak, but the two smaller ones shoved past it and darted toward the forest. It flinched, then broke into a complex, atonal collection of sounds with rhythms that slid over each other, merging in piercing tones that scraped along her nerves.

Heyoka, who had much more sensitive hearing, sank to his knees and clamped his hands over his pinned-back ears. For her own part, she could not move. It was as though she were caught in a web of sound, both terrible and wonderful, that bound her to the spot.

The two who had called themselves "breeders" stood

transfixed too, then returned slowly, step by step, to the heart of the village. Their posture was unwilling, their heads downcast. They had no choice, Mitsu realized.

When the song was over, she stood blinking in the sultry sunlight, trying to remember what she had been about to do before it started.

A few feet away, Heyoka muttered an expletive and lurched to his feet. She looked up. A line of dead-white flek stood at the edge of the village.

The laka hurriedly burst back into song.

Montrose breathed a sigh of relief when the three hrinn emerged from the forest. The black-coated one, Kei, was in the lead. The other two, yellow Visht and black-and-white Skal, trailed at his heels. This was new, he thought. That particular order obviously meant something had changed. Skal hadn't been with them before, and the other two certainly hadn't left for the mountain in that particular order. Hrinn never did anything like this casually.

Onopa's stocky form backed him up, stalwart and ready, as he lurched to his feet, heavily favoring his burned leg. "Kika should be here in a few minutes, then we'll head for the village and relieve Blackeagle and Jensen."

Kei regarded him with those enigmatic black eyes and the air between them crackled with the intensity of his gaze. Such a direct stare meant out-and-out defiance, Montrose remembered from Blackeagle's lectures on the psychology of hrinn. Don't ever hold such a stare, the sergeant had warned, unless you mean to back it up with your life.

The nape of his neck prickled. He was tempted to drop his own eyes and let Kei lead the mission but, dammit, this was critical. Blackeagle and Jensen were pinned down, maybe dying at this very moment, and he had more actual combat experience against the flek than anyone else here. Blackeagle had designated him in charge.

"I am Squad Leader, by Blackeagle's order," he said slowly. "You are my Second."

Kei snarled, soft and rattling beneath his breath, and his handclaws sprang free. He paced back and forth. He seemed bigger than Montrose remembered but, then, hrinn always had that effect on him when he came upon them unexpectedly. He'd never been able to decide whether they looked more like Terran wolves, bears, or jungle cats, probably an amalgamation of the most ferocious features of all three. "We don't have time to argue," he said. Sweat soaked the back of his uniform shirt. He was painfully aware he couldn't have taken a full-grown hrinn, hand-to-hand, even at the best of times, and, at the moment, he was not only crammed to the gills with pain killers from the medkit, but one-legged as well. "Blackeagle is depending on us. Come and sit down. We have to plan our attack."

Aliki Onopa watched, but didn't say anything, didn't even move. Naxk's feverish black eyes watched from where she lay on the ground. She was still too weak to do more than breathe, and walk for short distances, when it was required of her.

"There is a *pattern/in/progress* at work here," Kei said finally, then glanced aside at Skal. The black-and-white hrinn's nose wrinkled in what might have been a silent snarl and he looked quickly away. Kei turned his back and sat down beside Naxk. "I have been trying to smell it out, but I do not have its shape yet."

Patterns. Montrose nodded grimly. Religion again. Better not to get started on that subject. He'd be sure to stick his foot in his mouth.

The other two hrinn also took seats on the damp ground. Visht looked perfectly at ease, but Skal's ears kept twitching and bloody claw marks crisscrossed his neck, which made Montrose even more nervous. "As soon as Kika reaches our position," he said, dry-throated, "we'll head for the village. It's about five hundred yards to the northwest, near as I can figure. We heard laser fire earlier, but it's stopped now."

Kei's nose quivered as he sampled the air from several directions. "We should go on without Kika. She is traveling faster than our injured and will catch up."

And she would easily, Montrose realized. Kei was right. She could smell them out, just like the others had. He should have thought of that, but it was hard enough to think like a hrinn and plan for their special abilities under the best of circumstances, let alone under pressure. "You're right," he said. "Let's head out."

Without a word, Onopa took Naxk's arm and helped the tawny young female to rise. They had both tried to persuade her to remain here, when they made contact with the enemy at the village, but Naxk would not hear of it. "I would rather be dead," she'd said, "than lie here, safe, while my huntmates fall in my place!"

As for himself, Montrose had cut a staff from a nearby tree and could walk, or at least limp for now, as long as the medication in the medkit held out. He didn't like to think about the consequences of pushing himself like this that would surely come in the not-too-distant future, when the drugs wore off. But then, they might not even have a future, so he decided he would worry about it when, and if, it happened.

Water still dripped from the leaves, but the rain had stopped and shafts of green-tinted sunlight filtered down through the forest canopy. Tiny blue and gold avians burst into flight at their approach, screeching like out-of-tune violins. The dampness intensified all the smells so that Montrose was overwhelmed by the scent of leaf mold, wet wood, bruised leaves, and rich, black mud.

Hrinn lived in an even more concentrated sea of odors like this all the time, he thought, and wondered what that would be like, to know the world around you so intimately through this other underused sense.

Kei and Skal stopped at almost the same instant, their ears pinned, their black eyes darting. Naxk stiffened and looked at Onopa. Visht continued a few more steps, then flinched back.

"What?" asked Montrose in a low voice.

"A noise," Kei said. His ears swiveled. "Very strange."

"Fighting?" he said.

"No," Kei said. "Something else, but definitely not natural."

Montrose forged on, trying to be as silent as the hrinn, but it was difficult. They made no sound, except for wounded Naxk, traveling like ghosts, despite their bulk. Since his leg was stiff and wouldn't bear his weight, he had all he could do to put one foot in front of the other. If he gave them away with his clumsiness, the reason would not matter.

The others fell into line behind him, then he signalled Kei. "Take the point," he whispered. "Don't let us walk into a trap."

The big black's eyes gleamed. He disappeared into the wall of foliage without disturbing a single leaf. Montrose limped after him, wondering how something so big could move like that.

Then he heard what the hrinn had already picked up: a wretched teeth-rattling racket that grew louder with each step. It vibrated along nerve and bone, built up painfully behind the eyes. He felt as though he were wading upstream against a stiff current.

Kei halted and they bunched behind him. Naxk was breathing hard, her head back, eyes half-lidded. Onopa looked grim and weary beneath Naxk's weight.

Montrose peered ahead and saw a huge clearing with

concentric rings of neat thatched huts: the laka village. It was surrounded on this side by at least twenty, perhaps more, flek warrior-drones. The sun glinted off their luminescent white bodies as they stood there, frozen, laser-sticks raised.

The squad could not possibly take so many head-on, he thought. Their only chance was to ambush them. He motioned to Onopa to ease Naxk to the ground. No matter what she said, she wasn't mobile enough for this.

She sagged, then braced her back against a tree. He bent down in the shade and spoke close to her ear. "Stay here and guard our flank. We're going to slip around and drive them back this way. Don't let any get past you."

She was panting too hard to speak, but her hands tightened around her rifle. Damn, she was game, he thought and squeezed her shoulder.

Then he jerked his head at the rest. "Let's flank the line to the left," he said softly, "then pick them off one at a time. We can take out six or seven before they realize what's happening. Stay spread out and maintain your position. Don't give them a decent target."

The hrinn melted again into the trees. He and Onopa were left to follow. His leg was aching again and he was dizzy. Rainbow auras surrounded the light, wherever it pierced the leaves, and he knew he was running on raw nerve.

"You go first," he told Onopa. "I'll follow."

"Maybe you should stay with Naxk," she said. Her cheek was smudged with mud and her wet black hair was plastered to her head. "Make the best use of what mobility you have."

She was probably right, he thought, but he couldn't do it. As long as he could still move under his own power, he had to be with the squad. This was his command.

"No," he said, "I'll take the last position, but I can keep up."

She nodded, then her tall sturdy form disappeared between a pair of saplings into the foliage hrinnti fashion. Not a leaf stirred and he couldn't hear her footsteps above the torturous racket coming from the village. He checked his rifle, disengaged the safety, then limped after her.

The flek waited, a line of white statues at the edge of the village. Heyoka gritted his teeth, willing the laka to stop that goddamned awful racket, so he could mount some defense, even if it was just to take cover. In its own way, this was almost as bad as the transport grid revved up to full power.

"Tell them—to—stop!" he gasped. A red mist obscured his vision. "Tell them—they're killing—us!"

Mitsu was pale, but fortunately not as incapacitated. Hands over her ears, she darted forward and shouted at the assembled laka. When they didn't respond, she beat her fist against the one which had spoken to her a few minutes ago. It stumbled back, faltered, blinked at her with surprised pink eyes, then stopped singing. The rest trailed off into silence.

Mitsu questioned it, then turned back to him. "They have to sing," she said shakily. "It's for the Makers, the flek, as we call them, to keep them from—something. I'm not sure what. Their accent is different and I don't know all the words."

He glanced up at the flek. They were raising their laser-sticks, taking aim—

A laser bolt burst out of the trees and cut down the fourth flek from the end. Two more in quick succession killed the next pair, then the flek responded with fire into the forest.

"Come on!" Heyoka seized Mitsu's arm and hustled

her to dubious cover behind a hut. "It's the squad," he said. "They've re-formed and are coordinating an attack."

The laka were again milling in the line of fire as though they still had no idea of how much danger they were in. Several more died in the first seconds of fighting. "Tell them to take cover!" he said.

She poked her head around the hut long enough to relay the message. One of the laka broke off and joined them in their hiding place.

It spoke to Mitsu, its tone urgent. She shook her head. It repeated itself, gesturing at the fire fight.

"What's it saying?" he said.

"It wants us to break off this attack," she said. "They hate fighting and all forms of violence. They would rather die than be part of this."

"But the flek will kill them!" he said.

"They don't care." Her blue eyes were red-rimmed. She had a dark, purpling bruise across one cheek and he was suddenly reminded that he had stolen her back from the flek just hours before. Prior to that, she had been their prisoner. Was she accurately interpreting what the laka were saying, or was she just rewriting the scenario to the flek's advantage? Maybe that laka had really been begging for them to defend the village.

"They can't sing them down with all this going on!" she said. "The flek will hear, though, if you just call the squad off for now."

The Mitsu he knew would fight to the death before surrendering, he thought. She would never give up, no matter how hopeless the odds, and she would never let someone else fight her battles. This had to be the flek talking.

Another warrior-drone went down, then he heard a harsh cry in the thick underbrush. One of his squad was hit. He couldn't stand it any longer. Claws bared, he launched himself at the flek's unprotected flank.

Chapter Twenty-Four

Kika joined the squad just as it began the assault. Without thinking, Kei motioned the pale-gray into a gap at the far end of the line and then realized belatedly he'd acted as Leader. Well, Montrose with his injured leg was still lagging back in the forest. Kei was surprised he'd made it this far. The Ranger must be stronger than most humans he'd encountered during training.

They took out four of the flek before the enemy returned fire. That still left at least three times their number, not good odds. Though he had not been interested in the sacred patterns until recently, Kei wondered what sort might be at work here. Why would it have brought them so far just to let them fail?

Then he knew the answer. Patterns had to be deciphered, then ridden, like a current in a swift river. They didn't change direction to suit you or care what you did or wanted; they just *were*, coming into being to shape events. If you meant to use one, you had to sniff out what was arising. So, he asked himself, as he fired another bolt, what was the shape of the particular *something/in/motion* here? How could he merge with it and gain advantage?

Visht worked steadily on his left, firing and advancing, firing and advancing. Skal fought hard too, but not as carefully, risking open shots, then taking a second and even a third before retreating back into adequate cover. Kei was about to shout at him not to expose himself so blatantly when a flek laser bolt took the black-and-white full in the chest.

Skal bellowed and lost his rifle, fell back into the brush. Visht surged across to hold his position. Ears pinned, shoulders bristling, he took down two of the enemy in quick succession.

Kei was furious. Skal had no right to risk himself so! None of them did! If he weren't already dead, he would have been tempted to kill the idiot himself. With a roar, he blueshifted and crossed the clearing, able to see gaps in the firing pattern in his highly accelerated state.

The noise was replaced by an eerie, brittle quiet. The air grew nose-burning cold and he could almost feel frost forming on his ears. He glimpsed the mountains rising high and deep blue above the trees and thought of Bey. They had been huntmates their whole lives. It was strange fighting without him.

Claws extended, he ripped the head off the closest flek and went on to the next without waiting for the first to drift to the ground. Vaguely, he was aware of someone closing in and turned to see Visht's blue form moving with him in this chill blue place at the same speed. Neither of them could hold this state for long, he knew, and both would pay heavily for the energy expenditure when they fell out.

Motioning to Visht to take the next flek, he swerved after the one beyond. His breathing rasped in his ears and he felt his control slipping. So cold here. So cold. His hands and legs were going numb, his ears and nose.

They'd had little to eat and almost no sleep for the past day. Preparations were supposed to be made for blue-shift, excess energy absorbed. The scene flickered, *blue/ normal colors/blue*. A few more steps, he told himself. If Visht, who was considerably less able at this, could hold it, he could! Without Montrose, he was Leader, strongest of the hunt. He had to show the way.

He struck the flek, saw it begin to recoil, the weapon inch out of its startled hands. It oozed toward the ground and he ran on. How many left? He couldn't take time to count. Had to go on. Take out the next and the next.

His lungs burned and his legs were weakening. He was Levv, he told himself, strongest of all Lines, no matter that hrinnti males discounted maternal heritage. Traditionals had never been outcast as he and his agemates had been, never had to scratch and fight to wrest food out of the unforgiving mountains or redeem their stolen honor.

Let them all stay behind on Anktan, living their oh-so-proper lives and congratulating themselves on exterminating the flek on their own world. Through him, *Levv* would hunt flek across the entire universe!

With a shudder, he lost blueshift and found himself on his hands and knees in front of a startled flek. Drained from expending so much energy, he tried to lift his rifle, but his arms were too weak. He snarled and struggled to rise as the warrior-drone swung its laser stick around, took aim. His legs were dead wood, his arms stone. It was very bitter to come so far, only to die at the hands of this despised enemy.

A shot over his shoulder singed his fur and blasted the flek cleanly in the throat, its most vulnerable point. It gave a strangled cry and lurched backwards, clawing at the charred wound.

Kei jerked around to see Montrose's dark face peer out from the trees.

The human gave him that curious "thumbs-up" gesture humans were so fond of. "That's the last on this side," he called. "Sweep back the other way and see if there are any stragglers."

Kei hesitated, then found the strength to raise his trembling right hand in a salute. Montrose saluted back. Kei lowered his head and lurched to his feet to somehow sweep the remainder of the perimeter as he'd been ordered.

Kika reached Skal's fallen body just as he took a last shuddering breath. She knelt at his side. So much damage, she thought, as she surveyed the charred topography of the terrible wound across his chest. It had been a direct strike, searing through layers of skin. His eyes were glassy and staring. She was too late.

But the power she'd absorbed brimmed inside her like an inrushing tide, barely restrained. It wasn't meant to be contained like this, but to be used. That much she could feel, even though she had no training, nothing on her side except unhoned potential. She didn't know exactly what to do. When she'd set out, she'd only hoped the knowledge would come to her at the right time.

He is already dying, her mind whispered. She couldn't just kneel here while the life drained out of him and do nothing. A breeze threaded through the trees, stirred her mane, ruffled her fur as though trying to get her attention. No one else could do this, it was saying. It was up to her. She had to try.

Shots continued only yards away. Her ears flattened as something, or someone, very close, screamed and died. The air reeked of laser discharge worse than any firing range she'd ever trained upon. Trembling, she placed a palm on the motionless chest, closed her eyes, as she had seen other Restorers do, waited.

Stillness descended over her and she became aware of the blood flying through her body, the pathways for power crackling with blue energy. The wound was serious and painful, but it had not yet taken Skal's life. Some portion of him still lingered, though fading even as she watched.

She released a measure of raw energy into his limp form. He flinched beneath her hand, then quieted. Not enough, she thought. He needed more. How much, though? Surely too large an amount would kill him.

But he was dead anyway, unless she managed this. She placed her other hand on his chest, palm down, tried to quiet her mind, not think or plan, just be still and let the knowledge rise like a bubble from the bottom of a clear pond, feel the shape of this moment . . .

Power burst from her hands, and, once started, she could not hold it back. Skal convulsed beneath her touch, chest heaving, arms thrashing. It was as though she were the conduit for an immense wave, no easier to contain than a river in flood. She could not control any aspect of it, only hold on and endure until it spent itself.

The outpouring lessened, faded. Breathing hard, she opened her eyes and glanced around, dazed. Her entire body was alternately numb, then filled with tiny, prickling pains. The trees seemed to dip around her in great, sickening circles. Skal was staring up at her from the wet ground, more frightened than she had ever seen an adult hrinn.

With a snarl, he threw off her hands. She fell back, tried to speak, but words wouldn't come. It was as though she were still wide open to something so immense, there was no room left inside for her own thoughts. A pattern? She gazed at her shaking hands. What were the name of Restorers' patterns anyway?

Skal lurched to his feet and loomed above her, teeth

bared in a fierce growl. The raw, gaping wound on his chest had transformed into ridged yellowish scar tissue. And, bracketing the affected area, was the distinct outline of two outstretched hrinnti hands.

Heyoka saw Kei drop out of blueshift and fall, then saw Montrose take the flek out from behind. Montrose shouted something and then, after a long heart-stopping moment, miracle of miracles, the two *saluted* each other. His mane whipped in the breeze as he stared. Evidently a few things had changed while he'd been separated from the squad.

Kei picked himself up and slogged off around the village outskirts, weariness written into every line of his powerful frame. Fresh from blueshift himself, Heyoka knew that feeling. He was as boneless as a stewed tomato.

He prowled forward, keeping an eye out for concealed flek, then bent down to pry a fallen drone's laser-stick from its dead hand. The flek weapon was short and stubby, designed for spidery flek digits, not for human or double-thumbed hrinnti grips, but it felt good in his hand, like being whole again after days of illness.

Mitsu came up behind him, trailed by a number of laka. The bruise across her face had darkened and her left eye was nearly swollen shut. "Is this all?" she said and looked from one body to the next. "By my count, there should be at least ten more warrior-drones, not counting the world-architect. I don't see it anywhere either."

"World-architect?" Heyoka looked at her sharply, trying to decide if she was rambling or making sense.

"The Deciders sent one along to survey Oleaaka and see if it could be redeemed from their previous failure to convert it." Her brow wrinkled. "The architect must have split off to check the environmental engines while the rest came here. I bet the missing warrior-drones went along."

"There's more, then." Heyoka bit off a curse, then closed his eyes and tried to think. He massaged the bridge of his nose with one hand. He was so sodding tired! They had to intercept them before they went back through the grid. Once the exploratory party returned and reported, it was probably only a matter of time, and very little at that, before an invasion force came back through. With the flek lines sweeping back toward Oleaaka, it would be very much to their advantage to establish a base here.

"You should have let the laka sing them down," she said. "The flek are terrified of them and, if we can learn why, we might be able to use it too."

That nonsense again. Heyoka grimaced. "Those warrior-drones didn't look so damned afraid when they were shooting up the village. There must be at least fifty dead laka lying around here."

"But didn't you see how the flek reacted during that few moments when they were singing?" she said. "Those drones couldn't move."

"Hell, *I* couldn't move," he said irritably. "They were shorting out my neurons with that racket."

A large mauve-tinted native approached and spoke to Mitsu. Its tone seemed to be urgent.

She answered, then turned to Heyoka. "One of their females is missing."

"Then it's probably dead," he said.

"No, they haven't found her body. She was the pale-green one I overheard talking when we first entered the village."

"That one?" He looked around, but could not spot it anywhere. "I think she was the same one who spoke Standard to me in the forest."

"They say she's a translator," she said. "Apparently,

each caste speaks a different dialect so they can't communicate with each other. The translators are the only ones who speak across all caste lines. Their brains must be especially wired to decode and acquire languages, even one as alien to them as Standard."

Montrose emerged from the trees and limped toward them, using a rough staff to take the weight of his bad leg. "Well," Heyoka said, "I'm sorry about the translator, but, if she's alive, she'll probably turn up." He held a hand out to Montrose, who was ashen-faced and looked like hell. "Nice op, Corporal."

Montrose saluted, then reached out and took his hand. His grip was warm, but shaky. He looked like he needed some serious downtime. "Good to see you still breathing, Sarge." Then he glanced curiously at Mitsu. "You too, Jensen."

Mitsu nodded. "We've got to get back to the cave," she said. "What's left of the flek must be headed that way."

Kika and Skal emerged from the trees. The pale-gray female walked slowly, head down, as though she were dazed. Skal stalked well ahead of her, his lips wrinkled back in a snarl, ears flattened to his skull.

"Well, I'll be—" Montrose shook his head. "He took a direct hit back there in the trees. I thought he was a goner for sure."

"I think he was," said Mitsu. "Look at his chest."

Heyoka stared. Two shimmering double-thumbed handprints bracketed a patch of yellow scar tissue. "But there are no Restorers here," he said.

"I wouldn't be too sure of that." Mitsu fingered her own swollen eye wistfully.

From the far end of the firing line, Visht's yellow form appeared, rifle in his hand as though he'd done this all his life. Heyoka did a mental count. "Where's Onopa?"

"She's coming," Montrose said. "She went back for Naxk."

The laka were chattering at him urgently, but he ignored them. "Good fight," he said. "Everyone worked together, like soldiers are supposed to, like Rangers."

Kei finished his sweep for stray flek and returned, moving ever slower, just as Onopa and Naxk broached the forest's edge. Kei trotted over and supported the injured female the rest of the way.

"This is just the beginning, people," Heyoka said as they gathered before him. "Corporal Jensen here informs me there are more flek, probably out at the ruins in the forest, or headed back to the cave. We have to intercept them before they return to their own world and report."

"This is *her* fault!" Skal was bristling at Mitsu, stalking back and forth, radiating edgy defiance. "She brought the enemy back here!"

"They would have come anyway," she said, though her cheeks flushed. "They want information on the hrinn and what the Confederation is up to here, and they're talking about rebuilding the environmental engines to finish the conversion of Oleaaka for flek habitation."

Montrose looked stricken. "If the flek learn that the Confederation has pulled out—"

"If they want this world, they'll swarm in here and take it," Mitsu said, "whether the Confederation is in occupation or not. Face it, they've kicked us from one end of this quadrant to the other for decades. They never hesitate to engage us, if we get in their way, but for some reason they're very leery of the laka. These people drove them off this world forty-eight years ago and they've kept them out ever since, until we came along like meddling idiots, and reactivated the grid. We should be begging the laka to tell us how they did it all those years ago, instead of fooling around with laser rifles, one on one."

"You said the laka *were* flek," Heyoka put in, "that they speak High-Flek."

"Well, a form of High-Flek anyway," she said, then turned and studied the agitated natives. "Look at the configuration of their bodies, the shape of their arms and heads. They must be flek who decided at some point in their history not to be flek anymore."

"But the atmosphere," he said, "and the temperature, they're all wrong for them."

"They adapted, I guess." She spoke to the largest laka, whose carapace was pale mauve. It answered at some length. She pressed for what seemed to be clarification, then turned back to him. "She says long ago, the laka were Makers—"

"Makers?" Montrose said.

"That's what the flek call themselves." She ran a hand back through her straggling black hair. "They looked the same, thought the same, even came to this world to live as Makers live on all worlds, by ripping it apart and putting it back together in their own distorted image. But then one clutch was born whose bodies remembered something everyone else had forgotten—how to sing certain long-forbidden songs."

The laka interrupted.

She nodded. "This is Fourth Translator and she's amazing. In just these few minutes, she's already picked up enough Standard to understand a great deal of what we say and she's learning more with every word. She says the ones who were born were what we would call throwbacks, a coming together of all the recessive genes of many generations, and they remembered what the Makers were like, before they became Makers."

Heyoka faced Fourth Translator. "What does the singing do?"

The laka spoke again and Mitsu translated. "For drones, it scrambles the violent impulses and makes aggression impossible. For the rest of us, it soothes and reminds us who we are and what we must hold onto, if we are not to slip back into those savage, dark days."

They were tame flek, Heyoka thought numbly. Who would have thought such a thing could exist? All his adult life, he had fought this fierce, predatory species. Flek never gave up, never backed away, cared nothing about individual lives and could only be overwhelmed by superior numbers, greater firepower, or a combination of both, and now these pacifist natives said what had been needed all this time was only the proper tune?

"We have to get this information, unbelievable and sketchy as it is, back to headquarters," he said. "I certainly don't know what to make of it."

"What about the grid?" Mitsu asked.

"Ask Fourth Translator if we can leave Naxk here," he said, though the tawny young female jerked her drooping muzzle up and found the strength to snarl. "She can keep us apprised via the com unit if any hostiles show up back at the village. The rest of us will return to the grid and see if we can destroy it before they get there."

"Fourth Translator says Naxk may stay," Mitsu related, "and she and a number of her sister translators will go with us. She fears that is where they will find Ninth Translator."

Heyoka started to protest that this would likely be a fight to the death and no place for civilians, but then he realized that he did not have all the answers and this was, after all, their world.

"All right," he said. "Collect the rest of the flek laser-sticks and meet back here in five minutes. See if the laka can spare us some food. Those of us who used blueshift must eat or we'll going to be nose-down in the dirt."

They sorted themselves out and he noted even Mitsu and Kei did not give each other a second glance. Skal kept to himself, while Kika moved as though her mind were somewhere else entirely. Heyoka shook his head, humanstyle, and went to strip the flek dead of their weapons. It was going to be a bizarre assault force.

Second Breeder had not been to the echoing white ruins in some time. The keepers avoided this location, finding it too reminiscent of ancient troubles, and so he and the other breeders had only been able to slip off once in a while when their attention was otherwise engaged.

Even the hardiest of wandering vines shunned this place. Mottled red-trees, all that would grow here, towered over the fallen columns now and shed their leaves with greater frequency than usual. Some element in the soil pleased them and their leaves were much redder than trees of the same variety which grew elsewhere. Their shade was deep and cool, the air filled with a tantalizing hint of chemicals long ago leeched into the earth, balances that had once veered sharply out of stasis. The soaring walkways between the towers had fallen and lay shattered in the naked dirt, yet an elegance of line remained which called to him.

He tightened his grip on Ninth Translator and dragged her into the ruins' shadow. She averted her head at the sight. The dark green bruise beneath her shattered carapace had spread. She might die after all, as she had claimed. If so, he thought, that would at least be entertaining. They could watch, then have a Feast of Leavetaking of their own.

His brother breeders must be here somewhere, along with the gleaner they had captured. He sniffed the breeze, hoping to come across some hint of their scent. He detected the faint menthol of shellfruit upwind and the spice of a patch of ripening sweetcane, tiny green-furred rank-smelling climbers who made themselves pests at the colony and ate the thatching, and something else, strong and hearty, familiar . . .

A line of tall white figures emerged from behind a fallen column. Their red eyes gleamed in the dimness. They carried deadly weapon sticks in their first-hands and there was a uniformity to them that seemed both right and pleasing. The ones from the cave, the Makers, they had come to this ancient place too! Did they revere it as he and his fellow breeders did?

The largest one cocked its head and spoke. Its forceful voice carried through the stillness. A covey of shrieking scarlet avians burst from cover and flew away. Second Breeder thought he would die of joy. *He had understood the words*.

The Maker had said, "Sing one note and you will be destroyed."

Chapter Twenty-Five

The laka piled a rainbow assortment of fruit at the edge
of the village, then retreated, edgy and uncertain. Most
of the fires had been extinguished, but smoke still curled
through the outer ring of huts. Heyoka picked through
the choices, trying not to think of what his starving cells
really craved at this point—fresh meat. The laka, no
doubt, would be horrified if he snatched an avian out
of the bushes and tore it into pieces before their fastidious eyes.

He was intensely hollow in a way he doubted any
human could ever imagine. It was a fiery, yet glacial
hunger that ate all the way down into the core of his
cells and he knew only too well what spending oneself
this way without renewal could do. For months after
that last battle on Anktan, his vision had been stained
blue and every mouthful of food and water had tasted
like ashes.

Nisk, the hrinnti male who had administered his
delayed education, had advised him of the dangers
repeatedly. Though Heyoka thought he was exaggerating

301

at the time, he knew now Nisk had been using typical hrinnti reserve when stating the potential effects. Hrinn never said things they did not mean. He should have paid more attention.

It still amazed him that he had managed blueshift—twice—in the last twenty-four hours. He'd tried numerous times since his recovery back on Anktan, always after hours of soaking in a torrid thermal pool to absorb excess energy, and never managed it for a second. It just brought home to him that he still thought too much like a human.

Kei dumped an armload of thick green sticks on the supply pile, sniffed one with disdain, then threw it down. His manner was subdued, but Heyoka noted how Skal, skulking nearby, avoided meeting the big black's eyes. "What happened up there on the mountain, after I—left?" he asked, skirting the painful issue of his failure to thrash Skal himself.

"We sat vigil for Bey until the sun rose," Kei said. "Skal Challenged me and then we came back down to find the others."

So. Heyoka's ears pricked. Typical hrinnti brevity, leaving out everything of interest and trusting context to tell most of the tale. "And you won?"

Kei bristled. "Of course, I won!"

"Of course," Heyoka agreed. "So now you are Leader?"

"No," Kei said stiffly. "Montrose is Squad Leader." His black eyes drilled Heyoka. "You designated him such."

"But you haven't fought Montrose."

"Rangers do not fight one another," Kei said. "They fight flek." His black eyes narrowed. "You are the one who said that!"

"True," Heyoka said. "I'm just not accustomed to you paying attention. But Skal is a Ranger. Why did you fight him?"

"That is different. He is also hrinnti. We had to settle dominance." Kei's tone was one of an adult lecturing a backward child. "Even you should see that."

He would, Heyoka thought gloomily, *never* understand hrinn.

Mitsu emerged from the crowd with five variously colored laka, including mauve Fourth Translator. "They are ready," she said.

"Then let's hit the trail," Heyoka said, still doggedly chewing a grainy mouthful of fruit. It tasted like faintly sweet grit. He picked up another ribbed fruit to eat on the march. Three laser-sticks were tucked into the waistband of his uniform and he wished he hadn't been so quick to discard his shirt somewhere in the course of the last day.

Skal hovered until they all passed, then fell in at the rear of the procession, straggling behind even the laka. Heyoka smelled trouble there.

The leafy shade closed around them as though they'd plunged back into a lake of silver and green, and Heyoka still felt unutterably weary. But if Mitsu was right and they could stop the flek from returning home, they might yet find a way to destroy that grid and seal off Oleaaka.

"We breeders do know a few songs," Second Breeder said to the gleaming white Maker, "but most of them are very dull. I have just remembered a wonderful new one, though, bold and exciting, but I won't sing if you do not wish it."

The Maker leaned forward and snatched the alien *weapon* he'd been carrying out of his hand, smashed it against a tree and threw the shattered pieces to the ground. "You were whelped from the perverted ones," he said stiffly. "We are forbidden to listen to such."

All of these tall white Makers bore packs full of

equipment and carried *weapons*. One seized the translator's arm and Second regretfully released her. Well, perhaps they needed a translator too, he thought. They seemed to have brought none of their own, and he could always *steal* another. That would be amusing anyway.

"Will you *attack* the compound again?" he asked. "My fellow breeders are supposed to meet me here and we could all help! When I was at the compound earlier, the *attack* was going splendidly. I wanted to stay and watch, but I needed to *capture* this translator."

"You made contact with our other detachment?" The Maker glanced sharply at his fellows. They moved in and encircled Second with their gleaming white bodies.

"At the compound." Second crept even closer, letting their distinctive odor stimulate the chemical receptors in his brain. The scent seemed to linger *here*, *there*, unlocking even more previously inaccessible information recorded deep in his cells. He could feel new body-memories hovering just on the edge of consciousness, more *fierce* new words. "They were *fighting* the aliens." The wild, forbidden word lingered in his mouth and conjured up enticing images. Inside his head, he saw buildings burst apart in a fiery rain of debris; *explosions*, they were called.

"Wherever you're going, take us with you," he said. "The keepers forbid everything that is pleasurable, most of all *weapons* and *fighting*. And soon it will be time for the Feast of Leavetaking. Then we will have nothing at all."

"Be quiet!" The Maker's intense red eyes glared at him. "You talk too much! Obviously your early conditioning was sorely lacking."

Even this *rebuke* stimulated him so that he longed to *chastise* someone himself in turn. So many new concepts, so many new skills! Why were breeders never permitted these things on Oleaaka?

Another Maker emerged from the ruins, but this one was smaller, less sturdily made, though male like the rest. He carried a complicated machine of some type and referred to it from time to time.

The largest Maker strode forward. "According to this prisoner, the other detachment took the compound, therefore they will have encountered the perverted ones. We should return to the grid at once. They may well have been contaminated by the contact."

"Indeed?" The smaller Maker looked curiously at Second Breeder. "And is this one of the infamous perverted ones?"

"Yes. It has not tried to sing, so we have spared it for the moment in anticipation of gaining further information."

The smaller Maker sat back on his hindquarters with an air of fastidious disdain. "It is a very unsettling color."

"We are hatched white, just as you," Second said, "but then a tint is chosen for each. I requested red and Fourth Breeder wanted a deep dark green, but the guardians permit only pallid, washed-out colors."

The largest Maker swung its *weapon* in a backhanded arc and knocked Second to the forest floor. "Be silent unless you are questioned directly!"

Second lay blinking up at the sunlight seeping down through the leaves. His head spun and the hide was split across his brow so that hot ivory blood trickled down into his eye. It hurt more than any casual scrape or scratch he'd ever acquired. *Wound*, this was called. *Injury*. The Maker had *struck* him and this distress in his body was *pain*. He struggled back onto his feet, head and neck *throbbing*, vision distorted. "That was wonderful!" he said. "Teach me how to do it!"

In answer, the Maker raised his weapon and took aim

at Second's head, but the smaller one stepped forward. "Not yet," he said. "Does it not strike you that this one is curiously unperverted? Not only has it not attempted to sing, but seems eager to cooperate. We might well learn about the more dangerous ones from it."

"Architect, what about the other one, the female?" the largest Maker said.

"Oh, she's not dangerous now," said Second, forgetting the *painful* admonishment of a moment before. The tall Maker moved its *weapon* menacingly and his blood sang through his veins in anticipation of yet another *blow*. "It takes at least five females to sing properly so that we breeders are forced to listen."

"Five?" the smaller Maker said. He turned to the largest male. "See? Our young prisoner has already made himself useful. As long as you kill sufficient numbers of females so that they can never gather as many as five in one place, we could perhaps take back this promising world." He held out his machine which consisted of a dark-gray exterior with colors that flowed across its flat surface like water in a river. "By these readings, I calculate it would not take more than fifteen orbital periods to set this ecology to rights and establish optimum breeding conditions. There is still a chance to craft this world into a classic example of my hatching's best work."

Something rustled in the undergrowth, then a clump of bedraggled breeders appeared, herded by three more of the proud white Makers. Second Breeder recognized Eighth and Twenty-seventh Breeders in the lead, Tenth in the back, along with the cowering gleaner.

"They will help too!" he said quickly, hoping to divert any more talk of *killing* from being applied to their own potentially useful selves.

"This one is neuter," said another Maker, indicating the gleaner. "A worker caste of some sort."

"It's a gleaner," Second said. "We *stole* it so we could form our own colony out here in the forest, but we would much rather go to yours."

"Yes," said the delicately built Maker with the machine, the one they called Architect, "bring them along. Let the Deciders examine this lot with their own thorough methods." He turned to Second, who was standing now with his fellow breeders. "But if there is a single note of song, if you even think they are going to sing, kill them all."

The three human members of the squad ranged up ahead at the front of the column with the Black/on/black, Kei, and the laka. Visht and Kika took up the middle, while Skal relegated himself to the rear. The miserable forest was so choked with underbrush, he had to fight for every step and find his way by scent, rather than follow the squad by sight. Tiny scarlet insects buzzed around his eyes. It was hot and close and wretched in every way.

His ears flattened. He hated this claustrophobic place; it reeked of stagnant pools and decay and was filled with ankle-deep mud that sucked at the boots, entirely the wrong environment for a hrinn who was used to large, arid spaces.

Anger smoldered within him, a banked fire ready to burst into open flames. His chest still ached where the flek weapon had caught him, which made him even more irritable. The leaves rustled, then he glimpsed Kika's graceful pale-gray form momentarily before she disappeared in the curtain of foliage again. A snarl escaped him. He should have been standing beyond the Gates of Death right now, safely, and honorably, dead. What right had she to deny him?

All his life, he had sought to matter. He was of average size for a male and well enough marked, but there was always someone bigger at the time of Gathering who paired off with the female he had been tracking. He had stalked and killed several of these later outside of Challenge, something Visht had referred to back on the mountain. That fed his anger too. He had known it was wrong, even as he committed the crimes, and hoped to leave such dishonor behind on Anktan. A clean death in battle would have given him that.

As though she could hear his thoughts, Kika hung back, then gave him an appraising stare when he caught up. "You're still lagging," she said, her voice pitched low so as not to carry. "That was a very serious wound, even though it closed well, but I am not experienced in restorations. Why not save your strength and return to the village to wait with Naxk?"

With a roar, he sprang and carried her down to the forest floor. Her head struck a knobby root, but she was already fighting back as she fell, employing the Ranger tricks she'd learned in base camp, sliding out from under his claws and turning his momentum against him.

He was not weak, he was not, and no one would ever suggest such a shameful thing to him again! He struggled for a killing grip, but could not pin her writhing form. She caught him with her handclaws and opened a gash across his shoulder. The pain enraged him even further until he was white-hot with anger. All around him, the forest seemed stained white, and he realized it wasn't white at all, but a chill, heart-stopping *blue*. Kika lay motionless before him, her black eyes wide, her arms bent at unnatural angles. He had entered blueshift. Her unprotected throat lay exposed before him. She would not humiliate him again. He raised his claws for a killing stroke.

A hand caught his arm and he looked up into the scintillating onyx eyes of the Black/on/black himself. "She is your huntmate!"

Skal tried to free himself, but could not break his

grip. "She shamed me," he said in hrinnti, "denied me an honorable death! She shames me still with all this talk of weakness and injury!"

"You do not need an honorable death," the Black/on/ black said, and then he disappeared while the world turned green and brown and silver again. He had lost blueshift.

Kika scrambled up to face him, ears pinned back, loosened mane like a cloud around her face. "Come at me again!" she spat. "I will stuff your ears down your throat, one tiny piece at a time!"

The Black/on/black appeared between one breath and the next as he too left blueshift. "Stand down, Private!" he told Kika over his shoulder as he faced Skal. "I'll handle this."

She was breathing hard, bristling from nose to feet. "I will finish what lies between us!"

The Black/on/black put a hand on her shoulder and pricked through her uniform with his claws. She flinched. "I said 'stand down'!" He met her eyes until she dropped her gaze and gave way.

He turned back to Skal. "You don't need an honorable death," he said more evenly. "What you need is an honorable *life*. No matter what you did, or did not do, back on Anktan, this is another place, a chance to be part of an entirely new pattern. Fall in and guard our backs, as ordered, or I promise we will leave your bleeding corpse to feed the nits."

Skal stared. "I cannot be first again," he said. "Kei is the strongest and I will never be Leader."

"No one knows that for certain," the Black/on/black said. "We only know the shape of this moment, today, now. In the meantime, our enemy increases his lead with every breath, and you are holding us back. Choose now whether to hunt with us or stay here and eat death."

Death at such noted hands could be considered

honorable, Skal thought. He could make the Black/on/
black take his life, yet if there were a chance for something larger, something he'd never been able to find
anywhere else . . .

"We don't have time for this," the Black/on/black said.
"Choose!"

Skal dropped his own eyes and took up his place at
the rear of the pack. "No one will get by me," he said
solemnly.

The four young drones bore the distinct markings
of their castes, although, World-Architect 549 reflected,
they seemed to know almost nothing about themselves
or their intended function, stamped into their genes by
thousands of generations of careful breeding. One bore
the distinct mark of an outdated tech caste, rarely bred
these days, except on worlds where antique technology
required appropriate maintenance. The other three had
been bred out of decent, though not outstanding, warrior-
drone stock.

They were so eager, as though they'd just been
hatched. They wanted to know everything, go everywhere.
The warrior-drones had to be quite severe to keep them
from wandering off to explore the ruins, and each time
they struck one, the young drone actually seemed to
enjoy it. He supposed that was understandable after
being reared by this tainted colony. They had been
crafted for only one thing in this life, which had been
consistently denied them. How could they be expected
to have any pride of function, when they had apparently
been reared only to breed and die?

The other two, the so-called translator and gleaner,
refused to move unless beaten, but they, unlike the
drones, did not appear to enjoy it.

The architect decided it was time to return to the
transfer grid. He wished to present this valuable

information to the Deciders as soon as possible. They would know if conditions were optimum for retaking this world and carving it into something both strategically useful and appealing to the senses. It had the virtue of being located in a quadrant of space where the Makers had once held sway before their terrible Enemy had driven them out.

"I have completed my readings," he told Warrior-Drone 21487. "Escort us back now."

The efficient warriors fell into a standard combat pattern. "Take the middle," the warrior replied. "We may meet more resistance on the way back."

This pronouncement brought on wriggles of joy by the young drones, but the seasoned warriors took it in stride, readying laser-sticks, checking charges. They were experienced troops, rotated out from the front lines of several hot engagements. They had met the Enemy before on many occasions and prevailed. The set of their jaws, the line of their shoulders said they would do so once again.

They set off into the forest.

Mitsu didn't like having Skal at her back. She'd been around hrinn long enough to know a bad apple when she saw one. They should have left the black-and-white hrinn behind, even if they had to tie him to a tree.

She didn't say anything, though. Heyoka kept checking her as though he expected her to explode, and she could tell the rest of the squad didn't yet trust her either. They all thought her story was suspicious, that in her heart she'd gone flek again.

The rain forest thinned, then gave way to grass and sweet-smelling moss. A cloud of minute orange insects rose as they stopped at the mountain stream and she had to fan them away. She knelt beside the rushing water and bathed her perspiring face. Water trickled down her hot neck and under her uniform shirt. She tilted her head back, closed her eyes, dizzy with fatigue and hunger. She had eaten only a couple of bites of a sour red fruit back at the laka village, not knowing if it would agree with her. It would be stupid to incapacitate herself just before a battle.

Heyoka motioned to Kei and continued on toward the cave, ordering the rest to wait until they returned.

A lump of resentment rose in Mitsu's throat. He should have taken her. She watched as he disappeared over the rise. Then the laka knelt beside her, surprisingly graceful, despite their four-legged anatomy. They were all about the same size, though tinted different colors, smaller than flek, or at least flek warrior-drones. "Why did you come with us?" she asked in High-Flek.

Fourth Translator bent her mauve-colored head. "Because you cannot sing for yourselves," she said.

"I did sing, long ago, in a faraway place," Mitsu said. Unbidden, her fingers beat out a little flek working song of which she had once been fond.

Fourth Translator's high-pitched voice took up the cadence, and for a moment, it was as though she were back on Anktan, taking instruction from a surly egg-matron. She had a strong flashback of being surrounded by a thousand flek, each of whom was born knowing its purpose and skills. She could almost hear the shrill caterwauling of the huge grid being tuned, smell the flek's distinctive odor. *The white room. Pain. Disorientation. Loss of all sense of self.* It was as though they had extinguished her in that room and installed someone else in her place. In a way, Mitsu Jensen had been dead until Heyoka had brought her back. Cold sweat broke out on her brow and her hands shook so that she could not go on.

The laka broke off and regarded her with shimmering pink eyes. "You are distressed."

"The—Makers—took me prisoner, made me believe

I was one of them," she said. "When they were done, I
didn't know my companions anymore, or even myself."

"Did they sing?"

"Yes." Mitsu closed her eyes, fighting to hold on to
the here-and-now. For a heartbeat, she was back at the
Anktan grid. *Garish rainbow lights played over the
white walls, pinks, blues, purples, greens.* The traditional
colors of the flek—and of the laka too. Why hadn't
anyone noticed that before?

Heyoka reappeared on the opposite bank, and she
lurched to her feet, face still wet. Sometimes, like now,
when she was caught by surprise, she could almost see
him as a stranger might, tall and savage, black eyes
inscrutable.

"They aren't here yet. There was only a single tech-
drone down in the cave," Heyoka said, out of breath.
His ears were drooping and his jaws gaped between
words. "It scuttled into the back passage, so I left Kei
to keep watch."

He was pushing himself too hard, she thought. He'd
never been the same since Anktan.

The black-furred Ranger gestured for his odd force
to cross the stream. "Fall in! This is our chance to take
them out!"

Chapter Twenty-Six

Before Heyoka had led them a dozen paces, the crackle of laser fire charged the air. Damnation! His savage *other* urged him to plunge ahead, but he brought the ragtag column to a halt and turned to Mitsu, trying to gauge the effect her proximity to the flek was having. If he had any doubts, he could send her back with the laka. She gazed up at him with clear blue eyes, or at least one clear blue eye; the other was still swollen almost shut. But he detected no trace of that lost wildness that had possessed her on Anktan.

She looks all right, he thought. And maybe she is. The next few minutes will tell. "Tell the laka to take cover."

She spoke to the five translators, who turned and scattered back down the hillside without protest. Heyoka swiveled his ears, trying to pinpoint enemy positions. After a moment, he was fairly certain they had approached from the south, seaward along the beach. The wind was out of the mountains for now, which would have hidden their scent.

He motioned for Mitsu and Onopa to circle around

and back up to Kei. They nodded, scaled a tumble of
boulders up the closest ravine and headed for higher
ground to obtain a firing advantage. Onopa was nobody's
fool, he thought, and she knew Mitsu's history. She
would keep a close eye on her.

Heyoka dropped back down the slope to Montrose
who was struggling to catch up. He was drenched in
sweat and his hands shook with fatigue. "Stay here and
guard the laka," he said. "Don't let the flek break past
us and sweep back toward the village."

Montrose's dark face creased. Heyoka could see how
badly he didn't want to be left out of this. His jaw
tightened, but the younger man just saluted and
limped toward cover, his bad leg supporting almost no
weight now.

That left Kika, Visht, and Skal. The three hrinn
followed Heyoka over the next rise, then flattened to
the ground as they took in the scene before them. Kei
was perched above the cavern entrance in full view,
firing at anything that moved.

"Fall back!" Heyoka yelled to him. Kei's ears flicked,
then he faded into the rocks.

The flek, ranged in their standard star figure, kept
firing, though several peeled off and opened up on
Heyoka's position. He took advantage of the cross-fire
angle to take out one, then another, before they adjusted
their firing cadence and forced him back.

Visht and Kika were shooting steadily from just a few
paces behind him. The hillside's exposed black rocks
afforded some cover, but not enough. They needed to
improve their position. His com buzzed.

"It's me." Mitsu sounded out of breath. *"Kei thinks
two, maybe three flek made it into the cave before he
drove the rest back."*

Heyoka stiffened. "Damnation!" he muttered under
his breath. "That tech's already in there, so they can

transfer any time. It's not going to be enough to cut them off out here. We have to go in."

"*Affirmative,*" she said. "*That's the way I see it too. I'll go back up the hillside and enter the cave from above while you finish them off on this end.*"

His ears flattened. "Not by yourself, and that's an order!"

"*I'll take Onopa with me,*" she said. "*Even if the grid's fired up, once we get there, her ears can take it.*"

"We can all take it," he said grimly, "if we have to."

"*See you inside,*" she said and clicked off.

He squinted along the ridge line. After a few seconds, two figures in stained tan fatigues scuttled up and over without taking a hit, though more than one laser bolt slagged rocks at their feet. He shook himself, then turned his attention to the problem at hand. There was no way around it. They had to get inside.

With blueshift, he might be able to get through the flek firing pattern, but he'd already pushed himself to the limit. The gnawing hunger was still with him and would be, until he found some decent food. Kika, being female, couldn't blueshift, and he didn't know how much reserve Visht or Skal had left.

Visht fired three rapid rounds, then bolted across to Heyoka's side. He was panting hard, but his eyes were thoughtful. "I think I finally have its name."

Heyoka ducked as flek fire, drawn by Visht's dash, intensified. The air swelled with heat trails and the acridness of expended charges. "The name of what?" he said.

"This pattern!" Visht's nostrils flared with excitement. "I've been listening for the Voice to speak ever since we arrived on this planet, but it never did and I thought perhaps this place was just too far from Anktan for it to ever make itself heard."

Heyoka stared, jaws slightly agape with surprise.

During all the months of training, he'd never heard Visht put together that many words at one time.

"Then, just now, I realized we haven't ever taken the time to understand what's rising around us. We just keep blundering ahead, never thinking about the shape of events. That's why things have gone so badly."

Patterns again, those supposedly sacred *somethings/ in/motion* that almost all hrinn worshipped. His ears flattened with aggravation. Superstitious nonsense. They didn't have time for this. Too much was riding on the outcome of this particular fire fight. "We'll talk about it later."

"It's still *stars/over/stars*," Visht said as though he hadn't spoken. His black eyes gleamed and there was a new animation in his face. "I don't know why I did not see that before. It began on Anktan with your birth, continued on Earth with your rescue and upbringing, then returned to Anktan for the great battle. Now it has reached out to include Oleaaka. It's too big for just one world, or two, or three. Who knows how much farther it will stretch?"

"Even if you're right, that doesn't do us any good," Heyoka said, marking an overbold flek before he took it down. The laser-stick flashed. The flek fell, rolled, then regained its feet and took cover. "I never understood *stars/over/stars* to begin with."

"That's because you're an integral part of it," Visht said. "Trying to perceive *stars/over/stars* would be like trying to see yourself. No one can see his own back." He gazed at Heyoka with that worshipful hrinnti intensity he always found so unnerving. "It's into your birth, your very blood. You are the pattern itself!"

"Great." Heyoka sighted in on another flek warrior-drone that had become too bold and dropped it in its tracks. Two more swarmed over it and dashed up the hill after Kei. It was a feint. Damn, he'd fallen for that one. He keyed his com unit. "Kei, get out of there!"

Only static answered.

"Reach inside and listen to what the energy tells you. Whatever you do will be right," Visht said confidently.

Heyoka groaned under his breath. What reality was Visht inhabiting? The truth was nothing he did these days was right, from requesting Mitsu for this so-called "training run" to challenging Skal up on the mountain. He'd broken at least a hundred regulations trying to integrate hrinn into the Rangers, trashed what was left of his career by refusing to evacuate, reopened a transfer grid that had lain dormant for untold years, and then incited at least a portion of the apparently peaceful laka to run amok.

With a sudden burst of fury, he lurched to his aching feet. He was tired of fighting like a human, civilized, precise, always following protocol. Maybe it was time to fight like a savage. His vicious *other* surged to the surface, already whispering suggestions. "We're going in," he said to Visht, Kika, and Skal. "Stay on my heels!"

He laid back his ears and fired as he ran, weaving back and forth. The three closest flek froze, trying to adjust to this foolhardy strategy; then he was upon them, too close for either side to bring weapons to bear. He raised his laser-stick and bludgeoned the closest. Kika and Visht swept past him and fell upon the next, moving as a perfectly coordinated pair as though they'd hunted together their entire lives.

The warrior-drone went down with a startled squall even as Heyoka leaped upon the next. A laser bolt caught the edge of his right hand as it took the flek in the shoulder. He glanced back; the flek were firing upon their own troops in an effort to take out the hrinn.

It had been a good gamble, but he'd lost. He'd never find cover in time—

The first notes pierced the air just as Kika finished off her prey. She glanced up, claws ivory with flek blood, then shuddered.

The laka were advancing up the hillside, flanked by Montrose. They were singing the same strange, shrill song that wrenched at Heyoka's nerves and set his teeth on edge. It was too high, too piercing, full of odd harmonics that made it difficult to breathe.

He covered his ears, trying not to let his nerveless fingers drop the laser-stick.

Kika threw back her head and roared with pain.

"Run!" he told her. "Get out of range!"

She staggered a few steps, then crumpled to the ground, gasping. Visht's lips were pulled back in a fierce growl, his black eyes narrowed. Every muscle in his big strong body stood out with strain.

Montrose limped forward, one painful step at a time, his rifle trained on the remaining flek, who were dotted around them like a forest of statues.

Heyoka wanted to tell him to finish them off while they were helpless, but the words wouldn't come. There was only the terrible music, winding around through his head, slipping into unsuspected nooks and crannies, making him see bizarre colors that weren't there, smell odors that had never existed.

But the laka could sing all day and it wouldn't resolve anything, he thought. Whenever they ran out of steam, as they must at some point, the flek would still be here. His Rangers had to get into that cave and stop the one inside from returning to whatever world lay on the other side of the transfer grid. In the meanwhile, Mitsu was in there with only Onopa for support.

Panting, he fought to take a step, just one step toward the yawning black entrance of the cave. His right leg responded stiffly somewhere in that distant country beneath him as though it were made of robotics and under someone else's control.

If he could take one step, then he could take another, he told himself. Move, dammit! He was trembling with exertion, but the left leg shuffled forward.

The flek warrior-drones were transfixed as he edged around them, hands still over his ears. Kika writhed on the ground, but he couldn't help her, could barely help himself. Visht was watching him with a fervent intensity he had seen only once before, back on Anktan, when he had been forced to kill a priest to satisfy the expectations of a primitive culture he could never fully understand. They had called for him then by the name of a ancient legend, and he'd known all the while he was a sham.

If Visht could make himself heard through all of this, he thought numbly, the yellow-furred hrinn would be shouting it too. *Black/on/black! Black/on/black!*

But the Black/on/black was just an ancient legend with a tiny grain of truth at its heart. He knew better than anyone that he wasn't part of any so-called sacred *something/in/motion*. He was just a soldier, trying to do his duty. Another step. If he could get inside the cave, that might lessen the song's impact.

Visht's words came back to him—*"It's woven into your birth, your very blood."*

If only that were true, he wouldn't make so damned many mistakes. Another step, he told himself. He was almost there. One more—step.

The cave's entrance was a dark hole in the hillside set on an angle to the ground, and enlarged by all the activity. He lunged at it, grasped the sides and pulled himself through. He fell down the rocks that led down to the floor. Inside it was cooler and noticeably quieter. The laka song could still be heard, but was not so overwhelming. He lay for a moment on the cavern floor, trying to collect himself, then lurched down the passage toward the grid.

He could hear its terrible squeal in the distance.

The second entrance turned out to be farther back up the mountain than Mitsu remembered. The wind blew steadily in their faces, making it harder to climb Onopa followed on her heels, much taller and more wind-resistant, far too weary and out of breath to ask questions.

She couldn't find the cave, when they had finally climbed high enough. She rotated, examining the green-shrouded hills for familiar shapes. By her calculations, the abandoned base camp was about thirty minutes back to the east. She identified the outline of a stone cliff above, and a lightning-split tree about twenty feet away.

"It's around here somewhere," she told Onopa. "We can't be that far off."

Onopa shaded her eyes with one hand. Her face was splotchy with heat and exhaustion, her long black hair slick with sweat. "Think back," she said hoarsely. "You and Kei found the entrance first. What landmarks did you notice?"

Kei had been sitting on a huge boulder, cleaning his rifle, when she found him. They'd argued, then headed back to camp, going downhill all the way, so they'd been higher up. She squinted into the sun, then thought she spotted the flat-topped rock.

She let her eye follow the ravine downhill. She'd caught her heel on that variety of stupid slithering vine, which wouldn't stay put, and tripped, so she scoured the ground, looking for the same pattern of mottled green-and-white.

Then she saw it, a hole scarcely wider than a man's shoulders in the midst of a mat of the low-growing vines. They shuddered and slid aside at her approach.

"Here!" she said, kneeling, and motioned to Onopa. The rope ladder was still in place. She thrust her flek laser-stick through a belt loop, so that it poked her in the ribs, and started down the rope.

"Be careful." Onopa hovered in the circle of sunlight and blue-green sky above. "They might have set guards."

The cool darkness was a relief after the sultry steambath above. Mitsu inhaled the drier air gratefully and stepped off onto the rock floor. "Okay!" she called back up to Onopa and held the ladder while the stocky woman followed.

She felt at her waist for her coldlantern. "Damn. I lost my light somewhere."

"I still have mine," Onopa said and switched it on.

The cavern looked undisturbed. Mitsu placed her palm on the rock wall and felt it vibrate under her hand. "The grid is already activated," she said. "They're getting ready to leave. Come on!"

Onopa jogged in front, playing the light over the uneven floor. Mitsu kept one hand on the wall, guiding herself as much by feel as by sight. If only they had some explosives, they could seal this gate off forever, but of course the major had left nothing of that sort behind. He'd expected them all to be on the shuttle when it left.

The vibration became apparent in the cavern floor beneath their feet, then the squeal of the grid itself. Mitsu was sweating as they followed the twists of the musty passageway. The laser-stick seemed ridiculously light in her hand. She longed for a decent human-made laser rifle. How long did the charge in one of these flek weapons last anyway? She had no idea.

"Douse the light," she whispered finally as they drew close enough to see rippling blue interspersed now with other colors, not a good sign.

Onopa clicked it off as Mitsu edged ahead, trying to glimpse how many flek were already in the chamber.

It didn't sound as though anyone were firing, so either Heyoka hadn't made it yet, or it had taken them so long to find the entrance, the battle was already over.

In the center of the grid, the tech-drone was fine-tuning the crystalline matrix while three armed warrior-drones waited, covering the other entrance. Off to one side, the world-architect watched the tech with apparent patience. Its four hands danced over the crystals and with each touch the rippling lights accelerated. The grid must be almost ready.

She jerked back and pressed her shoulders to the wall. They would cut Heyoka and the rest of the squad down as they entered, and she couldn't warn him; coms didn't work down here.

"There's three, five, counting the tech and architect," she told Onopa. "They've set an ambush and are waiting for the squad. We have to take them out from this end."

Onopa nodded.

Mitsu thought for a moment. There was something she was forgetting . . . She cudgeled her brain. "Don't waste any shots on that tech. It's covered in some sort of protective sealant that works better than flek armor. All-Father help us if the rest ever start using it."

They checked their weapons, then nodded at each other, but before they could attack, the flek fired into the other passageway. The squad must be making their run.

"Now!" Mitsu yelled above the screech of the grid, skidded around the bend and threw herself to the floor just inside the chamber, firing at the warrior-drones.

Onopa followed, using the crystalline pillars for cover. Mitsu winged the drone on the far left, but then it whirled and fired back. She cursed under her breath. It required a direct hit to a vulnerable area to take out a flek. They not only wore body armor, but had the natural resistance of their chitinous bodies.

The screech from the grid wrenched into an octave higher and Mitsu felt waves of distortion sheeting off it. "Get out of there!" she told Onopa who was standing, one leg on the transfer pad, one leg off, but the other woman couldn't hear.

Desperate, she charged the flek and took a glancing bolt along the ribs. Her uniform protected her to some degree, but agony sizzled through her. She fell, rolled, and came up hunched over against the pain and shooting. The air crackled with laser fire, so acrid she could hardly breathe. Onopa ducked through the crystalline matrix, emerged on the other side and took down the warrior-drone on the far right.

The grid flashed a *blue* so bright, Mitsu could taste it, could feel it imprinted on her bones, stamped into her blood. She pressed back against the slick white wall, turned her head aside, held her breath. Her heart lurched into a sickening overdrive. Had Onopa gotten clear?

If not, half of her body was on its way to the flek.

Heyoka retreated at the first hint of flek laser fire. Kika, Kei, Skal, and Visht crowded up against him in the darkness. He felt their hot, eager breath on his neck; evidently they'd broken the song's hold too. "Wait until Mitsu and Onopa distract them, then we'll charge."

They could hear the grid's painful wail all too clearly from here, smell the reek of flek. Kika was already in distress from the sound, her ears being the most sensitive.

"Go back," he said. "You won't be any good to us if you go down again."

"I will not go down," she said grimly.

"You don't know that." His fingers checked the flek laser-stick, made sure he had the darn thing front forward.

"I do know," she said, and somehow, he believed her.

Kei edged around Heyoka, his ears pricked. "I can do it," he said. Fight pheromones were pouring off him. "Let me go first!"

"No, wait," Heyoka said. "Mitsu will get through and draw their fire."

The grid's racket cranked up another notch. Someone inside there was going to transfer soon. Then he heard human voices, increased discharge of weapons. "Now!" He made sure of the firing stud and charged into the transfer chamber.

Mitsu and Onopa had already dropped one drone, but two more were still firing and in the center of the room the grid had gone incandescent, the color sequence flashing by too fast to distinguish. Mitsu was pressed against the wall, her head turned away. Two forms stood inside the glow, glowing brighter and brighter until they disappeared.

Too late! Heyoka roared with frustration. They had gotten away. The two escapees would report back, the Flek would know this gate worked, and that this world was unprotected.

The grid's wail wound down as Visht and Kei threw themselves on one of the remaining drones, while Kika took out the other. Though their body armor and chitin were effective against laser fire to some degree, their neck joints were no proof against the strength of hrinnti muscles and claws.

Kika, so mild under other circumstances, tore the flek's head from its body, then stood over it, chest heaving. Kei and Visht made short work of the other, then wiped their gory claws on the stone.

"They're gone," Mitsu said. Her face was as pale as a newly risen moon. "I guess we could just wait for them here. Once they report, they'll be back."

Footsteps rustled in the outer passageway. Six laka,

led by the pale-mauve form of Fourth Translator, entered into the chamber hesitantly. Montrose, his face set with pain, limped at their heels.

"Where are the rest of the flek?" Heyoka asked.

Montrose shook his head. "It was the damnedest thing. They laid down their weapons and started singing too. I guess they're still singing out there on the hillside, if no one has told them to stop."

"Well, it doesn't matter. It's too late anyway," Heyoka said. "Two of the ones in here escaped through the grid."

Fourth Translator's pink eyes blinked at him, then she consulted the other laka, including an unfamiliar light-green one that hadn't come with them from the village. After a moment's discussion, the group parted and made way for the newcomer, who was smaller. It stared at the grid, then rushed over and touched a crystalline pillar with one hand.

The grid sprang back into life, though the sound was wildly dissonant. Fourth Translator bent her neck and spoke to Mitsu, who listened gravely, before turning to Heyoka.

"She says they are not beyond our reach, as long as the grid is here. The laka wish to quit hiding and take an active part." Mitsu's eyes were wide. "They want to go to the flek world on the other end of this grid."

Chapter Twenty-Seven

Mitsu stared. The grid's wail echoed in the constricted space, already waning. The air had a flat, almost brackish taste, as though somehow depleted by the transfer. "There is no way to go through the grid now," she told the laka. "The tech has already transferred."

"This young breeder comes of tech stock," Fourth Translator said, indicating the smaller laka dashing from column to column like a mad scientist. "The knowledge of how to operate this device is coded into his cells. He must only be stimulated in order to remember."

So, like flek, each laka was born with body-memories. Then perhaps it was possible. Mitsu felt sick at the thought of walking that stark, flek-infested world again. Her hands knotted together. "You have never been there," she said, fighting to keep her voice level, "so you do not know how many thousands of Makers wait on the other side of that grid. Whatever you did there, however much you sang, it would never be enough, not even if all the laka on Oleaaka transferred with you."

The pale-green laka limped forward. The dark-green

bruise beneath her cracked carapace had spread. "I am Ninth Translator," she said. "As you can see, I am broken, but before I die, I wish to sing down the madness."

"But you do not necessarily have to die. We have—" Mitsu broke off, unable to find a word in her flek vocabulary that meant doctor, healer, nurse, or anything comparable. "We have castes who mend broken bodies." She had to resort to a term meant for the repair of machines rather than living tissue. "There is much we may be able to do for you."

"Broken is broken," Ninth Translator said. She seemed quite unperturbed. "One equally able will be hatched in my place to serve the colony, but I wish to spend my last breath singing on that other, terrible world where all they know is violence and destruction."

Heyoka and the rest of the squad listened, unable to translate for themselves, while the young laka drone dashed around the grid, stroking first this crystal pillar, then that. With every touch, the sound altered, became less chaotic.

Mitsu turned to Heyoka and translated.

His ears drooped with doubt. "You've been there. Can you find your way around, if we could get back? Could we find the two who transferred in time to prevent them from reporting?"

"Maybe," she said. "But they have a good head start, and don't forget how toxic the atmosphere is there. I passed out after a couple of hours and could barely breathe by the time I persuaded them to bring me back."

"Then we would have to finish quickly, if we were to have any chance at all," he said.

"Of course," she said, "the laka are really flek, though they've obviously altered themselves genetically to adapt to Oleaaka. It's possible they may be much more tolerant of flekish conditions."

Montrose shook his head and limped closer. Lines of strain creased his face. "How can we be sure this laka can operate the grid? It's never done it before. For all we know, our atoms could wind up scattered across the galaxy."

"That's true." Heyoka's brow furrowed. "So I'm only accepting volunteers."

Mitsu closed her eyes, trembling, fighting not to give herself away. Inside, she was screaming—she couldn't go back there, straight into the arms of the flek yet again. It was a miracle she'd escaped the last time with her mind intact.

But they couldn't just hide here on Oleaaka, waiting for the enemy to return in the thousands either. She pictured cowering in the hills, trying to pick them off as they came through the grid, and shuddered. Perhaps it would be better to take the fight to them and use the advantage of surprise. That was certainly one tactic they would never expect.

"I'll go," she heard herself say and opened her eyes. The blue lights flickered over their grim faces as though they were all drowning.

"As will I!" Every hair on his body bristling, Kei glared at the rest of the squad as though someone meant to deny him.

"And I," Kika and Visht said together, then glanced at each other.

"I've come this far," Onopa said. Her broad face was determined beneath smudges of mud. "You're not leaving me behind now."

Skal edged forward and stood behind the human woman's shoulder, his eyes downcast, making his commitment understood.

Montrose gazed around, clearly in pain. The meds were wearing off, Mitsu thought. He was nearly out on his feet. "Me too, then," he said.

"Look," Heyoka said quietly, bending close, "you have a gimpy leg and it makes perfect sense for you to stay. If we don't come back, someone has to report to HQ."

"Then it will have to be someone else." A muscle jumped beneath Montrose's glazed eye. "Write them a message or paint a picture on the damned wall. If the rest of the squad is going, I am too."

Heyoka turned to Ninth Translator. "We'll all go," he told her, "but it has to be now, if we're to have any chance."

"Good," Ninth Translator said in Standard. "Stand there." She indicated the center of the grid, inside the irregularly spaced crystalline pillars.

They crowded together, laka and human and hrinn, as the little drone continued its dance between the pillars with what appeared to be joy. What was it like, Mitsu wondered, to be born for something, and never allowed to do it, not even to speak of it, your entire life? It was not surprising the breeders had run wild at the first hint of forbidden behaviors. The stress level of this society was very high. Even the slightest manifestation of aggressive behavior must awaken the outlawed inclinations written into their genes.

With each new adjustment, the grid's sound wrenched higher. Kika threw back her head in pain, held her ears with both hands. Kei snarled and knotted his fists. Heyoka paced, a difficult feat in that confined space. The vibrations doubled, doubled again. The coruscating blue light separated into purple and green and pink, brightened, flashed *white*.

Her eyes closed reflexively, but the light was so intense, she could see the chamber clearly through the flesh of her eyelids.

Between one breath and the next, cold swept through her body, penetrating to the marrow of her bones. The sound fell away, as though they'd been plunged into the still, frozen, blue heart of a glacier on some distant arctic world. She couldn't see Heyoka anymore, couldn't tell if she stood on her feet or her head. Directions swirled around her, traded orientation, then switched back again. Her head was whirling. Her stomach cramped.

Then, abruptly, they were *elsewhere*. She blinked at the appalling scene which had greeted her before, a barren yellow and brown landscape sloping downward in all directions. The white towers of the flek city stood in the middle distance and an overbright sun was rising in an incandescent mustard sky. The air assaulted her face, already too hot to breathe comfortably, thick with sulphur.

And downslope about thirty feet, two flek stood beside a pale-blue transport sphere, staring back up at them.

With a roar, Kei dashed out of the grid, but before he could reach the sphere, the laka surged behind him, singing. The strange notes shivered along his nerves, scraped as though trying to reshape something essential.

The two flek stood transfixed as the laka approached, singing, weaving something between them that almost had physical substance. Kei closed his eyes. He saw wild colors, dark, impenetrable blue mingled with moody rose and vibrant green, something altogether new, another way to think about the world, a new way to be.

But he did not want something new. He wanted only to follow the Black/on/black wherever this elusive *something/in/motion* took him, to drive the flek off every world they had stolen, to fight with all his strength until the despised enemy lay in bloody shreds beneath his claws. Without that, he was nothing.

He bowed his head and fought to hold on.

❖   ❖   ❖

Kika brought her hands away from her ears. Blood stained her fur again, but not so much as before, as though the sun-fueled restoration had not only healed her body, but made her stronger. She could still hear too, though her left ear was less acute than her right.

The laka song twined around her, dissonant to hrinnti sensibilities, but clearly of great effect on the two laka. She composed herself to endure. When the time was right, the pattern arising here would make itself known.

Onopa watched the hrinn from the back of the group. It was obvious they found the song unpleasant, but either the less sensitive hearing of human ears protected them or human nervous systems did not mirror the flek's so closely. To her, it sounded a bit like the grandmothers singing in her home village, off-key and thready, but with great warmth and sincerity.

She slipped through the stationary hrinn and laka and headed, rifle at the ready, for the strange semi-transparent blue globe waiting just beyond the transfer grid. Were those two the same flek who had just fled Oleaaka? If so, they had to be stopped.

One of the laka, the pale-green one, reached out and laid a restraining first-hand on her arm as she passed. *Stay,* the hand told her more eloquently than words. *Let what is going to happen be born.*

She bowed her head and stood aside.

World-Architect 549 stood, one foot inside the travel sphere, the rest without, his mind ripped open. Body-memories were being awakened by this terrible song, ancient ones, far older than any he had ever experienced, memories of a time before his kind had become Makers.

They had lived on only one world, very similar to this one, the memories said, *had in the end grown restless and* gone exploring. *The new worlds had called mutations into being, new castes who had given their species a militant focus, but in that quiet time before, they had been Singers and knew an entirely different purpose . . .*

He shuddered. That had been another species altogether! They were Makers now. They roamed the universe and crafted the raw material of each world into something more lovely than the last.

Listen, the song whispered, *it was/is you. Despite all that has happened, we are the same.*

No! He was a Maker, a world-architect! It was his function to remake entire planets so that they were both beautiful and useful, equipped with aromatic loveliness and utilitarian chemistries. Makers fashioned their own worlds. They were shapers!

Shape yourself then, the song said. *Remake yourself for each new world as we did. That is the real challenge. All else is foolish, vicious carnage.*

And it washed over him, how once the Singers had found joy in remaking themselves, how the genes could be twitched, just so, certain traits could be selected, others suppressed. In that light, there could never be any failed worlds because Singers could live anywhere.

Remember, the song insisted. *Open yourself and remember.*

They had been part of their worlds then, in perfect accord with each unique chemistry, so every planet had been a neverending song and his kind, its Singers. Then, sometime afterward, the warrior caste had come into being. After that, they had set themselves against each new environment they found, bent it to their own specifications, so that it no longer sang at all and they were the violent Makers.

But he was a world-architect. He understood nothing else.

Understand yourself, the song said. *Look inward and see. It has been done before and we had joy.*

The Singers had been content. Body-memories bubbled up, faster and faster until he was immersed in that ancient time. Emotions he had never before experienced flashed through him like storms until he was spent.

All the fighting, warrior-drones pitted against all opposition, lives spent in taking whatever they wanted, wherever they found it, then defending their acquisitions against the enemies accumulated in the process. So much energy expended, so many worlds tuned to the same exacting, difficult-to-achieve design. A waste, as well as a bore.

Before the Makers, world-architects had been something else, his body-memories whispered. *Something lovely and respected. They had . . .*

He strained, the lost knowledge shimmering almost within his reach.

Sing with us, the song urged and he found himself swept along. He could not help but do so. If the song ended, he would never know what had once been.

The transfer-tech was singing too. They were all singing and the song was much richer for the new voices carefully woven through the spaces.

They certainly had stopped at least these two, Heyoka thought, but this whole world must be full of flek. Those in charge would figure out what was going on shortly, and then this position would be overrun with warrior-drones. Five laka couldn't sing them all down.

Mitsu doubled over in a coughing fit. Her face turned red and Montrose thumped her back. She shouldn't have come, he thought. She'd already had a full dose of this poisonous atmosphere in the last twenty-four hours and it was hotter than any world he'd ever set foot on before. He wanted to strip out of his fur and he could see the rest of the hrinn were already panting and limp-eared with the heat.

"Are you going to be all right?" he asked her, fighting to make himself heard above the singing.

"It doesn't matter," she said hoarsely and wiped the cough tears from her eyes with one hand. "Even if I won't, we have to go on."

She was right, of course. He wrenched his mind back to the problem at hand and studied the sprawling city of slick white buildings in the distance.

The Confederation attacked flek-held worlds with bombs and laser cannon from orbit, when tactics dictated, but never landed and fought hand-to-hand. It wasn't profitable and worlds such as this one were useless to humans, after flek had ruined the atmosphere.

As he watched, hundreds of colored spheres, similar to the one downslope, rose from the city and drifted toward the hilltop. His ears flattened. "Okay, people, they've figured out we're here," he said. "Find cover!"

The laka turned their serene faces to the city and continued to sing.

Heyoka took Mitsu's arm. "Tell them to take cover!"

"I did," she said.

"They'll come out of those pods firing," he said. "The laka will be cut to pieces before any of the flek hear the first note."

Mitsu stared at the approaching flek, then at the blue sphere a few feet away. "All-Father, that's right! The pod!" She ran to the transfer-tech, who was now singing too. It looked dazed and unwilling to turn its attention away from the song. Mitsu spoke to it angrily and it shook itself, as though just awakening.

The swarm of colored spheres was closing. Heyoka estimated their number at least three hundred, maybe more. Panting from the heat, he took cover behind one of the crystalline pillars and readied his flek laser-stick. The breath rasped in his straining lungs; it was like breathing heated goo. Maybe they could pick the attacking warrior-drones off as they charged up the hill. At least the Rangers had the advantage of a defensible position.

Lights blazed from the city, the familiar garish pinks and greens and purples that fleks always employed. More spheres rose and headed their way. The fur on his back bristled. They were going to be inundated.

Mitsu dragged the tech into the transport sphere and Heyoka readied himself. The first wave of spheres was landing just out of range. In a moment, they would sweep up the hillside in one of their standard flek firing formations. He glanced back at his troops. Human and hrinn alike, they had taken up defensive positions and were ready. He felt a surge of pride, even though no one back at Headquarters would ever know of this, human and hrinn working smoothly together, adding strength to strength, instead of squabbling over differences.

The laka seemed not to realize their danger. They stood exposed halfway down the hillside, shoulder to shoulder, and sang. The world-architect sang with them, its eyes closed in apparent flekish bliss. Mitsu and the tech were in the other sphere, out of sight. What was she up to? he wondered, then sighted in on the closest craft as it approached. "Make every shot count!" he called to the rest.

Flek warrior-drones emerged from their transports and he fired upon his target. The flek stumbled, then regained its balance and headed up the hill. Cursing, he fired again and it went down. Two shots for a kill. Not bloody good enough! he told himself. He had to do better! They all did!

One dropped to the left, Kika's kill, then two more to the right, Onopa and Visht, he thought. The rest of the flek emerged, one by one, from their transports, but except for the crackle of Ranger lasers, he heard no return fire. He looked closer.

The flek were landing and leaving their spheres, but they weren't firing. Instead, they were standing at the foot of the hill and—singing.

"Hold your fire!" he called even as Kei took out another warrior. They were surrounded by a veritable sea of gaunt white warrior-drones, all armed and armored, but focused on the laka, who were still patiently singing.

Mitsu emerged from the blue transport, holding onto the side for support and wheezing. Her bruised eye stood out livid against her bloodless skin. "I opened the com," she said with effort, "so they heard the song before they landed."

She was going to die, if they didn't get her off this forsaken world soon, he thought. "Make the transfer-tech take you back to Oleaaka," he said.

"Soon," she said. Her lips looked blue. "Listen, this is just the beginning. If we can broadcast the laka song to the whole city, this entire world could go down."

And if that happened, he told himself, the Confederation would come in, before the flek rallied to take it back, see for once intact flek technology, including a working grid, possibly even divine how to put such devices to their own advantage. This could turn the whole tide of the war.

A shiver ran through him at the thought. "What now?" he said.

"We have to go to the flek city," she said. "Just point me in the right direction."

Kei's ears drooped with frustration. He paced back and forth, his extended claws empty. The enemy, so long sought, was just standing there in scattered clumps on the hillside, caterwauling along with the irritating laka.

As soon as this long-awaited battle had begun, it was over.

"Come on!" The Black/on/black beckoned to him. "We're going to the city."

His ears pricked. "There will be fighting?"

"We should meet plenty of resistance," the Black/on/black said. "I want you and Skal and Onopa to sweep ahead of the main group and clear the way for the laka. If they go down, we don't have a chance."

Kei glanced at Mitsu. She stood beside the transport, pale except for her cheeks, holding on to its edge with both hands. Her eyes looked dazed. He didn't like the thought of that one at his back, especially here, on a flek world. She could not be trusted.

"That's an order." The Black/on/black met his eyes with his own smoldering black gaze until Kei looked away. His pulse pounded and he wanted to Challenge, could taste the hot blood on his tongue, smell the fight pheromones dancing through the air.

But not here, not now. Perhaps one day there would come the right moment for him to pit his strength against the Black/on/black again, but for now, the flek were his enemy, no one else, and if the squad didn't hunt together on this day, they would certainly never hunt anywhere ever again.

With a roar, he charged, leading Skal and Onopa toward the gleaming white city.

Chapter Twenty-Eight

It was more difficult to walk this planet than Ninth Translator had expected. The yellow and umber landscape was strangely compelling, extending out to an almost invisible horizon lost in the haze. The carefully crafted atmosphere so closely mimicked the ancient world which had first given birth to her kind, it awoke sickening body-memories of strife and war and unending violence.

Part of her remembered what it was like to be bold and take whatever she wanted, to settle for nothing less than what she'd always known, though she had to turn whole ecologies inside out to achieve it. That fearful legacy was coded into her cells almost as deeply as the story of the Singers.

But they were becoming many now, as Maker after Maker was seduced into their song. A growing army of identical white forms turned and marched with them toward the city. Actinic green flashed through the murky air as the furred ones fired back at attacking Makers who had not yet responded. The waste grieved her, but then many lives also had to be sacrificed at the Feast of Leavetaking each year, and this was similar, the sacrifice of a relative few, so the rest could be returned to harmony.

The way was long, the air thick and hot. Her cracked carapace gave with each step so that the splintered ends stabbed tender skin and organs beneath, but she thought she might yet live long enough to sing amidst the canted spires of the city itself. Her participation was no longer vital, of course. They had acquired more than enough voices to be effective without her, but she found a curious strength of will sustaining her. It would be rewarding to walk that oddly familiar city, to have a part in turning its inhabitants away from wanton violence, before the pain forced her to terminate her body.

She misstepped, staggered, and nearly fell. Fourth Translator surged forward on one side so that she could hold fast to her, while Eighth pressed against her undamaged side on the other. They each took a portion of her weight, steadying her, and so, in tandem, the three sang their way toward the white city in the distance.

It was so abominably hot! Kika felt like snapping at the torrid heat of this terrible place. It deluged her until she was overflowing with it and no amount of panting helped.

A tiny blue spark bloomed at the tip of one claw, as she plodded along, then another, welling up like bright drops of light, and then she understood. This gruesome heat was fueling the special receptor cells in her body far more effectively than the milder sun of Oleaaka. But restoring took concentration, and, in the middle of battle, she doubted she would be effective. Still, she tried to relax and open herself to the heat. The moment might come when she was needed.

✧   ✧   ✧

The hodgepodge force moved through the noxious yellow haze in a sea of sound that was not music to Heyoka's human-trained ears. It scraped along the nerves, too shrill at its heights, deeply resonant whenever two or three of the sliding rhythms came together unexpectedly at a single note. He was growing accustomed to it, so that it was easier to function, but its effect on the flek they encountered was startling, the result of body-memories, as Mitsu had tried to explain. Long ago, the flek had been something else entirely, and, deep down, their cells retained the stamp of that other mind set.

Not so with hrinn, he thought. What they were now was what they had always been—fierce, proud, stubborn. It had been his job to help them adjust to human behavior patterns so they could leave Anktan and carry this all-important fight across space to the flek. They hadn't been able to remold themselves to fit human ideals though, and that had to be his fault. With Ben Blackeagle's guidance, he had done it, so obviously it was possible. He just hadn't shown them clearly enough, found the right words, used the proper examples. If only he had a medium as potent as the laka's, he might have been able to make them understand.

When they were nearing the city itself, with its irregularly spaced towers and soaring walkways, a new swarm of twenty or so air vehicles arose from its interior, not spheres this time, but tiny military craft, fleet individual fliers that would be impervious to laser rifles at this range. He had encountered them in battle on a dozen worlds. They would be armed, while his force was caught out in the open with inferior weapons and no cover.

"Run!" He took off, though his legs were leaden and his head felt as though it were solid wood. "We have to reach the city!"

Mitsu glanced up at the attack wave sweeping toward

them, then spoke urgently to the singing laka. The flek would surely know enough to keep their coms turned off by now and the transports were bound to be sound-proof.

The first bombardment took out the leading edge of their converted force in a hellish rain of orange fire. Burning bodies tumbled to the ground and lay scattered in smoldering heaps. The laka faltered, but he saw Mitsu urging them around the carnage. The pale-green one fell and her companions had to pull her back onto her feet. The attack wave swept past, then banked for another run.

"Split up!" Heyoka yelled. "Don't give them a decent target!"

Most of the combined force couldn't understand him though. Mitsu had to relay the message, which cost precious seconds as the flek roared back toward them and the city. Heyoka saw the architect staring up at the yellow sky, not even trying to hide. Being of a higher caste, it might be of use, once they reached the city. He reached inside for the speed to sweep it away from danger, then found himself nose-down in the rancid yellow dirt with no memory of having fallen.

He lurched back up, exhausted from even trying blue-shift and furious with himself. His legs threatened to buckle. Stupid, stupid! He couldn't afford the energy drain. They had too much to do here, too far to go.

Out of nowhere, someone else caught the architect, carried it twenty or so yards, then left it on its feet, out of the line of fire. Most likely Kei or Skal. Unlike him, they were both still whole. He ought to resign his commission and spend the rest of his days in some out-of-the-way males' house telling wild tales to cublings who didn't know any better.

The complex of white walls and walkways began abruptly a hundred yards ahead. Several laka had reached it now, though at least one had been killed along the way. He swerved over to Mitsu, who looked about to pass out.

He took her arm. She started to protest, but lacked the breath to do so and he hustled her into the white city.

The architect reeled, then regained his balance. Strong hands had gripped his arms for just an instant, then he was abruptly somewhere else, dazed, but out of the line of fire. It was as though a whirlwind had snatched him up, then released him some distance away, but he had fine-tuned this world's weather himself. No whirlwinds were possible.

He had heard reports about battles with the Enemy of course. Makers had been at war with humans for generations, but he had never once seen actual fighting before today. Dead and dying lay all around him now, their bodies smoldering with a sickly acrid odor. Even as he watched, the dying turned themselves off, winking out like stars, one by one. It was to be expected. They were now valueless to the community and there was no point in prolonging their own suffering. Their lifeless red eyes looked curiously empty and he found himself surprised not to be among them.

The furred ones, along with the surviving Singers, reached the city ahead and disappeared amidst its curves and crannies. The fliers zoomed back toward the city, seeking their quarry, leaving him out here alone with the bodies.

The song had broken off, but he could still remember what it had promised, that beguiling glimpse of another way to live, even more ancient than the culture he had been born into. Beside that, though, remained the imperatives of the Makers: *organize, build, possess, transform*. These had always proved satisfying and successful, and to some degree still appealed. It was as though two different conversations were raging inside his head at the same time and he did not know which to heed.

He stared around, trying to fathom his own reactions. It was his talent to craft worlds, tweaking chemical balances, pH, the mix of atmospheric gases, to produce something workable out of what had formerly been unsuitable; but crafting oneself, as the song had suggested, sounded far more challenging.

He wandered toward the city, his mind already at work on exactly how that might be accomplished.

Once again, Mitsu found herself inside the curving alabaster city, surrounded by white walls, staring up at bizarre lopsided towers. There was light everywhere, streaming up from every square inch of building surface so that the entire city was a source of light. Beams of colored light danced overhead, pinks and greens and purples. The stench of flek bodies permeated the air and there was an underlying chitter that she could feel in her bones.

Heyoka hovered over her like a black-furred duenna, ears drooping with fatigue. She wanted to tell him to back off, but couldn't find the strength.

Kei was suddenly there, between one blink of the eye and the next, then Skal, both dropping out of blueshift.

"Warrior-drones up ahead," Kei said.

Skal waited for orders, head bowed, breathing heavily, his piebald fur matted with thick ivory blood.

"Where would the communications center be?" Heyoka asked Mitsu.

"I don't know," she said. "Last time, I entered the city in a transport sphere and it landed on one of the upper galleries. We need one of the flek, maybe the transfer-grid-tech or the world-architect. Either one of them might have been there too."

The smaller tech was nowhere to be seen, but the architect was strolling toward them, its head craning casually as though on a sightseeing tour. Four laka were huddled against one of the white walls, staring about them with shocked pink eyes. Mitsu had a flash of anger at their naivete; they had thought they would just sing a few carefully chosen notes to the flek and they would cave in. Now they understood the full measure of what they had bitten off. She had tried to tell them, but it was too late.

A coughing spasm overtook her and she staggered back against the hot white wall. Montrose reached for her arm, but she waved him away. No one could help. Tears streamed down her face before she managed to control the fit, but the whole scene seemed unreal and distant and she didn't know how much longer she had before she passed out again.

"The—architect!" she wheezed at the laka. "Bring the architect—here. We have to—question him."

Fourth Translator ventured out across the bare, sulphur-stained earth hesitantly and urged him back with her into the city. Umber dust rose with every step, then settled lazily back to the ground. Mitsu waited, head down, hands clenched. Each breath was a struggle, far more difficult than the last.

The architect seemed in no hurry, as though he didn't realize his danger as the last few fliers headed back to the towers. He was not a warrior-drone, she thought, so quite possibly he really did not understand. The flek were very specialized and other concerns were coded into his genes.

Onopa slipped around the next corner, along with Kei and Visht. Scouting, Mitsu supposed. They probably had only a few moments more before the flek organized themselves enough to confront this combined force throughout the city.

Fourth Translator brought the architect to her. Mitsu raised her head and tried to focus. "The communications center," she said with great difficulty, "have you ever been there?"

"Of course," he said, then cocked his head owlishly.

"Do you know how to find it from this location?" she said.

"This way," he said, as though she'd asked directions to the nearest stream, and set off.

She nodded to Heyoka and he signalled the group, such as it was, to follow.

"Tell them to si——," he began in a low voice, but before he could finish, the laka were already singing on their own.

Heyoka trailed the architect through the bewildering maze of spirals and lopsided buildings. None of them had doors or windows or openings of any sort. Flek had no need of openings. They used a building material that could be rendered porous with the right sort of field generator. Otherwise, what they wished kept out, stayed out.

The gravity on this world must be higher than Oleaaka's. Either that, or his attempt at blueshift had drained him to the dregs. He doggedly put one foot in front of the other and plodded on.

Fourth Translator had taken Mitsu up on her back and he kept his eyes on that improbable sight. His partner was clinging to the laka and struggling to breathe. Under the double onslaught of heat and toxic atmosphere, she'd already stopped sweating, and he knew, for humans, that was a very bad sign. He had to get her out of here soon, or she wouldn't make it.

As for himself, the heat seemed a palpable presence, permeating his cells and lighting fires within. It was as though he'd steeped in a thermal pool all day and now was filled to bursting with power. He put that thought aside, though. The last time he'd overextended himself in blueshift, he'd nearly died.

The broad tilted walkways were the worst. Evidently flek had a much better sense of balance and didn't require adaptations like guardrails and stairs. The walkways rose abruptly and dropped off on either side. Montrose's bad leg slipped, and he slid perilously close to the edge. Kika pulled him up, her ears flattened.

He heard sporadic weapons fire up ahead, but the flek could not get close enough to kill without being exposed to the laka's song. Once they heard it, they were snared, and sang along with them. The sound reverberated off the sleek curves of the city, carrying far into the interior. Often, when they rounded a corner, a bevy of some utilitarian caste awaited, already echoing their song.

Ninth Translator fell finally at the foot of a steep ramp, her green sides heaving. "She is too weak," Mitsu said, after the ailing laka spoke. "But she says she has sung in the city and is ready to die now. We must go on without her."

Heyoka knew that flek always chose death when captured or disabled. That was why the Confederation could never capture prisoners to interrogate. But there was too much death here already today and, besides, long ago the laka had chosen not to be flek.

"Ask her to try a bit longer," Heyoka said and urged the injured translator back onto her feet. The cracks in her carapace had spread to the edges and the stain beneath was now very dark indeed.

Ninth Translator blinked at him, then spoke in recognizable Standard. "Why?"

"Because you are important to us," he said, "a friend. We can't just throw you away like a used-up power pack."

Mitsu passed a hand back over her clammy face.

"There is no word for 'friend' in High-Flek. I'm not sure we can make her understand."

Heyoka grimaced and took the laka's foreshoulders in his hands. "Don't die," he said to Ninth Translator. "Just *don't* die."

The laka spoke haltingly, then Mitsu translated. "She says she won't, for now, if you do not wish it."

"I don't!" he said more forcefully than he had intended. And they went on.

The architect led them up and up, threading through tiny crevices that surely could not have been meant as corridors, then along soaring walkways that seemed to lead only to precipices, where they had to scramble down, hand over hand. She peered over the edge at one point and saw how the walkways below formed swirls like the interior of seashells. There was obviously a flekish logic involved in navigating here, which Mitsu could not perceive. She found that oddly comforting. She never wanted to think like a flek again.

The air was hot and noxious, much worse than even the last time she had come here. Her eyes watered until she could barely see. Lower castes emerged through the walls as they passed, then followed them in droves.

If possible, it was even hotter on each new level as they climbed. Mitsu knew, if she had not been riding on Fourth Translator, she would have fallen by the wayside long before now. Ninth Translator struggled on, close to Heyoka. The injured laka watched him with fervent eyes, as though he were a star and she, a ship using him to steer by.

Six times, a wave of warrior-drones swept over them from out of the convoluted city byways, but always they held them off until the song took effect.

Montrose skidded over the edge of a walkway during one of those flek charges, then Skal disappeared after the next. She wasn't sure if the two Rangers were dead or just injured. They didn't dare stop to find out. They had to keep the remaining laka together and safe. She was sure, if their ragtag force didn't find the communications center soon, the flek would find a way to stop them.

They were at least a thousand strong when the architect stopped before a broad alcove made of three screens and open at the top. The laka song shrilled around them like a coat of armor, but insubstantial, a shield that could be disrupted any second.

From within the enclosure, several dozen warrior-drones emerged, already singing, leaving five great, hulking flek shoulder to shoulder beneath irregular screens that formed the three walls. Pink and green and purple lights bobbed just above their heads, tiny message couriers, she recognized from her stint on Anktan.

Her fingers tightened on Fourth Translator's shoulders. The architect was right. She had hazy memories of standing in this place or one very much like it. These flek were Deciders, perhaps even the same ones who had dispatched her back to Oleaaka.

"Spy-Drone 87650," one of the Deciders said, its voice amplified artificially to carry above the laka song. "You have disregarded your instructions by bringing the perverted ones back to us, rather than the information cache."

She rubbed her aching temples. Something was wrong. Why weren't the Deciders singing?

"But this does present an efficient way to deal with the taint." It craned its head at an approving angle. "It will be necessary to dispose of this facility, but we judge the opportunity to be worth the loss of one flawed garrison world, not even suitable for breeding."

Chapter Twenty-Nine

"They're not singing." Mitsu's heart raced. She slid off the translator's back, but had to steady herself as the garish scene seemed to darken before her watering eyes. Minute colored spheres bobbed before the screens as though they had an appointment elsewhere and were impatient to be off.

Radiating disapproval, Kei paced back and forth, glaring at her with his hot, black eyes. He always made her uneasy, but he looked ready to tear her throat out at the moment.

Heyoka was watching her closely. "What did it say?"

"It still thinks I'm one of their activated spies." Her fingernails bit into the palms of her hands. It was so hot, so bloody hot. Her lungs strained, but the oxygen content seemed depleted. "The song isn't affecting them like the rest." She gazed back at the throng which had accompanied them here, unable to make sense of it. Every other flek in this city within hearing distance was caught in the laka's trap.

"If we're going to get at their communications equipment," Kei said, "we'll have to rush them."

"We won't get access that way," Onopa said. Her long black hair had come loose and her cheeks were flushed with the terrible heat.

She looks magnificent, Mitsu thought, so tall and competent. Onopa never faltered, never seemed at a loss for what to do. She had a sudden intuition that the flek would never have been able to make scrambled eggs out of her mind.

"If we charge in there," Onopa continued, "they'll destroy all the equipment. Flek in danger of capture always do that. They never leave anything useful behind for us to pick over."

True. Mitsu ground the heels of her trembling hands against her eyes until all she could see were orange blotches. She breathed deeply, trying to clear her head, but her lungs seemed to be on fire. "They think I brought you here just so they could kill you."

Kei raised his muzzle and his bared teeth glinted with the pinks and greens. "Did you?"

"No," she said, then broke off in a coughing fit. She closed her eyes, fought for control. "But we can use this." Each word had to scrape its way out of her aching throat. "If I pretend to go along with them, maybe I can get close enough to open a circuit and broadcast the song into the rest of the city."

Heyoka's ears flattened. "They'll kill you the minute they see what you're up to."

"I'm dead anyway," she said. "We all are, unless we can turn this city to our side."

"Do not trust her!" Kei prowled forward, claws at the ready. The hazy yellow light shimmered along their curving three-inch lengths. "She betrayed us before! She will do it again!"

Mitsu faced the angry hrinn. The terrible, bubbling

cough waited in her chest like an angry hrinn, ready to spring out and take her down. "What I will do," she said carefully, "is whatever gets the job done, just like any other Ranger."

Heyoka shook himself. This was getting out of hand. "Be realistic," he said. "In your condition, you wouldn't get ten steps before you passed out. Stay here and translate for the laka. I'll take the squad in and secure the communications channels."

"You wouldn't know the right controls even if you did find them before the Deciders destroyed them," she said, so pale her skin was translucent. Her pupils had contracted to pinpoints and he had the impression she was looking through them all to another place, another set of faces altogether. "At least I know a little about flek consoles, which is more than any of you can say. Eldrich had me working on several, compiling information on Confederation forces, back on Anktan."

"No." He took her shoulders in his large hands and made her look at him. "It's a stupid idea."

"If you let her go, she will not open the channels!" Kei said. "Just like before, she is their creature and does not even know it. Once inside, she will betray us all, if she has not already done so!"

"I'm going," Mitsu said hoarsely, with what clearly was the dregs of her strength.

Inside the chamber, lights from the screens played over the Deciders' unreadable faces, green and pink and blue and purple. They were larger than any other flek he'd ever encountered, with solid, unwieldy bodies and oversized heads, feral red eyes. None were armed, but Heyoka knew every array of flek equipment was primed with a destruct mechanism. It would only take a second for them to trigger it. There was only one way to move fast enough to thwart the flek, and that wasn't an option for him. He would have to send Kei, who seemed as eager to kill Mitsu as the flek.

The hovering spheres suddenly rose in a single wave, swept out of the area altogether and dispersed. He swiped at one as it passed, and it burst, raining minute components.

All around him, the laka sang and the assembled flek sang with them, and further away, the sound of lasers sang a different, more deadly song, as Kika and Visht held off another warrior-drone attack, one level above this one. "All right," he said, in a voice that sounded nothing like his own. "Just figure out which console it is, then we'll provide cover, while you set the controls."

She nodded, as though she lacked the strength to speak, then released her hold on Fourth Translator and walked with all the assurance she could muster into the flek stronghold.

He had watched her back a thousand times in battle, and she had watched his. This was harder, he thought, than any of those. If he was wrong, if she had fallen victim to their tampering again, he might have to kill her himself this time. The fur bristled across his shoulders and he didn't know if he could do it.

Kei stiffened as she chittered at the Deciders. They did not respond. Mitsu cleared her throat and tried again. This time, one did answer.

Her face assumed unfamiliar curves, masklike, as it had been on that terrible day back on Anktan. Then she turned and slipped around the gaunt flek bodies.

Was Kei right after all, he found himself wondering. Was her conditioning taking hold again?

One of the Deciders uttered an unintelligible phrase, then, in a single motion, all five slumped to the floor, a tumbled pile of limbs and torsos and heads.

Startled, he approached, laser-stick at the ready. They looked—dead. Surely not, he told himself. It must be some sort of flekish trick to fool them into dropping their guard. In another minute, they would all leap up and attack.

Mitsu stared at him over the bodies. "They consider themselves and everyone else on this particular world hopelessly tainted by contact with the laka."

"So they just turned themselves off?" That made a gruesome sort of sense, he thought. They had preferred death to losing their identity as flek. "Open the channels!" he told her, scanning the consoles lining the walls underneath the screens.

"They're already open," she said, and he detected the thin edge of panic in her voice. "Their command to 'cease being' went out all over the city."

"Then they're all—"

"Dead," she said, "all, but those singing with us already."

"She may be lying," Kei said. "Remember that. She may be saying exactly what they told her to say."

Heyoka ran a hand back over his flabbergasted ears. No wonder they weren't fighting with the kind of single-minded ferocity flek usually employed. They'd already given up and cut their losses.

From the southern edge of the city, a distant *whump* sounded. A segment of the outer ring of buildings quivered, then fell in upon itself in glittering shards.

The laka faltered, staring at each other. Another implosion shook the city; then off to the west, a tower toppled to the lower levels, crashing through a series of the broad walkways. The shattered pieces followed like so much confetti.

"Before they died, they rigged the city to destroy itself!" Heyoka said. "Is there any way to stop it?"

Mitsu stared at him with stricken, bewildered blue eyes. "I don't know," she said. "I can try."

"No!" Kei blocked her way. "She knew all along what they were going to do and stalled to keep us here!"

Another explosion shook the city. Console lights flickered. Mitsu attempted to circle Kei, but he seized her arm, letting his extended handclaws pierce her unprotected skin. Red human blood welled up and ran down her arm. She reeled back, trying to free herself. "You idiot, I may be able to turn it off!" she said. "They must have some way of reversing an accidental triggering!"

"Private Kei!" Heyoka put all the force of years of Ranger training into his voice. "Stand back and let the corporal through!"

Kei's feral black eyes met his in brazen Challenge. They stood locked in one another's gaze, neither willing to look away.

Heyoka snarled and the desire to fight burned through him. *They were evenly matched,* his *other* whispered. *It would be good to finally give in and thrash that insolent arrogance within an inch of its life!*

His whole body trembled with anticipation, but then he took a deep, shuddering breath and drew back from the edge. *Not here,* he commanded the *other. Not now. Kei and I will settle this later.*

With a sudden roar, Kei threw Mitsu away from him and turned his back. She staggered, caught herself against a bank of equipment, then regained her balance. She examined first one array, then another, and another. The explosions wracking the city were coming closer. The laka had stopped singing so that the sound of the wind whistling against the high walkways was evident. The wretched-smelling air was choked with smoke and fumes.

"Damn!" she whispered, gazing up at the screens as she flipped through the flek information stores. Flek squiggles danced across the surfaces, replacing themselves over and over again.

Heyoka leaned over her shoulder. "Tell me what to look for," he said, then a nearby explosion shook the room. Debris rained in from a shattered tower and he shielded her with his body.

"I don't know," she said and pulled away. "It could be anything, a routine hidden within the most uninteresting list or program. I just don't know." She looked up at him, exhaustion written in every line of her body.

"What about the techs," he asked, "and the architect? Would they know anything?"

"They might," she said, "but we're almost out of time. I don't think the small grid has blown yet; I haven't heard an explosion that far off, but it can't be long."

Helpless, he stalked over to the opposite screen, but he didn't read flek, had never had any reason to familiarize himself with the symbols. He didn't have the slightest idea of what to look for.

"Of course!" she said suddenly behind his back. "Why didn't I see it before?" He turned and saw her fingers fly over the controls. Symbols danced across all three screens. "I should have known!"

"What—" he was saying, but caught a flicker of movement where none should be. One of the supposedly dead Deciders emerged from the tangled pile of bodies with a laser-stick and took aim at Mitsu's head. Without thinking, he found himself in that chill silent blueness only hrinn could ever inhabit. So *blue*. So *cold*. Every vestige of warmth leeched out of his body in a single heartbeat, even as he leaped toward the flek.

His fingers reached, but already, he could feel himself losing blueshift, though he tried desperately to hang on. Kei entered his field of vision from the left, moving swiftly, while Mitsu and the flek and laka were only statues.

"The Decider!" he tried to tell him, but the words were only a croak. His throat was numb. His vision was tunneling down to a single point—Mitsu's rapt, exhausted face as she studied the symbols on the board above.

Never turn your back on an enemy, Heyoka thought, not even a dead one, a premise of basic training. When had he forgotten that?

Kei seized Mitsu around the waist and—

Sound and color assaulted Heyoka. He lay on the floor, his nose pressed painfully into the slick whiteness. His limbs felt boneless as he fought to get to his feet. Mitsu was cursing weakly, struggling to free herself from Kei's grip.

"Let go, you rag-ear!" she cried and he found himself surprised she could think clearly enough to use such a particularly hrinnti insult at a moment like this. "I'm saving our sodding lives, whether you believe it or not!"

The laser bolt went wide of her head, burning a long furrow into the screen, then Heyoka was upon the flek. It was limp in his grasp, before he could tear its head off, no doubt, dead this time for real. He tore its head off anyway, then threw the reeking skull into the corner. Flek blood spurted hot and ivory across his black fur and his own blood pounded in his ears. His legs gave way and he sagged against the wall.

Mitsu whirled and boxed Kei's ears to make him release her. His hands dropped away and she went back to the console, muttering to herself, fingers flying over the controls. Kei froze, his massive body poised, claws sprung free.

"No!" Heyoka saw the *other* in Kei's fierce black eyes. She had struck him, in the ears no less, a hrinn's most tender body part, given lawful Challenge, in hrinnti vernacular. He had every right to respond.

He recognized the struggle going on inside Kei's head. It was the same struggle he himself had endured every day of his life while walking among humans. Sometimes the vicious *other* was easily subdued; at others, barely restrained at all, but he had warred against his own for years. He knew he always would, until the day someone carried his lifeless body to the barren top of some mountain and left it there.

"I did it!" Mitsu threw her hands up. "At least, I think I did." Her expression sobered as she cocked her head, listening.

Heyoka listened too. One breath passed, two, three. No explosions. Anywhere.

"I think maybe you did, shortstuff," he said, still monitoring Kei.

"And you said I couldn't!" She turned to Kei in triumph, then doubled over in a fit of coughing.

"No," he said, rigid with restraint, "you are wrong. I said you *wouldn't*."

"Oh." A bright trickle of blood appeared at the corner of Mitsu's mouth. Her eyes fluttered as she fought to remain conscious. "That's—different." She slumped to her knees.

"Come on," Heyoka said. "We've got to get back to the transfer grid and get out of here. The humans won't last much longer in this soup and whatever she did to their destruct routines may not hold either."

Kei nodded, a strange bit of human body language when performed by his big frame. He stalked out of the alcove and gestured to the laka.

Heyoka watched him. No one, he thought, except himself, Kika, and Visht, probably had any idea that Kei had never in his entire life suffered such a deadly insult and allowed the perpetrator to live.

He picked Mitsu up and carried her back to Fourth Translator, who took the semiconscious human on her back again. She shuddered in his arms as she struggled to breathe, heartbreakingly fragile. They rounded up what was left of their invasion force and made their way back through the eerie empty city. Dead bodies lay scattered everywhere like broken toys and the explosions had made lace of the beautiful soaring walkways, rubble of the towers.

The flek who had sung with them followed bewilderedly, some wandering off, then seeking them again, when they realized they were alone. There was no one left to command them to turn themselves off, no one to explain they had lost this particular battle.

"What will we do about them?" Onopa asked Heyoka. "We can't take them all back with us."

"We'll ask the laka," he said. "They should know what to do with converted flek."

"Makers," she corrected.

They found Montrose close to ground level, hiding out behind a shattered column. His leg was broken in two places. He hadn't been able to climb back up, but had splinted it as best he could and waited to see if they survived.

"Oh, we survived," Heyoka said grimly, "after a fashion."

"You all look pretty damn lively to me!" he said. His voice was hoarse and cracked from the atmosphere and pain was evident in his dark face.

Visht took his arm and hoisted him up onto his one good leg without being told. Montrose rested his weight on the hrinn and together they picked their way through the debris and bodies.

Heyoka touched Mitsu's shoulder. She roused enough to open bleary, reddened eyes. "Make sure they bring both the transfer-grid-tech and the world-architect back with us," he said. "Then ask what they want to do about the rest of these flek—Makers—who sang with us."

Groggily, Mitsu relayed his message to Fourth Translator, who considered before answering.

"She says they must all come to Oleaaka. If they stay here, without their city, they will die from lack of purpose."

He shuddered at the thought of that many untamed

flek running loose on the peaceful world at the other end of the grid. What if they reverted to their flekish personas, then refused to sing a second time? But it was the laka's world and, if that was what they wanted, he had no right to say no.

When they reached the grid, they found the single laka drone still joyfully tending the transfer crystals, running here and there, tuning each with reverence, its inherited knowledge almost fully restored.

"The humans should all go back in the first group," Heyoka said, and not surprisingly none of the three gave him any argument. Mitsu was nearly comatose and he directed Onopa to monitor her breathing. He put Ninth Translator in that group too, because the pale-green laka also was near death.

Kika stepped forward, her pale-gray fur yellowed with fumes. "Let me go with them," she said. "I might be able to help."

She had a new calmness about her that he recognized, but couldn't name. "They need a med," he said. "As soon as you go through, use the com up at the base camp to try and contact the Confederation. Someone may be in range by now."

"I will try," she said, "but I will also do what I can in my own small way."

Then he knew what he was seeing, the calm assurance of a fully trained Restorer, who possessed the power to address illness and injury. "As you did for Skal," he said.

"I have seen the shape of something big," she said, "which stretches between the stars themselves and binds us all together. In this something, there is even room for rogues like me who tried to be other than what they are and for a time wound up being nothing at all."

Looking into her serene eyes, Heyoka thought, whatever it was, he approved.

Chapter Thirty

The trip through the grid was still nearly unbearable, but when Kika's vision cleared, her ears did not hurt as much as before. Perhaps she was growing stronger, she thought, then helped Onopa herd the rest of the group through the cave's labyrinth until they reached the outside air.

Night had fallen on Oleaaka. It had just rained and the wind rushed over her muzzle, sweet with moisture and life. A faint tapestry of stars glimmered through the thinning clouds far out over the sea. When they first came to this world, she had found the vast expanse of water troubling, but now the crash of waves upon the unseen shore was soothing and she wished to sit by the shore again.

Montrose made it as far as the mouth of the cave and collapsed gratefully outside against the rocks. She judged him to be in pain, but not in danger of his life.

The smallest human, Mitsu, though, was indeed near death. Every breath she drew brought more of the startling bright red blood to her mouth. Kika settled beside her on rain-soaked moss and placed her palm flat on Mitsu's rib cage

Wrongness flooded up through her, imbalance, injury. To be so small, compared to a hrinn, this one was indeed very resilient, but her strength was nearly at an end. Closing her eyes, she reached for the wild blue power stored in her own cells and fought for control. Instinct told her this release had to be slow, very slow. Adult males often fought one another with this kind of power, and a strong jolt could easily kill. Skal's body had been much more resilient.

The energy seeped through the human's body cell by cell, repairing ravaged tissues, stimulating growth, banishing pain and swelling. It felt good to acknowledge the power simmering through her as well as her craving to restore imbalances. All those seasons when she had repressed this gift could never be regained. There were so many she might have helped who now lay irretrievably beyond her claws. But if she had not turned away then, she would have been forced to flee Jhii and present herself at a Restorers' House, and so never joined the Rangers.

That must have been part of the pattern, that she lie fallow for a time, so she might be in this place, here and now, and if it were indeed the intended shape of her life, then she need regret nothing. All was as it should be.

The night wore on and she lost all sense of the scene around her as she struggled to maintain control. Almost as much energy was being lost in her attempt to regulate it as she was managing to impart. If this pattern ever took her back to Anktan, she must present herself for training at a Restorers' House and fully master this gift.

When Mitsu's breathing finally grew more even, less labored, Kika withdrew and sat for a time, head down, gauging the depths of her own exhaustion. She had spent much, but perhaps there was enough left to help another. With a sigh, she moved on to the next most in need, the pale-green laka translator with the shattered carapace. The laka was too weak to raise her head as Kika placed a palm over the spider web of chitin.

Though her control was ragged and her skills poor, perhaps she could ease this poor creature's misery. She bowed her head and began.

Onopa went into the forest for lengths of wood, then resplinted Montrose's leg. It wasn't much, she thought, but it would have to do until they got him to a proper med.

That done, she decided to return to their base camp to use the bulky com unit left up there. Montrose tried to talk her into waiting for dawn, but she didn't want Blackeagle to come back and find her sitting on her duff when there was work to be done and orders to be carried out.

She climbed through the night, half-blind with weariness. Slimy vines slithered across her path and caught at her battered boots. The rocks were slick after the rain and she kept slipping, but they had casualties and she couldn't just sit around and catch a few winks while others suffered and died. At least she could breathe back here on Oleaaka. She could be grateful for that much. Her lungs still ached and her eyes burned, but Jensen was far worse off and Montrose needed more pain meds.

Finally, though, she had to admit she just didn't know where the hell she was. She took shelter beneath a cliff, which would protect her from the last of the rain's runoff, and waited for dawn. She rested her head back against the rock, too tired to sleep. Every inch of her body was bruised and aching and . . .

With a start, she felt the warmth of sun dance across her face. She opened her eyes and saw the emerald tapestry of the rain forest down below, the rise and fall of the diamond-topped sea all the way to the horizon, and a black-uniformed Ranger captain standing a few feet away, his arms crossed over his chest and his expression stern.

It seemed to take forever for the flek transfer-tech to retune the grid to its satisfaction. With Mitsu gone, Heyoka had to depend on the few words of Standard Fourth Translator had picked up, which proved altogether inadequate for the task at hand.

When the grid was finally pronounced ready, though, he went in the second group, along with Visht, Kei, the transfer-tech, and architect. That left mostly flek along with two laka, but their metabolisms could take the atmosphere far better than hrinn and humans. The actual transfer was as wrenching as before, cold as a Jovian moon and agonizing to his acute hrinnti hearing. If the Confederation ever did adopt this mode of transportation, they could forget about him using it. His ears were still ringing when he made his way out of the cave and up into the sweet morning air.

He had expected to see miserable survivors huddled together, somber faces, perhaps even a few dead, including Mitsu. Instead, he found an entire camp, complete with tents, a kitchen dispensing warm food, and a number of unfamiliar human Rangers.

Montrose lurched to his feet, his leg encased in a fresh clean professional-looking splint that couldn't have been fashioned from the materials at hand. He saluted. "Welcome back, Sergeant!"

Heyoka saluted back. "At ease, Corporal." He blinked at the bright sunlight and the organized bustle before him. "What is—all this?"

Montrose grinned, looking years younger than just a few hours ago. "The flek fell back unexpectedly, so the front has shifted again. It could even have something to do with the fall of the flek world on the other end of that grid. Once Oleaaka wasn't behind the lines anymore, the *Marion* returned to pick us up. Onopa found a search party up by the base camp and brought them down here. They transported Jensen and Naxk up to the ship for treatment, although they were already doing a lot better, but I requested to stay until the rest of the squad made it back."

"I see." Heyoka moved aside as Kei emerged from the cave and snarled with surprise.

"Master Sergeant Blackeagle?" A human came forward, male, fortyish, dark-headed, vaguely familiar.

Heyoka saluted somewhat sketchily, then nudged Kei to do the same. "Sir?"

"Captain Elias Tork," the man said and returned their salute. "Major Dennehy had to remain with the fleet, but he dispatched me in his place to pick up survivors, if there were any, and see if the transfer grid you discovered was still intact."

Heyoka blinked as a memory surfaced. "We were at Enjas Two together," he said. "I thought I knew you from somewhere."

"You were quite the legend back there," Tork said dryly. "It's not everyone who takes out an entire flek advance by himself."

"Those were special circumstances," Heyoka said, remembering the occasion of his first involuntary blueshift. "I don't think I could do it now."

"I heard you'd gone home," Tork said. "It looks like you put together a crack unit, though I think they tend to exaggerate. Your people have been telling me wild tales about transporting to a *flek* world and capturing the whole shebang?"

Heyoka could tell by the look in Tork's eye that he didn't believe a word of it. "It's true," he said diffidently, "for the most part."

Tork's eyes narrowed. "Exactly which part isn't true?"

"We didn't do it by ourselves, and we weren't able to capture everything and everyone there," Heyoka said. "To begin with, the laka provided what you might call 'covering fire.' We couldn't have gotten ten steps beyond the other side without them, and then the flek destroyed a large segment of their city before we were able to intervene. Most of them had already suicided at that point rather than be captured."

"But you *did* go through that grid?"

"Yes." Heyoka suddenly had an idea of how crazy this all sounded.

"And you could do it again—any time?"

"As long as we had one of the laka drones along who understands its mechanism, or a captive flek tech. We couldn't do it by ourselves. I'm not sure non-flek could ever operate that sort of technology. It seems to be as much an art as a science."

"Can I see the grid?" Tork asked. A fierce hunger burned in his eyes. "I want to be able to say I have firsthand knowledge when I report all this back to Major Dennehy."

Kei bristled and his handclaws flexed. He whirled upon Heyoka, outrage blazing in his eyes. "He does not believe you! I will tear his ears off!"

"Stand down, Private," Heyoka said. "Humans are different than hrinn, though that shouldn't exactly be news at this point. They're so doubtful, sometimes they don't even believe the evidence provided by their own senses."

"That is ridiculous!" Kei said. "No wonder they don't perceive the sacred *patterns/in/progress*!" He stalked away, snarling.

Tork stared.

"I'm afraid we're still training," Heyoka said offhandedly. "Don't worry, though. He hardly ever attacks without warning these days."

"I—see." Tork clasped his hands behind his back. "The grid?"

"Of course," Heyoka said. "With any luck, the next group will be coming through about the time we get there. You'll get to see an authentic flek transfer grid in operation."

"How many of your people are left back on the flek world?" Tork asked.

"One," Heyoka said. "A casualty, I'm afraid. Most of the rest coming through now will be lower caste flek, along with a few laka."

Tork's eyes widened. "Flek?"

"Tame ones," Heyoka said. "I'll explain while we walk. It's a long story."

When word reached Dennehy that the grid was operational and provided direct access to a relatively intact flek city, he returned to Oleaaka within forty-eight hours with three shipfuls of experts. The news about the laka's potent song was an extra bonus.

"I don't mind admitting I thought this project of yours was a complete wash," he said to Heyoka a few hours after viewing the now quiescent grid for himself. "Humans and Anktan-raised hrinn just didn't seem to be able to work together. I'm glad I can give you the green light now, as well as another well-deserved promotion."

"There is the matter of my insubordination," Heyoka said. "I did refuse a direct order to evacuate."

Dennehy winked. "You know, I think I forgot to write that up," he said. "I guess it's too late now. At any rate, you put your people first, and it's hard to fault an officer for that."

"Very generous of you, sir," Heyoka said, "but I'm going to refuse that promotion. In fact, I intend to resign my commission."

The older man sagged. "You can't mean that."

"I do," he said. "I've been going over this whole operation in my mind, replaying what worked and what didn't, and why. It's clear to me that it's neither fair nor efficient to ask hrinn to constrain themselves enough to function within human command structures. I could do it, but just barely, and only because I was raised by humans."

He gestured at Kei, working beside Kika now, taking inventory of the captured flek weapons. "They're amazing warriors, blessed with boundless heart and courage, but we just hold them back by insisting on petty rules and regulations meant for the human psyche. They've got strengths of their own that should be encouraged, not beaten back and subdued."

"You sound like you already have something else in mind," Dennehy said.

"I do." Heyoka watched Visht and Onopa emerge out of the rain forest, side by side, conversing easily, apparently oblivious of their different origins. "I want to take my unit back to Anktan and work out an entirely new command structure, perhaps a cross between a hrinnti Line and a males' house. If it works, we can still serve in the war, but as Anktan troops, not Confederation ones. We'll be your allies, rather than your subordinates, fighting at your side, but not under your command. We have to find our own way, a new pattern if you will, that fits us all."

"Don't resign," Dennehy said, "at least not yet. Take a leave of absence. Let me bring this to Headquarters. Perhaps we can work something out."

"All right, I'll hold off," Heyoka said. "For now, anyway." He turned to watch Visht, the reticent priest, who had followed the Black/on/black across space on the strength of his belief in this pattern; Kika, outcast from her own Line, who would have died by the hand of her own kin, had she not left with the Rangers; and

Kei, the rebel, born of outlawed Levv, like himself, and raised outside hrinnti conventions. Anktan had no role for any of them, and yet they all made fine Rangers, in their own fashion. Even Skal, with all his faults and quirks, had done well in the end. He doubted a squad staffed with only humans or hrinn could have been nearly as successful in this operation. Their strengths had combined in synergistic ways.

"What about your human recruits?" asked Dennehy. "They've worked hard on this project too. You can't just tell them 'never mind' and send them packing."

"They're welcome," Heyoka said. "I'll screen any and all applicants, as soon as I get set up. Those who have already trained with us can go now, or anytime later, if they wish."

Dennehy nodded. "Well, there's a shuttle due to land from the ship in a few minutes. I'm going back on it to the *Marion* and see if I can finish my reports. The holos of the flek city you sent back yesterday were magnificent! We've already learned more in the last few days than we have in years of long-range research."

Heyoka walked with him to the edge of camp and saw the major off, then found Kei waiting for him when he returned to the cave's entrance. The hole had been widened and stabilized by the Rangers for ease of access. The laka, busy with socializing their newly acquired flek, stayed away for the most part. The place still made them uneasy, but they had provided both a translator and grid-tech on duty all of the time.

"You told him," Kei said.

"Yes," Heyoka said. "And he seemed to understood. He thinks we might even be able to work this out and maintain an official relationship with the Rangers."

The noise of an incoming shuttle shrieked down through the atmosphere and he looked up in time to see it landing up on a terrace on the side of the mountain.

"That is good," Kei said. "I thought he would refuse. I still have difficulty predicting what humans will do, and the few times that I *have* been right, I always wished I weren't."

"I feel the same sometimes about hrinn," Heyoka said, "although I was glad to be wrong back in the flek city when Mitsu boxed your ears. I thought for a minute there you were going to tear out her throat."

"I was." Kei's black eyes, almost invisible against his black fur, blinked solemnly.

"What stopped you?"

"I glimpsed something in her face, for just a breath," he said. "I realized I had seen it before, in the faces of humans on Anktan, when we came together that night to attack the grid. She was part of what was arising both then and now, and I realized, no matter how great her offense, I had to let her live."

"You saw a pattern?"

"The one that was named before, *stars/over/stars*. Kika thinks she saw part of it too, and Visht. It's too big for one individual to comprehend, and it's not yet complete. It's still taking shape, even here in this distant place."

"You know, you didn't believe in patterns when I first came back to Levv," Heyoka said.

"Being caught up in one this large and overwhelming would make a believer out of anyone," Kei said crossly, "and all who come close to you will always be caught up in it. It's plain you are its center."

Heyoka had always been uncomfortable with this mystical stuff, but he supposed this sort of thing was the price of resembling an old legend. He rubbed his ears in frustration.

"Heyoka!" Mitsu's voice came from the slopes above.

"Down here!" He waved an arm, though he couldn't see her yet. Word was that she was much better, though the meds said she would not have survived the night, if Kika hadn't intervened.

In his new unit, there would be a place for Restorers, as well as cublings, misfits, and cast-offs of every rank. He would take them all, human and hrinn, male and female, and craft something unique that combined their strengths.

Mitsu crested the last rise and waved back. Her black hair feathered in the wind. She was pink-faced with exertion and grinning. "They wanted me to stay up there on the ship and interpret the flek data as it came in, but I talked them into letting me rejoin the squad."

"You look good," Heyoka said. And she did. Her cheeks had filled out again and the shadows that had haunted her eyes since Anktan were gone. She seemed much more her old self, but with a new assurance.

"Oh, I'm fine," she said carelessly. "I really didn't need to go back up to the ship in the first place. They made me."

"Glad I wasn't there, then." He gave her a broad hrinnti smile, pulling his lips back and revealing wicked double rows of teeth. Most humans, he knew, found it daunting, but Mitsu just grinned back.

"You were right all along about the laka and the flek," he said. "I should have trusted you."

"You couldn't know," she said. Her blue eyes sobered. "Heck, I couldn't know. The flek had messed with my mind so thoroughly back on Anktan, I could have been as crazy as a flea in null-grav and killed us all."

"But you held out," he said. "You made it."

"We made it." A smile crinkled the corners of her eyes.

"So, how do you feel about going back to Anktan? I've got a few ideas I want to discuss with you, after I bounce them off Command."

"I think I need to go back," she said. "I need to stand

on that plain beyond the mountains, where the grid used to be, so I can feel it's really, truly over."

They were companionably silent together for a moment, letting the bright Oleaakan sun stream over their faces, the breeze bathe them in pleasant green scents. It was going to be all right, he thought, watching her subtly altered expression. The impression of being wound tighter than a coiled spring had left her body. Mitsu was not precisely herself again—too much had happened for that—but she was on the road to someone that, perhaps, in the end, she would like to be.

She sighed, but he read contentment in the sound, rather than dissatisfaction, a safe coming to rest. "At any rate," she said, "Command is so wired about this find. They think it's going to make a huge difference fighting the war from now on. By the way, they've determined there definitely are no other cities on the flek world. It was just a single garrison, as the captured flek techs have been telling us." She shaded her eyes. "So, where's Kei, anyway?"

Heyoka looked around, but the hrinn had beaten a hasty retreat as soon as she'd come into view. He flicked an ear. "I think he's embarrassed. He had the perfect excuse to kill you back in the flek city and let it slip out of his claws."

Just then another of the around-the-clock exploratory teams emerged from the cave, complete with air tanks, sound dampers, and protective masks, back from a trip through the grid. At the tail end of the group, he was shocked to see a grimy hrinn, supported on either side by overwhelmed humans.

"Skal!" He bounded forward to take the piebald hrinn's arm. "I thought you were dead!"

"Probably too bloody mean to die," Mitsu muttered as she took the other arm and staggered beneath his weight.

Skal raised his head and regarded them with bleary encrusted eyes. "That is a terrible place," he rasped in hrinnti, then broke into a deep, rasping cough. His fur was patchy. One of his ears dangled and would not stand erect. "After we became separated, I could not find a single thing left to kill!"

Epilogue

Two weeks later, a few hours before the squad was to ship out for Anktan on the next scheduled shuttle, Heyoka decided to make a final visit to the laka village. He meant to slip off and speak to either Fourth or Ninth Translator alone, but Mitsu trailed after him.

Several flek looked up, as the two emerged from the rain forest's depths. Mitsu stared, then slipped closer and jogged Heyoka's elbow. "Look at their chitin," she whispered.

He narrowed his eyes, then saw what she meant. "They're *pink*!"

"Like the laka," she said. "Ninth Translator once told me their coloration was by choice, but I'd forgotten. They must dye themselves somehow."

Fashion-conscious flek, he thought. Now he truly had seen everything.

The village seethed with life, no longer the quiet place Confederation anthropologists had once found it. The vegetable patches and fruit arbors were again carefully tended. Most of the damaged huts had been repaired.

Lines of laka and flek bustled back and forth, as though there were no difference between them at all.

"I was here yesterday," Mitsu said offhandedly. "I would have asked you along, if I'd known you wanted to come back." She covered her eyes and stared up at the amber sun. "They aren't going to put their drones down anymore, you know."

He stopped. "What?"

"Their drones." She met his startled gaze. "They always put them down—euthanize them—as soon as they breed. It's called the Feast of Leavetaking. They couldn't think of any other way to preserve the peace. Once breeding has triggered hormonal surges, they start remembering things the laka would rather forget. You didn't know?"

"No," he said numbly.

"At any rate, some of them are natural techs, so now they can help maintain the grid and show us how to operate the remaining machinery in the flek city," she said. "Most of the rest carry warrior DNA, so they're not wanted here on Oleaaka, but Dennehy thinks we might be able to train them to fight for us. They don't care about politics or sides, but they sure do love a good fight. Command is even thinking of coating them with that stuff the transfer-tech dreamed up so lasers just bounce off."

"Well, they can count me out on that training assignment," he said fervently.

"Me, too," she said, then waved at a pale-green laka coming toward them. "Ninth Translator!"

The laka stopped before them, her elegant neck bowed, her eyes calm. "I have been practicing your language," she said, slowly and distinctly, "though it seems strange that your two species speak but a single dialect between them. Your forms are otherwise so divergent." She hesitated. "I have a new designation, Translator-to-Aliens. My descendents shall serve in this capacity as well, and perhaps even leave Oleaaka to travel with your kind and render assistance."

He glanced at her side, but the once-fractured carapace was smooth again. "You have recovered."

"You would not give me leave to die," she said, "so I did not."

"Kika had something to do with that too," Mitsu said.

"Both of the furred ones did," said Ninth. "Such a thing is unheard of among the laka, returning from the certain path to death. We are still trying to sort out the meaning of this event. For years, we fled contact with all other species, thinking them as violent and destructive as our forebearers. We valued the peace of our own hearts above all else, even our young."

"Humans can be violent," Heyoka said, "when the situation calls for it, and certainly hrinn can as well. Unfortunately, war is sometimes the price of survival."

"The gray one, Kika, spoke to me of a 'pattern,'" Ninth said, "something large and complex that has now reached out to include the laka too, but I do not yet understand what she meant."

"You aren't the only one," Heyoka said. "Don't let it worry you."

"We came to say good-by," Mitsu said. "We're leaving soon."

Ninth blinked. "All of you?"

"No, the laka have planted the seeds of a very powerful weapon here," he said. "I'm afraid the Confederation is going to remain on Oleaaka a long time, whether you want us or not, trying to puzzle out how to do what you already know. For years, humanity has been trying to exterminate the flek, or Makers, just as the Makers once tried to exterminate you, and it doesn't work. Pound for pound, they're incredibly effective fighters. The war has been essentially at stalemate for a long time."

He gazed around the village at the newly pink-and-green-and-blue tinted flek learning how to put their wartime skills to work in this agrarian setting and social organization, a bit like hitching cobras to plows. "The key lies in persuading the Makers to eliminate the aggressive castes, as you laka did, so that at some point coexistence between our species becomes possible."

"Our way was not without flaws," Translator-to-Aliens said. "We were forced to make difficult sacrifices."

"But you were on the right track," he said. "We want to record your song, study and refine it, then broadcast it whenever we come up against the Makers, compel them to listen to us too."

He looked up at the green-blue sky above and felt the immense blackness of space that lay hidden beyond. His fellow soldiers were fighting and dying on countless worlds out there this very minute, and the struggle would continue, the flek spreading across this quadrant with a speed and ruthlessness other species could never hope to match.

It had taken humans, hrinn, and laka to prevail in the flek city, many divergent voices coming together to sing one unique song. None of them could have done it alone. There was a sobering lesson here. It was time to combine strengths.

Settling back in the shade of the luminary tree, he watched Translator-to-Aliens practice her Standard on Mitsu, while, all around them, transformed flek assisted lowly gleaners and builders with their humble tasks, as unassuming in their new roles as old dogs.

Tiny orange insects buzzed around his muzzle. He could smell newly harvested melons being piled a few yards away, their scent a bit like astringent lemon spiked with vanilla. His eyelids sagged, then, overhead, tree limbs shifted in the breeze. The sun blazed through them and flashed as though reflecting off a mirrored surface. He blinked.

Just for a second, something had seemed to shimmer in the midday sun, a sinuous, wide-sweeping curve weaving through the village, linking laka and flek, human and hrinn, vast, complicated, as irresistible as a roaring river in flood, all leading back to him.

Something/in/motion.

He shivered. Blasted hrinn. Now they had him doing it too.

It was time to round up his troops and move on. After all, they still had a war to fight.